HOME FIRES

FIONA LOWE

JOIN MY NEWSLETTER

Also by Fiona Lowe

Daughter of Mine
Birthright
Just An Ordinary Family

Please join my VIP Readers and be first to hear about new releases,
competitions and giveaways.
fionalowe.com

Romance Novels 2006-2018
Fiona has an extensive backlist of romance novels. For a full list head
to fionalowe.com

PRAISE FOR FIONA LOWE

"The undisputed queen of Australian small-town fiction."—*Canberra Weekly on Home Fires*

"Fiona Lowe's ability to create atmosphere and tension and real relationship dynamics is a gift."—*Sally Hepworth, bestselling author of The Mother-in-Law on Home Fires*

"Lowe breathes real life into her characters...*Home Fires* is a profoundly hopeful tale, one of re-generation, of the strength gained from women supporting women, and of a community pulling together ... a powerful reminder of the resilience of the human spirit...a deeply Australian story that brilliantly captures our own life and times."—*Better* Reading on *Home Fires*

"Set to be the next *Big Little Lies*. Part-Liane Moriarty, part-Jodi Picoult, *Just an Ordinary Family* is a compelling drama about a seemingly 'ordinary' family that implodes after a domino effect of lies, betrayals, disappointments and regrets."—Mamamia on *Just An Ordinary Family*

Home Fires

First Published by Harlequin Australia in 2019
This revised edition published in 2020 by Fiona Lowe
Copyright © 2019, 2020 by Fiona Lowe.
All rights reserved.
www.fionalowe.com

Home Fires:

Cover Design by Lana Pecherczyk from Bookcoverology
Cover concepts by Barton Lowe

This is a work of fiction. Names, characters, places, and incidents are either the product of the author's imagination or are used fictitiously, and any resemblance to actual persons, living or dead, business establishments, events, or locales is entirely coincidental.

Published by Fiona Lowe

DEDICATION

*To my wonderful Tuesday tennis and coffee club women.
Thanks for getting me out of the home office and for being my
watercooler mates.*

*Be true to your work, your word, and your friend.—Henry David
Thoreau*

*Some people go to priests; others to poetry; I to my friends.—Virginia
Woolf*

CHAPTER ONE

The scent of the rainforest—leaf mulch, mud and a spritz of eucalyptus—prickled Claire's nostrils. A fine mist settled over her, the chill sneaking around the tops of her woolen socks and skating along her bones. Beside her, Matt pulled his hat down low before crossing his arms and shoving his hands under his armpits. The familiar oily smell of wool and dubbin rose off his coat, curling into the earthy perfume that said home. Sanctuary. Safety.

The reassuring aroma of Myrtle in winter.

It was very different from the summer smells of choking heat, dry dust and cow dung. Claire shivered, a combination of the insidious chill and sheer relief. Once she'd hated winter in Myrtle and had complained bitterly about the sun that crawled far too slowly to its zenith. Even when it finally reached its highest point, the weak light barely penetrated the canopy of the tall, straight mountain ash. Now she welcomed winter and the accompanying wet. It was harder to accept the rolling mountain fog that encased Myrtle in an asthma-inducing blanket, stealing the view down to the Southern Ocean. The low cloud dug up memories of another day when Myrtle was cloaked by impenetrable gray and isolated from the coast on one side and the flat plains on the other, where smoke smelled like fear, burnt flesh and cataclysmic change. A day no one wanted to remember. A day no one could forget.

A day that left a livid and jagged scar on the small township cocooned by the thick forest of Victoria's Otway Ranges.

She stamped her feet, trying to keep warm, and willing the proceedings to begin so they could all rush inside to hot tea.

Phil Lang stepped forward to the edge of the veranda, his moleskin-clad legs, blue-and-white check shirt and puffer vest marking him as a local and distinguishing him from the mob of Melbourne dignitaries—male and female—all wearing black suits. He tapped the microphone. "Testing, testing."

Claire flinched at the squeal of feedback reverberating through the speaker.

Matt slid an arm across her shoulder. "You should be anticipating that by now. What's this? The fifth opening we've been to?"

"Sixth." It was the same as the number of funerals she'd attended in one dreadful week. Of the six, only one burial had contained a single casket. At the others, there'd been two, four and five, respectively. She'd missed two funerals completely, because they'd been scheduled at the same time as others; no one had thought to schedule the funerals to avoid a conflict. Back then, thinking was impossible; existing almost too hard.

Claire flicked away a bead of moisture before it plonked into her eye. "Why didn't we bring an umbrella?"

"Because you love the rain." He squeezed her shoulder and smiled, the bold curve of his mouth filling with a special memory.

She allowed herself to tumble back two years to when life had been different—deceptively easy.

A wall of rain fell, pummeling her. Clay sucked at her boots, while her arms pushed high into the air and her head fell back to greet the crying pewter sky. Matt's arms wrapped around her, holding her close, and his deep, husky laugh warmed her skin.

"Matt! Feel it. Taste the sweetness."

"You're crazy."

"I've missed rain like this. I think I've been in the city too long."

His eyes sparkled like dappled sunshine on the rainforest floor. "Stay here then."

"Myrtle?"

"Myrtle. The farm. Right here. Marry me. We'll make a beautiful life and beautiful babies."

The microphone squealed again, fracturing the memory. Ricky Kantor, Myrtle's new—and self-appointed—AV guy, checked the cables and scratched his head. "Try it now, Phil."

"Testing."

A Melbourne woman clutching a clipboard said something to Phil before tapping her watch. Adam Petrovic, the local builder, turned from the group of dignitaries and spoke to Phil.

Julie Lang, Claire's mother's friend and her honorary aunt, slipped in next to her. "We're three minutes behind already."

"That's on time for Myrtle."

"Apparently the Minister has to be in Lorne by noon. You should see the running order his PA sent us. It included a request for vanilla custard slice. I told her that Myrtle specializes in light and fluffy scones and Otway jam and cream."

"With any luck, it means he'll have to cut his speech short," Matt said. His body tensed against Claire's. "Why are these things always such a bloody circus? Hell, we're struggling to field a cricket and football team, let alone trying to introduce basketball."

"That's now," Julie said quietly. "This is for the future."

"At the rate Myrtle's population's going backwards, the joint will be falling down by the time we've got enough people to use it. It's a perfect example of the gap between the state administration and the bush," Matt grumbled. "We've got people spending a second winter living in freezing campers and shipping container homes. They can't start building because of the bloody bureaucracy, but the same government's throwing buildings at us that we don't want or need."

Claire wanted to say *shh*, but she squeezed his hand hard instead.

His brows drew down and he shot her a look. She widened her eyes and inclined her head slightly toward Julie.

"Sorry, Julie. I wasn't taking a crack at you."

Julie gave Matt a small smile—half the size of the one she'd have given before the fires. BF, as Claire had taken to calling it. Now was AF—after the fires. One horrific December day that had scorched a demarcation line into their lives. Now everything was measured in BF and AF, from the big-picture things right down to the little things like reaching for your favorite cooking knife or wrench, only to realize it had been destroyed.

"I know you're not taking a shot at me, Matt, but the building's here now," Julie said. "We need to use it for more than just an evacuation center."

Matt's arm tightened around Claire. "Let's hope it never comes to that again."

They all knew hope didn't protect them from a damn thing.

"Rightio!" Phil's voice boomed through the speakers. "Let's make a start. Thanks for coming. Let's give the Minister a warm Myrtle welcome ..."

A scattering of applause broke out. Claire glanced around at the crowd. Despite eighteen months of experience, she couldn't stop the ache bruising her heart. Again. It was just like the previous five grand openings of the other new and shiny buildings; all she could see was the missing. So many absent faces. Some people chose not to attend these events. For others, that choice didn't exist.

"It's an honor to be in Myrtle today," the Minister said. "I was here a few days after the fires, stunned and horrified and barely able to comprehend only two buildings remained standing in your pretty town. Today, as I toured around, I'm heartened by how much has been achieved and how quickly. It's a testament to Myrtle's spirit, grit and determination."

"We still don't have a pub," a bloke called from the back.

The Minister's laugh was deep, hearty and practiced. "Sadly, that's not part of my portfolio, but you do have a state-of-the-art elementary school, a Men's Shed, Country Women's Association meeting rooms, a community health center, a playground and now this spectacular indoor multisport arena. Myrtle is back on top and kicking goals."

Was it though? All that remained of the stark lunar landscape that the conflagration had created—black ash, black trees, black bricks and blackened, crumpled iron—was the brittle lace of dead trees silhouetted on the ridge overlooking the town. Lifeless sentries gazing down on a carpet of defiant emerald green that wrapped itself around all the new buildings that made Myrtle look bright, modern and optimistic. Claire couldn't shake the worry that all of it was an illusion —one that could shatter at any moment. Underneath the veneer of Colorbond steel roofing, river stone and timber, Myrtle's heart remained charred and barely beating.

If the politician heard any gentle rumblings of dissent about the stadium, he didn't show it. "I know you're all keen to get inside and check out the facilities so without further ado, I declare the Myrtle Stadium open." He cut the ribbon and walked inside. Claire noticed Adam and Bec Petrovic slipping in immediately behind him, before his entourage, and well ahead of the rest of the rebuilding committee. Why didn't that surprise her?

The rest of the crowd moved and as Matt stood back to allow Julie and Claire to precede him through the double doors, Julie said, "Claire, I'm short a few hands. Can you help out with tea and coffee?"

"Sure. No problem."

This time it was Matt who squeezed her hand. Guilt flickered, but saying no to Julie wasn't an option. Julie was like family. Scratch that— Julie *was* family now and the closest thing Claire had to a mother. Not that she could say that to Matt. If she did, he'd look at her with hurt keen in his chocolate-lashed eyes and she'd experience a familiar tug of anger rising on a platform of shame.

No matter how many times he said, "You've got my mom," Louise Cartwright was very much Matt's mother—at best, she tolerated Claire's presence. Although Claire had originally met Louise when she was an eight-year-old Brownie and Louise was troop leader, twenty two years had passed before Matt introduced her to his mother as his girlfriend. That meeting had taken place on an unseasonably frigid late summer's day when a smattering of snow lightened the dark gullies and ice clung to the wide leaves of the tree ferns. Not much had thawed between the two women since.

As Julie walked purposefully toward the kitchen, Matt said quietly in a steely voice, "We had a deal, Claire. Apart from this bloody opening, we're spending the day together."

"And we are."

He snorted. "You just volunteered to pour tea. That'll kill another hour. Why didn't you tell her no? It's our first day off together in months. Hell, you're not even *in* the Country Women's Association. You've always said the CWA is not your thing and you never wanted to be part of it."

"I'm not and I don't." Claire sighed. "Matt, it's just pouring tea."

"It's not though, is it? Someone will ask you to look at a mole or listen to their kid's chest and you'll open the clinic and boom, the day's gone. With you it's always *just* something for someone." Tension ran up his jaw and she saw the battle he was waging between irritation and understanding. "Today, I wanted to be that someone."

She leaned in and kissed him. "You are my someone."

"Knock it off you two, it's only eleven in the morning."

"You're just jealous, mate," Matt said with a laugh.

Josh Doherty stood behind them, adjusting his squirming toddler on his hip. "Surely you've been married long enough now to be sick of each other?" he quipped.

Claire stilled, momentarily forgetting to breathe.

"Josh!" His wife Sophie threw him a dagger-laden look.

"What?"

"*Remember?*"

The stage whisper spun around the four of them. For a couple of seconds, Josh was as still as Claire had been, his gaze long and straight but vacant. Then he barked a laugh, the sound harsh, abrupt and loud. The child on his hip squealed in frightened surprise.

"That explains why you're still all over each other like a rash, then." He tousled the tight blond curls on his daughter's head. "Time you had a passion killer like this one and joined the rest of us poor bastards."

"I have tea to pour." Claire walked purposefully to the kitchen, shutting out the barrage of thoughts that threatened to intrude and ruin her day. Pulling a CWA apron over her head, she plastered a smile on her face and stepped up to the building line. "Tea or coffee?" she asked a woman from the Melbourne delegation.

"Do you have any herbal tea?"

"I've got bergamot." She flung a tea bag into a cup and wondered how long it would take the woman to realize it was Earl Grey.

"Is the Devonshire tea gluten free?"

Claire tried hard not to roll her eyes. "The jam and cream are."

"Oh. I'm lactose intolerant."

"I wouldn't say that too loudly," Claire said conspiratorially.

"Why not?"

"You're surrounded by dairymen."

The woman stared at the spoon Claire was handing her, nonplussed. "What's this for?"

"The jam. It's both gluten and lactose free." Before the woman could utter another word, Claire looked at the next person waiting, giving thanks it was a local. "Cuppa, Ted?"

"Thought you'd never ask, love."

"SHH, IT'S OKAY." Sophie lifted a crying Trixie out of Josh's arms. "Daddy didn't mean to scare you."

Josh's mouth tightened as he stretched his thumb out toward the tear on Trixie's cheek. "You're alright, aren't you, Trix?"

Trixie pouted and buried her face in Sophie's shoulder.

"Mommy's here." Sophie hugged their daughter close, soothing her and breathing in her scent of baby soap and dirt. Trixie wailed louder.

"Jeez, Soph. Now she's just bunging it on because you're making a fuss about nothing. She has to get used to noise."

"I'm doing what any mother does when her child's upset. And Trixie's not the only one upset," she said before she could stop herself. "Did you see the look on Claire McKenzie's face?"

"Flaming hell, Soph. It was a joke," Josh muttered. "Am I supposed to remember every little detail about everyone? Hell, we hardly know them."

"I s'pose not." Sophie regretted her unfair comment but each time she saw Claire, she was reminded of the vivid television images that had beamed into her mother's living room on that December afternoon when Myrtle burned. The memory was always accompanied by a wave of nausea and a quiver of anxiety.

Liam tugged at Josh's jeans. "Daddy, I'm hungry."

"Let's get some grub then." Josh caught their four-year-old son's hand and took a step toward a cloth-covered trestle table groaning under the weight of scones dripping with Myrtle raspberry jam and local cream.

Trixie's head shot up, all signs of her previous distress gone. She lurched sideways, throwing her arms out. "Dadda! Me! Me!"

A stab of irrational hurt caught Sophie under her ribs. "You little con artist."

Josh turned back, the smile on his face reminiscent of the ones he'd showered Sophie with before kids and mortgages. Before the fire. Instead of putting his arms out to Trixie so she could transfer over to him, he unexpectedly slid his spare hand into Sophie's. "Come on. We only came for the food, so let's all get something to eat."

Josh filled a couple of paper plates with the bounty and took the children over to the chairs while Sophie lined up for hot drinks. She smiled at Julie Lang. The older woman was her neighbor, and from the moment they'd moved to Myrtle, she'd taken Sophie under her maternal wing. As much as Sophie didn't like to admit it, Julie was more of a grandmother to the kids than her own mother.

"Tea for you and coffee for Josh?" Julie splashed hot water into the mugs. "While I've got you here, are you a knitter?"

Sophie blinked at the unexpected question. "Ah, no. I never learned." Sophie's mother eschewed anything she thought shackled women to the domestic sphere. This included housework, cooking and all craftwork.

"Perfect."

"Is it? I always thought it might be nice to know how."

"Excellent." Julie smiled. "I'm running a class and I'd love you to be there."

Life pulled at her. "I don't know, Julie. What with everything—"

"I'll text you the details." Julie pushed the mugs toward Sophie and looked expectantly at the next person in line. "What can I get you?"

BEC PETROVIC LISTENED to the Minister telling her what a brave and exceptional man her husband Adam was and smiled. What other possible response was there?

"Sacrificing his own safety to save those men ..." The Minister shook his head as if he couldn't fathom Adam's courage. "You must be very proud of him."

"Every day. It was a very special moment when he was presented with the Star of Courage by the state Governor, not to mention the afternoon tea at Government House." She laughed. "It makes today's offerings look a bit meagre."

The Minster nodded glumly. "I was told there'd be vanilla custard slice."

Adam appeared holding a white paper bag, which he handed to the politician. "The Nguyens make a mean vanilla slice, so I got someone to nick up to the bakery for you, Andrew. Just don't let any of the CWA biddies see you with it."

The man's eyes lit up. "Thank you. You're the right man to know."

"I do my best." Adam winked at Bec with his good eye and took her hand. "Don't I, babe?"

She smiled again because she couldn't fault him on that. Adam threw himself heart and soul into every task he took on. Her thumb automatically moved over the back of his hand. For months it had encountered a pressure bandage, but now it touched thick ridges of scar tissue, the legacy of disfiguring burns.

"Any news about the eco-tourism center?" Adam asked the Minister.

"You know I can't pre-empt anything."

"What about a nod for yes and a wink for no."

"I've got the number crunchers working on it. Any chance you can up the private-sector investment?"

Bec's concentration drifted. "Excuse me. I need to check on the girls." Leaving quickly, she pushed open a side door and stepped into a room containing a massive trampoline and gymnastics equipment.

"Mommy! Look!" Her eight-year-old daughter was jumping and somersaulting, sticking the landing perfectly and immediately repeating the action.

"That's great, Gracie. Where's your sister?"

"Dunno."

Bec glanced around despite knowing it would be a miracle if Ivy was on any of the equipment. She caught a flash of red hair and found her elder daughter sitting with her back pressed against a stack of blue gym mats, a book in her hands. *Oh, Ivy.*

Bec had never been a big reader and since the fires, her consumption of the printed word was reduced to flicking through magazines and glancing at the headlines of the paper. It was the opposite with Ivy, who now read voraciously. Bec had a love–hate relationship with Ivy's books. Part of her was grateful Ivy had something she loved but mostly Bec resented the books' intrusion into their lives. Not only did they take her daughter away from her, she was jealous Ivy had a place to escape to when the going got tough.

"I thought you were playing with your friends."

"I was but they've gone home now, because they've got *lives*. Why do we have to stay?"

"Because this opening's very important to Daddy. He's worked really—"

"Hard," Ivy said, rolling her eyes and sounding exactly like Bec. "I know, but it's *boring*. Why do I have to be here? I'm old enough to be at home on my own."

Bec tried not to sigh. The first year after the fires she'd worried for her daughters and just when she'd relaxed and dared to hope that the girls had survived the trauma thrust so violently upon them, Ivy hit puberty. It brought with it even more minefields to tiptoe through. "Have you had something to eat?"

"No."

"But you love scones. Come and have morning tea with me." She stretched out her hand and watched her daughter's internal battle play out in her sky-blue eyes—the girl who wanted to be both grown up and little all at the same time.

Ivy huffed out a dramatic breath and stood up. "I s'pose."

Bec threw her arm across her shoulders. "Remember how you used to make playdough scones for me."

"Mom! I'm not a little kid anymore."

"I know." It gutted her that the fire had stolen Ivy's childhood innocence. She blamed the inferno one hundred per cent; it was easier and far more palatable than looking elsewhere. "Gracie, do you want something to eat?"

"I just wanna bounce."

"Okay."

Bec and Ivy walked back into the main section of the stadium. The crowd had thinned considerably and she couldn't spot a single black suit, just the puffer-jacket attire of the locals. Her gaze sought out Adam and as soon as she saw him chatting to a couple of Country Fire Authority members, she relaxed. As she shepherded Ivy to the tea table, she anticipated being served by one of Myrtle's matriarchs who always made a fuss of her and the girls. Instead she got Claire

McKenzie—Casual Claire, as Bec had tagged her back in high school. There weren't many people Bec loathed but there'd always been something about Claire that made her jaw clench.

Growing up, they'd been in Brownies and Girl Scouts together. They'd clashed when Bec was patrol leader and Claire had cheerfully ignored all her instructions and done her own thing. Claire had always done her own thing—she still did. Whereas Bec was a joiner and loved nothing more than being part of a group. Before the fires, she'd always been involved with the girls' activities in some capacity, serving on the kinder committee, friends of dance club and the Parents and Friends Association. Unlike Claire, she enjoyed the company of other women. Recently though, due to Adam's burns, he'd needed her by his side and her involvement had dropped away.

A ripple of annoyance shot through her. Why on earth was Claire pouring tea? Had she joined the CWA? Bec shrugged the ridiculous thought away. Claire McKenzie was more likely to walk down the main street stark naked than be part of Australia's biggest women's group.

"Hi, Ivy," Claire said. She noticed Ivy's novel. "I love that book. It's a great series."

"Yeah, it's pretty cool." Ivy smiled shyly. "I'm re-reading it cos the next one's coming out soon."

"It's exciting, isn't it? I've ordered my copy already and when it arrives, I'm taking the day off to read it."

Bec wasn't familiar with the series—she had assumed the book was a kids' story. The fact that Claire not only recognized it, but had read it, irked her. "Two teas, please. Ivy and I are having a mother–daughter tea party."

She hit the words "mother" and "daughter" with added emphasis. Claire might have hooked the son of the district's most prominent farming family and have her own career, but Bec aced her with marriage and motherhood.

"Coming right up." Claire poured boiling water into a mug. "Unless you want a hot chocolate, Ivy?"

"Oh, yes, please." Ivy sounded as if she'd just been offered gold.

Bec's back teeth locked. "And a plate of scones ... please."

"Oh, you might be lucky. Julie, any food left?" Claire called over her shoulder.

Julie walked out of the kitchen holding a plate. "Lucky last. Here you go, Ivy."

"Thanks, Mrs. Lang." Ivy took her drink and the food over to a table and Bec was about to follow when Julie said, "Now the opening's over, you'll be pleased to get your husband back."

"Oh, you know Adam ..." Bec pressed her hand to her décolletage and fiddled with the neckline of her frock. "He's always got a project on the go."

"What about you?"

Everyone in Myrtle knew of Julie Lang, even if they didn't know her intimately. She was a mover and shaker and a woman people looked up to. Julie's daughter had been Bec's assigned buddy when she started school and her son had been Myrtle Elementary's student body president. As both Lang children were older than Bec they hadn't been friends and, even before her parents' divorce, the Sendos certainly hadn't mixed in the same social circles as the Langs.

Bec always enjoyed chatting with Julie—not that their conversations were deep or meaningful. They usually ran along the lines of pleasantries and the weather, Bec seeking advice on growing azaleas and camellias, and general chit-chat about the children. She would have liked the chance to get to know Julie better but there were scant opportunities when their lives were lived so differently. But now the older woman was looking at Bec as if seeing her for the very first time.

Bec felt a line of heat break across her cheeks. "Um, what about me?"

"Do you have a project?"

"Sorry?"

Julie gave her a sympathetic smile. "The last eighteen months, you've devoted your life to Adam and his recovery. But he's well and truly back at full speed, isn't he? It's probably time for you to do something for yourself."

The statement caught Bec off guard. "I ... I hadn't really thought. I mean, he still has difficult days ..."

"We all have difficult days," Julie said simply. "Adam's got the business and the Country Fire Authority as well as you."

Raucous laughter boomed around the stadium and Bec glanced toward the sound. Her burly husband, beer in hand, was surrounded by a group of men, almost certainly CFA volunteers, their heads inclined toward him, listening intently. If she blocked out the pink and puckered skin on his face, she was looking at a very familiar picture. Men had always listened to Adam and the fire hadn't changed that. If anything, his heroic actions that day had increased their attentiveness.

Adam turned toward her as if he knew she was watching him. He raised his beer in a salute. It was just the sort of thing he'd done before the fires when he was happy and content. She smiled back.

"I think you're right, Julie. Perhaps it's time."

CHAPTER TWO

A year before the fires

After a decade living in Melbourne, Brisbane, London and Papua New Guinea, Claire had forgotten what Christmas in Myrtle was really like. For years, her parents had travelled to visit her over the festive season or the three of them met at a vacation destination, but this year she'd come home to the heat and the flies and the Myrtle Christmas parade. What it lacked in professional floats, marching bands and Santa arriving in a helicopter, it made up for in so many other ways. Claire hadn't laughed so much in a long time.

She pointed to the Scouts, all of them in full uniform but with the added adornment of red and green foam antlers. Two of the them led a reluctant beast. "Where did they get the reindeer?" she asked her mother.

Heather rolled her eyes. "It's one of Syd Lidcombe's deer but it does the job."

Not to be outdone, the Girl Scouts—all dressed as penguins—were piled into Greg Rosetti's flatbed trailer. Smiling and waving, they enthusiastically threw candies into the crowd. Miss Myrtle's Dance Troupe, which consisted of twenty girls aged from three to eighteen and three self-confident boys, twirled and spun their red and green–sequined way down main street behind a Petrovic Family Homes utility truck. The "ute" was decorated with so much tinsel it was hard to see the original paint color. Shrieks of delight from excited children rent the air, adding to the whoop, whoop, whoop of a siren.

Claire hooked her arm through her father's. "I'm glad some things never change."

He grinned, his silver hair glinting in the late-afternoon sun. "It wouldn't be the Myrtle Christmas parade if the coppers didn't start it and the fire fighters and Santa finished it."

"Ron! Ron!" A little girl ran straight at her father's legs. "It's Santa!"

"Is it?" He bent down and swept her up into his arms. "Where?"

"There! There!"

"I can't see him," Ron teased, looking in the opposite direction.

"On the twuck, silly!"

"Oh, thank God." Julie Lang rushed in next to them, her face ashen. "She slipped out of my grasp and dashed across the road. I thought she was going to get taken out by the horses. Ami-Louise Tillerton, you must never do that again."

"Sorry, Nanna." But the child with large brown eyes didn't look very contrite. "I had to tell Ron about Santa."

"Claire!" Delighted surprise lit up Julie's smile and she hugged her. "When did you get home?"

Claire didn't correct her mother's closest friend that Myrtle hadn't been home in a very long time. "This morning. And who's this little cherub?"

"Penny's youngest. She and your dad are a mutual admiration society."

Claire looked at her father. He was busy with Ami-Louise, pointing out things in the parade just as he'd done for her when she was little. Ron's heart was huge and he loved children. Claire knew he'd hoped to be dad to a brood of kids but after she was born her mother had experienced eight miscarriages. Clare was an only child.

Julie leaned in and dropped her voice. "Ron's more than ready to be a grandfather."

"Hmm," Claire murmured noncommittally. She immediately shut down errant strands of guilt and a dollop of sadness that tried to sneak in.

"And you've just had your twenty-eighth birthday. Any chance a baby might happen soon?"

Claire blinked. It took a second or two to remember she was back in Myrtle, where everyone's life was considered a topic for discussion. "Not unless I do it on my own, and I'm not a big fan of that idea."

"Oh." Disappointment dimmed Julie's eyes. "It's just Heather told me you'd moved in with that fly-in, fly-out engineer so we were all hoping ..."

Heather noticed Claire's discomfort. "Leave her be, Julie. She's heartbroken."

"I'm not," Claire said emphatically. Was it even possible to be heartbroken when you'd spent more time on your own than with your boyfriend? "It wasn't a dramatic breakup, more like a long, slow fizzle. To be honest, the timing was perfect. My new job's so intense I don't have time for anything else."

Julie and Heather exchanged a knowing look and irritation crawled across Claire's skin. She loved them both, and she knew they only had her best interests at heart, but it was exactly this sort of conversation that drove her nuts. A career and a relationship were technically not mutually exclusive, but right now she was learning the ropes of working in healthcare management and handling a staff of twenty. The truth was, she didn't miss Stu, whose arrivals and departures had disrupted her life.

As for babies, well, she'd be lying if she said she hadn't noticed a new tendency to look inside strollers, or that cuddling the babies at the new mothers' groups she ran didn't make her happy. But right now, the urge to have a baby of her own wasn't strong enough to send her into the emotional see-saw of dating apps.

"So how's Hugo, Julie?" Claire's question moved the relationship microscope onto a safer topic: Julie loved talking about her son. "Is he still Myrtle's most eligible divorcee?"

"Sadly, yes." Her eyes suddenly brightened. "You're single now. You know your mother and I have always hoped—"

"No!" Claire shook her head so hard her brain hurt. "Hugo and I have known each other all our lives. He's like a brother to me."

"Told you, Julie." Regret furrowed Heather's brow, giving her a stern look. "Claire, I hope you know that friendship's the most important part of a relationship."

"Your mother's right," Julie said. "And you and Hugo are good friends."

Although Claire was standing outside under a wide, country-blue sky, she felt as if she were trapped in a tiny room with fast-closing walls. "I'm sorry to disappoint you both but there's no spark between Hugo and me."

"Spark!" Heather huffed. "What nonsense. Look at the Chatterjees. Their marriage was arranged and sparkless at the start. Now they're starry-eyed about each other."

"They got lucky!" Claire spluttered, feeling side-swiped by her mother.

"As exciting as lust is, darling, in the grand scheme of things, it's a one-minute wonder. It's not good looks or sex that gets you through the tough times, it's friendship and respect."

Get me out of here. Claire really didn't want to think about her parents and sex. She had enough trouble wrapping her head around the fact that they'd been married for thirty-two years. Her longest relationship had lasted two years, two months and two days.

"And what about Bec and Adam Petrovic? They were introduced by their families." Julie beamed as if she'd just laid down irrefutable proof that matchmaking worked.

"As Rebecca's biggest ambition in life was to get married and have babies, I'm not sure she was all that fussy."

"Claire!"

"What?" Her mother's censure at the catty comment only

intensified Claire's dislike of Rebecca. "So now I'm not allowed an opinion? You said it wasn't a love match."

"I didn't," Julie said firmly. "Adam worships the ground Bec and their daughters walk on."

"Good for Rebecca," Claire muttered, trying to freeze the rising frustration threatening to spill over into angry words she'd later regret. "Good for Adam. I'm glad it worked out for them, but I'm nothing like Rebecca, so it won't work for me."

"Santa! Santa! Santa!" Ami-Louise cried in disappointment as the fire truck passed and the distance between her and the smiling Santa— her grandfather hidden by bulky padding and a curly white beard —increased.

"Come on," Ron said. "Let's go and see Santa in the park."

"I'll come too!" Desperate to get away from the matchmakers, Claire fell into step with her father.

"I told them setting you up with Hugo wouldn't fly," her father said matter-of-factly.

"Thanks, Dad. I didn't know you'd heard all that."

"Just because I don't say much, doesn't mean I don't hear a lot."

They reached the park where the parade had ended. Families and couples were setting up picnic rugs in preparation for the community barbecue that always preceded the lighting of the Christmas tree. Carols by Candlelight followed, although due to daylight savings most of the littlies would have crashed by then, cuddled up asleep in their parents' arms. Right now though, children amped up on excitement hared around on bikes decorated with tinsel and family groups wandered around the floats. A line had formed to sit in the police car and to clamber all over the CFA fire truck.

Ron set Ami-Louise down in the Santa line. "Julie's right about one thing, though. I'd love to be a grandpa one day, but it it doesn't happen that's okay too."

Her father's words tugged at her heart. "I want to be a mother one day too, Dad, but it's only going to happen with the right man."

"There's good blokes out there, darling." He gently squeezed her arm. "I hope you meet him soon."

She smiled wryly. "Going by the demographics of this crowd, it won't be here." She kissed him on the cheek. "Catch up soon."

She walked toward the barbecue tent, tempted by the aroma of sizzling onions and hot oil. As much as she loved living in inner Melbourne and the access it gave her to food from around the world, right now she could murder a sausage in bread slathered in tomato ketchup.

It took her twenty minutes to reach the tent as she kept being stopped by friends of her parents and childhood acquaintances. "We must catch up while you're here," was said to her at least three times. She smiled, replying, "That would be great," knowing it was unlikely to happen. Even when she'd gone to school with these people and played netball with many of them, they'd never been close. Her natural tendency was to be a bit of a lone wolf, so although she was welcomed by several groups, she belonged to none. If she was honest, women en masse drove her nuts.

"Claire!" Hugo Lang picked her up and spun her around, which was no mean feat but Hugo was a bear of a man. He set her back on her feet, his hands firmly on her shoulders while he examined her intently. "Look at you, city girl. How long's it been?"

She kissed him on the cheek. "Was it the B&S ball?"

"I think you're right, although my memory's a little hazy."

"Beer with rum chasers has that effect." That night, Hugo had been understandably morose about life, love and how milking cows killed all chances of getting off the farm and meeting women. She'd suggested he audition for *The Bachelor*. "How are you now?"

"Yeah, good."

"You look good." In fact, if he was a woman she would have said he glowed, but perhaps that was just the natural tan that came from living a life outdoors. "Happy?"

He nodded. "Pretty much. And you?"

"Same. New job's a bit crazy but in a few months, I'll have a handle on it."

"And that fly-in, fly-out bloke?"

"Ah, no. That didn't work out." She read sympathy on his face and panicked. "Listen, Hugo, just a heads up. Our mothers have a crazy idea in their heads that as we're both single—"

"I'm not single."

"That's fantastic!" She loved Hugo dearly and this news, plus the grin that was streaking across his face, filled her with delight. "Hang on, how have you kept it a secret from Julie?"

"With great difficulty. Listen, don't say anything, okay? After Amber, this time I'm going slowly. I'll tell Mom and Dad when I'm ready."

"I get it. I have a three-month rule with my parents, so mom's the word."

"Thanks, Claire-bear." He hugged her again. "Sorry, gotta go. I'm late setting up the sound system for the stage. Make sure you come out to the farm before you leave town and I'll whip you up some scones."

Hugo, like his parents, was one of the most hospitable people on earth. Although he had a very limited cooking repertoire, he made a hell of a curry and light and fluffy scones, which had once got an honorable mention in the cutthroat world of agricultural fair cookery. "Is that how you won the heart of your mystery woman, whose name is ... ?"

"Nice try." He blew her a kiss and walked away.

With hunger pains cramping her stomach, Claire finally made it to the counter at the Lion's Club barbecue tent. With a can of soda in one hand and a sausage sandwich in the other, she moved clear of the crush. She leaned back on the boundary rail of the sports field and bit through the decadent white bread and savory onions into the hot-but-unknown-meat delight. She closed her eyes and as the indulgent carbs and fats exploded in her mouth she gave a small moan.

A deep, rumbling laugh surprised her and she opened her eyes. At first, all she saw was a bright yellow CFA helmet but then she noticed the dark brown brows arching over a pair of green eyes flecked with hazel. Eyes that were studying her with a warm and direct gaze and encouraging her to do the same. A tingle raced over her scalp before leaping down her neck. It quickly took off, raising every hair on her body, diving straight to her center and spinning there for a delicious moment before blasting out of her like electricity seeking earth. It left her heart thumping wildly and the rest of her body buzzing.

The man gave her a lop-sided grin that twirled an impish dimple into his cheek. "Going by the look on your face, the humble sausage in bread is your favorite food."

She remembered her moan and her cheeks burned. She laughed. "Not really. It's just been a while since I had one."

He was holding a hamburger in one hand and a beer in the other. "I haven't had one of these for a while either so I'm looking forward to becoming reacquainted."

"With the beer or the burger?"

"Both. Cheers."

He joined her, leaning casually on the rail, and bit into the hamburger. She tried to look away, knowing that staring was rude, but found herself watching the play of his jaw muscles. "Good?" she asked. The word came out slightly strangled.

He gave her the thumbs up.

She was mid mouthful of her own dinner when he said, "I'm Matt Cartwright. Have we met?"

She had vague memories of Matt Cartwright. He'd been a couple of years ahead of her at elementary school—a skinny kid with a mop of brown curls who'd been good at high jump and running. She didn't recall them ever sharing a conversation, and like most of the farmers' children, once he'd finished sixth grade, he'd headed off to boarding school. Matt Cartwright was still tall but he was definitely not skinny. His broad shoulders squared the shapeless yellow CFA jacket, hinting that the rest of his body might be worth looking at.

Her mother's recent hint that Claire preferred a certain type of man arrived unwelcome in her head. *He's not blond*, she countered silently.

Matt was looking at her expectantly and she swallowed the slightly-too-large mouthful, feeling the lump make its painful way down her esophagus. "I'm Claire McKenzie."

Recognition lit up his face. "Post office Claire?"

It was a Myrtle tradition to couple people's names with a defining characteristic. For men, it was usually their job. For women, it was often who they were married to—a tag that always riled Claire. Then there was a select group who got a personal tag such as Crazy Joe Rawlins, who leveled a shotgun at trespassers and anyone who pissed him off, Shorty McLeod, who was six feet tall, and Chatty Chris, who barely said a word.

"It's been a very long time since I was called Postie Claire. Are you still Roadside Mail Box 7650?"

"Yeah. That or Oakvale Park works."

"Can you be CFA Matt too?"

"Nah. That's the captain, Matt Holsworthy." He grinned. "So, if you're no longer Postie Claire, who are you?"

"Nurse Practitioner Claire."

"That's excellent but a bit of a mouthful. The four-syllable word goes against Myrtle convention. It doesn't exactly roll off the tongue."

She thought about her many years of study. "I suppose at a pinch I could be Nurse Claire."

He took a pull on his beer. "What about Caring Claire?"

"I like the alliteration, but Caring Claire makes me sound saintly. I'm definitely not that."

"Really? That's good to know. Personally, I quite like Cute Claire."

Her brain groaned at the corny line but her body sat up like a dog hopeful of a treat. "Are you flirting with me?"

He laughed again, only this time it held a hint of sheepishness. "The fact you have to ask means I'm not doing it particularly well."

"Oh, I don't know." She involuntarily tossed her head in an age-old action, letting her hair swing. "I think you're on the right track."

The dimple dived deeper. "Do you reckon if I workshopped it, I might get there?"

"It's worth a shot."

"Good to know." His face became thoughtful. Eventually he said, "Charming Claire?"

"Based on this conversation, you have no idea if I'm charming or not."

"You're playing along with me and I'm finding that pretty charming."

The compliment stole her attempt at a witty quip and she realized the gap between them on the rail had diminished. She wasn't sure who had moved—or if they both had. All she knew was that her body was hyper aware of just how close his elbow and dangling hand were to hers.

Matt pushed off the rail and faced her, the dimple now absent and his pupils large and inky black, almost obliterating the hypnotic green of his irises. "Charming and captivating."

The delicious effects of his low voice on her body swallowed her reply. Their eyes locked. The sounds of the crowd melted away and nothing existed except the two of them. The air between them vibrated with the seductive pull of desire and she let it tug her slowly toward him.

He moved unexpectedly, taking a jerky step backwards, and then his lopsided grin returned, overriding his serious look. "Come and meet Bert."

Her lust-soaked mind struggled to adjust to the rapid change. "Sorry?"

He laughed. "Now you're Confused Claire." He motioned with his hand toward the CFA tanker. "Bert."

"Bert?"

"Yeah. Big Expensive Red Tanker."

"You want to show me a fire truck?" She hated the squeak of disbelief in her voice. She may as well have said, "I thought you were going to kiss me."

"Have you been away from Myrtle for so long you've forgotten how Bert one and two keep Myrtle safe all year round, especially in summer?"

"Of course not," she said, frantically fighting for composure and at the same time berating herself for misreading the situation so badly.

"Glad to hear it." Matt winked at her and she glimpsed a little boy whose favorite toys were a red fire helmet and a Duplo fire truck. "Plus, Captain Matt's got a bar on the other side of Bert. Can I buy you a drink?"

Matt introduced her to the CFA crew as Postie Claire, and people who remembered her working in her parents' business welcomed her back while the strangers greeted her warmly. With their official duties as Santa's helpers over, some of the volunteers had joined their families but others, including Adam Petrovic, had stayed around to chat. Although Claire had grown up with Adam's wife, she didn't know the husband at all. He was ten years older than Rebecca and new to Myrtle. It didn't take her very long to notice how effortlessly he commanded a crowd: men—and not just the CFA members—gravitated toward him. The blue jokes probably helped.

Claire felt Matt's hand on the small of her back and she was suddenly facing a different set of people. It was a mixed group and she was thrilled to discover that four of the CFA team were women. This was a huge change from her childhood, when it was automatic for men to join the CFA and women the CWA. After a polite amount of general chit-chat, Matt extricated them.

They walked around the tanker and he gave her a tour of Bert. In typical guy fashion, he reeled off the specifications of the truck, including the 620 gallon water tank. He told her it included 170 gallons for the vehicle and crew spray protection system, which would be used if they ever got caught in a burnout. God willing, the crew would never need to activate it. He opened the cabin door and she swung up inside and then he joined her, rattling on about the air conditioning, electric windows, rearview camera, cabin support bar, fog lights and air horn. When he pointed out the seat belts, her bemusement gave way to laughter.

His usually wide smile was wry. "Sorry. Didn't mean to bore you."

"You're not. Well, not really. It's clear you're very proud of Bert."

"I am. And wait, there's more."

"Steak knives?"

"Better. These are the Thermaguard radiant heat protection curtains if we get caught in a fire front. Hopefully we'll never have to use them."

The rip of separating Velcro tabs was followed by the fall of silver curtains over all the windows, blocking out the sunshine and considerably dimming the cabin. For the first time in ten minutes, Matt fell silent. As Claire's eyes adjusted to the gloom, his hand lightly touched hers. Butterflies hurled themselves against the wall of her stomach.

He finally broke the silence. "Sorry for the deluge of stats. To be honest, though, it's mostly your fault."

"I ... um ..." His thumb was drawing circles on the back of her hand, sending addictive darts of longing all over her and reducing her concentration down to zero. "I don't follow."

"You're gorgeous."

"Um ... thank you."

"I haven't felt this jumpy around a woman in long time." Matt cleared his throat. "Are you totally bonded to staying for carols?"

"Not at all."

His fingers laced through hers, the touch warm and inviting. "Let's go to the beach."

Lorne was a half hour drive away down a steep and winding road. The nurse in her who'd treated far too many car-accident victims somehow managed to fight her way through the delighted internal squeals. "You okay to drive?"

"Yeah. I've only had a couple of light beers, but if you're worried, I'll ask Shane to breathalyze me before we go."

This time the dart that hit her wasn't just chemistry. She squeezed his hand. "Thanks. I'd love to go to the beach."

"Excellent."

He jumped down from the truck, came around to her side and extended his hand again. She didn't need any assistance climbing down but she accepted the offer, because why miss the delicious buzz that zipped through her whenever he touched her?

Once her feet hit the ground, Matt let go. "I'll get out of this gear and see Shane while you sort yourself out. Meet me in Noble Street in ten minutes."

Noble Street was two blocks away.

He must have read her uncertainty because he said, "My car's parked there."

That didn't exactly explain why they couldn't walk there together. She was about to say, "I'm happy to wait," but he was already striding across the oval.

As she watched his retreating figure—a tall, straight, bright yellow beacon—it occurred to her she should probably tell her parents her plans so they didn't worry at her disappearing act. A picture of her parents and the Langs lit up in her mind—four beaming and hopeful faces already mapping out a future for her and Matt. She pulled her cell phone out of her pocket.

Met up with friends. Will make my own way home. Love Claire xx

As she hit send, she realized the word "friends" was a rookie mistake. She didn't keep in contact with anyone in Myrtle and her mother knew it. Oh well, she had until morning to think up some names her mother wouldn't question.

CLAIRE LOVED the road that wound up and over the ridge then down to the coast. By far, her favorite part of the journey was the section where it twisted and turned through dappled light that penetrated the canopy of tiny-leafed beech trees interspersed with the world's tallest hardwood, the mountain ash. Ribbons of bark curled from their imposing trunks, draping themselves over the shorter and stockier blackwoods below.

Claire wished she'd known the forest before the timber-hungry white man arrived in the 1880's. They'd coveted the blackwood for its decorative timber, using it to build boats, kegs and musical instruments. They'd demanded the mountain ash and the beech for houses and public buildings in the burgeoning colony. Myrtle folklore insisted that the original section of the historically registered pub was built from the timber of a single giant mountain ash.

As Matt expertly navigated the tree fern–lined bends and drove out of the damp, lush forest, the vegetation changed again. Claire recognized the distinctively smooth white bark of the lemon-scented gums and the pretty salmon pink of the spotted gums. In spring, it was easy to pick the acacias with their golden fluff-ball flowers and the callistemon with their vivid crimson bottlebrushes but by summer, to her lesser-trained eye, the bush was just a mass of multiple shades of green.

Matt grimaced. "Geez, it's dry and the heat's hardly kicked in yet."

"Talking about the weather?" Claire laughed. "You really are a farmer."

"Believe me, drought's nothing to laugh about."

It was the first time he'd sounded serious and his tone sobered her. "But Myrtle's on the edge of the rainforest. It gets plenty of rain."

"Yeah, but not as much as when we were kids. We've had six years with well-below-average rainfall and the forest's bone dry. This year I'm asking Santa for rain."

The ocean's white foaming waves came into view over the tops of the shorter coastal melaleucas and tea tree. Claire sighed in delight. "I forgot how beautiful it is."

"It's a view that never gets old, that's for sure."

He slowed at the intersection with the Great Ocean Road but instead of turning into Lorne, he steered the ute the other way. Ten minutes later he pulled into a small parking lot with wooden stairs leading down to a beach. Unlike the main beach in Lorne, it wasn't crowded, but there were a few families beachcombing and half-a-dozen surfers out on the water.

"This is when I love daylight savings." Matt pulled beach towels out of a silver tool box on the back of the ute. "Fancy a swim?"

"Love one, but sadly, no swimsuit."

He rummaged through the box and then dangled a utilitarian one-piece swimsuit from his fingers. "Will this fit?"

"Maybe." For the first time since meeting him, a tiny slither of unease penetrated her euphoria. "Why do you have women's swimsuit in your car?"

He laughed. "I guess it looks bad but I promise you, these are my sister's. Sneaking off to the beach at a moment's notice when the farm gives us an unexpected break is a bit of a Cartwright family tradition. We keep gear in one another's cars."

"What else have you got in there?"

"Bodyboards and wetsuits. You in?"

"Definitely."

Matt handed her the swimsuit, a wetsuit and a towel before walking away and giving her privacy to change. He waited for her at the top of the path to the beach and then, hand in hand, they ran across warm golden sand and into the Southern Ocean. Despite the December heat, the first wave hit her with breath-sucking cold and she shrieked as water dribbled under the neck of the wetsuit.

Matt grinned. "Toughen up, princess."

"Hey! Be fair. I got used to swimming in the much warmer Bismarck Sea. Give me time to acclimate."

"You've probably forgotten how to ride a wave too."

Her competitive spirit kicked in. "Bet I haven't."

Twenty waves later, with eyes stinging with salt, muscles aching in a good way and her body alive with the joy of having fun, she signaled to Matt she was going in. He rode in too and they made their way back to the carpark and got changed.

Matt flashed her a familiar smile. "Hungry, Claire?"

"Starving. Let's drive into Lorne for fish and chips. My treat."

He threw a bag over his shoulder before lifting an cooler from another tool box. "I've got food. We may as well enjoy it, because Mom's going to have my guts for garters when she finds out I didn't deliver it."

It struck her as odd for a thirty-something man to be running errands for his mother. "Why didn't you deliver it?"

"I met you and I've been distracted ever since."

Her stomach flipped. "I've been suffering from a similar complaint."

"I'm glad." He caught her hand. "Let's picnic in the dunes and watch the sunset."

The white light of Venus had already pierced the pale sky and as they ate, the sun bid farewell to the day like an artist streaking vermillion and orange across a canvas. They listened to the chattering rosellas seeking a bed for the night in the banksias, the squawk of indignant seagulls fighting over something on the beach and the gentle thud of rolling waves in a calm sea. When the sky turned to indigo, the only things left of the avocado, tomato and herb salad and the lemon-roasted chicken were the bones.

"I know I was hungry but that food was amazing. The only thing missing was champagne," Claire said.

Matt leaned back on his elbows. "My bad. I'll do better next time."

The anticipation made her shiver.

"You warm enough?" He pulled a rug from the bag and threw it over their shoulders.

"Thanks."

"No problem." He slid his arm around her and she happily snuggled in. "Where's the Bismarck Sea?"

"Papua New Guinea."

"Vacation?"

"No. I spent a couple of years working for an NGO as a women's health practitioner. I split my time between tiny islands and remote villages on the Sepik River. I did everything from providing contraception to delivering babies and a lot of other stuff in between. I trained and worked with the island health workers, who were fabulous women doing a lot with very little."

"Sounds amazing and very different from Myrtle."

"So very different from Myrtle. Sometimes it was amazing, but a lot of the time it was heartbreaking. Despite the tropical setting and azure sea, many women lead tough lives. Often the pigs and chickens are valued more."

"Our pigs are treated like royalty but my mother and sister still get top billing. Mind you, Dad and I prefer a peaceful life."

She ignored the joke, too surprised by the mention of swine. "You're a pig farmer? I thought Oakvale Park was sheep?"

"It is, but five years ago we bought the farm next door and diversified. The acorns from the oaks are perfect for fattening up free-range pigs. We also grow pick-your-own summer berries and Mom and Tamara run the farm-gate café and handicrafts shop to catch the tourists. Mom's besotted with her alpacas and she spins their wool and sells it. I divide my time between the sheep and pigs with a sideline in bees."

"Wow! It really is a family business. Did you always want to farm?"

"Pretty much. What about you? Was nursing a calling?"

She laughed. "I don't know about that, but it certainly called me more than my family's business. The idea of working in the Myrtle Post Office and General Store wasn't something I ever considered. I wanted to see the world beyond Myrtle and Australia. With nursing I can work and travel. Every time I get sick of what I'm doing, I add another specialization to my belt and change direction."

"How often's that?"

She shrugged. "I guess, on average, every couple of years."

"Do you get bored easily?"

A bristle of indignation ran up her spine but she wasn't certain if she was irritated by him or by the voices of her parents and boyfriends past. "Not particularly. How is it any different from you diversifying from sheep?"

"Fair point. Mind you, we were chasing income, but you're right—I was up for a new challenge. I wanted a way of putting my stamp on the farm."

She dug her toes into the sand. "What's it like working with family?"

"I don't really have much to compare it to. After ag college, I was a ranch hand for a couple of years in outback Queensland and Western Australia, but it wasn't much different from when I'd worked on the farm as a teen, except my boss was a stranger instead of my father. I wanted to come home but I didn't want to be one of those sons who works on the family farm for no pay. I wanted to be part of the business."

"And diversifying offered you that?"

"Yep. It meant I didn't step on Dad's toes. As well as introducing pigs, I moved out of the homestead and into the manager's house. Thought that was the best way to reinforce I was an adult and a business partner."

"Did it work?"

"Pretty much. Sometimes it's hard to separate the family stuff from the business but when things get heated, I always find a fast gallop helps blow away the frustrations. Do you ride?"

"I was a complete pony-club failure. The jumps terrified me."

"You really are a townie." His exaggerated sigh tickled her ear and he tightened his arm around her. "And I had such high hopes."

"Hey! I can gallop with the best of them, farm boy."

"I'd like to see that."

Under a moonless, starlit sky, it was too dark to see his face but the unexpected sincerity in his voice undid her. That and the hours of lust battering at her, sapping her resolve until she had no energy left to resist. Her rational side insisted that overwhelming attraction like this was just Hollywood hype, or mythic legend like Lancelot and Guinevere—it had no sound basis. But right now, logic was struggling under the simmer of desire that had been fizzing inside her since she'd opened her eyes to his and tumbled into that forest-green gaze.

Despite her previous relationships, she'd ever experienced this sort of high-octane promise with a man. She'd never been a woman who made the first move either, but right now, not touching him was just too hard. Cupping his cheeks with her hands, she welcomed the prickly rub of his stubble against her palms and then she leaned in and kissed him. His nose was cold against her cheek but his lips were soft, warm and pliant. He tasted of avocado and tomatoes.

It took her a second or two to realize that his lips were perfectly still and that she was the only person actively involved in the kiss.

Shoot me now.

She dropped her hands and pulled back fast. Embarrassment burned her. She desperately wished for the world to swallow her whole and transport her back to her apartment. To a place where she didn't take risks with men she'd only met four hours earlier.

"Sorry. I—" *What? Got it all horribly wrong? Am useless at distinguishing between friendly banter and something more?*

He swore softly. "No. Don't be sorry. It's just ..." His arm was still around her waist. "You took me by surprise."

Oh God, this was going from bad to worse. A crackle of anger flared. "Surprise? Really? Are you telling me that I've misread every signal you've put out there since we met? That you haven't backed off moments from kissing me at least three times tonight?"

It took a few beats before he spoke. "No. Sorry. The last thing I want is for you to feel bad. Shit. I've totally stuffed this up." He rested his forehead against hers. "Can I make it up to you?"

"You can try."

His lips pressed so gently against hers it was as if he thought she was fine bone china. Everything inside her loosened and she sighed, opening her mouth. Hours of leashed desire broke free.

Claire didn't know if Matt pushed her or if she pulled him, but they fell back on the rug, mouths melding, legs tangling and hands pulling frantically at each other's clothes, seeking skin to touch, feel and explore. She loved the play of his muscles under her palms and welcomed the touch of his work-roughened fingers kneading her spine.

Her hands found his waistband. His hands found her breasts. The touch drove her crazy and her hips rose, pressing against him. He groaned and rolled her under him, burying his face in her neck and doing amazing things with his tongue.

It took the prickly feel of sand on her back to summon her common sense. Panting, she pulled her mouth from his. "Whoa! This is crazy."

"I reckon this is what they mean by instant attraction." He sounded as bewildered as she did. "It's like being hit by a truck."

She stroked his face. "Um, Matt, please don't get me wrong, I really want to have sex with you but—"

"Yeah. You deserve better than sex in the sand and the risk of chafing in all the wrong places. Besides, when it happens, I want to be able to see you in 3D rather than in silhouette."

Claire quite liked sex in the dark as it hid myriad imperfections, but the thought of seeing Matt naked sent another raft of longing through her. She was about to offer up options when he rolled off her, sat up and grabbed the abandoned blanket.

"Scooch over," he said.

She moved, readying for a quick pack up and fast exit to find a bed in Lorne. But Matt's hands were back on her, pulling her into him and rolling her over. When he stopped moving, she realized they were swaddled together in the blanket. Disappointment slugged her.

His fingers played gently in her hair. "Sex will be amazing, but this is nice too."

The touch was calm and caring—the complete opposite of the frenetic contact they'd shared a few minutes earlier. The sensible part of her was relieved that he was content to cuddle, because the cold hard reality was that she'd abandoned all sense of caution and safety and was alone on an isolated beach with a man she barely knew. Despite her gut telling her that Matt was a good guy, the situation could have easily turned bad.

Tucked in next to him with his body heat keeping her warm, her jittery and jangly nerves slowly settled and an unexpected feeling of peace rolled through her. She could wait a few hours longer for sex. Matt was right—this was good in a different way.

THE PALE PINK of dawn lightened the sky as Claire and Matt pulled into the driveway of Claire's parents' hobby farm. Matt immediately dimmed the headlights so as not to wake them.

"How long are you in Myrtle, Postie Claire?"

"I leave the weekend after Christmas."

He leaned in and quickly brushed her cheek with his lips. "I'll see you soon then."

"Great."

Claire got out of the car and stood at the gate watching the taillights disappear. Anticipatory delight at the coming week danced through her, making her want to laugh. Energized, she jogged the short distance to the house and prayed the back door no longer squeaked so she could let herself into the house quietly.

"Hello, darling. Did you have fun?" Heather stood at the kitchen counter holding a mug with both hands.

Claire's stomach dropped. Not only had she forgotten that her mother was an early riser, she'd been so distracted by Matt she'd completely forgotten to come up with a story about the evening. She decided that the best lies were born out of truth so she built on that.

"Great, thanks. A few of us went to the beach. We had a bonfire and drank too much. Thought it was wiser to sleep it off there than risk getting pulled over or running off the road."

Her mother took a mug off the hook and poured tea. "It was nice of Matt Cartwright to drop you home."

Claire's heart rate picked up. How was it that her mother couldn't find something under her nose but she had 20/20 distance vision in the dawn light? "Yeah. He was the taxi. I was the last one to be dropped off."

"I didn't see Taylor in the car."

Taylor? Her mother must mean Matt's sister, Tamara. "Ah, no. She wasn't there."

"Oh, I remember now. She's in Geelong at her company's Christmas party. She was pretty vocal they weren't paying for partners to attend this year so Matt couldn't go." She laughed. "*Partner* is the new word these days, isn't it? It used to be boyfriend, fiancée, and husband, and then it was de facto if they weren't married. Now even married couples say partner. Taylor and Matt have been practically living together for two years. Rumor is he's proposing at Christmas. I bet the next time I see her, she'll be flashing a ring and saying *fiancé*."

It was like being caught in a hail storm, only the balls of ice were inside Claire, stinging and burning. Matt wasn't single? Images from the night before assaulted her. His suggestion she meet him at his car instead of walking there together. Avoiding Lorne. His flirt and retreat tactics. The fact that she'd initiated the kiss.

Her breath froze in her lungs. What if she hadn't slowed things down? Would he have obliged?

The room spun. Hoping like hell her mother didn't notice her trembling hand, Claire managed to lower her mug to the counter without dropping it. "I'm pretty sandy and salty, Mom. I'm going to grab a shower and a nap."

"No breakfast?"

"I'll have something later."

"Come into town at eleven and have morning tea with me. I want to hear all about the bonfire and who was there."

Claire walked into the bathroom and threw up.

CHAPTER THREE

"I think you should go," Matt said. They were on their way home from the stadium opening and he slipped his hand onto Claire's thigh.

Claire put her hand over his. "Why?"

"Because joining in and getting involved is normal. After the last year and a half, normal's what we both need."

She stared at him. "Getting involved? What do you think I've been doing for the last eighteen months?"

"Work."

The implied criticism stung. "Hey, when I poured Leanne Riteski a cup of tea today and she asked me to look at the rash on her arm, I told her to make an appointment."

He shot her a smile. "Thank you."

"You're welcome. But I'm not sure that me joining a craft group comes anywhere close to normal."

"I dunno. If the fires hadn't vaporized life as we knew it, I reckon you would have rediscovered your country roots and joined something like this ages ago."

"Have you forgotten I was all set to join the CFA?"

"We've talked about this."

"I don't think you saying, 'No way in hell,' qualifies as us talking about it."

"Hell, Claire." His grip tightened on the steering wheel. "You know why."

She wanted to ask how it was different from her worrying about him but as she'd already eaten into a chunk of their time on this long-awaited day off, she took the path of least resistance. "I suck at crafts."

"No, you don't. You knitted me that beanie."

"I think lust made me delusional about my skill level."

"I like the sound of that. Feel free to channel those memories this afternoon."

She rolled her eyes. "I was living in Melbourne and you weren't around to see what a nightmare that beanie was. I spent more time unpicking the damn thing than knitting it."

"So, each stitch was a labor of love, eh?"

"Each stitch was infused with a swear word. I think I even learned some new ones."

"Nah." He squeezed her thigh. "I feel the love every time I wear it."

He still wore the beautifully soft merino beanie with its unique cable and wonky band that looked nothing like the pattern she'd so carefully followed. Claire wondered if his wearing of it had something to do with him believing they were still the same starry-eyed couple they'd been before the fires. Maybe he just hadn't noticed she'd changed.

He pulled up at Oakvale Park's gate and she jumped out to open it. As she swung it shut behind the ute and latched the chain over the knob, she wondered what her closing count must be after two years of living on the farm. The dogs barked, telling her to hurry up.

Hopping back into the cab, it suddenly occurred to her that Matt had been talking about this day off all week and hinting at "plans." Why were they at home?

"Uh, Matt, I thought we were going somewhere?"

His eyes sparkled. "We are."

A few brown and yellow leaves that had clung tenaciously to the trees long after the rest of the foliage had dropped fluttered onto the windshield as Matt drove along the oak-lined road that passed the big house—his parents' home. Oakvale stood serene, reminding her that in a sea of change some things stayed the same.Claire knew it was an illusion in more ways than one.

Although the exterior of the building had changed very little since it was built in 1899, the inside told a different story. But Claire adored the long clapboard homestead with its timber veranda, gingerbread wooden fretwork and the reassuring symmetry of windows and tall chimneys. As devastating as it had been for her and Matt to lose their house in the wildfires, she didn't hold a grudge that it had been sacrificed to save the homestead and the trees.

The one thing Claire disliked about the big house was its position. The only way for her and Matt to get to their house was to drive past the homestead. Despite a grove of oaks between it and the road, Louise and Bill always seemed to know when they were coming and going.

Instead of turning down their drive, Matt shot left and drove behind the old stables and outbuildings to the shearing shed. Slightly older than the homestead, it was a beautiful mix of mountain ash and corrugated iron. Claire often wondered if the shearers and roustabouts ever took time during the frenetic days of shearing to admire the bones of the building and appreciate the colors of the wood. She did.

"Are we dousing sheep?"

"Seriously? You're asking me that on this precious day off?"

"Sorry." Claire held up her hands in surrender, well aware she should have thought before speaking. Matt was the romantic in their relationship and if anyone was trying to pass off work under the guise of a date, it would be her.

He parked next to the empty stockyards. "Stay there." He hopped out and walked around to her door, opening it with a flourish. When she got out, he grabbed her gloved hand and walked her to the bottom of the stairs. "Close your eyes."

"Okay."

He led her and the moment the combination of lanolin, sheep dung and machinery oil hit her nostrils, she knew she was inside.

"Can I open my eyes?"

"Three more steps."

Their boots echoed on the boards as she counted to three and then she opened her eyes. Their patio heater was in front of her. Underneath it, and next to some wool bales, was a picnic rug, some throw pillows from their couch, Matt's old school blanket and a cooler. He'd even found the only two things flowering in the homestead's winter garden—lavender and hellebore—and put them in a vase. It looked like a set from *The Bachelorette* sans tea candles. Naked flames in the woolshed were verboten.

Had she forgotten an important date? Her mind roved across birthdays and drew a blank. Then she remembered they'd been standing outside the woolshed when Matt had asked her to marry him. Was today the anniversary of his proposal? Sweat broke out on her hairline. "What's all this?"

"Picnic. Get comfy and I'll pour you a drink. Figured your fave red on a cold day?"

"Perfect." She pulled off her gloves, trying to stay calm. "You're not proposing again are you?"

"No." The seal on the wine cracked loudly—almost disapprovingly. Matt silently poured two glasses of wine, handed her one and settled down next to her. "I don't need to propose. My ring's been on your finger for almost two years."

Her thumb played with the band of the beautiful tear-shaped diamond and she took a big sip of her wine to try to cut off the memory blast—her parents' happiness. Her own naïve and blissful delight.

She forced out words around the lump in her throat. "I love this ring and I love you."

"I know," he said. "And you know I'll marry you tomorrow or any other day. Just tell me when and where and I'll be there."

He opened the cooler as if he were expecting her silence on the topic and quickly set up the food: a rustic baguette, their favorite triple brie, Danish blue, duck liver pâté, salad greens, ham and pastrami, some slices of rare lamb, Tamara's homemade mayonnaise, a trio of dips, sushi and six oysters.

"Wow! Thank you." She kissed him. "What a smorgasbord of treats."

He handed her a plate and some silverware wrapped in a napkin. "Only the best for you."

She laughed. "Nice try but the blue cheese has your name written all over it."

"You got me."

They ate in the way couples who know each other well do—easy conversation, passing favorite foods—and all of it was interspersed with moments of companionable silence. As Claire ate, she was surprised to feel a coil of tension unfurl. Until that moment, she hadn't been aware it was inside her.

When they'd made a solid assault on the food, Matt said, "I've got coffee and some of those mini eclairs from Nguyens."

"Thanks, but I think I'll wait a bit. Especially as there's still wine in the bottle."

He smiled and refilled their wineglasses before settling back against the wool bales. "Come here."

She snuggled between his legs, pulled a blanket over them and rested her back on his chest with a long, satisfied sigh. "This is nice."

He slid his free hand into hers. "Yeah."

"You were right."

"Can I have that in writing?"

She gently elbowed him in the ribs. "I mean about taking some time just for us. Thank you."

"You're welcome." His chin rested on the top of her head. "It's been a crap eighteen months."

"Yes."

"But now, thank God, it's over."

Was it? "You're sleeping better."

"We're both sleeping better. I don't miss dreaming about burnt sheep, that's for sure."

Following the fires, Matt and his father had stoically undertaken the grisly task of putting down 1500 sheep and 200 pigs before commencing the massive re-fencing job. For three months he'd been very quiet. The nightmares lasted longer, waking him in the middle of the night, his skin slick with sweat. Claire knew it was his distress rising to the surface.

In the moments when she'd managed to penetrate the cloud of her own grief and despair, she'd always asked him, "Are you okay?"

"Yeah," he'd replied without fail.

"You'd tell me if you weren't, wouldn't you?"

He'd invariably nodded, leaving her unconvinced and worried—powerless against the unwanted force that had embedded itself in their lives. But thankfully, Matt was sleeping soundly again. On the nights Claire's nightmares still woke her, he didn't notice and she didn't tell him.

Matt kissed her hair. "I know we've still got boxes to unpack but the best thing is, we're living in our own place again."

They'd finally moved out of the homestead and into their brand-new house built on the site of the old one. Claire had pushed for a different position on the farm—one farther away from the big house—but she'd been thwarted not only by Louise and Bill but by the shire's local government. Despite their closest neighbors being more than two miles away, apparently one couldn't build a house just anywhere on a farm anymore.

"Moving into the house was definitely a turning point."

"We're luckier than most."

She heard the message buried in his words: *My family's very good to us.* And in their way, they were. After the fire destroyed everything she and Matt owned, Louise and Bill had created a living space for them in the far end of the homestead: a bedroom, bathroom and a room to lounge in. It gave them a certain amount of privacy but without a kitchen, the elder Cartwrights dictated meal times, the menu and the conversation, which was often a commentary on Claire and Matt's decisions, ranging from opinions on the new house plans and décor, to their choice of a vacation destination—"Is it really wise to be flying to Bali right now?"—and their choice of laundry powder.

There was no doubt at all that their new home was beautiful. With its sleek lines, state-of-the-art kitchen, mouse-proof pantry, mold-free bathroom and a view across the fields to the forest she adored, Claire was beyond fortunate to have it. However, knowing that wasn't enough to stop the pang she got whenever she thought about the loss of what the Cartwrights had always called "the manager's house." That quaint timber cottage with its wonky veranda had oozed character.

It had been the home where Matt and Claire's overwhelming lust and desire for each other had evolved into love. For Claire, it had been a magical place where they'd retreated from the demands of work, the farm and the Cartwrights, and wrapped themselves in a bubble of happiness. She'd loved curling up on the lumpy old couch with a cup of tea and the dogs, letting her mind wander as she listened to the walls whispering their stories of families past and strong women working hard to make a life with their man.

"So, I was thinking …" Matt said, his arms tightening around her.

She turned and ran her fingers up his chest. "Sex in the shed?"

He grinned. "Well, yeah, that goes without saying, but it wasn't what I meant."

She laughed and pressed her palm to his forehead. "Do you have a temperature?"

"Shush and let me finish. It's been tough but we've got the farm back on track, we're in our own home and, despite all the infighting and the issues with city hall, Myrtle's public infrastructure's been rebuilt faster than we expected.

"I know Adam Petrovic's not your favorite bloke, but you've got to admit that given the hell he's been through, the fact he made main street and the new shops a priority is pretty impressive. He's the town's hero in more ways than one. And Phil Lang told me today that the rebuilding committee's job is done. Everything's pretty much back to normal."

Claire thought of the new shops in main street. Half of them contained nothing more than a "For Lease" sign, because the fires hadn't just burned down Myrtle's infrastructure, it had destroyed many businesses. Of those that had attempted to trade for a year out of shipping containers, only two had successfully transitioned into the new shops. She thought about the firefighter and father of two who'd committed suicide a month earlier and the woman in her office only the day before who'd broken down in tears, saying she didn't know how she could keep going. None of that was normal.

"So, I was thinking," Matt continued. "You've given two hundred per cent to the town since the fires and I get that. People needed you and you've been a rock, but now it's time for us to get our life back on track too."

"It is and we are. I can't start planting the garden until spring."

He stroked her hair. "I'm not talking about the garden. I'm talking about a baby."

The cozy warmth inside her chilled. "A baby?"

"Why do you sound so surprised?"

"I ... it's ... we ..." *Breathe.* "It's just we haven't talked about having a baby in a long time."

"Which is why I'm bringing it up now. Life's good again and the timing's perfect." He laughed, his face filling with memories. "Remember when you first moved into the cottage? We spent hours talking about having three kids, two dogs and a cat. You even had a name book."

That book had burned to ash along with the rest of her library. She did remember them snuggling up together in their beautiful fallen forest timber bed and blissfully planning their future family. But now instead of wonder and excitement, she felt the jittery agitation of alarm. "We've got the dogs," she said inanely.

Thankfully, Matt didn't seem to notice her distraction. "Exactly. Now we add the kids. If it wasn't for the fires, this conversation would be about planning our second. Anyway, I've been doing some reading and if you stop taking the pill and start taking folic acid—although apparently they add that to bread now so you're probably good. Anyway, we can ..."

As he talked, the significance of his food choices for their lunch slammed into her like a runaway truck. He'd prepared her a last supper —the entire menu was food pregnant women were advised to avoid.

"You've been reading?" she asked faintly.

"Yeah. Doctor Google. Who knew there was so much stuff about pregnancy?" He sounded both thrilled and surprised. "There's even apps that give you a blow by blow of what's happening each week."

Bloody internet! God, most of her pregnant patients complained that their husbands weren't interested in doing any pregnancy reading and had to be dragged to classes. Why was she the one with an evolved man? Her heart pumped faster. "You didn't download an app, did you?"

"Not yet, I know you're a bit superstitious that way." His eyes sparkled. "But the moment I've knocked you up, it's going on my cell phone."

Panic jetted through her. Once, her long-held desire to be a mother had filled her daydreams. Now the idea only held fear. "I thought you'd want to get the house totally sorted first? I mean, once we have a baby, our time won't be our own. Are you sure you're really ready for everything that comes with being parents?"

"Postie." Her nickname caressed her tenderly. "I've been ready from the moment I met you. I know we probably shouldn't try until you've checked your folic acid levels are okay but"—his smile creased his face into deep and happy lines—"we can have fun practicing, starting now."

He kissed her then, long, slow and deep. She sighed, giving over to the thrill that jolted her, letting it stream through her until every cell vibrated with longing. She arched toward him, letting her body direct the play, embracing desire and running with it.

It was so much easier and safer than telling Matt she no longer wanted to have a baby.

CHAPTER FOUR

A YEAR BEFORE THE FIRES

It was five o'clock on a Melbourne evening and Sophie was feeding Liam his dinner while Josh sat at the table, skimming his email.

"Freaking hell, Soph."

"What?" Sophie's hand paused with the spoon midway to Liam's mouth. He squealed indignantly, grabbing for the spoon as Josh shoved his cell at her. It was impossible to avoid seeing the uncompromising figure. "How?" she asked faintly.

"You've got to stop using the reverse cycle all bloody day."

Josh's criticism burned. Their rented two-story townhouse was icy in winter and boiling in summer. Despite repeatedly asking the owner for better insulation or the installation of outside blinds, all they'd got was inaction and rising energy bills.

"It's alright for you. You get to leave the house and use the AC at work. Liam and I are stuck in this box."

"Rent and electricity aren't just eating into our house deposit, they're gutting it. You have to go back to work."

"No!" Her heart went into overdrive. All she'd ever wanted was to be a stay-at-home-mom. The thought of leaving Liam with strangers ten hours a day horrified her.

"We don't have a choice."

"But we've been through this. We've run all the numbers over and over. Liam's childcare will take a massive chunk of my wages."

"Yeah, but we'll save the rest because you won't be at home running up a huge electricity bill."

"Mom, Mom, Mom." Liam banged the tray of his highchair, demanding his dinner.

Distracted, she shoveled peas into his mouth. "I promise the next bill will be lower. Now the weather's nicer, I can take Liam to the pool and the park."

Josh gave her a hard stare, his brown eyes flinty. "You say that and I know you mean it right up until we get a string of days in the 90s. Then you'll be hunkering down here with the air on full tilt."

"It's not like I'm not trying! Do you have any idea what it's like to shop at the market with a toddler, but I do it because the food's cheaper. I haven't bought any new clothes in a year and I even had the horrible conversation with Mom and Kylie about doing a Kris Kringle this year instead of gifts for everyone. They looked at me as if I was an alien. I sat there dying, listening to Kylie giving me a lecture on Christmas spirit."

Josh grunted. "Your sister wouldn't know a budget if she fell over it."

Anger at his cheap shot at her family bubbled and spat. "Kylie doesn't have to budget, does she? Lex can afford to buy her whatever she wants."

"And poor Sophie's left slumming it with me." He grabbed his beer, rocked to his feet and strode to the couch. A second later the TV blared to life and a voice was telling them how a luxury spa with hydrotherapy jets would change their lives.

Guilt and aggravation swamped her. She hadn't meant to upset Josh but somehow the words always tumbled out unchecked and here they were again. Sighing, she lifted Liam out of his highchair and settled him on the floor with his favorite truck before kneeling on the couch and nestling her behind firmly on Josh's lap. He ignored her, keeping his gaze fixed firmly on the TV.

She stroked his face. "Never for one second have I ever thought I'm slumming it with you. I love you and I don't regret us for a second." Her hand fell to her side. "It's just I didn't think having Liam meant we were going to argue over money *all* the time. I hate it."

His gaze shifted to her face, his eyes sad. "I hate it too."

She leaned in and kissed him and when his arms finally circled her, she knew she was forgiven. "What if you asked for overtime? That would protect the deposit."

"They've put a freeze on it until February. Soph, we've done everything we possibly can to trim our budget. There's nothing else left to cut. You have to go back to work."

The thought of getting up before dawn, waking Liam and dropping him off at daycare just as the sun rose made her chest ache. She slid off Josh's lap and cuddled into him, lazily drawing a circle on his chest. "You know, some women are making a mint using social media to sell things. I could—"

"No." He trapped her finger in his palm.

"What do you mean, no? You haven't even heard what I'm suggesting."

"Don't have to. You have a pantry full of Tupperware you didn't sell and a bathroom full of makeup you promised me your friends would buy. If we want a house of our own, we can't afford for you to sign up and spend money on stuff you won't sell and don't need."

"The organized pantry makes our life easier," she said snippily, but she didn't push the point. As much as she hated admitting it, Josh was right. She was crap at selling things.

Liam grizzled and tugged on their legs. Sophie stood up and scooped him into her arms, inhaling his sweet post-bath smell. "Can you cook some rice while I put him to bed?"

Josh groaned. "I've had a huge day at work and you know I suck at cooking."

"*Cooking?* It's boiling water, Josh."

He tilted his beer bottle toward her accusingly. "You promised if you stayed at home with Liam, you'd do all the cooking."

"And you've just told me I have to go back to work. That means you're going to have to step up on the cooking and cleaning."

"Yeah, well, you're not at work yet."

Rage fizzed so hot and hard she thought she might explode. "Here!" She dumped Liam in Josh's lap and their son gave a surprised cry. "Put *your* son to bed and I'll cook the damn rice."

"We wouldn't be having this argument if you hadn't got pregnant two years earlier than we planned."

His betrayal stung. "Me? Don't you dare pin this on me. You were there too, Josh. We got pregnant using the pill. We made a joint decision to have Liam. *We!*"

He shot her a mulish look before dropping his forehead onto the top of Liam's bald head. When he looked up, she saw regret in his eyes. "Sorry. That was a crap thing to say. Liam's the best mistake we've made, but it's just so fu—"

"Swear jar!"

"Fine! But it's freaking frustrating that we're going backwards."

"I get that you want a house, but is it really worth it if it means we're arguing about money all the time? Is it worth me going back to work if other people get to spend more time with Liam than us? And you're right, you suck at cooking and cleaning so when I go back to work, instead of arguing about money, we'll argue about who cleans the toilet."

Her heart ached at the look of desolation on his face. She wrapped her arms around her husband and son. "And why are we doing this to ourselves? None of my cousins own their own home. Everyone rents."

And they were back to the crux of the problem—she didn't have the same need as Josh to own their own home. When her parents had moved their small family to Australia, they'd never discussed buying a house, being content with full employment and a comfortable rental. Her mother, Aileen, still lived in the same house they'd moved into three months before her father died far too young at thirty-eight. Aileen now shared it with her landlord, enjoying a life rich in the travel and trinkets she'd always craved.

"Yeah, but we don't live in Ireland! I'm twenty-nine, Soph. My parents bought their first house at twenty-two. My grandparents did the same."

"Josh, you're comparing apples and oranges. Your family bought and built when there was more land surrounding Melbourne *and* there wasn't a massive property boom. We need to be realistic. Right now we can't even afford the outer-outer suburbs. Wouldn't it be better to sit it out and wait until the property bubble bursts?"

"No! That could be years away and we'll just get further and further behind."

"Not necessarily. We can use this time to have another baby. If the kids are close in age they'll be playmates. When they're both at school, I'll go back to work full time. We'll buy a house then. How's that for a new plan?"

His face hardened. "Just promise me you'll call Rixtons tomorrow and get your job back."

The following morning, she fought her reluctance and did as Josh asked. She gave her name to the new receptionist and while she waited for her call to be transferred to personnel, she silently chanted, *No vacancies, please no vacancies.*

"Sophie!" Deb from personnel squealed down the line. "Are your ears burning? I was just about to call you. One of the case managers just quit. Can you start back Monday?"

WHEN THE MALE voice on the GPS said for the third time, "Turn around when possible," Josh swore.

"Swear jar, Josh," Sophie muttered, crossing her arms. "After all, this was your idea."

Liam squealed from his car seat, siding with his mother.

Josh almost swore again, but instead he channeled his frustration into tugging hard on the steering wheel. The moment he'd pulled partially off the narrow road, he changed the natsav to a female voice. He should have done that before leaving home—he hated a bloke giving him instructions.

"Just admit it, Josh. We're lost, we're hot and it's time to go home."

Josh was admitting nothing.

The reason they were currently geographically challenged in the Otway Ranges, outside a town neither of them had heard of six weeks earlier, was because of that bloody electricity bill. Since Sophie's return to full-time work, their house deposit was steadily building but all three of them were exhausted and their relationship was deteriorating fast. Today was all about stopping that slide. Today was about new beginnings. It was about him stepping up and being the man his family deserved—and it would be as soon as he worked out where the hell they were.

They'd left Melbourne more than two hours earlier, but the last ten minutes seemed to have lasted longer than the rest of the time put together. Surely they were close to their destination? They had to be. Hell, he'd followed Adam Petrovic's instructions to a T.

"We're not lost." Josh grabbed for the map on Sophie's lap but she moved it out of his reach and turned it around. This need Sophie had to turn the map when the car turned drove him nuts. "Seriously?"

"Shut up. At least I have a better idea of where we are than the GPS. *It* says we're in a field."

"Are you sure we took the right road back there?"

"You said it was a bit over a mile from the turnoff and that's where we turned. Mind you, I'd hardly call this a road."

"It's the country, Soph. Gravel is a road." He made another grab for the map and was successful.

"You dragged me away from a massive list of Christmas jobs just to get lost in the middle of nowhere? Some surprise, Josh." Sophie swiveled in her seat, passing a fractious Liam his water bottle. "Please can we just go home?"

"Not until we've found what I'm looking for." He regretted the grit in his voice but this was too important to admit defeat. "I reckon if we drive back to the turn-off we'll pass it."

He backed up to a gap in a grove of trees and turned into a secluded driveway marked with impressive stone pillars. The sign on the freshly painted white wooden gate said, BEECHSIDE.

Sophie peered through the windshield down the long tree-lined drive looking for the house. "Impressive. But we're nowhere near the beach. And why would they spend big bucks on an entrance like this and misspell the name?"

"That spelling's the name of a tree."

"Oh! Clever. How do you know that?"

"I've got hidden depths you're yet to discover," he quipped, dodging the question. Now wasn't the time to tell Sophie how he knew the difference between a blackwood and a myrtle beech. That information would come after he'd laid the groundwork of his plan. He maneuvered the car back onto the road, driving slowly. "Keep your eyes peeled for a sign. It's around here somewhere."

As they crawled along at a snail's pace, Josh lowered his head and peered under the visor. Just as he saw a flash of silver, Sophie yelled, "Stop. Go back."

Peeking out from behind some rangy bushes was a sign that read, LAND FOR SALE. CONTACT ADAM PETROVIC, BUILDER.

Josh gave a woot. "This is it."

"*This* is your surprise? A field?"

"Sure is." Josh unbuckled Liam from his car seat and put his hat on before hoisting him onto his hip. Sophie remained inside the car so he opened her door and took her hand. "You do realize that pouting like that just makes you look sexy."

Her frown cleared and she laughed. "Okay, I'll get out of the car. But if there are snakes, I'm outta here."

"We'll make lots of noise and protect, Mommy, won't we, mate?" Josh said to Liam, who was tugging on his hat.

Liam blew a raspberry. Laughing, Josh passed him to Sophie so he could open the gate. As he hooked it closed, a grazing sheep with a massive coat of dirty wool gave them a disinterested glance before returning to munch on the brown grass.

Heat shimmered in the air around them. The top section of the property was cleared to the point where the land fell sharply away. The slope was heavily wooded with black-barked eucalypts, along with some stringy barks and the occasional blue gum. Josh glimpsed some huge tree ferns at the bottom of the gully, which told him there was a creek. In the distance, the rolling hills of the adjacent farmland gave way to a rippling blue-green vista that stretched to the horizon. Was it sea or sky? Probably both. Josh had spent hours studying Google Earth and he knew the Southern Ocean lay on the other side of the range.

Excited by the potential of this serene place, he turned to Sophie. "What do you think?"

"It's eerily quiet."

"At dawn and dusk, it'll probably be noisy with birds."

"How is that a selling point?" She glanced at the ground as if anticipating marauding creepy crawlies and reluctantly released a squirming Liam. He squatted down, studying an ant.

"Birdsong's gotta be better than the 5:18 whistle of the first train and the buzz of freeway traffic."

"I guess."

"Use your imagination." Josh led her up the small rise. "If we built our house here, we'd get a clear view of the mountains one way ..." He put his hands on her waist and turned her. "... and cows the other. This block of land's much bigger than what we can afford to buy in Melbourne."

"Josh, it's in the middle of nowhere."

"It's five minutes to Myrtle."

"There's nothing in Myrtle. If you blinked you'd miss it."

"You're exaggerating. I saw a bakery, a small supermarket and a pub. There's more off the main road and besides, Colac's only forty-five minutes away. It's got an Aldi and Woolies supermarket plus Target. Not to mention the library, the arts center and a cinema."

"Forty-five minutes? That's not close."

"It takes you longer than that to get from our place to the mall. Out here there's no traffic."

His mind raced, seeking compelling reasons to persuade her that living here would remove them from the precariousness of renting. How it would give them the opportunity not only to build their dream home but to make their money work for them instead of lining the pockets of landlords. It would be solid financial security in the form of bricks and mortar.

He pulled her in close. "We can build a sustainable home that's cool in summer and warm in winter. We can stop arguing over energy bills. Just think, Soph. No shared walls. No more of Kabir's sitar music or Zac yelling at his missus. No neighbors on top of us. Hell, we can have floor-to-ceiling windows. We can walk around naked and no one would see us."

"And we do that so often."

"But wouldn't it be nice to know that we could?" He grinned then kissed her.

She pulled back. "But we don't know anyone out here."

"We'll meet people. Country people are friendly. You saw the signs in Myrtle advertising Carols by Candlelight."

"Yes, but we haven't seen any actual people. And what about our families?"

He knew if he was careful, he could score points here. "Your mother and Kylie pretty much ignore you unless they want something, so what's to miss? Of course, if I've got that wrong, we can build a spare room so they can visit."

"No need to go that far."

He laughed. "Well, I was thinking about a spare room for my parents when they're not off doing the gray nomad thing."

"I like that idea. Liam would love it."

"So you can picture it?"

"Maybe. What about our jobs?"

"Remember all those pine plantations we passed? They're owned by Sustainable Timber. The company's hiring and I did a video interview on Monday. They offered me a job on a Myrtle plantation. I'd be working outside instead of in a stinking factory and the money's awesome. I've run the numbers, Soph. I've talked to the bank. If I take this job we can afford to buy this land and build our own home."

"Let me get this straight. You're asking me to give up the job you forced me to take, move to the middle of nowhere and get another job? Is there a job for me out here? Is there even childcare in the sticks?"

He tried not to grin as he played his trump card—the gift he so desperately wanted to give her. "If I take the plantation job and we move out here, we can afford for you to give up work and stay at home with Liam."

Her mouth fell open. "Are you serious? You're prepared to change jobs and move just so I can stay at home with Liam?"

"Yes, I'm bloody serious. Do you think I liked asking you to go back to work? I hated it. I felt like I was letting you and Liam down. We both know since you went back to work things have been crap. We're always tired and strung out and we've hardly had sex. I want you to be happy. I want both of us to be happy." He cupped her neck with his palm. "Let's be honest. We're both happier when you're not working."

"You just hate having to do the vacuuming and you're missing sex."

He grinned. "Hundred per cent. So, are you in?" *Please say yes.*

But she didn't say anything and disappointment snuck in under his euphoria.

"Soph?"

"Staying at home here will be heaps different from staying at home in Melbourne."

Josh gave a silent vote of thanks that he'd not only researched jobs and house and land packages, he'd also investigated what was on offer for families. "According to the internet, there's a toy library in Myrtle so I reckon they'll have a playgroup too."

He bent down and scooped up Liam, who was busy eating dirt. "Come on, mate. Let's go and check out what Myrtle's got to offer."

ON THE SHORT drive back to town, Sophie's mind spun like a top. That morning, when Josh had told her that the day's destination was a surprise, she'd assumed it was something to do with her Christmas present. Although why she'd thought that made little sense—Josh didn't excel in gift giving or in the writing or speaking of romantic words. Although today he might have just made up for years of lousy gifts. But could she give up everything familiar and move to the country?

Josh braked at a road block and a bloke wearing a pair of vivid orange overalls and clutching a stop sign leaned down to window height.

"The parade's finished but there's food and carols at the sports ground. Chuck a U-turn and take the first left."

Josh threw her a questioning look. "Wanna go?"

"Why not? I'm starving."

Five minutes later, they stood on a sports field surrounded by families with excited children. A row of white tents was pitched near a truck that appeared to be doubling as a stage, complete with two large black speakers. Sophie wasn't sure if it was a Christmas market, a community picnic, or both.

Josh glanced around. "I reckon we just found the population of Myrtle."

"Oh, look, Liam. A jumpy castle."

"Twuck! Twuck!" Liam, who was sitting on Josh's shoulders, threw himself forward in excitement, waving his pudgy hands toward the fire truck.

Josh laughed. "I think the fire truck wins over the jumpy castle."

As they struck off across the grass, a clown tied a balloon to Liam's wrist and girls dressed as penguins offered them candies. It wasn't until they reached the truck that they saw a rotund Santa sitting on the back.

A man wearing a bright yellow uniform approached. "Would the little tacker like to sit on Santa's knee?"

Sophie hesitated. Two weeks earlier, they'd taken Liam to the mall to see Santa and he'd had a meltdown worthy of an Oscar performance. "I'm not sure. He—"

"Twuck! Twuck!" Liam jerked so far sideways, Sophie thrust out an arm to steady him.

Josh lowered Liam to the ground and he made a beeline for the truck and the big man with the white beard.

"Up! Up!"

Santa's blue eyes twinkled. He didn't try to touch Liam but he patted his knee.

"Do you want to sit on Santa's knee?" Sophie asked.

"Twuck! Up!"

Sophie lifted her son. "He might scream."

"He won't be the first. And if he does, you just scoop him up into your loving arms."

Reassured, she settled Liam on Santa's red-clad knee, held her breath and stepped back.

Liam beamed up at Santa. "Fire."

Stunned, Sophie called out, "Quick, Josh! Get a photo."

Grinning at her, Josh pulled out his cell and took several photos. "His first Santa pic. It's the perfect present for Mom and Dad. Forget fake reindeer and bright lights in a noisy mall. All he needed was a country fire truck."

She laughed. "He's such a boy."

Santa's helper—a woman dressed in the same yellow uniform as the man who'd invited them to see Santa—produced a plastic toy fire helmet that said CFA on the front. Liam proudly put it on his head and immediately disappeared underneath it. Josh took more photos.

"What does CFA mean?" Sophie asked the woman.

"Country Fire Authority. Are you from Melbourne?"

"Is it that obvious?"

The woman laughed. "Only because most people around here know who we are and what we do. We're the volunteer fire brigade."

"And Santa's sleigh."

"Every year. If you've enjoyed the country Santa experience and you'd like to leave a gold coin donation in the tin or buy a candle for the carol service, it all helps."

Josh put two dollars in the tin and Sophie thanked Santa before removing a protesting Liam from his knee.

"Why don't you take him over to the playground and I'll grab some food," Josh suggested. "Saves him being stuck in line and unhappy."

"Good idea."

The playground consisted of two old swings and a primary colored play area with a slide, ladder, stairs and a platform that resembled a boat. Two young girls who looked like sisters immediately adopted Liam.

"Can we take him up to the boat?" the older girl asked. "Please."

"Um ..." Sophie wasn't used to this sort of request at her local park. "Okay, but hold his hand." She hovered, standing close to the stairs and then next to the platform in case Liam got upset or toppled over but he was glowing with delight under the full-beam attention of the girls.

An attractive woman with blonde hair that fell across her shoulders in waves stood at the edge of the play area. She wore a knock-out cream frock splashed with a vivid red poinsettia and cut in a silhouette that lifted and sculpted her in all the right places. High strappy sandals set off the look.

Sophie immediately felt fat and frumpy in comparison and wondered how hard it must be to walk in such high heels on ground that was baked into wide cracks. But despite the stunning dress and the shoes, the thing that struck Sophie was the way the woman twirled her fingers in her hair and the almost secret smile on her face as she spoke on her cell phone.

"Watch me." The younger of the two girls clambered up onto the top rail of the boat and held onto the supporting bar above her head.

"Sweetie, that's very high. Perhaps you better come down," Sophie suggested, fearing potential broken bones.

"Gracie. Mommy told you not to do that."

The girl ignored Sophie, gave her sister a mulish look, and with the sure-footedness of a tightrope walker, took a couple of steps, wrapped her knees over the bar and hung upside down.

"Mommy! Look at me!"

The beautiful woman on the cell phone spun around. The starry-eyed smile disappeared and her pink cheeks paled. Sophie didn't know anyone could move that fast in six-inch heels.

"Very good, Gracie," the girls' mother said breathlessly. "Now I've seen the trick, you can get down. Carefully."

Gracie swung up, slipped off the rail and spun around, planting a kiss on her mother's nose. "I knew that would make you look. You've been on your cell *for. Ever.*"

"And you know that I'm only on my cell if it's important."

"You sound like just like Daddy," Gracie said morosely. She suddenly brightened. "Mommy, this is Liam. And that's Liam's mommy."

Sophie smiled politely, feeling as uncomfortable as if she'd been caught eavesdropping instead of keeping a close eye on her son. "Your daughters are very friendly."

"Thank you. It's always a relief when they do what you hope they will." The woman's tinkling laugh held a tight edge. "They love to mother the littlies. Makes me wonder if I should have had a third."

"Are there many young families here?"

"Lots. Myrtle's having a renaissance. We're in a perfect position really. It's cooler in summer and we're surrounded by forest but not too far from the coast."

"Is there a playgroup?"

"Yes, they use the hall and the park. We've got a terrific preschool and elementary, and I think one of the new residents is starting up a toddler music program. Marylou runs the playgroup. I can introduce you if you like. She's just over there."

Sophie was taken aback by the woman's thoughtfulness. "I ... um ... thanks but we don't live here."

"But you're thinking about it?"

"I don't know. Maybe." Based on the woman's clothes, Sophie decided she must be part of the new population. "Did you find it a big adjustment, moving here? I mean there's so much space and it's quiet. And snakes. There's snakes, right?"

"Actually, I grew up here and it can be really noisy when the magpies, kookaburras, cockatoos and wattlebirds all try to outdo each another. Not to mention the roosters. And yes, there are snakes. They still freak me out." She laughed. "Sorry, I should have introduced myself. I'm Bec Petrovic."

"Sophie Doherty. We've been looking at some land today and the builder my husband's spoken to has your surname."

"Oh, that's my husband, Adam." Bec smiled. "We're Petrovic Family Homes. Are you the couple interested in the land next to Beechside? It's such a pretty spot. When your little boy's older, he'll love yabbying in the creek at the bottom of the block." She checked her watch and gasped. "Excuse me. Sorry. I have to go. Ivy! Gracie! Time to meet Daddy."

Josh arrived with the food and they sat under the shade of a tree to eat the best hamburger with the lot they'd ever tasted. "It's got pineapple!" they said simultaneously and then laughed.

After they'd eaten, they strolled past the tents selling Christmas crafts. Liam toddled happily between them with one chubby hand in each of theirs until they reached the nativity scene. He bravely patted a sheep but kept a safe distance from the cow, declaring, "Big moo." By the time the carols started, he'd fallen asleep in Sophie's arms with the fire helmet still on his head.

"That was the most laid-back carol service I've ever been to," Sophie said as they walked back to the car.

Josh laughed. "It was pretty funny when the cow in the nativity scene did that massive dump."

"And did you see Liam's face? He loved everything."

"Yeah. You know what struck me about tonight?"

"Tell me."

"Even though it's hot, everyone's happy. Well, a lot less stressed than most people in Melbourne are a week before Christmas. The whole thing had a positive vibe. When I came out of the food tent, I saw a bloke leaning in close to a woman. He was definitely trying to hit on her."

Sophie slipped her arm through Josh's and nudged him with her hip. "True Christmas spirit, eh?"

Josh grinned, his teeth flashing white in the moonlight. "Let's hope he got lucky."

After strapping Liam into the car seat, Josh closed the door and pulled Sophie into his arms. "What do you reckon now? Can you imagine living here and bringing up our kids?"

Her heart skipped a beat. "Kids?"

"If we take the plunge and move here, not only can we afford the house, we can have another baby. That sounds bloody fantastic to me. Are you in?"

She squealed, threw her arms around his neck and kissed him.

Later that night, Josh got lucky.

CHAPTER FIVE

THREE MONTHS AFTER THE FIRES

Josh wrenched the top off a beer and downed half the bottle. His heart was pounding, but it wasn't because of his fast walk back to their unit in Myrtle's temporary housing village—accommodation for fire victims. It was because of what he'd learned at the community meeting that night. How the hell was he going to tell Sophie?

He ached to protect her and his young family. Sophie was exhausted from caring for the new baby and was already dealing with enough stress without him adding to it. He'd do just about anything to shelter her from the news, but this time he couldn't hide it from her. Nothing could sugar-coat it so he went with cold, hard facts.

"The block's been zoned BAL FZ."

Sophie held the baby high on her shoulder and was pacing back and forth across the tiny width of their living space as she did most nights, trying to pacify their daughter. She didn't break her stride. "What's BAL when it's at home?"

"Wildfire fuckin' assessment level."

"Swear jar," she said flatly. Automatically.

"Fuck the swear jar!" Agitation pulsed and his body clenched. If

Sophie didn't know about BAL, he was going to have to explain everything. "Do you remember the time we saw the platypus splashing in the creek and we said it was a sign that we'd totally done the right thing moving here?"

"Mmm." Sophie reached the wall and turned yet again.

"Well, signs are bullshit. The creek does nothing as a fire break. The trees on the bottom half of the block add to the intensity of the fire and just blast us with ember attack. But the killer's the steep rise from the creek. It makes the whole freakin' fire travel faster."

Trixie squealed and Sophie patted her more firmly on the back, a comforting, rhythmic thud. Josh craved something that would comfort him and lessen his impotence against the force of their circumstances.

"You know how we always wanted to win the lottery?"

Sophie's feet slowed. "Yeah?"

"Well, today's our lucky day. We've hit the jackpot. Want to know what the prize is?"

The look on Sophie's face said she didn't want to hear. He got that. He'd sat in the meeting wishing he'd never been introduced to the acronym BAL. That he'd never learned all the ratings. He wished he'd never seen the pity on people's faces that was directed at him or their relief when they realized the topography of their own land gave them a get-out-of-jail-free card.

He threw his head back and gulped more beer, needing the blunting effects of the alcohol.

"What, Josh?" Sophie finally asked.

"Our block's got the highest BAL rating there is."

"What does that really mean?"

"It means the price of the new house went up $150,000 just like that." Josh snapped his fingers.

"But our insurance will cover it, right?"

"Oh, sure. They're such a kind and generous mob, always willing to help a brother out."

"So that's a no?"

"It's a definite no. They insured the house based on what it cost us to build it. We built a regular house on a bush block. To get a building permit for the new house, we need to add a heap of extra stuff like window shutters, a reinforced concrete slab and a special roof with ember guards."

"That's crazy money. Let's sell the block and move back to Melbourne."

"You say that like it's easy."

"Of course it's easy. You put up a board and place some advertisements online."

Something throbbed behind his ear and he dug deep, trying not to yell. "Myrtle hit the national news, Soph. People died. No one in their right mind's gonna buy a block of land up here now."

"Why are you being so negative? You can't possibly know the block won't sell until we put it on the market."

He wasn't being negative. He'd heard the talk from men who'd put their land up for sale three months earlier. None of them had received a single nibble of interest. His skin itched and he scratched his lower arms hard. "Even if the block sold, it won't come close to clearing the mortgage. We'd still be up to our eyeballs in debt. Plus, my job's here."

He loved his job. Right now, work was the only thing keeping him sane. It also kept him thankfully busy so he had no time to think about anything else.

"Why can't we extend the mortgage?"

"We're maxed out. We can't afford higher repayments."

"So, what are you saying?"

"I'm saying..." His throat thickened against the words he didn't want to say. "We can't afford to leave Myrtle and we can't afford to build."

The throbbing behind his ear spread over all over his body and his hand curved into a fist. He slammed it into the door, welcoming the biting pain.

A muffled shout of "Shut the fuck up" travelled into the room from the other side of the wall, immediately followed by a surge of doof-doof music.

The noise startled Trixie and her newborn cry broke over them like shattering glass.

"Josh!"

He cradled his hand. "Do you get it? We're stuck in this hellhole."

"But we need to live somewhere!"

He wanted to disappear through the floor and hide. Be anywhere but here with Sophie's anxiety and her disappointment in him. Be far away from Trixie's accusatory cries—*you brought me into the world then let me down.*

He hauled open the fridge and grabbed another beer.

Trixie screamed louder.

"When the hell is she gonna stop crying?"

THE PRESENT

Sophie startled awake, taking a moment to realize she was in Liam's bed. She must have fallen asleep reading him a story.

It had taken her and Josh a few weeks to work out the best way to get the kids to sleep in this open-plan steel shed that was now their home. Their insurance policy had paid for twelve months of emergency accommodation in the temporary housing village—the period of time insurance companies considered reasonable to rebuild a house. Reasonable didn't take into account that the wildfire not only destroyed their brand-new dream home and changed their physical environment so dramatically they barely recognized it, but its impact reached further into their lives than they could ever have imagined. Never in her wildest dreams had Sophie imagined she'd be living in a shed on their block of land and servicing a mortgage on a house that didn't exist. The cost of the rebuild hung over them like a lingering toxic plume.

Holding her breath, she raised her head from the pillow. Liam's little hand was tucked up under his cheek and his chest was rising and falling evenly. Love swelled her heart. Some days, she was convinced that the reason children looked so angelic in sleep was so after a tough day, parents instantly forgave them everything and stayed around to do it all over again. But as she calculated how she was going to extricate herself from the bed, she hoped that doing it all over again was going to happen tomorrow and not in thirty seconds.

Getting up without waking Liam was easier said than done. For weeks, he'd been as clingy as a limpet, each night insisting, "Don't want Daddy. Mommy, you read me a story," and refusing to fall asleep unless she lay down with him too.

Lowering her right leg to the floor, she carefully shimmied her behind to the edge of the mattress, trying to avoid any jerky movements. Generally, once Liam was fully asleep, he didn't wake up, but if she rushed her departure it added another half an hour to the process.

Confident her son was deeply asleep, she slid her other leg from under the bedsheet and tip-toed out from behind the partition. The room spun and she pressed her hand against the wall. Falling asleep at seven o'clock was the worst—it always left her feeling like she was swimming up from the bottom of a vat of thick molasses.

More than anything, she wanted to collapse into bed and abandon herself to blissful sleep, but she couldn't do that. There were always jobs needing doing—washing dishes, folding laundry, packing up toys and general tidying up. It was easy for people to think they were being helpful when they said, "The world won't end if you leave it all and sit on the couch," but they didn't live in a 450 square feet space. What they failed to understand was that the interior of the shed was one of the few areas in her life where she could exert any control. The rest was chaos.

Josh walked in bringing a blast of cold air and an armful of logs for the Coonara wood heater. The cold weather was only a week old, and already she was wondering how they were going to survive three long months. She cast a glance at the full sink of dishes, stomped on her guilt and picked up her handbag. "I should be back around nine, nine thirty."

The logs tumbled abruptly out of Josh's arms, crashing into the basket with a dull thud. "You're going out?"

"I told you at breakfast. It's that knitting thing Julie invited me to."

Josh turned around slowly, his face taut with disappointment. "Do you have to go?"

When they'd been living in Melbourne, Sophie remembered asking him the same question. She'd been an exhausted new mom, wanting nothing more than to collapse on the couch with Josh for company, but he'd happily head out the door to play basketball with his mates. Sophie didn't have to go out tonight and initially when Julie had invited her she'd been reluctant, but she'd woken up looking forward to it. If Sophie were honest, these days she took every opportunity that came her way to get out of the chilly shed.

"When we moved to Myrtle, we talked about getting involved. With everything that's been going on, we haven't done that. I thought craft group might be a good start."

"When we moved here we didn't expect everything to turn to shit," Josh muttered, brushing dirt and wood chips off his fleece.

As the debris fell onto the floor she'd swept before dinner, she fought a surge of aggravation and bit off indignant words. Now wasn't the time to talk about any of the crap that clung tenaciously to their life —she desperately wanted a night off. "Why don't you go out tomorrow night and I'll stay home?"

"Where exactly? This stinking town doesn't even have a pub anymore."

"Maybe you could put up a flyer on the noticeboard at the indoor sport center? See if anyone wants to play basketball."

He grunted. "You know it's a football and cricket town."

"Join a team in Colac?"

"We can't afford the petrol."

She wanted to shout, "Don't try then. Be miserable!" But that would only trap her there. "I better go or I'll be late." She moved to kiss him goodbye.

He dodged her. "Great! So you're skiving off and leaving me with the dishes?"

"Sorry. I'll do them when I get back. Promise."

"And wake me and the kids up with the crashing and thumping? Don't bother." Josh walked to the area they called the kitchen—a fridge, a two-burner gas camping stove, a stainless-steel sink balanced on Masonite with some storage underneath, a zippered three-shelf pantry and an island cart. He filled the electric kettle from the cold-water tap before flicking it on.

The rigid set of his shoulders almost undid Sophie's resolve. Almost made her stay, but the need to leave won out. "Bye," she said softly. When he didn't respond, she slipped out into the night.

Unlike when they'd lived in Melbourne, these days whenever she was out at night she automatically glanced up. No wonder it was cold; there wasn't even a sliver of insulating cloud wafting over the inky sky, only a carpet of silver stars. She huffed out a breath, watched it vaporize in a white puff and wondered how, despite everything that had happened, she'd not only got used to the endless space and sky, but somehow needed it. When things pressed down on her so heavily that it hurt to breathe, she came outside. She'd sit on a plastic chair in the middle of the new concrete slab that she both loathed and loved, and she'd stargaze. Sometimes she managed to convince Josh to join her but more often than not he stayed inside with his wireless headphones clamped to his ears, watching TV.

The drive to the CWA meeting rooms took her less than five minutes. Built with wildfire relief money, the new building had two distinct areas: the CWA at the front and the Men's Community Shed at the back. Not that it looked anything like a galvanized steel shed. Despite the men wanting a simple steel construction, architects had got involved and Myrtle now owned the most luxurious "shed" in the country.

When Sophie had accepted the invitation to the craft group, she'd assumed the gathering would be held at Julie's place, given it wasn't connected with the CWA, but the older woman said it was important to use the new buildings. There were a few cars in the carpark and Sophie's stomach lurched with a combination of anxiety and excitement. Since moving back to their block of land five months earlier, part of her missed the company of the women in the temporary housing village. All of her missed her life before the fires. Sometimes the memories were vividly 3D and taunting and at other times so ephemeral and fleeting that Sophie wondered if they were tricks of the mind. When she summoned the courage to look at the photos on her cell phone that she'd taken in the few short weeks they'd lived in their Myrtle home, she often got the feeling none of it had been real. It felt like someone had photoshopped Josh, Liam and a pregnant Sophie into the picture as an advertisement for Petrovic Family Homes.

Slipping out of the car, she walked into the well-lit building. The large meeting room was empty but a bubble of conversation drifted from another doorway. She entered the smaller carpeted room, which was tastefully decorated with couches, comfortable chairs and local artwork. A low table groaned under the weight of a cheese platter with three types of cheeses, crackers, grapes, figs and strawberries. It was the white bowl filled to overflowing with the rainbow colors of chocolate balls that caught her eye.

"You made it." Julie greeted her warmly.

When Sophie had met Julie for the first time, she'd been struck by how the older woman looked so much younger than her years. Not anymore. Her once blonde hair was now white. Her round face, which had previously been lightly dusted with lines, held deep furrows around her mouth and eyes.

"It was touch and go there for a minute, but I left Josh with the dishes and here I am."

"Good for you. You know, Bec, don't you?" Julie gestured toward an elegant woman standing chatting with two women Sophie didn't know.

"Sure." The correct answer was "Sort of, not really." Sophie didn't know the woman other than she was a lapsed hairdresser and a busy stay-at-home mom of two daughters. Any chance of a possible friendship had, like so many other things, been exploded by a fireball on a blazing December day.

"We're just waiting for one more and then we'll make a start," Julie said. "Help yourself to something to eat and drink."

Sophie poured herself a mineral water, bypassed the cheese and, ignoring a critical voice in her head telling her she was yet to lose the baby fat, selected a chocolate. Worrying about calories came at the bottom of a very long list of issues currently taking precedence over her weight.

"I'm a sucker for salted caramel." Bec plucked a turquoise green–wrapped ball. "I try hard but I can't resist them."

In the first year after the conflagration, Bec had lived in Melbourne, close to the hospital and Adam. More than once, when Sophie was trying to soothe a crying child upset by a neighbor's noise in the temporary village, she'd been struck by the paradox—she was homeless in Myrtle while the award-winning Petrovic family home three miles away sat untouched by flames and empty. The uncharitable thought was always followed by drenching shame.

Sure, she and Josh wouldn't wish their situation on anyone, except perhaps her sister whose self-obsession prevented any level of understanding of what they were going through. But at least the four of them were safe and together. Adam Petrovic had almost died ... technically he *had* died in the burns unit but the staff had successfully restarted his heart. When Bec and Adam had finally returned to Myrtle, Sophie wasn't sure what had shocked her more: Adam's ugly scars or Bec, who'd dropped two dress sizes. Thankfully, Bec had gained some weight and no longer looked like she had a terminal illness.

"It's great to see you here, Sophie." Bec smiled. "How are things?"

A litany of words rose, almost choking her, but she swallowed them down. The question was purely social. "Oh, you're a mom," she said vaguely. "You know how it is."

"Busy, busy, right? It's great you're taking a night off for yourself. I always think it's a good thing for the men to spend some time at home alone with the kids like we do. There's nothing like some hands-on parenting reality to make them appreciate all we do."

"Actually, Josh—"

Julie clapped her hands. "Everyone's here, let's make a start. Grab a seat."

Sophie sat next to Bec on one couch while the two unknown women settled themselves on the couch opposite. Claire McKenzie plonked herself hard and fast onto one of two chairs, her cheeks bright pink as if she'd rushed to get there.

Julie sat on the other chair. "There's only six of us, so we don't need nametags, but let's go around the room and introduce ourselves anyway. I'm not sure Sophie, Erica and Layla know everyone."

As Bec was saying, "Great idea," Sophie heard a groan. She was surprised to see Claire rolling her eyes.

"I'll go first, shall I?" Bec didn't wait for confirmation. "I'm Bec Petrovic and if the name rings a bell, it's probably because my husband's company built your house."

"Not ours," Claire muttered.

Sophie felt Bec stiffen. This snarky version of Claire was very different from the professional nurse who'd visited her at the temporary village during her lowest point with Trixie. That Claire had been caring, reassuring and practical. She'd cut through the chaos with steady calm and the reassuring words, "You're doing your best under very difficult circumstances, Sophie. No one can ask for more than that. You need to be kinder to yourself."

"Anyway …" Bec said firmly, ignoring Claire, "… I think craft group is a great idea. I'm looking forward to it and getting to know you."

"You've all met me before in my preferred domain at the clinic. I just want to put it out there that I totally suck at crafts." Claire glanced around hopefully. "Is there wine?"

"If you behave, there's cake at the end," Julie said mildly.

Layla, who wore a headscarf and spoke with an accent, looked slightly askance. "Why do you come if you don't enjoy making things?"

"Claire's like a naughty girl at the back of the bus, Layla." Bec smiled brightly. "Don't believe everything she says."

Layla smiled politely and Sophie felt sure she was probably unfamiliar with the back-of-the-bus analogy. "I'm Sophie or Soph," she said hurriedly to prevent Bec or Claire saying anything else. Julie obviously knew both women well so why had she thought inviting them to join the same group, let alone sitting them together in a small room, was a good idea?

"I've got two kids. Liam's at preschool and Trixie's eighteen months."

"Such fun ages." Erica's friendliness leaped around the room like a playful Labrador. "That extra gap between kids is great, isn't it? You get some one-on-one time with the younger one when the older one's at preschool."

"It's worked out great," Sophie heard herself saying enthusiastically. No way was she admitting to this bouncy, cheerful woman that *nothing* had worked out great. That was tantamount to admitting to being a total failure as a mother. Wondering if lying at craft group was against the rules of craft group, Sophie studiously avoided Julie's gaze and changed the subject.

"I don't know if I suck at crafts or not, because I've never done any. I'm really looking forward to learning how to knit. We're currently living in a shed on our block while we ..." *Why did you mention the shed? Now what will you say? Avoid bankruptcy? Dodge homelessness?* "... owner-build."

Owner-build—it sounded like something off *Grand Designs* when the reality was so far removed it was laughable. "Anyway," Sophie rushed on, "I thought I could learn to knit and make a blanket for the sofa at the same time."

"Wow! How exciting that you're building your own home," Erica gushed. "That must be giving you the most amazing sense of achievement."

Sophie tensed, instantly visualizing the barren concrete slab and the distinct lack of steel struts it was designed to support. Those weren't any closer to being erected than the day the slab was poured months earlier. "It's so rewarding."

Was God going to strike her down for that outright lie?

"Your partner must be a lot handier than mine," Erica prattled on. "Don't get me wrong, I love Nathan to bits, but he doesn't know a screwdriver from a wrench. Fortunately, he's a lot more talented with the stock market so we left everything to Bec's clever husband. We're so excited to be in Myrtle, but I don't have to tell you girls anything. You've had the luxury of living the country life for longer than me."

The room quieted so fast it was as if everyone stopped breathing. Sophie waited for Julie, Bec or Claire to mention the elephant in the room but they all looked as stunned as she felt. She stared at her knees. She didn't know if her throat was tight with anger or the shock of being side-swiped. Coming here tonight was supposed to be an escape—a couple of hours away from her fire-impacted life. A place where she could spend an evening talking about inconsequential things like knitting. A chance to be normal. Who was she kidding? She wanted to leap across the coffee table and slap Erica's friendly face.

Sophie shoved her hands under her thighs. "I don't consider a wildfire burning down my home a luxury."

Erica's brows drew down, giving her a doleful and perplexed look. "I'm sorry. I didn't mean to … It's just with all the new public facilities, I assumed the rebuilding was finished. I mean the fires were ages ago, weren't they?"

"The fires were a lifetime ago and yesterday." Grief cracked Julie's voice.

Without thinking, Sophie reached out and squeezed the older woman's arm. Julie's ability to appear together and serene always made Sophie feel calmer. Sometimes she forgot the terrible toll the fire had exacted on Julie and Phil.

Julie patted Sophie's hand and gave her a wobbly smile. "Sophie's blanket idea has hit the nail on the head. I think it would be great if our mission is to make things for people who are doing winter tough. Socks, gloves, beanies, blankets, that sort of thing."

"Socks and gloves?" Claire shuddered theatrically. "Doesn't that involve four needles? I tried it once and all my stitches slid off the end."

"Stick to making a blanket and leave the complicated things to the more experienced knitters," Bec said coolly.

"Can you crochet?" Layla asked. "Is easier than to knit. Only three or four stitches."

"Oh, I like the sound of that." Claire hacked hunks off the Camembert wheel with the urgency of someone who hadn't seen food in days. "Can you teach me how to make an Afghan?"

"I don't know. I'm from Turkey not Afghanistan."

Julie laughed and pulled a brightly colored rug from her basket. "Layla, we call this an Afghan rug."

"Oh, yes!" Layla smiled. "I can teach Claire this. I think it's what you say is easy-peasy?"

Claire smiled wryly. "You haven't tried teaching me yet."

They paired off naturally—Julie and a subdued Erica, Claire and Layla and Bec and Sophie.

Bec picked up a ball of wool. "I'll teach you how to cast on using the long-tail technique."

"Is it hard?" Sophie was suddenly anxious that she might not be any good at knitting. Unlike Claire, the idea of publicly announcing her deficits petrified her.

"When I first learned, I was all fingers and thumbs but it's like anything. Practice makes perfect."

Sophie glanced at the beautifully groomed woman beside her. "Is that a personal mantra for you?"

Bec's fingers stilled on the wool and a beat passed before she laughed. "Heavens no. It's just something my babushka used to say."

Sophie followed Bec's instructions, wrapping the wool around her forefinger and thumb and trapping the length of the strand against her palm with her other fingers. Ducking the needle through a loop, she caught the wool and drew it back. Suddenly she'd created a stitch. "This feels like that wool game I played as a kid."

"Or tying shoe laces with the bunny going through the hole."

Claire glanced up from her chain of crochet stitches. "I'd forgotten all about the wool game. When I was in third grade, it was huge at Myrtle Elementary. I could do cup and saucer and the cat's whiskers but all I really wanted to do was the parachute. I spent hours on it but I never managed it."

"It's really not that hard." Bec held up her hands. She'd woven wool through the fingers of her left hand creating the shape of parachute silk and her right hand held down a strand of wool to represent the parachute lines. "See?"

"Rebecca was queen of the wool game at school." Claire's smile didn't reach her eyes. "And skipping. Oh, and I think her Tamagotchi was the only one that didn't die."

"That's so cool! Can you teach me how to do it?" Erica asked, oblivious to the tension that arced between Claire and Bec. "I'd love to show the kids."

"Of course," Bec said. "I'll show you and anyone else who wants to learn when we're having supper."

Sophie noted that Claire didn't take Bec up on the offer.

JULIE WALKED into Beechside and found Phil on the recliner with his feet up and Taffy, their aging beagle, on his lap. Both were watching television.

He glanced up when her hand touched his shoulder. "How did it go?"

"Do you want a nightcap?"

"That good, eh?"

She poured two ports and carried them over. "Remind me why I thought it was a good idea."

"Because Bec and Claire have got the stuff Myrtle needs."

"Individually perhaps, but after what I saw tonight, definitely not together. I thought after their shared experience of the fires ..."

"We all experienced the fires in some way or another. Doesn't mean we shared anything."

Julie sighed. "I suppose not. Tonight was like their school formal preparation all over again. Bec was doing everything a little too perfectly and although Claire wasn't outside smoking with the boys, she was misbehaving."

"And the newbies?"

"Erica's enthusiastic but she's got foot-in-mouth disease. Layla's lovely. She seemed a bit overwhelmed at times. Claire adopted her."

"Of course she did. Did Sophie go?"

"Yes." Julie sipped her port. "Unfortunately, we both had a bit of a moment."

"We all have those, Jules."

She patted his knee, remembering the week before when she'd found him hammering in the stakes for the tree roses, tears streaming down his face. Fortunately, it was a coping day for her so she'd been able to support him. It was the times when they both fell apart that terrified her.

"I see a lot of moments at the Men's Shed," Phil continued. "Were punches thrown?"

"Very funny. The moment wasn't between Sophie and me. It was sparked by something Erica said. Am I foolish thinking Myrtle can build a bridge between the old community and the new?"

"In the grand scheme of things, Sophie and Josh are relatively new."

"You know what I mean."

"Yeah. Wildfire veterans versus wildfire virgins." He picked up her hand. "These things take time."

"I suppose."

"And time's about the only thing that bastard inferno didn't change."

CHAPTER SIX

A **YEAR BEFORE THE FIRES**

Bec hurried toward the happy Christmas crowd as fast as her heels allowed. She'd been so busy answering Sophie Doherty's questions about Myrtle she'd lost track of time. Squinting into the sun, she spotted Adam across the sports' ground. He was glancing around, looking for her and the girls.

"Sorry, I'm a tiny bit late," she said breathlessly, getting the words out before he said them to her.

Adam's gaze skimmed her appreciatively. "I'm never wrong. I said you'd look hot in that dress and you do." He cupped the back of her neck and pulled her head in close while his other hand squeezed her butt.

Even before his tongue sloppily claimed her mouth, she tasted the beer. She gave him a quick flick of her own tongue before sliding her mouth away. "Adam. G-rated family gathering. Business image."

"You're right." He sighed, dropping his hand from her behind, but leaving the other in her hair. "But I'm cursed with a beautiful wife. You're on notice, babe. The moment this carol service's over and the girls are in bed, so are you and me."

Even if he hadn't said it, Bec knew they'd be having sex. Adam was always horny after events like this. Whether it was because the company was sponsoring the Christmas picnic and parade this year and he'd been enjoying the slaps on the back and multiple thanks from people all evening, or if it was the booze—or something else entirely— she'd learned a long time ago that nights like this were not the time to have a headache.

He looked over her shoulder. "Where are the girls?"

"Buying an ice cream with the money you gave them. Don't worry, they'll be here in a minute."

He gave her an indulgent look. "Relax. We've got plenty of time. Where were you?"

"At the playground. I met Sophie Doherty."

"Who?"

"She's the wife of that bloke you told me was interested in the Beechside block. She was asking me questions about Myrtle so I didn't want to rush away."

"That block's starting to cost me money. I hope you sold her on it."

"I did my best."

"You always try."

"Have you had anything to eat? I ordered your favorite chicken salad from Oakvale Park and—"

"I had a ham—" He suddenly stilled, his eyes fixed straight ahead. "What the hell are the girls wearing?"

She turned, watching their daughters approach with smiles on their faces and dripping ice-cream cones in their hands. Gracie wore an old pair of shorts and last year's Christmas T-shirt, which was slightly too small for her. To offset the look, she'd slung a pink tutu around her waist. Ivy sported cut-off jeans and a tank top. Both had sneakers on their feet.

"They look like they got dressed at the thrift shop."

She laughed. "Hardly. They look like every other kid here."

"Exactly!" He shook his head. "It's hardly a recommendation, is it?"

"Do you remember that article I told you about? The one that said lots of girls' clothes prevent them from playing freely? Tonight's all about fun. Ivy's been riding her bike with her friends and you know what Gracie's like. She hangs off every available bar. They couldn't do any of it in a dress."

"There's no way they're going up on stage with us looking like that."

"Oh. Okay."

"Okay?" His nostrils flared. "It's not anywhere near okay. They're going up on stage with us as planned and they're wearing dresses."

"I ... um ... I didn't bring their dresses."

His usually warm, dark-chocolate eyes flashed with anger. "Are you trying to ruin the business?"

"No!" Given everything she did to help promote the company, his words seared like sunburn. "That's not fair. It's a casual night and—" She suddenly realized that arguing surrounded by the entire district's population was unwise. "I'm sorry. I should have thought."

"Damn straight, you should have thought. You're the one who just reminded me about business image. We *are* the family of Petrovic *Family* Homes. Take the girls home and bring 'em back looking like my daughters instead of someone else's dirty street kids."

Agitation tumbled her gut. "Adam, there's not enough time—"

"Listen to me." His voice dropped to a low rumble. "Go and put them in the dresses you bought for the marketing photos and get them back here on time." He turned away from her, greeting his daughters with a hug. "Girls, go home with Mommy and put on your dresses so you can come on stage with Daddy."

Bec put out her hands. "Let's go."

Gracie pouted. "Aww. Do we have to?"

"Yes." Adam smiled but his tone was implacable.

"But I don't wan—"

"Okay, Daddy." Ivy glanced quickly between her parents and grabbed her sister's hand. "Race you to the car, Gracie."

Bec followed the girls, uncertain if she should be grateful to Ivy for making the situation easier or worried about the fact that she had. "We have to be quick. Take your shoes and socks off in the car."

Giving thanks that Myrtle's police officer was enjoying the social, Bec broke the speed limit down Platypus Creek Road, making the three mile journey in record time, only to be left groaning in frustration as the automatic gates Adam had installed opened at a snail's pace. At the three-quarter mark, she maneuvered the SUV around the gate, gunned it along the drive and pulled up in a spray of crushed gravel next to the fountain. Releasing the door locks and deactivating the security system, she yelled, "Run."

Ivy, bless her, quickly and quietly got changed while Bec dealt with a squirming Gracie. In desperation, she finally grabbed a candy cane off the Christmas tree and thrust it at her five-year-old. "Suck this and keep still."

Minutes later, they were back in the car and Bec was blessed by two miracles: no dusk-enticed wildlife crossing the road in front of her and pulling in to the sports ground with three minutes to spare. "Okay, girls, hold hands. We're going straight to the stage truck."

"Mommy ..."

Bec turned at the worry in Ivy's voice. "What?"

"You need to put on your lipstick and perfume then fluff your hair."

Out of the mouth of babes. Bec tugged the rear-view mirror toward her and grabbed her makeup bag out of her voluminous handbag. She quickly set to work to repair the damage the evening's sun, dust and a dollop of stress had wrought. Concealer and powder were her friends, along with a lipstick pencil in Adam's favorite shade, Berrilicious. Finally, she finger-styled her hair, blasted it with hairspray and spritzed herself in perfume.

Ivy smiled at her. "Daddy will be happy."

She checked her watch. "He will be if we run."

Despite his medium height, Adam was easy to pick because of his breadth and his distinctive red Petrovic Family Homes polo shirt, which was tucked neatly beneath a black leather belt and pressed chinos. His shoes shone. The first time Bec met him, she'd teased him that he was the most neatly dressed builder in the country; even in his work clothes, he managed to stay relatively clean.

Adam was standing next to the stage truck's stairs and chatting easily with Hugo Lang. Her husband always appeared relaxed in other men's company but Bec knew it was an act. Adam was extremely competitive and every conversation was either information gathering or a quest in one-upmanship. She doubted Adam thought the dairyman was a threat to him in any shape or form but Hugo owned land that Adam considered prime real estate.

Her heart was hammering so she deliberately slowed and took a couple of deep breaths, regaining her composure before approaching the men.

Hugo was handing Adam a box the size of a cigarette packet. "Put this in your pocket and when you're ready to talk, slide this switch."

"Too easy." Adam noticed Bec and his mouth curved into an endearing smile. He mouthed, "Well done," and stretched out his hand.

Something tight inside her let go and she slid her hand into his.

"Hugo, look at my three gorgeous girls. How lucky am I?"

Bec winced at Adam's insensitivity. Hugo's ex-wife was a woman kind people called a free spirit and everyone else called a self-centered bitch. For her part, Bec had never worked out if Amber had fallen in love with Hugo or the farm. Either way, for two years, Amber had embraced the bucolic lifestyle and been hell-bent on self-sufficiency. Her one positive contribution to the community was the establishment of Myrtle's farmers market.

Hugo Lang might be a third-generation dairyman but he was very much on the grid. Everyone in town had watched and wondered why and how he'd put up with the stream of hippies who'd accepted Amber's open invitation to camp on the farm. Before Amber finally ran off to northern New South Wales with a guy from the Bellinger Valley, it was rumored her mantra of "love and acceptance for all" meant she'd slept with half the football team.

"No contest there at all, Adam. Definitely lucky." Hugo turned to Bec, bestowing on her the same easy smile he gave everyone. "Good to see you, Bec. Merry Christmas."

Before she could return the greeting, Hugo turned his attention to the girls, squatting down to their level.

"Is Santa bringing you two coal this year?"

"No!" Gracie said indignantly. "He's bringing me a trampoline."

"And what about you, Ivy?"

Ivy glanced at Bec and Adam with hope in her eyes. "A puppy."

Bec swallowed, torn between destroying the Santa illusion and heading off Ivy's disappointment. She'd already lost the puppy argument with Adam. Twice. Experience had taught her that raising it a third time would not be the charm—more likely a hex—and this year, more than anything, she wanted a happy Adam over Christmas. When Adam was relaxed and happy, they were all relaxed and happy. Many would say blessed.

Adam grunted. "Santa's not bringing you a puppy."

Ivy's face fell and Hugo rose. "Bring the girls out to the farm one day, Adam. They can get their puppy fix there."

"Work's crazy, mate. I've got the pub extension and four houses."

"Daddy, please!" Ivy begged.

Bec watched Adam closely, wanting to decline the unexpected invitation, except Hugo had explicitly issued it to Adam. Her husband hated her making any decisions on his behalf but he also hated being put on the spot and both Ivy and Hugo had done exactly that. Then again, Adam loved to be seen as magnanimous. Like so many things with Adam, nothing was predictable—this could go either way.

Adam tickled Ivy under the chin and winked at Bec. "If you can convince your mother to overcome her aversion to cows, she can take you."

Bec shuddered theatrically. "There's no way I'm going if there's a bull anywhere near me."

Ivy turned back to Hugo, her features pinched with worry. "Is there a bull?"

"Tell you what, Ivy. If you call me before you come, I promise I'll put the bull in the back field that day."

"Yay!" Ivy looked at Bec with shining eyes. "Mommy did you hear that?"

"Yes, darling," she said faintly. Just the idea of visiting the farm threatened to spark a panic attack.

"Righto, that's enough," Adam said briskly, taking control. "Let's get this show on the road."

Hugo cut the Christmas music and, with the girls on one side of Adam and Bec on the other, the four of them walked onto the stage.

"G'day, Myrtle. You totally rocked the Christmas parade this year."

Cheers and woots soared into the evening air along with applause.

"I hear the Scouts are in a spot of bother, having lost Santa's reindeer. If anyone finds Rudolph on their way home tonight, don't be tempted to make venison sausage but give Syd Lidcombe a call. He'll come and pick it up. I hope you've all managed to drop a gold coin or two into the CFA tins and you've got your candles ready to go. I know many of the blokes have done a great job this evening lubricating their voices in preparation for the carols ..."

He paused for laughter and the crowd obliged, sending a wave of sound rolling over them. "But on a more serious note, Christmas is a time to gather with family and friends and reflect on the year we've had. Myrtle's had an awesome year. Of course, the farmers want more rain and higher prices—don't we all—but the great thing is, Myrtle's welcomed twenty-six new families and four businesses, not to mention the expansion of others. Petrovic Family Homes is proud to employ ten Myrtle tradesmen and subcontract to local businesses. We're honored to sponsor tonight's event. I don't know about all of you, but I couldn't achieve half the things I do without the love and support of my family, especially my amazing and talented wife."

As expected, Adam choose that moment to lean in and kiss Bec full on the mouth, and she played her part. The retro 1950's dress lent itself to a dip and she added a Marilyn Monroe leg pop for extra measure. The crowd, high on the joy of the season and three hours of drinking, cheered wildly. As Adam righted her, Bec glimpsed Hugo giving a thumbs-up sign.

Adam grinned at the appreciative crowd. "Merry Christmas, Myrtle. May the New Year be a good one for us all. Now, kiss your family, kick back and enjoy the carols."

They filed off the stage and the Disgraced Rockers, Myrtle's resident rock band—average age of fifty-one—opened with the Aussie version of the "The Twelve Days Of Christmas." The Petrovics walked to their picnic blanket and Adam lit the girls' candles before settling in behind them next to Bec.

"Great speech," she said, squeezing his arm.

"Yeah. We nailed it. Sorry about before, babe, but you know how important it is to get everything right."

She knew it well—she just didn't always pick what constituted "right." "I shouldn't have dropped the ball. It was stupid."

"Doesn't matter. It all worked out in the end." He pulled a bottle of Veuve Cliquot from an insulated bag, popped the cork and poured her a glass. "Peace offering?"

Whenever he lost his temper, there was always an apology. Always a peace offering. "Thank you."

He flicked his tongue in her ear and murmured, "Later, you can thank me properly." Then he scooted forward and joined the girls singing, "Go Santa Go!"

CHAPTER SEVEN

SIX MONTHS BEFORE THE FIRES

The first time Bec realized her husband had moments of being a stranger was on his first weekend leave from the hospital. After the long months spent in the burns unit and far away from Myrtle, Bec had assumed Adam would be desperate to come home. She'd planned a mostly quiet weekend so Adam could play with the girls, but knowing how much he loved company, she'd invited a few close friends for Sunday lunch. When she'd mentioned it to Adam, he shook his head.

"I'm not wasting five precious hours of my first weekend out of this prison in a car. Get your mother to mind the girls and book us a weekend at Crown."

"Crown?"

He gave her his new smile—tight and constrained by burns' scarring. "Of course, Crown, babe. We've got some celebrating to do."

The strangest thing about being in a luxury hotel was the complete absence of nurses, doctors and various allied health professionals suddenly appearing in their doorway. It was the first time in six months that Bec had been alone with her husband—the first time since

But these hot and heartfelt tears reset something inside her and the long months of duty morphed into affection.

Hope fluttered in her chest. Affection grew into love, didn't it? *This* was their new start.

Bec cupped his cheeks in her palms and she leaned in, gently kissing his eyes, his nose, his jaw and his neck. Her fingers opened the buttons on his shirt and she slid the soft cotton off his shoulders, pressing her lips to the pressure bandages on his arms and chest. Then she unbuckled his belt. Adam's hands stayed by his side. It was the first time in twelve years he'd ever allowed her to take the lead.

THE PRESENT

Bec stood in her award-winning kitchen with its sleek lines, stainless-steel appliances, black granite and the occasional juxtaposition of pockets of polished wood to honor the bush. With her hip against the island counter, she idly listened to the familiar clunks and whirrs of the coffee machine grinding beans and heating water before forcing it through the grounds. She hungrily watched the dark caffeine-loaded fluid drip into a glass. It was two in the afternoon and fatigue ran like glue in her veins.

Her tiredness bothered her. Even during the difficult days and weeks straight after the fires when she'd been consumed by shock and grief, when Adam lay in an induced coma fighting for his life, when the girls needed constant reassurance, when the pain of being wrenched away from Myrtle and missing the funerals of people she'd known and loved all her life had bent her double, she'd swear her concentration had been sharper. She didn't understand it, especially as Adam had been back at work for ten months, giving their lives a familiar pattern. But some days she felt like she was living in her own personal fog, although unlike Myrtle's winter nemesis, it wasn't clearing by ten in the morning.

Right now, all she wanted to do was nap but Adam was dealing

the wildfire—and bursts of agitation kept zapping her, thumping her heart and raising itchy red splotches on her skin. Adam, on the other hand, looked jubilant and relaxed. His hospital clothes of tracksuit pants and T-shirts had vanished, replaced by a new suit. The formal clothing hid the pressure bandages he wore twenty-four seven.

"Ready for a big night?"

Before she could object, Adam ushered her across the opulent foyer and into the casino. As they made their way to the gaming tables, Bec heard conversations falter, immediately followed by curious whispers.

"What the hell happened to him?"

"Burns?"

"God, do you think he ever looks in a mirror?"

If Adam heard the comments, he didn't show it. He confidently took his place at a roulette table as if he'd sat there only yesterday.

Adam played, his attention focused the way it had been before the fires. Bec stood behind him with her hand on his shoulder and acting her part, while the warning words of his health team to "not overdo things," played in her head. The high-octane excitement of the casino was hardly taking things easy. Neither was drinking. Adam ordered a second drink for them both. Was that one too many for him? She didn't dare mention it. She'd already suggested they return to their room and Adam's gaze had razed her with derision.

"Seriously, Bec? Why would I walk away from a winning streak?"

The small crowd who'd gathered to watch the players looked as if they agreed with Adam so she'd quietly sipped the Toblerone cocktail he'd chosen for her, making sure she smiled and kissed him each time the croupier pushed a stack of winner's chips toward him. When he summoned the waitress to order a third round of drinks, she tried again.

"Maybe now would be a good time to stop. The doctor said—"

"To enjoy myself." His happy face tightened. "And that's what I'd be doing if you weren't such a killjoy." He pressed chips into her hand. "Come on, babe, let your hair down. Have some fun."

Bec could think of a hundred other things they could be doing that she considered fun instead of being here in the company of strangers. Reluctantly, she placed bets on red and the number seventeen, remembering another time and place. The ball spun and landed on black. She lost. Adam won. Was that an allegory?

The anxiety that had been with her all day pirouetted in her gut as she tried to think of a way to quietly and unobtrusively extract Adam from the roulette table. Bec slid off her chair and whispered in his ear, "Come and have supper with me."

"Let's try blackjack," Adam slurred. He stood and Bec staggered as his bulk slammed into her. She couldn't remember the last time Adam had been so drunk he couldn't stand. Then again, he didn't usually combine alcohol and opiates.

A black-suited security guard appeared beside them and relief slid through her when Adam agreed to the man's suggestion that "Sir might appreciate a lie down in his room." The moment the obsequious man had backed out of their suite and the door clicked shut behind him, Adam slumped on the bed. He stared out into the colorful city night.

"Pretty view, isn't it?" God, she sounded so tentative but being with Adam now was like being with a stranger.

He grunted.

"Can I get you anything to help you sleep? Make you some tea?"

"Come here." He patted the bed, his contracted fingers preventing his palm from connecting with the mattress.

Bec sat and the mattress sagged, tilting her toward him. A messy mix of feelings made her stiffen, keeping a space between them. She didn't want to hurt him but part of her didn't even want to touch him. She knew she had to. Knew she needed to find a way to love him again when she'd never expected to have to try.

"Look at me," Adam demanded.

She turned and stroked his less damaged cheek.

He closed his hand around her wrist, the grip surprisingly strong despite the damage to his hand. "You're a shit actress, Bec," he said softly.

It was a joke that had started on their third date and it always made her laugh. Tonight was no different and she relaxed into giggles.

"I repulse you."

The vitriol in his words shocked her. "No. Adam. Not at all."

"Liar," he growled. "I've seen it on your face."

Her heart raced as her mind spun to that defining and awful night when a nurse had ushered her into the burns unit. Nothing about Adam's black and bloated face or his red, raw body was familiar. Shock made thinking impossible but she'd been vaguely aware that a machine was breathing for him. She remembered recoiling so violently at the terrifying sight of him that her back had hit the wall and she'd vomited onto the floor. Adam had been in an induced coma then and completely unaware of her reaction. By the time he'd been weaned off the machine, her responses to him and his burns were the practiced ones of a loving wife.

"When have you seen it on my face?"

"Every time you do a dressing."

The nursing staff were teaching her how to change Adam's dressings in preparation for his discharge home. She wasn't a natural nurse and each time she pulled back the gauze and exposed the graft her hands shook.

"That's not repulsion. That's fear. I'm terrified I'll hurt you."

"I don't a want a nursemaid, Bec. I want a wife." He jerked her hand and pressed it hard against his badly scarred cheek, immobilizing it. "Touch it."

Her mouth dried at the feel of the rippled and puckered skin under her palm.

Adam didn't flinch. Three beats passed then he dropped his head into his hands. A snotty, strangled noise filled the room.

Was he crying? In all their years together, Bec had never seen or heard him cry. Not even in the first couple of months after his injury when his level of pain would have reduced most men to tears. There been moments when his stoic endurance tempted her to curtness. After all, what sort of man didn't experience moments of vulnerability?

the wildfire—and bursts of agitation kept zapping her, thumping her heart and raising itchy red splotches on her skin. Adam, on the other hand, looked jubilant and relaxed. His hospital clothes of tracksuit pants and T-shirts had vanished, replaced by a new suit. The formal clothing hid the pressure bandages he wore twenty-four seven.

"Ready for a big night?"

Before she could object, Adam ushered her across the opulent foyer and into the casino. As they made their way to the gaming tables, Bec heard conversations falter, immediately followed by curious whispers.

"What the hell happened to him?"

"Burns?"

"God, do you think he ever looks in a mirror?"

If Adam heard the comments, he didn't show it. He confidently took his place at a roulette table as if he'd sat there only yesterday.

Adam played, his attention focused the way it had been before the fires. Bec stood behind him with her hand on his shoulder and acting her part, while the warning words of his health team to "not overdo things," played in her head. The high-octane excitement of the casino was hardly taking things easy. Neither was drinking. Adam ordered a second drink for them both. Was that one too many for him? She didn't dare mention it. She'd already suggested they return to their room and Adam's gaze had razed her with derision.

"Seriously, Bec? Why would I walk away from a winning streak?"

The small crowd who'd gathered to watch the players looked as if they agreed with Adam so she'd quietly sipped the Toblerone cocktail he'd chosen for her, making sure she smiled and kissed him each time the croupier pushed a stack of winner's chips toward him. When he summoned the waitress to order a third round of drinks, she tried again.

"Maybe now would be a good time to stop. The doctor said—"

"To enjoy myself." His happy face tightened. "And that's what I'd be doing if you weren't such a killjoy." He pressed chips into her hand. "Come on, babe, let your hair down. Have some fun."

Bec could think of a hundred other things they could be doing that she considered fun instead of being here in the company of strangers. Reluctantly, she placed bets on red and the number seventeen, remembering another time and place. The ball spun and landed on black. She lost. Adam won. Was that an allegory?

The anxiety that had been with her all day pirouetted in her gut as she tried to think of a way to quietly and unobtrusively extract Adam from the roulette table. Bec slid off her chair and whispered in his ear, "Come and have supper with me."

"Let's try blackjack," Adam slurred. He stood and Bec staggered as his bulk slammed into her. She couldn't remember the last time Adam had been so drunk he couldn't stand. Then again, he didn't usually combine alcohol and opiates.

A black-suited security guard appeared beside them and relief slid through her when Adam agreed to the man's suggestion that "Sir might appreciate a lie down in his room." The moment the obsequious man had backed out of their suite and the door clicked shut behind him, Adam slumped on the bed. He stared out into the colorful city night.

"Pretty view, isn't it?" God, she sounded so tentative but being with Adam now was like being with a stranger.

He grunted.

"Can I get you anything to help you sleep? Make you some tea?"

"Come here." He patted the bed, his contracted fingers preventing his palm from connecting with the mattress.

Bec sat and the mattress sagged, tilting her toward him. A messy mix of feelings made her stiffen, keeping a space between them. She didn't want to hurt him but part of her didn't even want to touch him. She knew she had to. Knew she needed to find a way to love him again when she'd never expected to have to try.

"Look at me," Adam demanded.

She turned and stroked his less damaged cheek.

He closed his hand around her wrist, the grip surprisingly strong despite the damage to his hand. "You're a shit actress, Bec," he said softly.

It was a joke that had started on their third date and it always made her laugh. Tonight was no different and she relaxed into giggles.

"I repulse you."

The vitriol in his words shocked her. "No. Adam. Not at all."

"Liar," he growled. "I've seen it on your face."

Her heart raced as her mind spun to that defining and awful night when a nurse had ushered her into the burns unit. Nothing about Adam's black and bloated face or his red, raw body was familiar. Shock made thinking impossible but she'd been vaguely aware that a machine was breathing for him. She remembered recoiling so violently at the terrifying sight of him that her back had hit the wall and she'd vomited onto the floor. Adam had been in an induced coma then and completely unaware of her reaction. By the time he'd been weaned off the machine, her responses to him and his burns were the practiced ones of a loving wife.

"When have you seen it on my face?"

"Every time you do a dressing."

The nursing staff were teaching her how to change Adam's dressings in preparation for his discharge home. She wasn't a natural nurse and each time she pulled back the gauze and exposed the graft, her hands shook.

"That's not repulsion. That's fear. I'm terrified I'll hurt you."

"I don't a want a nursemaid, Bec. I want a wife." He jerked her hand and pressed it hard against his badly scarred cheek, immobilizing it. "Touch it."

Her mouth dried at the feel of the rippled and puckered skin under her palm.

Adam didn't flinch. Three beats passed then he dropped his head into his hands. A snotty, strangled noise filled the room.

Was he crying? In all their years together, Bec had never seen or heard him cry. Not even in the first couple of months after his injury when his level of pain would have reduced most men to tears. There'd been moments when his stoic endurance tempted her to curtness. After all, what sort of man didn't experience moments of vulnerability?

But these hot and heartfelt tears reset something inside her and the long months of duty morphed into affection.

Hope fluttered in her chest. Affection grew into love, didn't it? *This* was their new start.

Bec cupped his cheeks in her palms and she leaned in, gently kissing his eyes, his nose, his jaw and his neck. Her fingers opened the buttons on his shirt and she slid the soft cotton off his shoulders, pressing her lips to the pressure bandages on his arms and chest. Then she unbuckled his belt. Adam's hands stayed by his side. It was the first time in twelve years he'd ever allowed her to take the lead.

THE PRESENT

Bec stood in her award-winning kitchen with its sleek lines, stainless-steel appliances, black granite and the occasional juxtaposition of pockets of polished wood to honor the bush. With her hip against the island counter, she idly listened to the familiar clunks and whirrs of the coffee machine grinding beans and heating water before forcing it through the grounds. She hungrily watched the dark caffeine-loaded fluid drip into a glass. It was two in the afternoon and fatigue ran like glue in her veins.

Her tiredness bothered her. Even during the difficult days and weeks straight after the fires when she'd been consumed by shock and grief, when Adam lay in an induced coma fighting for his life, when the girls needed constant reassurance, when the pain of being wrenched away from Myrtle and missing the funerals of people she'd known and loved all her life had bent her double, she'd swear her concentration had been sharper. She didn't understand it, especially as Adam had been back at work for ten months, giving their lives a familiar pattern. But some days she felt like she was living in her own personal fog, although unlike Myrtle's winter nemesis, it wasn't clearing by ten in the morning.

Right now, all she wanted to do was nap but Adam was dealing with end-of-financial-year matters and interviewing for new apprentices to cope with the burgeoning business. A steady stream of men tramped through the house and she was required to be on hand if Adam needed anything. So far that had been morning tea, lunch and some painkillers. Even so, with the doorbell ringing every forty-five minutes, a nap was totally out of the question. So were all noise-creating household tasks, including listening to the radio. Today was a bit like being on house arrest. Who was she kidding? Many days felt like she was in prison.

An ache that ebbed and flowed but refused to completely leave her suddenly throbbed. She picked up her cell phone, her fingers scrolling through folders to a photo taken before the fires. Staring at the picture, she hardly recognized herself. That time held a mythic quality. Had any of it existed? Had her life really been that optimistic and full of promise? And if it had, why had she so cavalierly deleted most of the evidence?

It was a rhetorical question. She knew exactly why she'd deliberately sent the photos to trash, watching them spiral down and vanish forever. The knowledge didn't help her or ease the loss that rushed back, poleaxing her as if it was fresh and new instead of being nineteen long months old. She abruptly flicked off the screen and put her cell face down on the counter.

The coffee machine clunked and steam shot through the milk, frothing it before it poured into the glass and lightened the coffee from deep chocolate to latte brown. Of course, the silver and black coffee machine was Italian. Bec had chosen it because it was the best. Everything inside and outside this house was the best.

It started with the majestic turn of the driveway that brought visitors up to the imposing modern mansion with its nod to French Colonial style. The foyer took over with its sweeping staircase, welcoming people into the well-appointed interior with its luxurious fittings. Its opulence extended out into the rear terrace, which was perfect for al fresco family dining and overlooked a tropical-blue swimming pool and manicured gardens. Adam called it aspirational—

the perfect house to represent Petrovic Family Homes. It was why Adam had insisted on a home office as well as the commercial space in Myrtle. That choice had proved wise; the Myrtle office had burned to the ground but the fire hadn't touched the house.

Although the office had a separate entrance for the employees, potential clients always came to the glossy black front door. Bec's job was to greet them, walk them past some carefully staged family clutter —sheet music scattered on the piano, a packet of pencils and one of Gracie's drawings on the table, an open novel on the ottoman, a steaming cup of coffee on a side table—items that turned a display house into a home. Clutter that made her fingers twitch and her gut churn.

Each time she escorted a couple to the office, she'd murmur appreciatively at their compliments about the house before handing them over to Adam, who greeted them ebulliently. There, in that light-filled space with its glimpses of the Southern Ocean, prospective customers would sit browsing through house designs. Bec, who'd grown up in a bog-standard brick veneer home, sometimes wondered if the opulence of this house had the opposite effect on people. It certainly had the ability to overwhelm her. Many days she craved something less grandiose.

At least you have a house. The thought stung like a slap as did the memory of the way Sophie Doherty had said "owner-build." Erica had totally missed the hidden meaning in the words but Bec had seen Sophie's deer-in-headlights look and felt for her. Perhaps if she mentioned the Dohertys' situation to Adam he might be able to help. Choosing when to mention it was the tricky bit.

"Bec!"

She jumped at the sound of Adam's voice. Their new start she'd pinned her hopes on all those months ago at Crown hadn't played out quite as she'd imagined.

With a twinge of regret, Bec left her just-brewed coffee on the counter and walked to the office. She stopped in the doorway, studying the back of Adam's head as if the pink skin would broadcast his state of mind before he turned to face her. Even if it could, some days his moods were so mercurial, they changed in the time it took for him to swivel the chair. Checking her watch, she calculated that the painkillers she'd given him earlier would have kicked in.

"Can I get you something?"

The chair turned. The severe scarring on one side of Adam's face meant his expression was often blank, but the less impacted side of his mouth tweaked into a crooked smile. He held out his arms. "Come here, babe."

She didn't hesitate—she just walked straight to him. The days of playful flirting and sexy, pouty faux-resistance were long gone. When she reached him, he pulled her forward until the edge of the chair slid under her bent knees. She rested them on either side of his thighs before lowering herself onto his lap.

He held her gaze. "Aren't you going to ask what's making me so happy?"

"I'm just happy you're happy."

"This is going to make you happy too."

These days, not much made her happy, but she desperately wanted to believe him. "Is it?"

"Hell, yeah. The end-of-financial-year statement's in and it's the best we've ever had. Part of me almost wants to give thanks for the fire."

She shuddered. "It almost killed you!" *It killed part of me.*

"Yeah, but with the all the rebuilds, that bastard fire's the best thing that's ever happened to our bank account. I'm taking you shopping in Melbourne next week to celebrate."

"Should we? Sometimes I'm uncomfortable about how we're benefiting."

But he didn't hear her. His attention was fully consumed, studying her as if he'd only just noticed what she was wearing—a fine black merino top, black leggings, suede ankle boots and an elegant cardigan that swept to her knees. It was perfect Myrtle winter wear that was both stylish and warm. She'd bought the outfit the year before when

Adam was in rehabilitation. While he'd been attending physio and occupational therapy, she'd gained a few precious hours to herself and indulged in some liberating solo retail therapy. Adam had never commented on these clothes, in stark contrast to his opinions on her pre-fire wardrobe.

"I'm buying you some dresses," Adam said. "You always rock a frock."

"In summer, sure." Bec worked hard at not sounding resigned. She could already picture the shopping trip—her modeling clothes and Adam buying the ones he liked the best regardless of their practicality or winter warmth.

"You rock frocks in winter too. Clear your calendar for Wednesday."

Apart from craft group, grocery shopping and taking the girls to and from school and their after-school activities, these days her calendar was almost empty. It had been stripped bare by Adam's months in the hospital, followed by months at home helping him get back to normal—whatever the hell constituted normal. She thought about Sophie living in a cold shed.

"Instead of shopping, what if we donate the money to help out people like the Dohertys?"

His bad eye twitched. "You're making it sound like they've suffered more than I have. That I don't deserve some good fortune after all the agonizing pain I've gone through. Still go through."

"That's not what I meant. I—"

"Good, because the last thing I need is my wife being ungrateful for all do for our family. We're going shopping and I'm buying you a showstopping evening gown. Petrovic Family Homes has been nominated for a Master Builders Regional Award."

Relief poured through her, followed by delight. *Do I squeal first? Say congratulations? Kiss him?* "Oh my God!" She kissed him full on the mouth. "What a massive achievement, especially on top of all your rehab—"

"You didn't think I could do it?"

"Of course I thought you could do it. I've watched you do it. You're amazing."

"And?"

Get it right. She stroked his damaged cheek, having learned it upset him if she favored the unscarred parts of him. "I'm so proud of you."

"Show me exactly how proud you are."

She instantly relaxed and blinked back the urge to cry at the sheer and blessed normality. Not many things in their complicated dance of post-fire life remained untouched by the blaze but this, *this* was the same. Adam always celebrated good news with sex.

"I'll cook you whatever you want for dinner and you choose the wine. I'll make sure the girls are in bed early tonight so we have plenty of time to do justice to this great news."

"That's hours away."

She laughed at his petulant tone and began to slide off his lap, her mind already running through logistics. Did she have enough time to shop before school pick-up? Or should she drop Ivy off at her piano lesson and, instead of staying, go and shop? Lately, Ivy had wanted her to stay so—

"I don't want to wait hours." Adam's arm tightened around her back, halting her progress and keeping her firmly on his lap.

It was impossible not to feel his erection. "But Scotty's due any minute."

"So?" His free hand slid under her top to the waistband of her leggings.

"So, since you made him a partner, he just walks into the office unannounced".

"I've noticed that. This might just teach him to knock." He tugged down her leggings and cool air hit her butt.

Adam had never suggested they have sex anywhere other than their bedroom and the idea of being caught by someone, let alone Scotty, horrified her. She tried wriggling off his lap. "I'm not having sex here."

The moment the words left her mouth she knew she'd chosen the wrong ones. Adam's eyes flashed and the flexible side of his mouth flattened at her outright refusal.

"In that case, we've got a problem."

"I'm not saying no to sex," she soothed. "I just think we can have more fun in the bedroom and—"

"No!" The word sliced the air like a knife.

Breathing hard, he tugged and pulled at her leggings until the heavy-duty elastic waistband sat tight across her thighs. It took her a second to realize this prevented her from standing up. With his strong builder arm pressed hard against her back, she couldn't move.

Faint ripples of unease fluttered inside her. "Adam?"

He pulled her head down, his guttural voice jagged against her ear. "Never wear these bloody leggings again."

"No. Sorry." The words tumbled out automatically. Anything to prevent his simmering anger from exploding into a full-on boil.

"We're celebrating work, Bec, so we're doing it in the office. Right here, right now." He loosened his fly and lifted her. "Ready?"

"Yes." Despite the notice, she gasped as he drove up into her.

She was intimate with his erratic temper—had been since he'd returned home from the hospital, but sex with this raw edge was different. New.

He rocked into her. "You proud of me, babe?"

"Yes."

He thrust again. "Are you lucky to have me?"

"So. Very. Lucky."

"Do you deserve me?"

"No."

"Of course you do." Adam grinned at her then—his smile full of love and devoid of even the slightest hint of anger. His rutting changed to long, slow caresses. Familiar. Reassuring. Normal.

She drew in a deep and reassuring breath. If only she'd said yes from the start, they could have avoided any unpleasantness. After all, they'd been having sex for twelve years. Where was the harm in spicing things up a bit by trying something new?

Afterwards, Adam was exuberant. "Next time we're using the desk."

Bec was on her feet and smoothing down her clothes when Scotty walked in. Thank God he hadn't been two minutes earlier. He shot her a questioning look and her racing heart hit overdrive. Scotty always saw too much—it both unnerved and heartened her.

"Sorry I'm late. I've been dealing with morons at the city hall." Scotty slumped into a chair. "You're looking good, Bec. Do something different with your hair?"

No, Scotty. Don't. "I—"

"You shouldn't be noticing my wife's hair, mate," Adam said lightly.

Bec knew the lightness was the thinnest of veneers. When she was younger and Adam's jealously had been an occasional narrow streak of dark green, she'd delighted in his possessiveness. But since surgeons had rebuilt sections of his face, arms and torso with skin grafts, that streak had both widened and deepened. It had moments when it bit her hard.

"I'm noticing everyone's hair, mate," Scotty said easily. "I reckon the whole town's gone to that new hairdresser since she opened."

"She's good," Bec said brightly, trying to rise above the disappointment that the salon wasn't hers.

Before the fires, her laundry had doubled as a home salon for relatives and a few past clients who'd preferred her to cut their hair. Adam had grumbled about it, but he'd often called in when she was working and sat chatting with her clients. After the fires, when Adam had got the all clear on his hands from the occupational therapist, she'd asked if she could lease one of the new shops.

"Myrtle needs a hairdresser and I could offer waxing and—"

"Sorry, babe. We've just rented to a hairdresser."

"What? Why didn't you ask me?"

"Seriously, babe? It's bad enough that the rels expect you to cut their hair but salon hours? No way. Besides, no wife of mine needs to work."

"I want to work."

His jaw tightened. "You have a job right here helping me, not to mention the girls."

Adam's words were familiar and she'd told herself that nothing had really changed: this was the same as her pre-fire life. Deep down, it felt different. More constrained. Smaller.

Now a burn of betrayal raced along her veins. First Scotty's compliment then mentioning the salon. What the hell was he playing at today? Was he trying to bait Adam?

"Let's hope Salon Eva keeps its customers," Scotty said. "The commercial strip's taking longer to lease than we hoped. Bec, you're a woman who shops. What sort of business do you think we should target next?"

Adam leaned forward, clicked on the computer's mouse and the large screen flickered into life. "Bec hasn't got time to yak with you. She's heading out to pick up the girls, aren't you, babe?"

Apparently she was going an hour early, but she didn't mention that. Instead she said, "Ivy gets worried if I'm late." At least that was the truth. "Will I switch the telephone through to here?"

"Nah. It can go to voice mail. Scotty and I've got a lot to discuss."

When Adam had been in the hospital, Scotty ran the business. Unlike her husband, he'd involved her in the decision-making and sought her opinions. For eight months she'd known more about Petrovic Family Homes than she had during any other time in her marriage. Given that everything else in her life then was a ball of worry and grief, the business became an escape. The moment Adam had resumed work, all consultation had stopped. Now, whenever Adam said, "Scotty and I've got a lot to discuss," it meant *go away and let the men talk business.*

Bec closed the office door behind her.

𝄞

CLAIRE STOOD in the community health center's carpark rummaging in her handbag for her car keys. It suddenly dawned on her that she'd specifically left them on top of the work fridge so she'd remember to bring home the ice cream she'd bought at lunchtime.

"Damn!" Going back inside meant deactivating the security system and calling the company so they didn't call her. Still, it was better to do all that than arrive empty-handed. It was bad enough she was going to be a little bit late. She punched in the numbers on the security keypad with one hand while she used the other to bring up the company's number on her cell phone, all the time cursing the Melbourne architects who thought Myrtle—population two hundred and dropping—needed this level of security. Any drug addict who broke in was going to be sorely disappointed.

A screeching sound engulfed her, making her jump. She frantically punched more numbers into the keypad. The sound continued, ripping into her eardrums and vibrating in her chest. She ran inside, trying to get away from it, or at least get the muffled version. After talking on the cell to the security company and explaining what happened, she pulled open the freezer and shoved the ice cream into an insulated bag before zipping it up. Then she grabbed her car keys, made her way back to the front door and plugged in the new code. Just as the agonizing sound ceased, Shane Radley pulled up in the four-wheel-drive police vehicle and got out.

"Everything okay, Claire?"

"Yes, sorry. I'm the culprit. I was in a hurry and I must have pressed a wrong number. I had to go back in and rescue the ice cream for tonight's dinner."

"I'm sure Matt will appreciate it."

"Actually, it's his father's favorite."

"How are Bill and Louise?"

"Yeah, good." She heard her voice squeak and cleared her throat. "Actually, tonight's a first. They're coming to our place for dinner."

"Matt told me the new house is finished." Shane smiled. "When we moved into the new residence, I think Sally invited someone around for a meal every weekend for two months. It felt good to be normal again, you know?"

She nodded, despite having no idea what normal felt like anymore. But if Shane was experiencing normal, surely she could too. Shane was a good country cop and Claire had a lot of time for him. He knew his community and was especially connected with the pre-fire residents. He was well respected and on first-name terms with model citizens and criminals alike. Not that there'd ever been many lawbreakers in Myrtle before the fires razed the town. There were even less now.

"I saw Lucy the other day. Great hair."

Shane grimaced. "Teenagers, eh? I'd just got used to the pink ends. I gotta say it was a struggle not to yell at her when she came home with her beautiful long hair hacked short, spiked and blue."

"You should take it as a compliment," Claire teased. "It's pretty close to Victoria Police blue."

"I really don't care what color her hair is. Sally and I are just relieved she's finally settled back at school and found her concentration. It was touch and go there for a while. Last year we weren't sure she'd even finish tenth grade. Now she's talking about going to university."

"That's great. Lucy's lucky to have you and Sal."

"I dunno. Maybe we got lucky."

Claire thought about the men and women of Myrtle and how many were barely coping. All their energy was sucked out of them just trying not to sink under the weight of trauma, red tape and rebuilding. It didn't leave much in reserve for emotional support for their kids.

"Too many teenage girls are wiping themselves off with vodka on the weekends then coming to see me on Monday terrified they're pregnant. I'm terrified they've got an STD too. Some of them tell me they were so out of it, they're not sure if they even had sex or if they had it with more than one person. Shane, we've got traumatized young people self-medicating and indulging in high-risk behavior. We need to offer them something. Provide a safe place they can hang out."

He rocked back on the heels of his regulation black boots. "We've got an indoor sports center."

"I guess we do. How do we make that uber cool so they turn up?"

"Blue Light Disco?"

Claire didn't want to rain on his parade by saying that "cool" and "Blue Light Disco" hadn't gone together when she was a kid, let alone twenty years on. "Oh! What about a trampoline disco? Get Lucy's opinion on that for me, will you? We can apply for funding and—"

Her cell phone bleated—Matt's ringtone. Her heart sank. He only rang if she was more than twenty minutes late and she'd promised him, hand on heart, she'd be on time tonight. "Sorry, Shane, I've gotta go. Say hi to Sally for me. And I'm serious—ask Lucy and get back to me."

Shoving her cell phone to her ear, she ran to the car. "Honey, I'm on my way."

When Claire pulled up outside the nameless house that she still didn't recognize as hers, there were no waiting dogs with tails wagging enthusiastically. Obviously, they were far too busy inside idolizing the visitors. She grabbed the ice cream and half-walked, half-danced across two long, skinny planks of wood balanced precariously on top of rain-sodden soil. For months after the fires, everything she'd touched had left a streak of black ash. Now, on the very same site, winter rains were rendering what would one day be her front yard to a morass of black and sticky mud. Sometimes, Claire didn't know which was worse: mud or ash. Whenever that happened, she slapped herself. Hard.

Reaching the veranda, she kicked off her shoes and stepped over mud-encrusted elastic-sided boots, gum boots and a very nice pair of knee-high black leather boots. Louise's. Claire paused in the laundry and stowed the ice cream in the freezer before hanging the insulated bag on the hook that Matt had installed for the purpose. She was halfway across the kitchen on her way to the bathroom to check her hair and swipe on some lipstick when she heard Louise's voice.

"Claire! There you are. Matt was starting to worry."

It was a familiar greeting—one that had been said to her on numerous occasions during the time they'd shared a house.

"Hello, Louise. Good to see you." Claire leaned left to kiss Matt's mother and Louise leaned right. Flustered, Claire pulled back and tried again, finally landing a tense kiss on Louise's cheek. God! She and Matt had been together for two and a half years. Why the hell hadn't she got better at this?

The fact Louise wasn't holding a drink reassured Claire that Matt's parents must have only just arrived. "Welcome to our new home. Would you like a tour?"

"Matt's already given us one."

"Oh." She hadn't thought she was that late. "Can I get you a drink, Louise?"

The dogs raced into the kitchen, their claws clacking on the floorboards as they made a beeline for Claire. Her heart rolled in appreciation at their visible and uncomplicated emotions. With dogs, whether they were happy, sad or in pain, what you saw was exactly how they were feeling. With Louise Cartwright, Claire could never tell what she was thinking or feeling. It left her on tenterhooks.

Bill appeared in the kitchen, followed by Matt, who immediately slipped his arm around her waist and kissed her hello. She whispered, "Sorry."

Matt gave her a half-annoyed, half-indulgent smile. "You're here now. Mom and Dad brought some of the good stuff to wet the house's head."

"How lovely. Thank you." Claire always led with gratitude even if she didn't feel grateful. After her excruciating official introduction to Louise as Matt's girlfriend, her own mother had advised her to always be polite and appreciative and never ever get between a mother and her son. "Do that darling and you'll win her round in the end."

Did Heather ever look down on these tense gatherings and admit that perhaps she'd got it wrong?

"Hello, Claire." Bill kissed her on the cheek. "You've done a great job. The house is lovely."

"Thanks, Bill. We're getting there."

"As soon as the ground dries out a bit, I'll bring the bobcat over and make a start on the flower beds.

Matt deftly popped the cork from the sparkling wine.

"Such a good sound," Claire said, desperate for a drink.

He poured four flutes with the fizzing pinot before handing them around. Claire noticed that compared with the others, the tide on hers was seriously out.

Bill raised his flute. "May this fine house ring with love and happiness."

They all murmured their agreement and clinked the delicate crystal. Claire drank, savoring the dry honey taste and the tingling effervescence on her tongue.

"May it soon ring with the sounds of a gurgling baby," Louise added.

Bubbles raced up Claire's nose and she coughed.

"No need to be coy, Claire," Louise continued. "Matt showed us the room you've set aside as the nursery. Although I think the one you're using as the office would be better."

Stunned that Matt had mentioned baby plans to his parents, Claire shot him a look, but he was smiling at her unperturbed. She reached for the bottle to refill her wineglass. "As we're not pregnant yet, we've got plenty of time to decide which room works best."

Matt's hand reached the sweating bottle first and he shoved a stopper into it before returning it to the fridge. Claire decided not to insist on more lest Louise comment. It wouldn't be the first time she'd passed judgement on Claire's enjoyment of alcohol.

"We're just glad you're finally trying." Bill smiled. "Now Tamara's kids are at school, I miss having little ones around. There's something special about seeing the farm through the innocent eyes of a child. Not to mention the years they idolize you. Precious times."

Claire blinked rapidly, desperately trying to hold back tears as the memory of her father saying, "I'd love to be a grandfather one day," came back to her. *Oh, Dad. I miss you so much.*

"Look at you getting all emotional and you're not even preggers yet," Matt said fondly.

"I'll help you decorate the nursery," Louise said. "Tamara

appreciated my decorator's eye and my wallpapering expertise."

Tiny explosions of anxiety detonated all over Claire, cramping her stomach and raising her pulse. When she and Matt were living in the homestead, Louise and Bill's encroachments into their personal life happened a lot. Moving into the new house was supposed to stop them. But here she was standing in her new kitchen with the senior Cartwrights talking about creating her garden and discussing yet-to-be conceived children as if they not only existed, they were old enough to ride in the tractor!

It was time to change the subject. "What needs to be done for dinner? Will I cook the rice?"

"All sorted," Matt said.

"My son, the modern man," Louise said admiringly.

"I wouldn't get too excited, Mom. I just followed Claire's curry recipe and chucked everything into the slow cooker. I hope it works. I'm also test driving the rice cooker." He gave Claire a tentative look. "I thought it was time to break out the replacement wedding presents."

"A replacement wedding would be a good idea too," Louise said. "Before the baby."

The air in the open-plan living area turned thick, viscous and choking. Claire's chest fought to rise against a crippling spasm. "I'll just wash my hands for dinner."

By the time she reached the bathroom and locked the door behind her, her skin blazed with heat and her armpits and hair were slick with as much sweat as if she'd run the twenty miles from Myrtle. She stared into the mirror, barely recognizing the wild-eyed woman looking back at her.

"THAT WENT WELL," Matt said cheerfully. They stood shivering on the veranda, waving goodbye to his parents.

Did it? Sometimes Claire wondered if she and Matt attended the same family gatherings, but there was no point voicing it. "Now we've practiced on your folks, maybe we should invite some other people over when the weather's better?"

"Sure, as long as you're not distracted like you were tonight."

"I wasn't distracted."

The taillights of the quad bike disappeared around the bend and Matt steered her back into the warmth and the purring sound of the dishwasher. "You were quiet."

"Not really. It can be hard to get a word in when the Cartwrights are animatedly discussing bees, sheep, alpacas and pigs."

"The bees are as much yours as they are mine."

"I know."

He sat next to her on the couch. "You used to be more interested."

The criticism was faint but it rankled. She loved the bees more than the sheep or Matt's precious acorn-eating Wessex Saddleback pigs. It wasn't that she liked the insects more than the animals, but she associated bees with her love for Matt. On her first visit to the farm, they'd tended the hives and extracted the honey. Matt had explained the architectural genius of the hexagon honeycomb that tripled as a container for pollen, honey and baby bees. It had been a special time— the day she'd called him "honey" for the first time and glimpsed a future with him.

"I'm still interested in the bees. I was the one who chose the elegant new jars and redesigned the labels that got Oakvale Honey into that trendy fruit and veggie shop in Geelong."

"I meant we used to look after the hives together. You haven't come out with me in ages."

Claire fought against a flash of irritation. "It's been hard to come out when we didn't have hives or anything for the bees to feed on."

"I s'pose, but it's all coming back. Some of the eucalypts flowered in Feb and winter's so ridiculously wet, spring will be loaded with flowers for busy bees to feed on." He picked up her hand, wrapping it in his. "Promise me we'll do the next extraction together."

"Sure. As long as it doesn't clash with anything at work."

His mouth flattened. "What held you up tonight?"

"You'll laugh."

"Will I?"

"Yes." She elbowed him playfully, wanting to banish his doubtful look. "I accidently set off the security system going back inside to get your dad's ice cream. Shane arrived and we got chatting about what might work to engage the teenagers."

"Surely that's up to the school."

"If Myrtle had a high school, sure, but we don't. Our kids are getting lost in the system at a school where most of the students didn't lose horses, houses ..." Her voice cracked. "Family."

"*Our* kids? Hell, *we* don't have any kids yet. This isn't your responsibility."

"You know what I mean. And as the community health nurse, it *is* my responsibility. Health and wellbeing for all ages and stages."

Matt tensed. "I thought you were looking to rein in your hours, not extend them? And when the baby comes—"

"I'm not even pregnant!" The leash she'd clipped on her frustrations during their pre-dinner-drinks conversation gave way. "And God! Why are you telling people we're trying? Stop it. Stop it right now."

He flinched, his forehead creased. "I haven't told anyone."

"You told your parents."

"Yeah, but that's not 'telling people'."

Her hands flew up into the air before slapping her thighs. "It is! And it's too much pressure. Now your parents will be glancing sideways at me looking for signs I'm pregnant. Humans aren't like sheep or bees or cows, Matt. We're pretty inefficient at conceiving. It might take us a while and even when we do, there's always the risk of miscarriage and—"

"Hey, shh, Postie, don't get upset." He stroked her hair. "Forget all that nasty medical stuff. We won't have any problems. We're fit, healthy and ready. And besides, the universe owes us big time after what it's put us through."

His confidence terrified her.

CHAPTER EIGHT

"Have you seen my knitting?"

Sophie had spent ten minutes searching in the usual but limited number of storage places in the shed but none had yielded the cloth bag with her wool and knitting needles.

"Josh?"

He looked up distractedly from the laptop—he'd been studying their bank statements for the last five minutes. "What?"

"My knitting. Have you seen it?"

His eyes drifted back to the screen. "Didn't you leave it on the sofa?"

"Yes, but it's not there."

"What's this payment of two hundred and fifty dollars?"

She pulled out the sofa cushions. Her knitting wasn't there but she discovered the Duplo construction worker Liam had thrown a tantrum over a few nights earlier when it went missing. She also found a two-dollar coin, a piece of shriveled apple and a bread crust. Shuddering, she gingerly picked up the food. "Josh! You let the kids eat on the sofa."

"So?"

"So they dropped food."

When they'd moved into the shed it hadn't taken long to discover they were sharing it with rodents and some terrifyingly enormous spiders. On Julie's advice, Sophie now stored everything, including soap, in plastic containers and traps were permanently set. For the first couple of weeks, the random snap of a trap going off made her jump. But like so many things she'd never anticipated getting used to, now when she heard the loud clap of the spring release, she made a resigned mental note to tell Josh. He dealt with the trap horrors, but not even he was prepared to reuse the device. Fortunately, they didn't cost much.

She dropped the offending food items into the trash, which she emptied religiously each night before going to bed, otherwise it became a mouse theme park. "You know any scraps are an invitation for mice and rats. Besides, we had an agreement that the kids ate at the table."

"You *told* me they had to eat at the table. I didn't actually agree."

Josh's words activated the spores of discontent that permanently hovered just under the surface. "Just because we're living in a shed doesn't mean we drop our standards. I don't want them being little savages who think they can just eat anywhere."

"Where's the damage? They were tired and grumpy so I plonked them in front of the TV and gave them a sandwich. We all got twenty minutes of downtime. You need to chill, Soph."

She didn't want to chill. She wanted the children to have routine. Manners. "When I was at home—"

"Yeah, well you're not. I am. Deal with it."

She stared at him, stupefied. "Deal with it?"

"Yeah." His face hardened. "Just like I have to deal with it."

She shoved the cushions back on the sofa with punishing force. So often it felt like all she did was deal with her life instead of actively living it. As she stooped to pick up the TV remote, she glimpsed a flash of pink. She got down on her knees and reached under the sofa, grabbing at the strand of wool. Expecting the skein to follow, she stared at the yarn in her hand. Instead of the neat and even square of stocking stitch she'd worked so hard to make, the entire thing was off the needle in an unraveled and knotted mess.

"Josh." She tried to keep her voice quiet and low so as not to wake the children. "Did you let the kids play with my knitting?"

"Yeah. I'm exactly the sort of father who lets his kids play with something sharp that can poke their eyes out."

She shoved the ruined square at his chest. "Look at it! They've wrecked it."

"They've done a number on it, that's for sure."

His lack of empathy poured oil on the fire of her aggravation. "How could you let them?"

"Jeez, Soph. I didn't *let* them do it. I didn't even know they'd done it."

"Why didn't you know? It's not like they can escape to another room to cause havoc."

"You shouldn't have left the bloody knitting out for them to get at."

"You should have noticed them destroying it."

He threw up his hands. "How is this my fault?"

"Because it's parenting 101! When the kids are really quiet they're usually doing something wrong." She suddenly remembered what he'd said about downtime. "You weren't supervising the kids, were you? You were playing on the bloody computer."

"I was *working* on the computer. I'm trying to build us a house, remember? Unlike you, I don't have the luxury of the peace and quiet of an office where no one interrupts me every five freakin' minutes."

"Luxury? You've got to be kidding me!"

A startled cry rose from the other side of the partition and Josh scowled, his face twisting into harsh and unforgiving lines.

"Great going, Sophie."

"I'll go."

Guilt whipped her as she crouched down beside the portable crib that was Trixie's bed. Her daughter had been a light sleeper from day one. She'd entered the world screaming, indignant at being torn from her safe cocoon, and Sophie understood. Trixie had arrived when their world was black and still smoldering. A war zone, where death and destruction dominated.

It was the arbitrary nature of the fire that hurt the most. When Sophie had finally been allowed back on their land, it wasn't the sight of the buckled and twisted remains of their home that undid her. It was seeing two tiny rompers, Liam's shorts and T-shirts and Josh's workwear—clothes she'd pinned on the clothesline the morning of the fire before leaving to visit her mother. She'd doubled over at the everyday sight, sobbing at nature's taunting. How dare she have taken normality for granted.

Trixie stood in her crib, clutching her blankie with one chubby fist and rubbing her eyes with the other. She took one look at Sophie and screamed, "Dadda! Dadda!"

"Mommy's here," Sophie said softly. She stroked Trixie's hair and tried to lay her down so she could tuck her back under the covers.

"No!" Trixie's back arched and she stiffened like a board. "Dadda."

Sophie sang the goodnight song she'd created for Trixie on the long nights of walking the floor in the temporary village—nights when Trixie only slept when she was snuggled in Sophie's arms. Despite the sleep deprivation, the fact that they'd lost everything they'd owned, Trixie's almost constant fractiousness and Sophie's feelings of hopelessness, it was in those early hours that love grew. When Trixie had gazed up from the breast, her large, dark eyes full of adoration and trust, the rush of solicitude that had expanded Sophie's heart had physically hurt. In days riddled with bewilderment, angst and unreliability, those moments had kept Sophie going.

Tonight, instead of the goodnight song soothing her daughter into a dreamless sleep or prompting looks of adoration, Trixie's wails continued to increase in volume and shrillness. She pounded the top of the crib with her free fist.

Josh appeared, his presence critical even before he opened his mouth. "At this rate, Liam's going to wake up too."

"Dadda." Trixie hiccupped and stretched out her arms. "Up."

"Come on, you little terror," Josh said affectionately. "Time to lie down."

"Okay." Trixie shoved her thumb into her mouth and obediently snuggled down for her father.

Sophie stood rooted to the spot, eviscerated by inadequacy and feeling like an outsider in her own family. Then anger hit with the dry heat blast of a furnace. It took conscious effort to walk away instead of staying and giving in to the temptation to yell. No wonder Trixie preferred Josh over her. He didn't parent, he just let the kids do whatever they wanted.

She looked at the remains of her blanket square and fought tears. How could she go to craft group tonight with this sorry example? It would be too embarrassing.

Sophie suddenly remembered Claire saying she sucked at crafts, as if the statement was a badge of honor rather than something to be ashamed about. Could she pretend to be equally blasé and unaffected? There was only one way to find out. She shoved the wool into its bag, grabbed her keys and headed out the door.

THE WARMTH of the CWA room greeted Sophie, as did Erica, Layla, Julie and Bec. Claire was yet to arrive and Sophie wondered if she'd attend a second time. As the town's only healthcare provider, Claire was composed and caring, but outside of that role it seemed she excelled at stirring the pot. By the end of the first evening, Sophie had felt sorry for Bec. Perhaps the group would be calmer without Claire's presence.

Tonight, the food on the table was a little different. The cheese platter remained the same but instead of chocolates there were three small plates of sweet-looking food. Sophie recognized the contents of one.

"Is that Turkish delight?"

Layla smiled. "You like it?"

"I love it. Did you make it?"

Layla nodded. "And the baklava, but I buy the halva."

Stricken, Sophie swung around to Julie. "Was I supposed to bring a plate?"

Understanding crossed Julie's face and she shook her head. "Layla enjoys cooking so she's treating us. Sit back and enjoy."

"I will. So what's halva?"

Layla was busy explaining what halva was made of and telling her about tahini when Claire walked in, her work I.D. lanyard swinging around her neck.

"Hi, everyone."

"Hi, Claire," they all murmured.

"Sorry I'm late."

"Are you?" Bec's smile was tight. "Because you've been saying that for as long as I've known you."

The chatter in the room stalled.

Claire laughed, but the edges were cool. "Back in the day, Bec and I were Girl Scouts. She blames me for our patrol losing the Camp Otway Cup. I was late for dinner and lost us points. The fact the Warrnambool girls aced us in almost every activity doesn't seem to factor into her logic. Oh! Is that baklava? Matt will be jealous." She loaded a plate and added some figs.

Julie sighed. "Didn't you manage dinner?"

Claire shook her head. "Tuesdays are frantic and family planning ran late."

"Please, take some baklava home to your husband," Layla offered.

"If Tuesdays don't suit, I'm flexible," Erica said amicably. "Any night except Monday works for me."

Bec's chin lifted. "Claire's known from the start that craft group's on Tuesdays. Once we start shifting dates and times, it impacts on other people."

Claire's brows shot to her hairline. "Did I ask for a—"

"How's everyone getting on with their project?" Julie interrupted firmly.

"I bought some of Louise Cartwright's beautiful wool." Bec held up a completed glove before passing it to Erica.

"It's so soft." Erica pulled it on, modeling it. "And elegant and warm."

Bec smiled appreciatively. "I chose black because it's such a classic color and can be worn with just about anything. I should have its partner finished by next meeting. Then I thought I'd try knitting socks."

Claire shoved another piece of baklava in her mouth.

"I knitted a chunky beanie for a bloke." Julie held up a charcoal gray ribbed beanie with a cuff.

"Wow, you're fast." Erica passed Bec's glove to Layla for inspection.

Julie laughed. "Not really, just experienced. Over the years, I've knitted this pattern many times to keep my family warm. It's cold milking cows in winter."

Claire fingered the gray wool as if it was precious. Sophie thought she heard her say, "Hugo," but it was so soft and indistinct she wasn't certain. She glanced at Julie, but the older woman's demeanor was open and friendly, so perhaps Sophie heard wrong.

"Layla, have you got something you'd like to share?" Julie asked.

"I'm not fast like Julie and Bec but I start a çorap." She produced a colorful sock with an incredibly intricate design of diamonds, dots and squares.

Sophie gasped. "That's amazing. It's like a tapestry."

"Goodness." Bec tensed and re-crossed her legs. "Perhaps I better leave the sock knitting to you."

Layla smiled shyly. "It's traditional Turkish design. My grandmother teaches me but I'm slow. Perhaps I should knit plain socks?"

"No way," Claire said. "Those will not only keep someone's feet warm, they'll warm their soul. After all the sh—everything, we need color in our lives."

"Could you teach me how to knit a pair?" Erica asked. "The kids would love them as slippers."

"Did you manage to make anything, Claire?" Bec's tone left no room for ambiguity. Clearly, she doubted the nurse had created anything.

At the first meeting, Sophie had got the impression that Claire was the instigator of the animosity between the two women. Now she saw it ran both ways. If they disliked each other so much and Claire struggled with crafts, why didn't she just drop out of the group?

"Ta-dah!" Claire held up a multicolored square. "Thanks to Layla's fabulous instructions and infinite patience, I've managed to crochet an Afghan square and ..."

Sophie's stomach dropped to her feet and an irrational spurt of dislike for the nurse coursed through her. This wasn't fair. Claire was her partner in the I-suck-at-crafts stakes.

"... only nineteen to go. Hopefully, I'll get quicker. What's surprised me is how much I'm enjoying it." Claire smiled at Julie. "It's made me stop and sit at night. Mind you, that might just be because I finally have my own sofa to sit on."

"Have you just bought a new sofa?" Erica leaned forward. "Nathan and I are looking. He wants leather but I'm wondering if we should wait until the kids are older and—"

"Erica," Claire said patiently, although Sophie heard the strain. "I've got new everything. Our house was destroyed in the fires and up until a month ago we've been living with Matt's parents."

"Oh, right. Sorry." Erica sounded flustered. "I keep putting my foot in it, don't I? I don't mean to. Don't get me wrong, I know some of you went through dreadful experiences that I wouldn't wish on my worst enemy, but it's very hard being new in this town. We were so excited about moving here but I feel like I've hit an invisible wall. Those of us who didn't experience the wildfires find it impossible to break in. That's why I was so excited to join this group, but even here ... Sometimes I think I should ask people as soon as I meet them, 'Were you here that day? What happened to you?' Just so I know!"

"Don't do that! Not everyone wants to talk about it," Claire said tersely.

Erica opened her hands as if to say, "See!"

Claire sighed. "Sorry, Erica. We're not trying to be exclusive. It's just really complicated, because whether people were in Myrtle on the day or not, everyone was impacted in a different way. We're all struggling. Please give us some time."

Erica gave a resigned nod. "I'm sorry you lost your house, Claire, but it must be great that you're in your own place again. And kudos for surviving the in-laws." She shuddered theatrically. "Nathan knows better than to ever suggest that to me."

"Louise and Bill are lovely people," Bec said, stoutly defending the Cartwrights as though Erica had cast aspersions against them. "When I was a kid, they lent me a horse so I could be part of pony club."

Just as Sophie was wondering if Claire would correct Erica on the fact that the Cartwrights weren't officially her in-laws, the vivid television images of the nurse on that catastrophic December day lit up her mind. A wave of nausea hit as it always did any time she thought about that night. It was the reason she actively tried not to think about it.

"Sophie?"

"Sorry?"

"How did you go with your blanket square?"

Five sets of expectant eyes were suddenly trained on her and her mouth dried. This was as bad as telling her year eight science teacher that a dog ate her homework—it had been the truth but he hadn't believed her. She clutched the tea-towel bag on her lap.

"Oh, so, funny story. It was going really well ..." she tried feigning nonchalance and pulled out the remains of the square, "... but then the kids got to it."

"Oh no." Bec's hand touched her arm sympathetically. "Don't you hate that? You turn your back on them for two minutes and chaos."

Erica groaned. "Scarlett got to my wallet last week and mailed all my cards though the central heating vents. They're gone for good."

"My son opens the fridge when I say goodbye to a friend. I didn't know he can do this. He drops twelve eggs to see if they bounce like his ball," Layla added with a groan. "So much mess."

Julie smiled. "We've all been there."

"Not me."

Sophie couldn't decide if Claire was sad about being childless, or relieved. "I know I should have put the knitting out of their reach but some nights I'm just so tired ..."

"It's easy enough to fix." Bec lifted the knitting out of Sophie's lap. "If we can't untangle the wool we'll just salvage what we can. I'll show you how to pick up the stitches. It's a lesson all knitters need to learn."

A lump formed unexpectedly in Sophie's throat. "Thanks."

"No problem, but you have to promise me not to be so hard on yourself. So many people don't understand what a hard job being a stay-at-home mom is. You're busy juggling so many balls and sometimes you drop one."

Bec gave Sophie a reassuring smile. "But for all the little hiccups, we wouldn't swap it for any other job, would we?'

It was like being sucked into a dark, stifling tunnel. Sophie's chest ached, desperate for air, but she couldn't seem to take a deep breath. Her warm skin turned clammy and the tips of her fingers tingled painfully. Her head was spinning and tremors wracked her body as if she were freezing, which was crazy because she was hot. She was vaguely aware of an awful noise—the cry of an animal in distress—which made no sense because she was inside. Nothing was making any sense except for a terrifying premonition of doom and a desperate need to flee. She tried to stand. Her legs refused to move.

"Oh God."

Sophie was vaguely aware that Erica was out of her chair but her voice sounded far away.

"Sophie? Are you okay?"

"I was trying to help."

Bec's distress piled on top of Sophie, pressing her deeper into the couch.

"I doubt you're the cause, Bec," Julie said quietly. Sadly.

Words formed in Sophie's head but her mouth wouldn't deliver them. Why couldn't she move her body? What was happening? Panic soared.

"You're okay." Claire's kind voice spoke quietly in her ear. "I'm going to put a paper bag over your mouth and nose. I need you to take long, deep breaths, okay?"

"I'll get water," Layla said.

"Breathe in ... and out. In ... and out. That's it," Claire instructed. "You're doing great, Sophie. Keep breathing like this and everything else will follow."

Sophie's mouth still wouldn't function, but her frantically beating heart started to decelerate and her pulse moved toward a more normal speed. With it, her spinning head steadied, her dizziness receded and her blurred vision sharpened at the edges.

"Can she drink this?" Layla asked.

"How are you feeling, Sophie? Have your fingers stopped tingling?"

Sophie nodded, wondering how Claire knew.

"Want to try breathing without the bag?"

Sophie nodded again and slowly lowered her lifeline. That's when she saw the sea of concerned and anxious faces. A wave of humiliation hit. She gasped and her breath hiked again.

"I think Sophie needs some space," Julie said. "Probably best if everyone sits down. I'll make tea."

The women retreated and Sophie felt both grateful and guilty. "Sorry. Thank you."

"Don't apologize. We're just glad you're feeling better." Erica glanced around at the other women, who all nodded in agreement.

"Have a drink of water and some of Layla's Turkish delight. The sugar will help," Claire said.

"Here." Bec shoved the plate at her so fast the pale pink squares wobbled.

"Thanks." Sophie put a piece in her mouth, closed her eyes and savored the taste of rosewater and pistachios. When she opened them, Julie was back with the tea tray.

"You're looking brighter. You had us worried there for a minute." Julie handed her a cup of Earl Grey.

Bec's immaculately made-up face was pulled tight and haggard with consternation. "I'm so sorry, Sophie. I didn't mean to upset you."

Sophie wanted to say, "That's okay," but that wasn't fair as Bec had only ever been kind. "It's not you. I ..." Her hand trembled and the tea cup clinked against the saucer. "I feel so stupid falling apart like this."

"I had a panic attack once," Erica said matter-of-factly. "It terrified me. I thought I was going to die."

As if choreographed, everyone's heads swung toward the perpetually chirpy woman, their faces stunned.

"It was three weeks after Rafi was born. I'd had a dream pregnancy and was determined that no baby was going to slow me down. It was crazy sauce. Even though I wasn't getting any sleep, I'd convinced myself I could do anything and everything and then some. When Nathan asked me to attend an industry function with him, I was there with bells on. One minute I was drinking champagne at a fancy hotel in Melbourne and the next I was rocking back and forth on the plush blue carpet in my Alex Perry dress, barely able to breathe." She gave a shrug. "I struggled with post-natal depression for a couple of years. It's part of the reason we moved here."

Sophie couldn't believe Erica was so calm about something so awful as post-natal depression. Or that she was prepared to admit to having a mental illness. "Are you okay now?"

"Pretty much. Sometimes I wonder, but then again, we all have good days and bad days with the kids, don't we?"

Sophie was about to murmur her agreement when she censored herself. She'd been pretending to everyone in Myrtle for weeks. If Erica could talk about her PND to women she barely knew, perhaps Sophie should get over herself, ride out her shame and tell them the truth. "That's my problem," she said softly. "Right now, I'm not having good or bad days with the kids."

"Where are the children?" Claire asked, one hundred per cent the health-care worker.

"The kids are—Josh will kill me if he finds out I'm telling you this. He doesn't want anyone to know but he lost his job. The bloody fires destroyed the plantations. They kept him on as long as they could but ..."

She shredded the tissue in her hands. "I've been working full time for weeks. Part of me knows we're lucky I found a job so quickly, otherwise we'd have lost the land and be homeless. But I can't be grateful. I'm working full time and driving back and forth to Colac while Josh is at home ..."

Tears fell hot and hard and the words tumbled out of her. "God. Is a shed even a home? Josh's desperate for a job. The last thing he ever wanted was to be Mr. Mom. He's not great at it. He let the kids destroy my knitting. Everything's back to front. He hates it. I hate it and the kids ..."

She couldn't talk about the kids in case the guilt and anger that often roared through her hit without warning. Then she'd totally lose it. Again. "All I've ever wanted is to be a stay-at-home mom. We totally changed our lives and moved to Myrtle to make it happen. We had six glorious weeks and then everything turned bad."

The room was silent, humid with unspoken words. Sophie understood. No words could change her situation. Miracles, like someone stepping up and saying, "I can give Josh a well-paying job," didn't happen to people like them.

"Oh, Sophie, I'm sorry." Julie sounded like a missing piece had suddenly been slotted into a puzzle. "This explains why I haven't seen much of you and the kids lately. I thought you'd got busy with playgroup and kinder."

Sophie blew her nose. "I'm sorry, Julie. I wanted to tell you but Josh ..."

"Men, for all their macho strutting, can have remarkably delicate egos," Bec said succinctly.

"And a tight job market doesn't help." Julie sighed. "The fires destroyed so much and then left a whopping vacuum in their wake. Phil sees good men at the Men's Shed every day, all desperate to work."

"We've got pretty new buildings but we don't have an economy to support them," Claire said. "Just empty shops. I wish I could wave a wand and fix it."

"It's tough for both of you," Bec said.

You have no idea. Jealousy struck Sophie like a blow to the back of the head. Did beautiful Bec, who didn't work despite having school-age children, who was married to a man whose business benefitted from the fires and who lived in a stunning home, really have any idea how tough things were for her and Josh?

"Would your husband come to playgroup?" Erica asked in her eager way. "I promise not to tell him anything that us Stitch Bitches talk about here."

"Is that our name? I love it!" Claire high-fived Erica. "It's worth learning to crochet just so I can say I'm a Stitch Bitch."

"I'm not sure that's what we should be calling ourselves," Bec said crisply. "I was thinking more along the lines of Crafty Women."

"Stich Bitch is a joke, yes?" Layla smiled. "I like it. Turkish women gossip when we sew."

"So do Australian women," Julie said. "Talking's as important as the knitting."

But Sophie didn't agree. She was already regretting talking and now all she wanted to do was knit.

JULIE SAT in Beechside's kitchen, staring into her flower garden as she'd done for over forty years. During that time, she'd watched her children grow, leave home, return and leave again. She'd weathered the ups and downs of a long marriage, the rise and now seemingly continuous fall of milk prices, and she'd gained and lost friends. Throughout it all, her garden was her constant companion. Her pride and joy.

Today, despite the perpetual green of the native pines, the purple and green hellebores and the cheery white snowdrops, the sight was mid-winter dismal. Once she'd appreciated the bare deciduous trees—found beauty in their skeletal limbs silhouetted against a steel gray sky—but now she ached for spring color. Ever since the fires and the unavoidable sight of cadaverous trees and scorched black earth, she'd found her need for color had intensified to the point it hurt. Winter, with its achromatic gloom, oozed into her already scarred soul, too often stifling fledgling moments of delight.

When she and Phil had returned from their honeymoon and moved into what was then a new house, the garden was just a tussocky meadow. With tens of thousands of hours of love, care and devotion, not to mention physically exhausting work and tons of cow-manure compost, the garden was the recipient of numerous awards. According to the Colac *Herald*, it was "a jewel in the crown" of the district's gardens. For years she'd happily opened it to raise funds for local charities and twice for local families in need. Back then garden tours had been simple: charge an entry fee, offer raffles, get the CWA to run the Devonshire tea tent, invite the Native Plant Society to sell pots of the area's indigenous plants and watch people enjoying themselves. Count the money. Donate it to the appreciative charity. Clean up. Job done.

Now, just the thought of opening the garden again in the hope it may help struggling Myrtle families daunted her. She wasn't deterred by the amount of work involved—hard work had never fazed her. It was more to do with the fact that the garden lived when people had died. When so many had lost the basic stays that tethered them to their everyday lives.

Not that her green oasis was completely unscathed: it held evidence of that dire day when nature had foisted its blistering fury onto them, first withering plants to the point of death, then hurling fireballs. But its wet and faithful heart had held firm and in turn helped to save the house. Her garden was a badly injured and scarred solider—enduring amputations and grafts—but it had gone on not only to recover, but to thrive.

Sometimes, she hated that it had. Sometimes she'd be tending to it and an overwhelming urge to hurt it would hit her. Without being aware of how it happened, she'd find herself holding a bare-rooted plant in her hand. Sobbing, she always replanted it, but these episodes scared her. She'd always considered her garden a haven but now it was a double-edged sword. It turned from heaven to hell and back again without warning.

Julie knew it was topography, not fate, that had played a role in her house and garden's survival on a day that took few prisoners. The knowledge didn't make it any less cruel for people like Josh and Sophie, who lived on the next rise over and had lost everything. Or for herself. She would have offered up every possession she owned to the greedy jaws of the fire if had meant Hugo was still alive and milking cows. Still dropping by a couple of times a week for dinner. Still helping her in the garden. Not dead.

The revitalization of the garden was her memorial to Hugo. He loved it almost as much as she did. Had. Did. God help her!

The sound of Phil's footsteps and the click of the kettle's switch made her turn away from the window.

"Did you forget you offered me a cup of tea ten minutes ago, love?"

She sniffed and pulled a tissue from her sleeve. "Sorry. I was having a Hugo Moment."

Phil squeezed her shoulder. After months and months of unrelenting grief bending them double and making walking, talking, thinking and breathing an agony, the feeling had slowly changed its form. Now, when the sun rose, there were many more days with anticipation for the hours ahead and what they might offer—time with the grandchildren, bedding down the annuals, a nap in the sunshine, coffee with a friend.

But grief was a conman in disguise. One minute it was admiring the day and cozily drinking tea with you. The next it was revealing its yellow teeth before sinking them in deep and stealing your concentration. Mini vague-outs punctuated their week and Julie had named them Hugo Moments. Admitting to one didn't always prevent an argument or save a misunderstanding, but it helped.

"There's been a round of layoffs at Sustainable Timber. Josh's lost his job."

Phil swore softly. "That's the last thing those two need. Will this push them over the edge financially?"

"Sophie's working so I gather they're hanging on for now."

"That's something at least. Can't Josh get a transfer to a different plantation?"

"The only vacancies are in South Australia, so he's home with the kids. Sophie's an accounts manager at Sustainable."

"That's gotta be a kick in the guts for him."

"It's an indignity he didn't need on top of everything else."

"How is he?"

"Judging by the fact Sophie's kept all of this a secret for weeks, I'm thinking not good. He loved that job and a man without a job is never a good thing."

"Do you want me to drop in on him? Invite him to the Men's Shed?"

"Sophie doesn't want him to know we know."

"Secrets don't always help."

"We could invite them up here for dinner? See if he tells you over a beer?"

Phil placed his hand over hers. "You sure? It's been a long time since we've had anyone over other than Penny, Jack and the kids."

"If it's a bad day, we just tell them and reschedule. Like you say, secrets don't help." But she knew in her heart that everyone in Myrtle was keeping secrets, including her.

CHAPTER NINE

Each week, the senior Cartwrights hosted the almost non-negotiable Friday-night family dinner. Bill and Louise always presided, sitting at either end of the polished oak table while Matt and Claire, Matt's sister, Tamara, her husband, Lachlan, and their two children, Piper and Max, took their positions down the long sides.

"Sorry I'm late."

As Claire slid into the Oakvale dining chair next to Matt, she realized she'd forgotten to wash the day off her hands. Matt immediately leaned in and kissed her on the cheek, his eyes sending her an undecipherable message.

"Sorry, Claire. Matt said you'd be later than this so we started without you." Bill's hand was on a bottle of red wine and he cocked a questioning brow at her wineglass.

"Oh, I didn't expect you to wait." Claire picked up the crystal stemware and passed it to Bill, seeing disappointment flash in his eyes. *This* was exactly why she'd got cross with Matt for telling his parents about the baby plans.

She took a sip of the bold red, holding it on her tongue and savoring the flavors for a moment or two before swallowing and welcoming its warmth. "For once me being late was because of good news." She raised her glass. "My submission was successful. Shane and I got the funding for the teen trampoline disco and an ongoing youth group. Well, for a year anyway."

Matt murmured congratulations but everyone else at the table looked at her, their gazes critical. Although she'd been the recipient of such looks before, this time Claire was at a loss as to why. Couldn't they see the funding was a win for Myrtle's youth?

"Your dinner's in the warming drawer," Louise said briskly.

Claire swallowed a sigh. She reminded herself it was a thoughtful gesture—something Louise did for any member of the family who got held up. It was just that whenever Louise did it for her, Claire couldn't shake the feeling that thoughtful veered toward critical and the meal became evidence of her deficits. "Thank you."

"It's my birthday, Claire," Piper announced proudly.

Claire's feet stilled on the way to the kitchen. Holy crap! Of course it was Piper's birthday. She knew it was. She'd chosen, bought and wrapped her niece's gift, written the card and left both articles on the kitchen counter for Matt to bring to dinner. But the sweet success of scoring the youth-group funding and her rush to get to family dinner had momentarily driven the birthday right out of her mind. Now she understood what Matt had been trying to signal to her and the reason for the family's disapproving looks. The Cartwrights made a big deal of birthdays and Claire had inadvertently slammed Piper's party.

"It is!" Claire gave her a hug. "And you're sensational seven. Happy birthday. Have you opened your presents?"

"Yes! Matt gave me a book and stars for my room. I can lie in bed and watch them twinkle. And he's going to read the story to me."

"Pipes, the presents are from Claire too," Matt said. "The stars were her idea."

Claire almost blew him a kiss.

"Okay. Thank you," Piper said obediently.

"I'm glad you like them." Claire turned toward the kitchen and just as she reached the door she heard Tamara say, "We've just painted Piper's room, Matt. Those things leave marks on the ceiling."

Just fabulous. Strike two against Claire for the evening and she'd only been in the house five minutes.

When she returned with her meal the conversation had shifted away from talk of presents, and Piper and Max had been excused from the table to play on their mother's iPad. Claire quickly worked out the adults were discussing Tamara's visit to Geelong and her meeting with Geelong Otway Tourism. Claire ate with half an ear on the conversation. The part of her that was a mature and confident woman knew she should participate, but the fourteen-year-old girl deep down inside her, who was still smarting from the crack about her present choice, was saying why bother taking an interest in their work when they didn't seem capable of taking much interest in hers.

"I showed Mark the figures so he couldn't argue the sixty per cent income drop at the farm-gate store and café," Tamara said. "We need the tourists back. The store won't survive another summer without them."

Matt drummed his fingers on the lace cloth. "The problem is, people remember the images on TV and Facebook. They still think of Myrtle as a post-apocalyptic disaster zone. We need to show them we're not. We need to put the farm back on the map."

"How, exactly?" Lachlan asked. "Tam's got the café and store all over social media but it's like yelling into a void. There are only so many ways I can take photos of honey, wool, candles and tea towels, not to mention all the menu items."

"Tourists want more than just the farm," Louise said. "They want to wander up and down main street and browse in a bookshop. They want to discover the perfect something in a second-hand store and drink a beer in a country pub or microbrewery. Myrtle has none of that now."

"They need accommodation too and Myrtle falls short on that front as well," Bill added.

"But we've got the bush and it's back." Lachlan's usually even tone rang with enthusiasm. "The DSE—"

"It's DELWP now, Lach," Tamara reminded him. "The Department of Environment, Land, Water and Planning."

"Whatever. It'll change again at the next election. Anyway, they've promised that the new mountain-bike paths will be finished by the end of November. That'll bring the cyclists and their wallets back."

"And we'll have berries again this year," Tamara said. "Mark suggested advertising in the regional tourist magazine. I thought we could also put signs in Lorne to tempt the summer crush to take a drive up the road."

"What about glamping on the farm?" Louise said. "We can target families."

"First berries, then alpacas and now glamping? At the rate you're commandeering fields, we won't have enough for the stock." But Bill's gaze was filled with warmth and admiration for his wife.

"It's an idea worth considering, Mom. We'd need to offer more than just accommodation and berry picking. Maybe some stuff like hay rides, pat a sheep and—I know! Ride an alpaca," Matt said.

Louise pursed her lips but it was purely for show. She rarely disapproved of anything Matt said or did. "I don't even have to object to that suggestion because my darlings will just spit at you."

Matt laughed, the sound deep and melodious and so very dear to Claire. In their early days, cocooned in the cottage and far away from the real world, she'd spent hours snuggled up with her ear pressed to his chest, listening to it rumble inside him. Now his laugh relaxed her and she acknowledged with some discomfort that it was more important for her to contribute to the conversation than sulkily hold onto her pique. It would also avoid Matt saying sadly on the way home, "You were quiet at dinner." He'd been saying it a lot lately.

Claire glanced along the table. "The shearing shed is a piece of history. I've often thought photos of it taken at different times across the year like at shearing and at rest would make a great coffee table book or cards. You know, highlight all that beautiful wood. Some people might be interested in seeing it."

Under the table, she ran her foot along the back of Matt's calf. "I know it's one of my favorite parts of the farm."

He squeezed her thigh and she knew they were silently sharing the memory of their afternoon.

"They're all good ideas but we're already busy. Who's going to run this farm-experience venture?" Bill asked.

Matt's eyes crinkled up at the edges as he smiled. Claire knew the look. "You could take it on, Postie. It's the perfect way for you to get really involved in the business."

Another four sets of eyes swiveled to her. She read varying emotions—expectation, duty, doubt and curiosity. Dread trickled through her.

"Mommy," Piper called from the other room, "is it time for cake?"

"Soon," Tamara replied before resuming the conversation. "Mark made some other suggestions, which I'll type up. We can discuss them at next week's meeting ..."

Tamara had instigated family farm meetings, which Claire thought was a good idea, in principle. Not that she managed to attend many of them, because they usually took place in the middle of the day when the kids were at school and she was at work.

"... I think it was worthwhile," Tamara continued, "and afterwards I had lunch at a funky place in Little Malop Street. You'll never guess who I ran into ... Taylor!"

Claire's dinner curdled in her stomach.

"How lovely!" Louise gushed. "How is she?"

"You know Tay—still gorgeous. She's cut her hair sporty short and of course it looks amazing. She sends her love to everyone." Tamara looked straight at Matt. "I sent all of ours."

Say something, Matt, Claire pleaded silently. She was so very weary of this game of Tamara's but sadly not immune to it.

Matt studiously continued chewing the piece of lamb he'd speared off Claire's plate.

Claire swiftly drained the contents of her wineglass.

"I can't imagine Taylor with short hair. Did you take a selfie?" Louise asked.

"Sure did." Tamara reached for her cell.

"No devices at the table, Mommy," Max said sternly, appearing at his mother's side.

Claire wanted to hug him.

Lachlan laughed. "He's got you there, Tam."

"*Now* is it time for my ice-cream cake?" Piper asked with a hint of a whine, her patience running thin.

"As soon as Claire finishes her dinner," Louise said.

Claire could have weathered the imploring looks of Piper and Max but she'd lost her appetite. Silently, she placed her knife and fork together.

"Are you sure you've finished? I didn't mean to rush you."

"You're not and the meal was delicious. Thank you. Can I help clear?"

"No, you sit here and rest after your busy day. Tam will help. She has to come into the kitchen anyway to prepare the cake."

And to show you the photo of Matt's ex-girlfriend you're so desperate to see.

CHAPTER TEN

A YEAR BEFORE THE FIRES

Christmas for Claire meant good food, family and fun—the joy of doing nothing for a few days. For weeks, she'd been looking forward to her first Myrtle Christmas in years and things had started off so well. Almost perfect, really, until Matt Cartwright, with his captivating eyes and easy yet caring manner, turned her world upside down.

Four excruciating days had crawled past since their night on the beach and now Claire was packing for an early return to Melbourne. She wasn't sure how she'd survived Christmas without falling apart—probably a combination of willpower and sheer bloody-mindedness. If her parents had noticed anything amiss they'd put it down to her breakup with Stu. Claire hadn't disabused them.

She wasn't immune to the irony that after a year-long relationship with Stu, their breakup had been devoid of any regret, yet after one night with Matt, she felt like she'd lost a limb. She knew it was crazy to feel this way but her gut and her heart told her they'd shared something special—something neither of them had expected.

"It's like being hit by a truck," he'd said at the beach. He'd sounded as bewildered as she'd felt and she'd believed him. The slick two-timing bastard!

More than once, Claire had contemplated driving out to Oakvale Park, finding Matt and screaming at him. She wanted to pummel her fists into his chest and hurt him as much as he'd hurt her. It was only the risk of running into his family and his by-now fiancée—the unknown Taylor—that had stayed her. Did Taylor have a clue what she was getting herself into with this guy? Should Claire find a way to contact her and tell her he was a rat bastard of the highest order?

She set the idea aside, knowing the messenger always got shot. What she hated most about the situation was the lack of justice. His fiancée was duped, she was left feeling used and Matt bloody Cartwright got off scot-free, ready to rinse and repeat.

Thank God they'd stopped short of sex. But that thought wasn't enough to temper her flailing emotions. In the last ninety-six hours, she'd lurched from fiery fury to excruciating embarrassment to soul-sucking sadness and back again, hating herself as much as she hated the farmer who'd scammed her. Today was no different.

Throwing herself onto her bed, she pressed her face into the mattress and screamed. It was becoming a habit and one that had to stop. Soon she'd be back in her apartment and back at work. By then the aberration that was Matthew Cartwright would be a bitter memory she never planned to revisit.

Her cell phone rang. She sat up and rummaged under a under a pile of clothes until she found it. "Hugo, darling!" She'd called him that ever since they'd spent a wet afternoon years ago watching an old black-and-white British movie, the title of which neither of them could remember.

"Hey, Claire-bear. How's the post-Christmas slump treating you?"

"Not bad," she lied. "I'm heading back to the big smoke tomorrow."

"You promised you'd come out to the farm before you left, so get your sweet behind up here around three."

"Short a relief milker, are you?"

He laughed. "Now that you mention it. Bring your gumboots too. See you soon."

Happy for a welcome distraction, Claire finished her packing and then went and found her parents. They were reading under the shade of the veranda. "I'm going to Hugo's. Either of you want to come?"

Her parents exchanged a hopeful glance. "We're comfortable here, love," Ron said.

"It's only salad for dinner so no need to rush home," Heather added.

Claire lacked the energy to reiterate that she and Hugo were never going to be a couple. "Is that code for you don't want me to spend my last night with you both?"

"We've spent five lovely days with you, darling. Give Hugo our best."

Subtle as a brick. "Will do."

When the car crested the ridge, Claire pulled over at a row of mailboxes and admired the expansive vista: the shimmering blue-green hue of the forest and the distant rippling mountains. No wonder Hugo loved living here; this part of the farm was like being on top of the world. Putting the car back in gear, she negotiated the notorious and pothole-riddled road that wound down to Hugo's house. On the way, she passed the corrugated iron milking parlor where a few eager cows were already waiting patiently for milking to begin. When she finally pulled up outside the home pasture, she was surprised to see two other cars. Hugo hadn't mentioned a party. Grabbing her milking gear, she approached the garden gate.

"Hello, Claire."

Her head jerked up and her breath stalled tight and heavy in her chest. Matt Cartwright stood on the other side of the gate. Half of her wanted to turn around and flee but the other half wanted answers. Somewhere in the mix, a traitorous part of her just wanted him.

Matt's smile was warm and inviting. He opened the gate for her and as she passed through, he leaned in close. "It's great to see you."

She shied away from him. "Are you for real?"

"Um, yes. Are you okay? You sound pissed off."

"Pissed off is barely the tip of the iceberg. Listen, Matt, I don't play games. I came here to see Hugo, not you. To be honest, I really don't care if I never see you again."

"Because I didn't contact you over Christmas?" Confusion wrinkled his brow. "I thought you'd be busy with your family so I held back. It wasn't easy. If it helps, I haven't been able to stop thinking about you."

Betrayal bit her. "Believe me, it doesn't."

"I'm sorry, Claire. I wanted to see you but things my end have been ... difficult."

"I bet," she muttered.

"I've been waiting for you to arrive so we can talk."

"I don't think so."

Claire took three steps toward the house before Matt caught her hand. Her stomach lurched. Her skin tingled. Her knees wobbled. Her mind furiously berated her body's easy capitulation and she tugged her hand free from his loose grip.

"Talk about what? Your fiancée?"

He flinched as if she'd slapped him. "Whoever told you I'm engaged has their wires crossed."

"Is that so." She crossed her arms, trying to steady the trembles that shook her from top to toe. "But you do concede you have a long-time girlfriend you conveniently forgot to mention when we spent the night at the beach."

"I can explain. Hell, I want nothing more than the opportunity to explain. But not here." Children's laughter drifted from the house, followed by the yapping of dogs. "Hugo's got guests. Let's walk to the falls."

The sincerity on his face and in his voice wrapped itself around her, tempting her to listen. The pain of the last few days twisted again. *Do not fall for his candor. It's tainted. He lied to you.*

Matt's gaze suddenly shifted across her shoulder and she followed it to see what had caught his attention. In the distance, a woman wearing a farm-inappropriate dress and high heels stood staring across the fields. Her fingers rubbed at her temples as if a blinding headache had her in its vice-like grip. At least Matt had been telling the truth about Hugo having guests.

She turned back to him. "Let's go up to the house and talk. That way I'll have witnesses to verify the truth of your story."

"Claire," Matt implored. "Please. This needs to be private."

"Matt?" A bitter female voice suddenly hurled itself between them. "You've got to be kidding! It's Claire McKenzie? Have you totally lost the plot?"

Claire's spine stiffened. It had been years since she'd heard the dulcet tones of her childhood adversary but some things weren't easily forgotten. Claire swung around to find the woman in the dress standing next to her. The intervening years hadn't changed Rebecca much. She still carried herself with an air of superiority that crawled under Claire's skin.

"Hey, Rebecca Sendo. How are things?"

The woman's berry-red mouth pursed. "I'm Bec Petrovic and you know I have been for a long time. Why are *you* here? This is low even by your standards. Go back to your very busy city life instead of causing heartache and pain for decent people."

Not even Claire's deep understanding that she and Rebecca barely tolerated each other could have prepared her for this attack. It was like being slammed into a wall of rancor. "Listen, Rebecca, I haven't done—"

"There's two sides to every story, Bec," Matt said quietly. "You've only heard Taylor's."

"And that's all I need to—"

"Claire-bear!"

Hugo was striding across the lawn with Adam Petrovic and his daughters. Four puppies accompanied them, playing around their feet. Despite wearing pretty sundresses, the little girls fell onto the dry grass with squeals of delight and tumbled and rolled with the dogs.

Adam nodded briefly to Matt and Claire before shaking Hugo's hand. "Thanks for giving the girls some puppy time, but it's best I get my skittish wife off the property before she sees that bull. Come on, girls."

The older daughter immediately stood up but the younger one ignored her father.

"Gracie! Now!"

Gracie stood clutching a puppy and sashayed over to her father, batting her long lashes. "Can we take this one home, Daddy? Please."

"Not today." Adam plucked the puppy out of his daughter's hands and released it onto the ground before putting his hand on Rebecca's back and guiding her through the gate.

"Safe drive to Lorne," Hugo called out cheerily.

Claire suddenly found herself in the awkward position of standing between Hugo and Matt and waving goodbye to the Petrovics. It was like being unexpectedly catapulted onto a movie set and acting a part.

"Well, that was unfortunate." Hugo shot Matt a rueful glance as the SUV disappeared around the bend. "They were supposed to visit this morning but you know Adam. His time's more important than anyone else's."

"Bec's going to hold a grudge," Matt said softly. Miserably.

Hugo slapped a beefy hand onto his shoulder. "Half of Myrtle's going to do that, mate. Just give it some time. It'll blow over soon enough. I've gotta start milking so apart from the puppies, the house is all yours."

Claire, who was feeling not only invisible but utterly flummoxed, rounded on her friend. "I'm coming with you."

"No need, Claire."

"Hugo, what the hell's going on?"

"Matt'll explain."

"I don't want Matt to explain anything!"

Matt wrung his hands. "I need to talk to you, Claire. I need to explain. I'd have come to your parents' place but I thought it might make things complicated for you. That's why I asked Hugo to invite you here."

"*Might* make things complicated?" Her voice rose to a screech. "Hugo, you've got no idea—"

"I have a good idea. Do you trust me, Claire?"

"Of course I do." She pointed an accusatory finger at Matt. "It's *him* I don't trust."

Hugo wrapped his big arms around her and she sank into his embrace, comforted by the safety he always offered. Was her mother right after all? Did she let attraction get in the way of making sensible decisions about men? Should she go with reassuring and secure rather than with tantalizing and exciting?

Hugo moved his hands to her shoulders and took a step away, his face serious. "Claire-bear, we both know relationships can suck. Listen to what Matt's got to say and when you've got all the facts, *that's* when you make up your mind."

Before Claire could spew out her many objections, Hugo walked away, whistling. His reasonableness irked her and she wished she had a missile handy to hurl at the back of his head.

"Can we sit?" Matt indicated a bench in a garden nook that had Julie's handiwork written all over it.

Unable to decide if she was feeling angry, betrayed, let down by men in general, curious or all of the above, Claire stomped ungraciously to the seat, sat and re-crossed her arms. She had no intention of making this easy for him.

Matt joined her. "Claire, I'm beyond sorry you heard about Taylor before I had a chance to tell you."

"Chance?" She ground her teeth. "You had *eleven hours* to tell me."

"Yeah. It looks bad." He rubbed his stubbled cheeks with the back of his fingers. "The thing is, if I'd told you I had a girlfriend but I wasn't happy and I was intending to break up with her, would you have believed me?"

"Probably not. And the fact that less than an hour after you dropped me home, I found out the town expected you to propose to her on Christmas Day bears that out."

"The town's wrong. I was never going to propose."

"So why did they think that?"

He sighed as his fingers shredded a gum leaf and the pungent scent of eucalyptus filled the space between them. "Taylor and I've been together for over two years but for the last few months, I've been coasting. I wasn't unhappy but I was starting to feel something was missing. We were in Melbourne over the Melbourne Cup weekend when she started hinting hard that an engagement ring would make the perfect Christmas present. I realized she saw it as the natural progression of our relationship and for a few weeks, I wondered if committing to marriage was the thing that was missing. But the closer it got to Christmas, the more I knew that getting engaged was the complete opposite of what I wanted."

"I'm guessing you didn't tell her that?"

"Don't look at me as if I'm a moron! I thought she deserved better than having her heart broken right on Christmas or New Year. I'd planned to wait until January third or fourth." A pained look crossed his face. "And yes, in an ideal world, I should have told you about Tay at the beach, but I didn't think it was fair to her that you knew I was breaking up with her before she did. I was trying to do it the right way."

Despite his ethics on this point, a green bomb detonated inside her heart. "The right way? You should *never* have invited me to the beach."

"I know. You're right. The thing is, Claire, I didn't go to the parade with any intentions of cheating on Taylor. Hell, it's Myrtle. The chances of meeting anyone new are virtually zilch. And even though I knew I was ending things in just over a week, I had every intention of doing it the right way."

He gave a wry smile. "And then I saw you and half my good intentions vanished in a heartbeat. I convinced myself that if we went to the beach it was just a chance to get to know you and enjoy your company without crossing a line. I mean, it wasn't that big of a stretch. I'm a grown up. I've got control.

"Only every time you looked at me, I was a goner. It was like someone else took over my body. All I wanted was you. Right up until I met you, I'd always thought that 'eyes across a crowded room' thing was bullshit. But there you were. It was like electricity arcing between us. I know you felt it too."

She'd be lying if she denied it. She'd felt it—she felt it. It zipped between them, an overwhelming pull that defied common sense. An energy that made her behave recklessly and without regard to the consequences. All that mattered was being with him. If he felt a tenth of what she did, she understood his dilemma. It certainly accounted for his push-and-pull, hot-and-cold behavior at the beach.

The fact that he wanted her as much as she wanted him made her dizzy with longing, but as hard as it was, she clung tightly to her unravelling common sense. "And what about you and Taylor now?"

He blew out a breath imbued with the remnants of distress. "I broke things off with her on Christmas Eve."

"That was the day you—"

"Dropped you home at dawn. Yeah."

Joy expanded her heart so fast a sharp pain caught her under the ribs. Matt hadn't waited until January to break up. He'd done it within twenty-four hours of meeting her. Claire's mind veered toward Taylor, who'd been expecting a marriage proposal at Christmas but had instead got dumped. She pulled back fast. The unknown woman had nothing to do with her. The thing to focus on here was the fact that Matt had put her first.

"Thank you."

He shrugged and for the first time since they'd sat down together, he fixed his gaze on her. "I didn't have a choice. Meeting you crystallized why I should have done something months ago. But I didn't and it's been a bugger of a Christmas. Mom and Dad aren't exactly thrilled by my decision and Tamara's not talking to me. Taylor's devastated and furious. Yesterday, she slashed my tires. I'm currently driving one of the farm utes."

That explained why Claire hadn't recognized his car when she'd pulled up. "Two years is a long time to be with someone."

"It is. I'm sorry I couldn't give her what she wanted."

"She would have asked you if there was someone else."

"Yeah, she did. But as I'd planned to break up with her before I met you and I didn't want to add to her hurt, I told her and my family there's no one else. The only person who knows is Hugo."

It's low even by your standards. Rebecca's vitriol came rushing back and Claire closed her eyes as if that would protect her. "Not anymore. Rebecca's worked it out and she's not a big fan. By the end of today, all of Myrtle *and* the shire will know."

He grimaced. "Yeah. Sorry. Meeting here was supposed to head off any chance of gossip and give us some time."

"Time?"

"Time to explore this thing that ... that ..." He floundered.

She knew what he meant. "Breathes between us? Steals our concentration? Consumes us?"

"All that." He laced his fingers with hers and her stomach fluttered. "Do you want to explore it?"

Her heart sped up and her body sang. She squeezed his hand. "More than anything."

"Thank God."

His hands rose to her cheeks and he kissed her. At first all she tasted was his relief. It flowed into her, scooping up her own and merging with it. It hovered, suspended in liberation and suffused with hope, assuaging the days of hurt. Then need took over, blasting aside everything except overwhelming desire.

It was a kiss for the ages.

Matt pulled away first, his chest heaving. He rested his forehead on hers. "I'd take you home right now but—"

"It's probably best we don't appear together in Myrtle just yet."

"Thanks for understanding. I promise you, it's just for a bit. Just long enough for things to die down and for people to get used to the idea of us."

She stroked his cheek. "I love the idea of us."

"Me too. And I want to see you. Any ideas how we can make these next few weeks work?"

"Too easy. I live in the big bad city. How often can you visit?"

"WHAT DO YOU SAY TO DADDY?" Bec turned to Ivy and Gracie while Adam drove them away from the puppies.

"Thank you, Daddy," their daughters chorused.

Adam put his hand on the back of Bec's neck. "Do I get a thank you for coming along and protecting you from those scary cows?"

Bec's head throbbed but she made herself smile appreciatively. "Thank you. I wasn't expecting it. I know how busy you are trying to sort things out so you can come to Lorne with us."

She didn't mention that what he considered to be a chivalrous gesture had thrown her day into chaos. Instead of taking the girls to the farm in the morning to see the puppies, which would have defused their excitement and contributed to their cooperation in the afternoon, she'd had to contend with irritable and at times disobedient children along with reduced packing time for their annual summer vacation. God, she hoped she hadn't forgotten anything.

Adam grinned. "I didn't completely trust the girls or soft-touch Hugo not to twist your arm to bring home a puppy."

"I wouldn't do that. I know how you feel about a dog."

"Good." His fingers rubbed her neck. "Looking forward to the vacation?"

"So much." Since Christmas, Adam had been in an expansive mood and Bec didn't plan to be the pin that popped his happiness balloon.

"There's just one thing I have to do on the way."

"Daddy!" the girls groaned. They knew as well as Bec that "just one thing" meant they'd be hanging around waiting for him for at least half an hour.

"Be good and we'll have fish and chips on the beach tonight."

Adam slowed and took a right turn toward the struggling vineyard he'd bought last year, "for a song, babe."

"Are you going to make wine?" Bec had asked him, curious about the purchase.

"Not bloody likely! But we'll sell the grapes to other wineries while we're waiting for the rezoning to come through. Then we'll sell the land and make a killing."

The wait for the rezoning was taking longer than expected but in typical Adam style, he was making the property work for him. Scotty Ferguson, his lead builder, had moved into the house and was paying rent and the big green shed that had once stored stainless steel wine vats was now being used for framing. Despite some issues with a couple of the seasonal workers, the first grape harvest had been a financial success. Now he was planning a second.

"Can we come with you, Daddy?" Gracie asked.

"No. There's too much dangerous equipment in the shed."

"But I want to say hello to Scotty."

"He's busy. Stay in the car."

Bec shot her youngest child a look but Gracie was too much like her father. Crossing her little arms, she pouted and kicked the back of the driver's seat. "But it's hot!"

"Stop that!" Adam released his seatbelt with a jerk. "And don't move."

His happiness balloon was leaking fast and Bec moved to tie a knot in it to prevent it spiraling away completely. "Please leave the keys, Adam. I'll run the AC."

"Fine. Just keep them in the car, okay?"

She nodded, knowing it wasn't a question. At least Adam had parked in the shade of a scraggly gum. It was a reasonable distance from the buildings and as she watched him walk away, she saw Scotty's familiar height in the doorway of the shed. From that distance, it was unlikely he could make her out through the tinted windows but he tilted his head toward the car anyway, acknowledging her as he always did—silently but with care. She went to wave but stalled her hand in case the girls noticed. The two men disappeared inside the cavernous corrugated shed.

She'd always liked the well-mannered and polite Scotty, a feeling that didn't extended to some of the men who worked for Adam. He complimented her and made her feel so much more than just the boss's wife—not that she could ever say anything like that to Adam. Although he cheerfully told her if he thought a woman was hot, she'd learned early on to limit her observations about other men to their negative qualities. She'd never mentioned to Adam that Scotty always asked her how she and the girls were doing.

"Mommy, this is boring!" Gracie said. "Can we watch a movie?"

"Sure." Bec rubbed her temples, trying to alleviate the grinding throb that had started as a mild ache at breakfast and had escalated over the day. Reclining her seat, she closed her eyes and welcomed the red-tinged light through her eyelids. It was as close to dark as she could get and she concentrated on trying to empty her mind.

Her cell phone buzzed. She reluctantly popped one eye open and Taylor's name came into focus on the screen. The thought of another excruciating call with the distraught woman was more than she could bear right now. It had been hard enough that morning. Taylor had sobbed to Bec that although Matt insisted there wasn't another woman, she didn't believe him.

"Why else would he dump me? I'm going to find out who she is if it kills me."

Bec had managed to make the appropriate sounds of outrage at Matt Cartwright's despicable timing as well as soothing noises for Taylor's obvious distress, but part of her had wanted to say, "Marriage isn't everything it's cracked up to be. Maybe you dodged a bullet. You've got the sort of freedom I dream of."

When she'd been standing alone in Hugo Lang's garden, looking out across the fields, the idea of freedom had hung tantalizingly like the sparkle of a glittering diamond. Not that Bec knew exactly what constituted freedom, but at that moment she knew it wasn't the life she was living. Those unwanted thoughts and feelings had swirled and bumped inside her like bumper cars, leaving her flustered and uneasy, and then she'd spotted Matt Cartwright.

He was the last person she'd expected to see and his drawn face and anguished look had immediately suggested that, despite his diabolical timing, perhaps his treatment of Taylor wasn't as heartless as she'd been led to believe. It was obvious he was hurting too. But any threads of sympathy she'd been weaving together were ripped apart the moment she'd recognized Claire McKenzie—the woman who'd been given the freedom to leave Myrtle that Bec had been denied.

The moment Claire's supercilious voice had spoken Bec's maiden name, she'd seen red. She'd gone in guns blazing, defending Taylor, who, although they played netball together, Bec didn't count as a close friend. Still, did that matter? Shouldn't women stick together, especially when one of the sisterhood was behaving badly? If anyone was capable of behaving badly, it was Claire McKenzie.

Bec sat forward with a start and grabbed her cell phone. Taylor deserved to know about Casual Claire and Claire deserved everything she got and then some. With fingers flying, she typed, *Ask Claire McKenzie how well she knows Matt.* Her thumb was set to press send when she recalled Matt saying, "There are two sides to every story."

Bec slumped back against the seat. She knew all about two sides and how only one was ever public. Reluctantly, she tapped the back button, emptying the text box of the incriminating words. She hadn't deleted them to protect Claire. She was protecting herself.

"Mommy, who's that?" Ivy asked.

Bec looked up from her cell phone. "Who?"

"Over there." Ivy pointed.

An underweight man with heavily tattooed arms and wearing black pants and a black death metal T-shirt was walking out from between the vines. His pale skin said he didn't spend much time in the light of day.

"He looks scary, Mommy."

Bec understood why her sheltered daughter thought this, and to be honest, the man's presence made her uneasy too. She pressed a button on the console and the locks engaged with a loud clunk. "I'll ask Daddy."

She texted Adam. Skinny carny-type guy in vines.

Settle petal. That's Travis. He's harmless. Doing community service weeding around the vines.

The fact that a guy wearing a T-shirt featuring a skull dripping with blood was on mandated community service didn't sound harmless to her. "It's okay, Ives," she said brightly. "The man works for Daddy."

"He doesn't look like he works for Daddy."

Bec knew what Ivy meant. All of Adam's tradesmen wore the company's red polo shirts.

"I don't like it here, Mommy. I want to go to the beach."

"Me too."

But it wasn't the glistening ocean and the golden sands that called her. It was somewhere else entirely.

CHAPTER ELEVEN

THE PRESENT

"Ivy wants to stop piano lessons."

Bec and Adam sat in a patch of winter sunshine on the deck, eating lunch. She'd made borscht and rye bread, following her babushka's recipes. Not only was it hearty winter fare, it was also one of her husband's favorite lunches.

"That's okay." Adam ripped off a hunk of bread and dunked it into his soup. "But clients like to picture their kids learning an instrument so keep the sheet music up and the piano lid open so it looks like someone's playing it."

"It's not so much giving up the instrument. She's dropped out of dancing and you know how much she used to love it. She says she hates being on the student council and she doesn't want to try for student body president next year. Now she's talking about quitting Girl Scouts. What worries me is she isn't replacing any of the activities with something else."

Bec's frustration with Ivy spilled over. "All she does is read!"

"She's got to stay on student council to get a leadership position next year. And she's a Petrovic, so it's important she does one community activity."

"I know. I told her that and she got snarky with me saying, 'Why? You don't do anything.' And she's right. Compared to before the fires, I'm not doing anything ..."

"You're going to that craft group."

"Yes, but it's not like being on a committee driving change." Bec concentrated on sounding casual. "There's a vacancy on the school board and Ross McPherson's invited me—"

"No."

"No?"

"You don't need the hassle."

"But it wouldn't be a hassle." It would be something that took her out of the house and challenged her.

Adam shook his head. "You've got enough on your plate here."

"It's only one night a month and Ross said they need more women. It's the sort of example Ivy needs to—"

"I said no." The timbre of Adam's voice warned her that if she pushed it, he'd tip into anger. These days she never knew if that would be as mild as irritation or involve volcanic yelling. He reached out and lightly touched her hand. "Sorry, babe but you know I need you here. I'll talk to Ivy."

Since the fires, "I need you here" was Adam's default reply whenever she wanted to do anything. It was on the tip of her tongue to ask him how craft group was any different from attending a school board meeting once a month when a new thought niggled: there were no men at craft group. For all of Adam's bravado about surviving the fires, Scotty's and Travis's ongoing thanks, the town's hero worship of him, and the government's acknowledgement of his courage, Bec knew deep down he abhorred the scarring on his face and body. She hated the scars too—not because they disfigured him but because they trapped her.

A jagged spike of pain rent her from head to toe. She immediately closed off her thoughts and distanced herself from the freedom that had beckoned her on the eve of the hateful fires. Her emotional survival demanded it. She focused instead on her elder daughter's worrying behavior.

"I think a puppy would help Ivy. Puppies demand attention so she'd have to put down her book to play with it. And taking it to puppy school is social."

"Jeez, Bec. Not this again. We are not getting a puppy." Any hopes she had that a near-death experience might have softened Adam's attitude to a dog were dashed. "Find someone who's lost interest in their dog. Ives can take it for walk and our house and garden won't be trashed."

"Okay. I'll ask around. By the way, parent-teacher conferences are soon." She wanted to add, "I think you should come," but "should" was a word she now avoided with him. "It would be great if you could come."

Adam rolled his eyes. "All they ever say is "Ivy's a delight and Gracie needs to sit still more." Why would any of that have changed?"

"Because we spent a month thinking you might die."

He jerked his spoon, streaking the air with purple flecks of soup. "Christ, Bec! That was almost two years ago. I didn't die. The girls know I'm very much alive and kicking. Why do you keep harping on about it?"

Because I still can't believe you lived. "I was the one by your bed day in, day out, scared out of my wits."

His face softened. "But you know me, babe. I'm a fighter, I'm tenacious and I get what want."

The burns specialist, the nurses and the allied health professionals had all said to her at different times, "Your husband's remarkable, Mrs. Petrovic. He's got inner strength. It saved him."

It was Adam's confidence and drive that had attracted her nineteen-year-old self to him. She hadn't expected to like him and truth be told, to spite her mother and grandmother, she hadn't wanted to like him one little bit. The day they'd insisted she dress up for her cousin's birthday, she hadn't twigged to their subterfuge. It was only when they arrived at her aunt's house that she'd discovered they'd tricked her. There was no birthday party—her cousin wasn't even home. Instead, it was a small gathering and Bec was the gift, all wrapped up in her best dress—the potential present for her mother's brother-in-law's cousin's son.

On Bec's thirteenth birthday and every birthday that followed, her babushka had told her that that one day she'd find her a nice husband. Bec always thought it was a joke. Not that she hadn't wanted to get married and have babies, but like her friends, she wanted to choose her own boyfriend and ultimately her husband. Standing in her aunt's living room with an elaborate afternoon tea laid out on her mother's best cloth, the full significance had hit her like a train.

"It's Australia not the Ukraine, Bubbe," Bec had shrieked before turning to her mother. "Tell her!"

"He's a nice man," her mother had said calmly. "Matchmaking is the sensible way of doing things. We know his family. We know their values, they know ours. We share the same heritage. It's safer for you than meeting some random man at a pub or club."

"It's the new millennium, Mom!"

"Pah! It's only afternoon tea." Her mother had smoothed a strand of Bec's hair back into place before dusting powder on her nose. "And you never know, you might like him."

"I won't!"

The doorbell chimed. Bec intended to be monosyllabic for the entire meeting.

"G'day. I'm Adam Petrovic."

Bec blinked at the man standing in front of her. *He's old.* Well, not exactly old, but older than her. He made the guys she'd been dating look like boys. He wasn't much taller than her but his arms were broad like tree trunks and he was smiling at her as if he already found her fascinating.

"I'm Bec," she said and immediately kicked herself for not staying aloof and insisting he call her Rebecca.

"Mom said you were gorgeous and she's not wrong." Adam

inclined his head toward the assembled relatives before leaning in close. "How long do you reckon before we can ditch this lot? It'll be way more fun to go for a drive than hang out here."

She'd been peeking through the curtains and had seen his car—a red, low-slung Mazda RX Sports. She was a sucker for a flash car. "What about now?"

His laugh boomed, full of energy and whizzing around her like starbursts. "We'll leave as soon as I've eaten your babushka's yabluchnyk and I've told her it's the best apple cake I've ever tasted."

True to his word, he ate the enormous slice her grandmother cut him, all the time making appreciative sounds. Her babushka's smile was wider than Bec had ever seen it. When Adam set down the empty plate, his stomach must have been set to explode. Her mother immediately offered him her cherry solozhenik.

He winked at Bec before fixing his full attention on her mother. "How did you know cherry's my favorite?"

He ate a serving fit for two. It wasn't until they'd been married eighteen months that Bec discovered Adam hated cherries.

After his second cup of coffee, he took Bec's hand firmly in his as if he'd not only received her permission, but it was something he did every day. "I promise to bring her back in time for dinner."

Their relatives exchanged knowing glances and smiled approvingly. He led her out to the car and opened the passenger door for her with a bow. He climbed in next to her and with the flick of a switch, the soft top rolled back.

It was the first time Bec had sat in a convertible. The first time sitting on leather seats. She tried not to show it. She tried to sound unimpressed and bored. "Not bad."

"It's a bit different from the work ute." His square hand caressed the top of the compact steering wheel. "I promised myself once I'd paid off my first house, I'd buy an impractical car."

Her head snapped around so she was looking at him. "Do you own other impractical things?"

"Not yet, but I plan to."

A thrill raced across her skin.

"Any destination requests?"

Bec took in her aunt's small house, sunburnt grass and wilted flowers. It shared similarities with the modest house where she lived with her mother and grandmother. Her gaze brushed the leather seat before her head fell back and she faced the vast country sky. This car didn't belong in Myrtle. This car could take her into the wider world she was desperate to explore.

She clicked her seatbelt into place. "Take me anywhere that isn't here."

They'd sped down main street, flashing past the salon where she spent five and a half days a week working as an apprentice hairdresser. They whipped past the elementary school, the Scout hall, the pony club—her childhood. More than anything she wished her friends could see her but no one was in town on a Sunday afternoon. She'd assumed Adam would drive to the beach, because that's where every guy she'd ever dated took her. He unexpectedly headed west.

Racing through the gears, Adam expertly steered the car through the dense rainforest, around the tight bends of Turtons Track. The mountain wind whipped her face. Her carefully blow-dried hair unraveled and words blew away before they'd been heard. She dropped her head back, stretched out her arms and laughed. It was the most exciting thing she'd ever done in her life. She never wanted the exhilaration to stop ...

Adam's spoon clinked against the soup bowl, bringing her back. "Stop worrying, Bec. I'm here and I'm not going anywhere. You know I'd never leave you and the girls."

She did know that. Family was everything to Adam and he'd been upfront about it right from the start. "When we get married," he'd told her in a voice devoid of any doubt a month after they'd met, "it's for life. Divorce isn't something the Petrovics do, so if you can't see us together forever, tell me now."

High on the excitement of experiencing the world beyond Myrtle he'd introduced her to, and dazzled by his generosity—gifts for her and practical help for her mother with house repairs—she'd thought his declaration not only romantic but a much-needed promise. Her father had left to start a new family in Sydney when Bec was eleven. Bec hadn't wanted that sort of abandonment for her future children. Now, Adam's previously comforting promise had moments when it felt like a threat.

If his love of family had reassured her, it was his love of Myrtle that took her by surprise. She'd never entertained a single doubt that when they married, they'd move into his Melbourne house. She'd planned exactly how she was going to shed her small country life and embrace the big city and everything it offered. Instead, impervious to her pleas, Adam had insisted on buying land in Myrtle: "Untapped potential, babe."

He'd built their first house. Their current house was their fourth—each one bigger and better than the previous, but always showcasing exactly what Petrovic Family Homes was capable of building. Then the fires had added an extra and unanticipated dimension to the business and Adam, along with Scotty, had ventured into commercial real estate.

Leaving Myrtle was less of an option than it had ever been.

"I think it would be good for Ivy if we both went to parent-teacher conference," she said, trying again. "You know, just in case she doesn't get her usual report."

So you hear it from the teacher, who is harder to ignore than me.

"What did I just say about not worrying? Ivy's fine. It's elementary school, for God's sake. Junior high's when things gets serious. I'll come then, I promise." Adam pushed away his empty bowl. "Anyway, Scotty and I've got that meeting with Lawrence Philpott about the eco-tourism development. You know how important it is."

"Fingers crossed," she said, thinking of Ivy but knowing Adam would assume it was about his precious eco-tourism project.

"Not just fingers, babe. Cross the lot." He pointed at her toes. "If we can get this over the line, it's gonna be huge. Not just for us either, but for Myrtle."

Bec started clearing the table but Adam stopped her. "Sit. I've got a present for you."

Confused, she sat. "A present? But I don't need anything. I mean, last month you spent a fortune replacing my entire wardrobe."

"Not quite all of it." He produced a plain package addressed to him. "After the fun we've had in the office, I thought you might enjoy this."

They'd replicated sex in the chair a few times, as well as on the desk. Bec was yet to be convinced that desk sex was particularly exciting, comfortable or safe. Her head had been far too close to a pile of discarded staples. Thankfully, over the last couple of weeks, sex had returned to the bedroom and night-time hours. Blessedly back to normal.

As she gingerly opened the box she got a fluttery feeling in her stomach that couldn't be called excitement. She sensed this "present" was about to change things again. Inside the box, pale pink tissue paper was sealed with a gold sticker proclaiming the name of an unfamiliar company. She broke the seal and pulled back the fragile sheets, surprised by the contents.

Nestled inside the tissue paper were seven pairs of underpants. They came in a variety of colors and styles from boy brief to thongs, but all were made from beautiful lace. Over the years, Adam had bought her many things—jewelry, clothes, cars—but he'd never bought her underwear. As she picked up each one, she realized they all had something in common.

"Um, did you buy the wrong ones? None of them have a crotch."

He grinned. "That's the point."

"Oh, right." She laughed but she heard the strain. "I'll wear them in bed."

"I didn't drop 500 bucks so you can wear them in bed. I want you to wear them during the day."

"During the day?" Bewildered, her mind went directly to all the new clothes he'd bought her—dresses—and then to his anger over her leggings, before finally settling on the girls. She didn't want to wear this sort of underwear during the day. "But they're not very practical."

"Fuck, Bec!" His hand hit the glass-topped table and the cutlery jangled.

Adam loved giving presents but he expected them to be received with gratitude and praise. A lot of praise. This need of his to be appreciated and respected had, like so many other things, been heightened since his injuries. "Put on a pair and I'll show you exactly how practical they are."

She flinched at the vitriol in his voice and instinctively leaned back even though he'd never raised a hand to her. She back-pedaled fast.

"Thank you. They're gorgeous. Of course I want to wear them for you."

His face, which had deepened to puce, returned to its new normal red. "Good."

"But ... can we agree that I only wear them during school hours and not when I'm out of the house?"

"Honestly, Bec." He shook his head indulgently. "Sometimes I wonder about you. I bought them for us to enjoy. They're not for wearing out of the house or when the girls are home."

A feeling rolled through her—not exactly relief but a definite reduction of anxiety. Yet again she'd misunderstood him—an increasingly common occurrence. What on earth was wrong with her? Why did she get it wrong so often and leave herself wide open to his displeasure? It only upset them both.

Adam was smiling and leaning forward, looking at her expectantly. She wasn't chancing the loss of his good humor. Picking up a handful of the expensive lace, she let it fall from her fingers like a waterfall.

"Which color would you like to me to wear first?"

CLAIRE WAS LEANING in close to the mirror and brushing on some mascara when Matt came up behind her, snuggled in and wrapped his arms around her waist. Her hand slipped and a black streak smudged her cheek.

"Matt!"

"Sorry. You were just too tantalizing not to touch."

She laughed and wiped away the smudge. "You've been touching me non-stop for the last half-hour."

"And it was great. Thanks for coming home before your craft group. Are you sure you have to go?" He nuzzled her neck. "We could go back to bed."

"I'm sure."

The words came out firmly, surprising her. She'd never expected to enjoy the group and she wasn't completely certain "enjoy" was the right word, especially as Rebecca was part of it. But instead of dreading Stitch N Bitch, she found she looked forward to it. She liked checking in on the progress of everyone's projects. If she was honest, tonight she wanted to brag just a little, because much to her surprise, she was managing to crochet three squares a week.

"Besides, you're the one who told me I should join."

"I did, didn't I." He stepped away and rested his behind on the vanity. "Have your periods come back yet?"

This time the mascara hit her eyebrow. "My periods?"

"Yeah. I've been reading and some women get their periods as soon as they stop taking the pill. For others, it takes longer. It's just you haven't said anything about them and I haven't noticed any evidence."

Evidence? Her pulse quickened.

"Do you think you should have a blood test? You know, to make sure your hormone levels are okay?"

She dabbed at the streak and recapped the mascara, using the time to restore her calm. "It's still early days, honey. Let's wait one more month."

For a moment, Matt looked like he was going to argue the point, then he blew out a long sigh. "It's hard, isn't it? I mean, once we made the decision to have kids, I was ready for them."

She squeezed his arm. "I did explain that it might take a while."

"I know." His doleful face was reminiscent of a kid whose candy money had dropped into a storm drain. "Thing is, I want it to happen straight away. I can't wait for you to be a mom and for me to be a dad. We'll be amazing parents."

The lamb chops she'd cooked for dinner congealed in her stomach. "I'm going to be late," she finally managed to say, desperately hoping she sounded perfectly normal.

He laughed. "So what's new?" As he walked her to the door, he sternly told the excited dogs to settle before picking up her craft bag and handing it to her. "It's drizzling, so drive carefully."

"Always." She kissed him. "Love you, honey."

"Love you too, Postie."

She ran to the car and drove the familiar half mile along the oak-lined road to the gate. Leaving the engine running, she pulled on the handbrake but instead of hopping out of the car, she leaned over, unlatched the glove box and rummaged about until her fingers closed around the foil packet of pills nestled under the service manual.

She'd been taking oral contraceptives for years, always skipping the seven sugar pills each month so she didn't have to bother with the inconvenience of a period. Habit meant she was still doing it, which was a mistake. Matt thought she'd been off the pill for two months and apparently was waiting for her period with almost as much nervous anticipation as a woman after a drunken one-night stand. She needed to give Matt a period so he didn't push for blood tests.

You need to tell him you don't want a baby.

Just the thought of broaching the subject terrified her, let alone having the conversation. Pressing a white pill out of the packet, she put it in her mouth and swallowed it. One down, six to go before she took another protective, hormone-loaded tablet.

SOMEHOW, despite the rain, Claire arrived at the CWA rooms five minutes early.

"No need to do that exaggerated watch-checking thing tonight, Rebecca."

"I don't know what you mean." Bec didn't glance up from adjusting a plate of blinis decorated with curls of smoked salmon and perfectly placed strands of dill.

"Yeah, you do," Claire muttered quietly.

Ever since Layla had brought her Turkish sweets, Claire had noticed that Rebecca had upped the ante in the food stakes, bringing something Insta-worthy each week. She probably posted them on social media before she came; not that Claire followed her. This competitive homemade food thing women did to one another drove her nuts. Each week, Claire noticed Sophie's anguished face when she caught sight of the escalating food offensive. Despite Julie's reassurances that no one need bring a plate, Claire knew the young working mother felt her lack of an oven and a real kitchen keenly.

In unspoken solidarity, Claire refused to contribute anything homemade to the supper. The week before she'd brought salt and vinegar chips as more of a statement than anything else. When she'd poured them into a pretty bowl—she wasn't a total philistine— Rebecca's eyebrows had hit her hairline. Sophie had thrown Claire a grateful look, but it was ex-socialite-Erica who'd surprised her most: she'd dived onto the chips as if they were rare and expensive caviar and scarfed them down.

"Salt and vinegar chips and lemonade are my weakness," she'd said sheepishly, licking her greasy fingers. "They remind me of happy childhood summers on the beach."

"Why is it so cold in here tonight?" Claire asked no one in particular as she picked up her crocheting.

"There's a problem with the heater." Julie's knitting needles clacked. "For some reason it's only working intermittently. I'll get Phil and the blokes to take a look at it tomorrow."

Layla's second sock lay across her lap. "Lucky we knit with wool. It keeps us warm."

"It's a shame we can't wear Julie's beanies." Sophie was knitting in fingerless gloves.

Claire noticed everyone was wearing some form of trousers—fleecy jersey to fine corduroy—except for Bec. As usual, the former Miss Myrtle was dressed in her signature impractical frock, only instead of at least wearing tights or knee-high boots, she sported ordinary stockings and ankle boots. Claire remembered how Bec and her gaggle of giggling girlfriends had always hogged the heater at school, elbowing out anyone not in their group.

"Aren't you cold, Rebecca?"

"No."

"Really? You look cold."

Bec's chin rose. "I think I'm in a better position to judge."

Claire shrugged and ate a blini. She might be philosophically opposed to the food wars, but she had no qualms about eating the offerings.

"It's a gorgeous dress," Sophie said admiringly. "You always wear the most beautiful frocks."

"Thank you." Bec's hand jerkily smoothed down the flared skirt that fell from a tight waist. "Adam chose it."

The look on Sophie's face was priceless. "You're kidding."

"No."

"Wow! That's incredible. The most personal thing Josh's bought me without my help was a beach towel. Even then he got the color wrong. I hate pink."

Erica laughed. "A few years ago, Nathan, bless him, gave me a Thermomix. He honestly thought he was being helpful and he couldn't understand why I left it on the kitchen counter unopened."

"That's a lot of money to leave sitting in a box," Julie commented dryly.

"I know, and that's what I was banking on. Eventually, Nathan couldn't stand it so he unpacked it. It's such a toy and he's such a boy, he fell instantly in love with it. He and the kids use it every Sunday to cook dinner while I sit in the reading nook or the bath. Either way I have a glass of wine and a book."

Erica shot up a couple of notches in Claire's estimation. "That sounds like a win to me."

"Damn straight."

"Has Adam bought you other clothes?" Sophie asked, obviously fascinated that such a man existed.

"Oh, you know. A few things. Usually it's clothes but just recently he bought me ..." Bec dipped her head and fiddled with the hem of the dress, which sat just above her knees. "Does anyone's husband buy them underwear?"

It took every gram of restraint Claire had not to roll her eyes. This woman's ability to turn almost every conversation into a bragging opportunity never ceased to amaze her. "Matt bought me some cotton panties from Aldi last week when he was buying a log splitter."

Claire's intention was to make the women laugh so they didn't feel bad that their husbands didn't splash money around like Adam Petrovic. It worked, but as the giggles spread, an uninvited memory shoved its way into Claire's mind: the exquisite touch of beautifully embroidered tulle and silk georgette against her skin.

Buy it, darling. Spoil yourself. You're only a bride once.

Since the fires, the memory of her mother's voice—both the tone and volume—had faded so much that she struggled to hear it in her mind. But now it was suddenly so loud and clear that she turned, expecting to see Heather standing behind her, eyes shining brightly behind her glasses, her loving arms wide open.

All Claire saw was empty space.

Blinking fast, she vigorously wrapped the wool around the crochet hook and yanked it hard through the stitches, keeping her gaze well away from Julie. The last thing Claire needed was to be asked in front of everyone if she was okay. That question belonged to her—she owned it fully and she'd been asking it of Myrtle's residents almost continuously for the last twenty months. It wasn't a question she ever directed at herself.

"When my husband travels overseas, I give him a shopping list," Layla said. "He says, 'Never doubt my love for you. I show you how brave I am by going into lingerie store to buy your favorite silk underwears.'"

Sophie's mouth gaped. "But you're Muslim."

Layla shrugged. "There are no rules against wearing silk underwears. It makes me feel sexy."

"Good for you, Layla," Erica said wistfully. "I remember feeling sexy once."

"Perhaps you need to buy some silk underwear," Julie suggested.

"Perhaps when I've lost twenty pounds." Erica sighed. "The problem is, without an exercise buddy, I lack motivation. When I was in Melbourne, I used to sign up for all the fun runs."

"Are you a runner?" Claire was surprised.

"God, no! Well, I mean I'm not a running junkie. I signed up because if I paid the money, I'd train. I love the preparation boot camps and the whole women-supporting-women vibe. It's a shame Myrtle doesn't have a fun run."

"You could organize one," Julie said.

Erica laughed. "As Nathan so politely puts it, I couldn't organize a piss-up in a brewery."

"That's a bit harsh," Claire said.

"Oops, that came out all wrong. Poor Nathan. He doesn't say that about me. It's just one of his favorite expressions when he's complaining about some of the less competent people he works with and I've adopted it."

She smiled wryly. "The thing is, since the PND, I've learned that if I take on too much, I risk getting overwhelmed, so I pace myself. I'm more of a worker bee. Give me one task at a time and I'll get it done, but I won't take on the big-picture planning and coordinating stuff. It does my head in. I'll do just about anything to avoid having another meltdown."

"I love organizing things." Bec sat forward so she could see around Sophie. "And I think a fun run is a great idea. I'm sure Adam would happily provide some sponsorship money so we could get T-shirts and caps printed."

Claire could see it now—red T-shirts with white writing proclaiming Petrovic Family Homes Fun Run. "Adam's a generous guy."

Bec's eyes narrowed as if she couldn't detect if Claire was being sincere or taking a cheap shot. "He cares a lot about Myrtle."

Claire swallowed the words, "He cares a lot about his profile," and ate another blini.

"Does Myrtle even have enough people to run in a fun run?" Sophie sounded skeptical.

Claire thought about their struggling town—the vacant shops and the empty blocks of land abandoned by people who couldn't face staying and being reminded of everything they'd lost. The "For Sale" signs on empty blocks were bleached and faded after more than a year of being out in Myrtle's unforgiving weather. They represented the rising cost of property tax to help cover the shire's dwindling revenue. Just like Oakvale Park needed tourists, Myrtle needed people with disposable incomes and ways to spend their money.

Claire glanced around at the Stitch Bitches. "Sophie's got a point about numbers, but if we think more broadly, a fun run might just be what we need to put Myrtle back on the map."

Layla's forehead creased in confusion. "Myrtle is already on Google maps."

"It is, but tourists have forgotten about us. Myrtle's in a catch-22. Since the fires, it's only the locals who are spending money in town, but because of the fires, there's hardly any places to spend it, so we drive to Colac or Geelong or shop online. All the bureaucrats were so focused on rebuilding the town, no one thought about the fact it's incredibly difficult to repair an economy when the population's dropped by fifty per cent."

"Claire's right." Julie laid down her knitting. "We need to offer outsiders a reason to come to Myrtle."

"But we need to give them something to spend their money on."

"A fun run's just a registration fee," Erica said.

"That's just the down payment." Bec pulled out her cell phone and started swiping. "Once they're here they'll buy lunch and water and they'll bring their family with them to cheer them on. They'll need lunch and ice creams too. The men will want beer."

"We have one bakery and no pub." Sophie doggedly started a new row. "It sounds like a lot of work to me."

"There's the CWA." Claire turned to Julie. "If we did a fun run, would they run a Devonshire tea tent?"

"I'm sure they'd agree to that."

"A fun run *and* scones?" Erica laughed. "I'd sign up for that."

"In France, they offer wine and chocolate on the route," Claire said.

Bec held up her cell phone like a stop sign. "We're not doing that!"

"Why not? It might be a drawcard. A point of difference. We could offer it as an option to the strollers rather than the runners." Claire's mind buzzed with ideas. "Lachlan said the bike tracks will be open this summer. If we organized a fun run that could be run, walked or ridden, then perhaps we could coordinate it with some sort of official opening of the tracks. You know, piggyback off the government's advertising. We might even be able to drag a few Lorne holiday makers up from the beach."

"Why would they leave the beach?" Layla asked.

"Some vacationers get sick of endless beach days and go looking for different activities," Julie said.

"You know, Josh and I ..." Sophie trailed off.

"What?" Bec encouraged.

"It doesn't matter."

"Yes, it does. What were you going to say?"

"Well, one of the things that clinched our decision to move to Myrtle was the community feel we got the night we strolled through the mini Christmas market."

Claire tensed. "We can't do anything too close to Christmas."

"I wasn't suggesting that," Sophie said sharply. "I meant you could run a market and invite stallholders from all over and charge them to attend. One of the women I work with makes beautiful jewelry."

"A fun run with craft stalls ..." Bec typed on her cell phone.

"If you're thinking of doing something like that, you'll need a committee," Julie said sagely. "And office bearers."

"We're not seriously doing this, are we?" Sophie's look was pure horror. "I mean, I don't have any spare time and Erica has already said she struggles—"

"Hey!" Erica said with uncharacteristic force. "It's fine if you don't want to be involved but please don't use my mental health as your excuse."

Two red spots flared on Sophie's cheeks. "I didn't mean—"

"I think it's a good thing," Layla said.

"Let's do it." Claire spoke the same words at the same time as Bec. Surprised, she glanced at the woman with whom she shared nothing in common and barely tolerated. In all the years they'd known each other, not once had they done a single thing in unison. Was it a sign? And if it was a sign, did it mean stay or run, and run fast?

"In that case, I think you should consider forming an evening branch of the CWA," Julie said. "It offers you support and insurance."

Claire tried not to groan. "Surely we don't need such a formal structure? It takes the 'fun' right out 'fun run.'"

"I agree with Julie," Bec said in her annoying "dot the I's and cross the Ts' voice. "If we're doing this, we have to be professional about it."

"If Bec's going to be president, then I'll be involved." Sophie's reluctance appeared to be vanishing under the weight of her veneration for Bec.

"If that's a nomination, I accept." Bec was on a roll. "I need a seconder?" Erica waved. "Thanks. Are there any other nominations?"

"Don't look at me." The last thing Claire wanted was to be an office bearer. Truth be told, she didn't even want a formal committee. She just wanted to get on with the job and not be bothered by the mud-sucking tendencies of protocol.

"Thank you. I accept the position of president." Bec bestowed a dazzling smile on Sophie. "Will you help by being secretary?"

Sophie nodded.

"Great. Layla will you second Sophie's nomination? Excellent. Thank you. Anyone else? No? Congratulations to Sophie, our new secretary. Now we need a treasurer." Bec glanced around expectantly.

Erica shook her head. "Layla and I are very happy to be committee drones."

"Okay, well, I guess that makes Julie treasurer, then."

"I'm very happy to be a mentor for the group, Bec, but as I'm already on the other CWA branch's committee, I have to decline your very kind offer."

"Oh ..." Bec shivered, goosebumps rising on her arms. "That's disappointing."

The nurse in Claire, who'd been watching the underdressed woman battle the cold all night, finally won out over disparaging teenage Claire. She grabbed her old waterproof, fleece-lined coat that Matt teased her wasn't even farm chic and threw it at Bec. "For God's sake. Put this on before you get pneumonia."

Bec picked up the coat with the tips of her fingers, holding it away from her as if she thought it was either going to bite her or permanently mark her as a fashion failure. "I'm. Not. Cold."

"Actually," Julie continued smoothly as if she hadn't been interrupted, "Claire balances a rather large budget in her day job. She's the perfect choice for treasurer."

Claire didn't know who was more stunned and horrified—her or Rebecca.

CHAPTER TWELVE

"If I said I'd get it done, Soph, I'll get it done." Holding the cell phone against his ear with one hand, Josh picked up a bag of apples and slung them under the stroller.

"The problem is, Josh, you've been saying that for weeks and now it's overdue. It's important. Do you want her to get sick?"

"What sort of a bloody stupid question is that?"

"Well, I sometimes wonder—"

"Is that all?"

"Can you buy a bag of yo-yos from the bakery? I want to take them to the fun-run meeting tonight."

Josh didn't know what pissed him off the most: the fact that Sophie had got herself onto a damn committee that took her out of the shed on another night, leaving him at home with the kids, or that she wanted to spend money on expensive gourmet cookies. "Yo-yos are not part of the budget."

"I know, but all the other women bring food. If I take them, I can pass them off as homemade."

"Aren't you forgetting something?"

"What?"

"We don't have an oven."

The line was silent for a couple of beats. "Fine. Can you make hedgehog slice?"

That was one assault on his masculinity too far. "No."

"No? Seriously, Josh, just like that? When I was at home and you were working—"

"Yeah, well you're not at home and hedgehog slice isn't part of my job description."

"You know, you can be real prick sometimes." The line went dead.

"Yo-yo!" cried Trixie. It took him a moment to realize that his daughter hadn't understood the call but was straining against the restraints of the stroller, her arms reaching desperately toward the supermarket fridge. "Yo-yo."

"You just had a cookie. You can have yogurt at home."

Trixie squealed in protest, pummeling her feet on the support.

"Yeah, like that's gonna convince me."

Not once had Josh ever thought to add "go supermarket shopping on my own" to his bucket list. But after weeks of being the main caregiver to his children, it was there along with "going to the loo without an audience" and "fully completing any task in one go."

A woman smiled at Trixie. "Got your hands full there. My granddaughter's that age and she can throw a tantrum at the drop of a hat."

"She likes to test the limits, that's for sure."

"You're a hero, giving your missus a break on your day off." The woman shot her husband a death stare. "You'd have got more sex if you'd babysat the kids more."

Josh wasn't touching that. He grabbed for the milk and moved himself and Trixie out of the aisle. Before he'd lost his job, he'd probably only taken the kids grocery shopping on his own a couple of times and he couldn't remember if anyone had ever said anything to him then or not. Now that he regularly shopped with Trixie while Liam was at preschool, he'd noticed a couple of things: women praised him for babysitting and men ribbed him about getting in the good books with the wife.

He knew when Sophie took the kids to the shops, no one ever suggested to her she was babysitting. While Josh hadn't willingly put up his hand to be an at-home dad, the fact that people assumed he was babysitting ticked him off. Sometimes he came close to yelling, "I'm doing the cooking, cleaning and the all the childcare, but I'm getting less sex than ever."

He bent down and grabbed a big can of tuna off the shelf. He was just straightening up when he noticed in his peripheral vision, a pair of black work boots and navy blue drill pants. His gut churned. Was it one of his old workmates? A bloke whose job had been preserved and whose masculinity was still intact while Josh was living in a shed and wading in dirty diapers, half-eaten food and a sea of toys?

"G'day, Josh."

"Scotty." Josh shook the hand of the builder who'd supervised the construction of their first house. He liked the no-nonsense man better than Adam Petrovic, who was just a bit too slick. He also appreciated that when they'd been building the house, Scotty had found opportunities for Josh to labor, which had helped offset some of the costs. He'd learned a lot, although at the time neither of them had ever expected Josh to be using the knowledge again so soon.

"Got the day off, mate?"

Josh tried not to wince. When he'd first lost his job and people made this comment or asked if he was on vacation, he'd nodded, allowing them to think that was the case. Admitting to people he was unemployed wasn't just acutely humiliating, there was something about hearing the word spoken aloud that made it very real. But as the weeks rolled on and he'd started running into people on a more regular basis, trying to hide his unemployment behind a nod in a tiny town was impossible. He'd come up with a stock phrase instead, one he knew was BS but it was far more palatable than "I got laid off" or "I lost my job."

"I'm between opportunities."

"Jeez, sorry, mate." Scotty sounded genuine. "Didn't realize you'd got squeezed by the last round of cuts at Sustainable. Much work out there?"

"Nothing within a hundred miles."

"That's tough."

"Yeah." Josh didn't mention it was even tougher that Sophie had walked straight into a job at the same company that had let him go.

Trixie babbled and Scotty scooped up the toy she'd dropped before handing it back to her. "I s'pose the flip side is, it gives you plenty of time to work on the house."

Josh's hand involuntarily tightened around the stroller's handle. A house required both time and money to be built. He had not much of one and even less of the other, but it was easier to blame the kids than admit to being strapped for cash. "Ever tried wrangling two kids and building a house? It's slow progress."

Scotty laughed. "I'll have to take your word for it. I'm still on the lookout for a woman who'll have me."

During the build of the first house, Sophie had declared Scotty "a catch." They'd had long discussions about him, searching for reasons why a good-looking, easy-going, apparently straight, hard-working and successful guy like Scotty didn't have a woman in his life.

"Either you're not looking that hard or someone got her first," Josh joked.

Scotty looked away before scratching the back of his hand. "You might be right. Listen, I don't s'pose you're interested in some casual work? You know, just while you're between jobs."

Josh's heart rate leaped. *Don't sound desperate.* "Yeah. Might be."

Scotty checked his cell phone. "You still got the same number?"

"Yep."

"Great. I'll give you a call."

"No worries."

"Catch ya later."

Josh finished the shopping with more enthusiasm than usual and then jogged down the street to the clinic. If he didn't get Trixie's vaccination sorted today, Sophie would go even more ballistic than she usually did when she got home.

He was struggling with the stroller and the door when a man appeared on the other side of the glass. Josh closed his eyes for a second, hoping when he opened them, he'd see a different bloke. It didn't work.

"Good to see you, Josh. You too, Trixie, my gorgeous girl." Phil Lang bent down to Trixie's level.

"Pill!" Trixie immediately offered Phil her Terry the Toucan toy—an act of unprecedented toddler generosity.

Josh liked Phil. He had a lot of respect for the older man who reminded him of his father. When he and Sophie first moved to Myrtle, Julie and Phil had welcomed them as if they were family, inviting them to swim in their pool and enjoy their English-style garden with its towering rhododendrons and camellias; so very different from their own bush block. Sophie had commented more than once in their happy pre-fire weeks that Julie was more of a mother to her than Aileen. Josh couldn't argue with her about that. For his part, Phil had advised Josh to buy a fire pump.

The suggestion had surprised him. "I thought if there was a fire, the CFA comes."

"They do, but it's not like the city. You need to be prepared."

"Work's giving me some fire training in the new year."

"Great. You might want to think about joining the CFA too. It's a good way to meet people. Either way, go down to the station and have a chat with the volunteers. They'll give you some information booklets to help you with your fire plan."

But with getting settled into the house, getting ready for the new baby and the crazy time that was the run-up to Christmas, Josh had never made it to the station. That conversation with Phil seemed a lifetime ago.

"Phil."

The older man rose from Trixie's level. "I was just talking to

Claire. We're organizing a guest speaker as part of the Spanner in the Works men's health program we're hosting at the Men's Shed."

"Right." The Men's Shed! Bloody hell, he was thirty-two, not sixty. Josh had no interest in listening to a guest speaker for a group of old codgers with prostate problems.

"She suggested a bloke with experience in wildfire trauma."

Josh tasted metal in his mouth. "Survived one, has he?"

Trixie shrieked for her toucan.

Phil's hand touched Josh's shoulder. "I'll let you know the date."

"No need. I'll be busy that night." He shrugged away the touch, shoved the stroller forward and entered the building. At least Claire McKenzie was ready and he didn't have to wait.

Pulling Trixie's green health center book out of the stroller basket, he handed it to the nurse with a shrug of embarrassment. "She's overdue for a jab. I've tried to get here a few times but ..."

Claire smiled. "Time's got a habit of getting away from us."

He thought about the weeks of chaos where most days he had no idea what the hell he was doing. How he needed to force himself to get out of bed every day. "It's harder than I thought it would be."

"What's that?"

"You don't have to pretend. I'd bet my bottom dollar Sophie's told you I'm at home with the kids."

"I have to separate my professional and personal lives, Josh, otherwise people wouldn't feel safe here. What I hear at Stitch N Bitch stays there."

Despite Josh's best efforts, his mind slid to that stinking hot December night when inky darkness glowed red and the roar of fire struck terror into both their souls. Had Claire McKenzie separated from that night too? God knows, Josh had tried. Was still trying.

"The important thing is that you're here now," Claire said. "Leave the stroller and bring Trixie into the office."

He did as instructed and Trixie happily toddled after Claire to a low table with blocks scattered over it. She started playing with them.

"Great tower," Claire commented as Trixie stacked four blocks.

"It's not many," Josh said.

"It's above average."

"Really?"

"Yep. It probably helps that she has a brother who likes building things."

"She hates missing out on anything. Sometimes I help them stack all the Lego blocks into a tower as tall as me. They love pushing it over and hearing the smash of plastic on concrete. The blocks go everywhere but they're not as keen about picking them all up. It drives Sophie nuts."

Claire laughed. "Tell her you're helping Trixie develop her fine motor skills. With all the screen time kids are getting, this stuff's really important. I see preschoolers whose pinch-and-swipe tech skills are way beyond mine, but they can't hold a pencil."

Josh didn't tell her how many times a day he gave Trixie his cell phone for five minutes of peace. "Yeah, I read the other day that some five-year-old got hold of his mother's cell and ordered McDonalds on Uber Eats. Lucky we live in the country."

"How's Liam?"

"Yeah, okay."

"You don't sound convinced."

"He's pretty clingy. Preschool drop-off's never pretty."

"He's dealing with a lot of changes. Sophie going back to work, the house—"

He flinched. "I doubt he even remembers the house."

"You might be surprised. If you're worried about him—"

"I'm not. He's going to school next year so it's time he stopped being such a mommy's boy."

Claire's frown said she disagreed. "Hey, Trixie, where's Daddy?"

Trixie pointed to Josh.

"Where's Daddy's nose?"

Trixie ran over, scrambled up onto Josh's lap and put her finger on the tip of his nose. Claire asked about hair, feet and shoes, and Trixie pointed to the correct items. Josh got an unexpected shot of pride.

"Is she saying many words?"

"She jabbers a lot when she's playing. Sometimes she says something like kettle, clear as a bell."

"Do you talk to her much?"

"What do you mean?"

"Oh, general patter describing what you're doing."

He grimaced. "I'm not doing anything worth talking about."

"You are. You're Trixie and Liam's portal into the wider world." He must have looked blank because she added, "You said Trixie can say kettle. She's learned that because she hears you and Sophie saying, "Put the kettle on" or "The kettle's boiled." When you're doing the household stuff like dishes or putting a load of laundry on, tell Trixie what you're doing. Name things and her vocabulary will take off."

"I read to her."

"That's great. Are you taking her to playgroup? I think she'd eat it up."

"Not yet." He heard his reluctance. Sophie had suggested he go, but he'd held off because attending seemed like conceding defeat— admitting that his lack of a job wasn't just a temporary aberration. That, and he'd be the only bloke.

Claire scooted her chair backwards and picked up a colorful leaflet from a rack. "Do you know about occasional care?"

"What is it?"

"It's childcare for when you need a bit of time. Say, you had a job interview or you needed a couple of uninterrupted hours to achieve some goals on the house or just an hour to be Josh instead of Daddy. It can be as short as an hour and as long as five."

He thought about the temporary work Scotty might offer him. "Is it expensive?"

"You'd probably be eligible for Child Care Benefit."

The words sparked images, harsh and bright in his head. Him standing in a tent, his mind blank yet screaming while he tried to summon up answers to questions a public servant was asking him. The bitter frustration of having lost everything and needing assistance but having no ID documents to prove he was Josh Doherty.

Itching with the strangeness of wearing a set of clothes that had once belonged to another person. Standing in Country Target feeling nothing like himself and desperate to choose his own outfits, but being overwhelmed by the array—walking from the store without making a single purchase. Standing in line at the shire offices attempting for the fourth time to get a planning permit to rebuild. Consuming his limited resources of patience trying not to reach across the counter and collar the pedantic guy who lived in a house and had never lost every freakin' thing he'd owned in a fire. Stuck on hold for forty minutes listening to the "very many ways the agency can help you" only to be told they were unable to help.

His knee jigged up and down of its own accord. "Child Care Benefit? That involves a government application, right?"

"Yes. You apply on the myGOV website. It's pretty straightforward."

Josh barked a laugh.

Claire jumped.

Trixie cried.

"PENNY FOR THEM?" Phil asked as he pulled out from behind a large green tractor on the road into Myrtle.

Julie waved to Mick, their tenant farmer, as they passed. "I just got the notification that the craft group is now officially Myrtle CWA Nightlights." Julie laughed. "Can you tell Claire about the name change?"

Phil laughed. "You reckon she'll take the loss of the name Stitch N Bitch better from me, do you?"

"Hugo was the one with the knack for calming her down, do you remember?"

"Yeah. Those two shared something special. That Christmas when

Claire broke up with the engineer, I really thought Hugo was in with a chance."

"I did too. He'd always joked Claire was his back-up plan, but then after the debacle that was Amber and that B&S ball, I knew it wasn't a joke. He loved her. I was convinced it was just a matter of timing, but ..."

"What?"

She ran her hand along the door handle, thinking about Hugo and trying to picture him.

"Come on, Jules, spit it out."

"That Christmas at the sports field... It's just when I told him Claire was single, he didn't react the way I expected."

"How was that?"

"To thank me for the very good news and dash off and find her."

"What did he do?"

"He said he was sorry to hear that she'd been part of a breakup and he hoped she wasn't too upset. Then he said he had to rush off and fix something with the AV because Adam Petrovic was waiting to give his speech."

"All that proves is empathy. For all you know, Hugo was planning on finding Claire after the AV was sorted."

"It was the way he said it, Phil. He used to regularly ask me about Claire. That Christmas was the first time in years both of them were single at the same time. They should have got together." She shifted in her seat. "I've always wondered ... Do you think he'd met someone?"

"No." Phil shook his head firmly. "Think about it. Whenever Hugo fell in love he was dreamy and useless and we all knew more than we wanted to about the relationship. Granted, Amber did a hell of a number on him, but even if he'd kept a new relationship quiet, it's unlikely he'd keep it from Penny. She'd have told us, after ... Besides, any woman who loved him would have come to the funeral and introduced herself. Shared her grief with ours."

"Not if she died too."

"He was alone except for Turbo."

"I know." Not for the first time, Julie ran through the names of the women who'd died in the fires but she couldn't imagine Hugo falling for a teen or a single mother a decade older than him, and the other three women had been in solid relationships. Once again, she came to the same frustrating conclusion as Phil.

"I guess you're right. Anyway, even if Hugo had delayed setting up the AV and gone straight to find Claire, she'd already met Matt."

Phil thumped the steering wheel with the heel of his hand. "And *that* should never have happened."

Julie sighed. "Don't. Claire got enough of that sort of nonsense from the town and the Cartwrights in the first few months. The important thing is, it's worked out for them."

Phil slowed at the speed limit sign on the outskirts of town. "They're not married yet."

"Stop being such a grumpy old man. Your own daughter lived with Jack for two years before she married him."

"Doesn't mean I was happy about it. If Ron was still here, he wouldn't be happy about this either and because he's not it's my—"

"Stop!"

"Hell, Julie, there's no need to—"

"No. Stop. Look!" Julie frantically pointed out the window to a vehicle parked near the bakery. "Hugo!"

Phil sucked in a sharp breath and braked hard.

Julie almost fell out of the car in her haste before running to the smiling dog in the back of ute. She rubbed her hands along the animal's head and behind his ears. "Hello, boy. I've missed you so much."

Phil appeared next to her and silently squeezed her shoulder.

"One blue eye and one brown eye, Phil. Can you believe it?"

"It's not Turbo, Jules," he said softly. "And this isn't Hugo's ute."

She glared at him, anger blowing through her like a treacherous northerly. "You think I don't know that? Of course I bloody know it's not Hugo and Turbo. But give it to me, Phil. Let me believe just for a few moments that Hugo's in the shop buying a pie and the paper and

Turbo's here waiting patiently for him to come back. Damn well give it to me!"

Phil made a strangled sound and wiped his nose with the back of his hand. "Sorry, love. Thing is, when I first saw ... I hoped ... I hate hoping. Makes it harder."

The Australian Shepherd licked their hands. Julie buried her face in the dog's coat and let her tears fall.

When she raised her head a few minutes later, Phil was saying unsteadily, "Great dog."

She dug a tissue out of her pocket and wiped her eyes. As her vision came back into focus, she noticed a short man standing beside them. He was wearing black tracksuit pants with a matching hoodie, and he held a white bakery bag. He looked nothing like her tall, handsome Hugo, who'd worked in jeans and overalls and hadn't owned a pair of tracksuit pants.

"Yeah," said the stranger. "I'm taking him down to a mate's farm at Simpson."

"You're taking a circuitous route," Phil said, sounding a bit more in control.

"I like a drive. Never seen the Twelve Apostles so thought I'd tick 'em off me bucket list."

"Our son had a dog with a merle coat just like this one." Julie made herself look at the man. "We miss them both."

Understanding crossed his face. "Sorry."

Julie nodded, not trusting herself to say anything more.

"I'm taking him over to the park to give him a run if you wanna come."

"Thank you. I'd like that. I'm Julie, by the way, and this is my husband, Phil."

"G'day. I'm Kane and this is Gizmo." He opened the truck's tray and the dog jumped down, immediately nuzzling Julie's hand. "He likes you."

They crossed the road to the park and in between throwing the ball and fussing over the dog, Kane told them about Gizmo's pedigree and his quirks. Julie and Phil shared Turbo stories.

Forty minutes later, after waving goodbye to man and dog, they got back into their car. Julie turned to Phil. "I felt him at the park."

"Hugo?"

"Yes."

"Sure it wasn't just memories?"

"Does it matter?"

"S'pose not."

The constant ache inside her had changed shape over time—narrowing in width, stretching in length—but it still throbbed. "Hugo was stolen from us. With every passing month, I'm finding it harder and harder to stay connected to him."

Phil squeezed her hand and turned on the ignition. "That dog's so much like Turbo. Remember when he was a puppy and he snuck inside and chewed Hugo's boots?"

The memories of Hugo and his puppy—the farmer and his dog—tumbled through her mind like water cascading over a sheer rock face, bringing her closer to her son. "Gizmo gave me something today."

"Happy memories?"

It was more than that. "What do you think about us getting an Australian Shepherd puppy?"

"Taffy'll get her nose out of joint."

"Taffy can help train the puppy."

Phil stared at her. "You're not thinking straight. Have you forgotten all the holes Taffy dug? How you threatened to give her away? A puppy will cause chaos in the garden for a couple of years at least."

"Perhaps it needs some holes dug."

"You're serious?"

She nodded. "The garden's not the same without Hugo."

"A puppy won't change that."

"No, but it might change us."

"We're getting older, Jules. Losing Hugo's hammered our health. Think about it. A puppy's exhausting."

"Good."

"Good?"

"Phil, I'm numb a lot of the time. I want to feel something even if it's exhaustion. I want to feel close to Hugo again. Do you remember the name of the bloke Hugo sold Turbo's puppies to?"

CHAPTER THIRTEEN

"Josh! When I'm at work do you do any housework?"

Sophie jerkily polished the sink, rubbing the stainless steel hard until it gleamed as much as an old sink could.

"Sophie! Can you treat me with a bit of respect?"

"I would if you admitted that when I was at home with the kids, I looked after them *and* did all of the domestic crap."

"When I was at home full time, I did all of it too."

Initially when Scotty had offered Josh some temporary work, Sophie had been torn. What was the point of adding more stress to their lives and putting the kids in childcare if the cost absorbed all the money he earned? Then again, Josh was happier when he worked, which made home a far more pleasant place to return to each night. But the unexpected frosting on the cake was Scotty paying Josh in cash. It meant their government child benefits weren't impacted and the money was going straight into the house fund. They had everything crossed that the work would continue until Josh found a full-time job.

"You're only working for Scotty four hours a day. That gives you time to do stuff. I'm working full time, commuting and I'm still doing more housework than you."

He leaned against the broom. "Only because you're a martyr. You're cleaning stuff I've already done."

She threw her cloth hard into the sink. "Like what?"

"I'd cleaned the portaloo."

"When? A week ago?" Tears pricked the back of her eyes. "It's not fair, Josh."

"What's not fair is you taking your constant bad mood out on me. It's not my fault you're ruining your Saturday. Why the hell did you invite your mother and sister here anyway?"

"I didn't exactly invite them. Mom invited herself."

Aileen had unexpectedly called her at work, doing her best to guilt Sophie into visiting, despite it only being three weeks since she'd driven the 124 miles to Melbourne for her mother's birthday. This time, Sophie held firm, telling herself that as she was working full time and her mother was now retired, if Aileen wanted to see her and the kids, she should be the one to make the drive.

Josh shoved the broom into its closet. "You should have told her no."

"Would you tell your parents no?"

His nostrils flared. "My parents don't even live in the same state to say no to!"

Craig and Janet had once again decided to winter somewhere warm and they were managing a campground in the Gulf of Carpentaria country, ten hours' drive west of Cairns.

A car horn beeped.

"Gran's here!" Liam ran to the door.

"At least someone's happy to see them," Josh muttered. He scooped up a wailing Trixie, bereft that her brother had disappeared on her.

They walked outside into late-winter sunshine that blessedly took the edge off the usual cold and hinted at spring. After the hugs and kisses and Aileen saying, "We never thought we'd get here," Sophie's mother and sister briefly admired the view before rushing to use the portaloo.

Sophie thought Josh would walk her relatives over the slab and outline the position of future rooms like he'd done months ago with his own parents, but he was morosely silent. It was Liam who danced across the concrete, showing them where his bedroom and playroom would be.

"One day, Nanna, my bed will be here but with walls."

Aileen and Kylie dodged the puddles from the earlier rain before tentatively stepping inside the shed. Sophie, who'd got up at six and spent five hours cleaning and tidying, couldn't help feeling proud at what they'd achieved, even if it had come with an argument. Her recently completed knitted blanket was draped over the sofa, giving it a fashionable retro look, and the battered kitchen table looked unrecognizable with all its scars hidden under a cloth.

She'd cut some cheery daffodils from a clump that was flowering by the side of the road and stuck them in a mason jar in the center of the table, which was set for lunch. Josh had done a good job keeping the fire stoked so the room was toasty warm. Even the kids had managed to confine their toys to one corner—probably because she'd screamed at them. She wasn't proud of losing it, but her guilt over her shrewish outburst was tempered by the fact the toys had stayed in their rightful place. The shed had never looked homier—welcoming even.

Aileen and Kylie looked around silently.

"Take a seat at the table. Lunch is ready. I've made minestrone and the bakery made the crusty bread."

Aileen shivered despite the cozy warmth. "It's perfect soup weather."

Kylie took in the makeshift kitchen. "You made soup on *that* stove?"

"Where else do you expect her to cook?" Josh sawed jaggedly through the loaf of bread.

Sophie shot him a warning look and felt her smile tighten. "I'm the queen of the one-pot meal these days. It's perfect winter cooking." She handed around bowls of steaming soup. "When it gets warmer, we'll go back to barbecuing."

Kylie picked up her spoon. "Ever since we built the outdoor kitchen, Lex loves to cook. We practically live on the deck in summer."

"Sounds great." She hoped she sounded neutral. Living outside on a deck when there was an air-conditioned house five steps away was nothing like their stifling hot summer, inside or outside the shed.

The conversation waned while everyone ate. Sophie helped Trixie with her soup and supervised Liam's liberal use of the parmesan cheese.

"Very tasty soup," Aileen said. "And healthy."

"You really should buy a Thermomix," Kylie said. "They're amazing. If you had one, you wouldn't miss having a kitchen. I wouldn't be without mine."

Sophie ground her teeth. She was living in a shed next to a bare slab, and her sister was suggesting she buy a $2,000 appliance. *Stay calm. Think happy thoughts.*

"I'm content with my cooking pot."

"Oh, Sophie. You can't be serious?"

The derision in her sister's voice lit the fuse she'd been trying so hard to keep damp. "What do you want me to say, Kylie? That unlike you, I can't afford a Thermomix, let alone a kitchen? Would that make you feel happily superior?"

"There's no need to be rude! I was only trying to help."

"Help? Hah! You were judging. If you really want to help, lend me your Thermomix until I have a kitchen."

Kylie's face blanched under her makeup.

Memories rushed Sophie: her younger sister always putting herself first. Kylie's propensity to borrow and not return. Her inability to share. The selfish and unreasonable bride who'd refused to compromise. The housewarming party invitation that arrived a year after the wedding with a gift list attached.

Sophie made an exaggerated facepalm. "Oh, that's right. You've always preferred bragging to me about your possessions rather than sharing them."

"Sophie!" Aileen said. "Be nice to your sister. She's driven a long way to see you."

"To see me or to show off her new car?"

Kylie huffed. "Honestly, Sophie. I know things are a little bit difficult for you but that's no reason to be spiteful."

"A little bit difficult!" Sophie stood fast, her chair scraping loudly on the concrete floor. She released a startled Trixie from her highchair. Liam slid off his chair and immediately took his sister's hand, leading her away from the table as if he wanted to keep her safe. "Look around, Kylie. Do you see a bathroom? A laundry? A hot-water tap?"

"You were the ones chasing cheap house and land packages. You chose to move down here to the middle of nowhere. No one held a gun to your head."

"Oh, so it's my fault a wildfire burned down my house?"

Kylie waved a manicured hand. "All I'm saying is, we make our own decisions. Then we have to live with them."

Josh, who'd been unusually quiet, made a growling sound not dissimilar to a possum defending its territory. "You're a fuckwit. Get out of my house."

"Josh!" Sophie stared at him. Josh had only ever treated Kylie like an annoying puppy: with resigned tolerance. Not once in seven years had he lost his temper with her, let alone sworn at her.

"You can't talk to me like that," Kylie spluttered.

"I can talk to morons however I want."

Kylie's hand went protectively to her belly and tears spilled down her cheeks.

"Your sister's pregnant," Aileen hissed at Sophie. "Today was supposed to be a happy day. Are you going to stand there and let him upset her like this?"

Pregnant? Sophie wanted to be happy for Kylie, she really did, but now the reason for their surprise visit struck her with the viciousness of a backhanded slap. It was all about Kylie. Still, what did she expect?

She was familiar with her sister's histrionics but she was baffled by Josh's pinched face and clenched fists. Her allegiances were not exactly torn. "Josh?"

"Get her out of here before I get back." He stormed out the door.

"I never liked him!" Kylie sobbed.

"You introduced us!"

"He's always had a chip on his shoulder. All this nonsense about buying a house," Aileen said.

Sophie bristled. "How does Josh wanting to buy a house for his family mean he's got a chip on his shoulder?"

"He wants things too fast. You should have stayed in Melbourne and saved up."

"What don't you understand? We had our dream home and a wildfire burned it down!"

"Because you built here instead of waiting until you could afford a place somewhere safe."

Astounded, Sophie struggled to find words. "Oh my God! You think we *deserved* to have our house burn down and for Josh to lose his job?"

"I think Josh was greedy and he's convinced you to be the same. Now it's come back to bite you. I mean, look at how you're living. And Josh swearing like that in front of everyone. None of it's good for the children."

"The children are fine." But even as Sophie ground out the words, she heard the lie. Since she'd gone back to work, Liam alternated between hanging off her, desperate to be cuddled, and pummeling her chest with his little fists, pushing her away. "When Josh gets a full-time job, we'll finish the house and everything will go back to normal."

Her mother looked both unconvinced and unsupportive. When Sophie and Josh had lived in Melbourne, she'd told herself that her mother helped her a little bit with Liam, but Trixie's birth had opened her eyes. It took less than a week for Aileen to tell Sophie that Dennis couldn't cope with having her and the kids living in the house. With Josh working and camping on the block, she and the children had moved in with her in-laws until the temporary village was up and running. Even after they'd moved out, Janet and Craig had been amazing, visiting each Wednesday with frozen meals. Occasionally, they'd even taken Liam back to Melbourne to give her and Josh a break.

Just before they left on their latest trip, they'd offered the use of their house in Melbourne whenever Sophie and Josh wanted a weekend break from the shed. Josh had flatly refused and as much as Sophie craved a few nights in a space bigger than 450 square feet, she didn't think the pain of re-entry to shed living would be worth it. Neither would the arguments with Josh to convince him to go. She wished her in-laws didn't head north for half of every year, but if wishes were fishes, Aileen would mother her and offer practical support instead of long-distance criticism.

Kylie stood up. "Aren't you going to congratulate me?"

"It's great news, Kylie. When's the baby due?"

If her sister noticed her flat intonation she ignored it and as Sophie and the kids walked them out to the car, she cheerfully prattled on about the woes of early pregnancy, her wonderful obstetrician and how the hospital she'd chosen had private rooms with double beds, an à la carte menu and staff who would mind the baby so she and Lex could go out for dinner.

It's a hospital, not a vacation destination! "It all sounds great," Sophie managed to say.

"Dadda?" Trixie asked as they walked back inside after waving goodbye.

"He'll be home soon."

"Can I watch *Paw Patrol?*" Liam asked.

As it was only 1.30 P.M., Sophie would normally say no, but after the disaster that was lunch, all she wanted was quiet time. She slid the DVD into the player and stacked the soup bowls on the sparkling sink that neither her mother nor Kylie had noticed. As she waited for the kettle to boil so she could wash the dishes, she stood in the doorway, her gaze seeking Josh. Despite his unexpected outburst, she'd assumed he'd return the moment Kylie's BMW purred out of the gate. Their own car was still parked in its spot by the tank so he couldn't have gone far. Perhaps he'd finally gone down to the creek?

When they'd first bought the block, they'd wandered along the creek, breathing in the scent of the bush—eucalyptus, moss, wombat poo and fresh water. After the fires had rendered the landscape charred and naked, murdered the wildlife and blackened the creek with ash, they'd avoided it. Now the fresh green regrowth shrouded much of the charcoal tree trunks, tempting her to forget the destruction and remember the joy they'd shared. Recently, Sophie had been suggesting that they go platypus spotting, but Josh never showed any enthusiasm for it. These days, Josh exhibited little enthusiasm for anything.

She sighed and zippered up her polar fleece against the chill. She had a sneaking suspicion that Josh was missing his father. Not that he'd admit it. When they Zoomed Janet and Craig each week so they could read a story to Trixie and Liam, Josh was always there. But now that she thought about it, lately he hadn't said much more to his parents than ask about the weather. Back in the day, he'd had long animated chats with his dad about work and the house but he'd barely mentioned his job with Scotty. Instead, he sat staring at the screen, listening to his parents talk. He sat a lot at other times too, although Sophie wasn't convinced he was always listening to her.

She stepped beyond the veranda and scanned the horizon. There was no sign of her rangy husband crossing the meadows, only grazing Holsteins. As she turned back to the house, something flickered in her peripheral vision. Shielding her eyes, she squinted. What the hell? She slipped her feet into her work boots and strode across to the car. Josh sat, his shoulders hunched forward and his forehead resting on his hands, which were crossed on top of the steering wheel. She pulled opened the door.

"What are you doing?"

Josh didn't move.

She shook his shoulder. "Josh!"

He raised his head and rubbed his face on the sleeve of his fleece before looking at her. His eyes were red-rimmed and bleary, his nose snotty, and moisture lingered on his cheeks.

The thought that he might have been crying sent a jag of fear slicing through Sophie before she quickly told herself she was being ridiculous. Josh wasn't a crier in good times or in bad. He was more likely to joke than sniffle during a sad movie. After her long and difficult labor with Liam, the closest he'd come to being "emotional" was to laugh at Liam's cone head. Sure, he got grumpy, but cry? Never.

"What's going on?"

"Nothin'."

"Then why are you sitting in the car?"

He shrugged.

"You look like you've got hay fever."

"Or Trixie's cold." His head fell back against the headrest as if it was too heavy for him to hold. "I feel like shit."

That would explain his outburst with Kylie—Josh was always irritable when he was sick. He was also clueless at connecting those feelings with being unwell so instead of being proactive and taking cold and flu meds or putting himself to bed, he got cross. She placed the back of her hand on his forehead as if he were one of the kids.

"You feel hot. Come inside."

"Okay." But he didn't move.

"Hurry up, Josh. It's freezing out here."

"Are you going to give me crap for swearing at your sister?"

"I probably should, but I think I'll give you Tylenol instead and send you to bed. We need you well by Monday. Every job you do for Scotty puts us one step closer to the frame."

JULIE LAUGHED at the antics of their captivating ten-week-old Australian Shepherd puppy. Charger had been part of the family for three weeks and she was utterly besotted.

"Charger! Come!"

The puppy's ears shot up and he raced toward her across the field, losing his balance as his feet hit a fresh cow pie. Julie groaned as he rolled in it for extra measure. Picking him up gingerly, she got a full whiff of eau du pong.

"Bath time for you, buddy."

By the time she'd washed his squirming silken body in the laundry sink, she needed a bath herself. With Phil at the Men's Shed, she decided to treat herself and use her birthday present from Penny. She lit the candle, opened the pomegranate-scented soap and luxuriated in a deep bath. As she enjoyed the simple pleasure of being cocooned in warm water, she felt the dull ache that was, and always would be, Hugo's absence, but she gratefully acknowledged that the darkness was slowly lightening.

With the soap bubbling on her hands and the delicate fragrance delighting her, she set about washing herself, starting with her face and working downwards, gently kneading her skin.

Her fingers froze. She swallowed hard.

There was a pea-sized lump in her breast.

No. It wasn't possible; she was imagining it. She forced her fingers to move again, repeatedly fleeing and returning, but each time they found the ominous lump.

The morning's joy turned to cold, hard dread.

JULIE SAT QUIETLY in her role as mentor while Bec opened the Myrtle CWA Nightlights meeting with the reading of the Collect, a short prayer. Neither Layla nor Claire ever read the first or last line. Although Julie understood Layla's hesitation, she knew with Claire it was sheer bloody-mindedness. For some reason, Claire was railing against inadvertently finding herself a member of the CWA. It was crazy. The organization had been close to her mother's heart and it represented everything Claire believed in: helping others. Helping

Myrtle.

I did it for you, Heather. It's what you wanted and I hope you approve.

Julie's friendship with Heather had started inauspiciously. After a misunderstanding in the kindergarten playground that had resulted in sand being thrown, tears and a furious teacher, Heather had been Julie's best friend for sixty-two years. If Hugo's death had taken part of her heart and a piece of her soul, Heather's felt more like losing a limb. For decades they'd sought advice from each other, shared secrets, moaned about their husbands, bragged about their kids, cried and laughed. They'd laughed so much. She missed Heather's sense of the ridiculous and she ached for her friend's unconditional and unwavering support.

More than ever, Julie needed it right now.

If Heather were alive, Julie would have confided in her about the breast lump. Heather would have held out her phone and insisted she make an appointment with their GP, Colin, right then and there. It would have been Heather saying briskly, "And I'm driving you, no arguments," and she'd have sat holding Julie's hand when she got the results.

But Heather was dead and perhaps Julie would be joining her whether she did anything about the lump or not. After losing Hugo, the thought of being told more grim news threatened to fell her. Worse than that would be telling Phil and Penny she had cancer. She'd see the flash of fear on their faces then feel their need for her support and reassurances. They'd want her to tell them that everything would be alright. That she'd be fine.

Julie had spent more than a year and a half caring for them after Hugo's death, holding them up and getting them through the bad times until they'd finally reached this point of acceptance where they spent more time looking forward than looking back. The thought of going through that all over again *and* dealing with medical appointments and treatment overwhelmed her. She couldn't do it. Not without Heather.

After two long and agonizing days, she'd come up with a plan. She was ignoring the lump. When she showered and dressed, she kept her fingers well away from the spot and she kept busy. If her mind ever veered in the direction of lumps and cancer, she immediately changed tack and thought about something else entirely, just like she was doing now.

Watching the way Claire's silver crochet hook flicked rainbows around the room reminded her of a conversation in the bakery she'd had with Matt a couple of weeks earlier. He'd been his usually upbeat and happy self and he'd dropped a couple of hints that he and Claire were trying for a baby. Claire hadn't mentioned baby plans but now that Julie thought about it, lately Claire had been remarkably quiet about anything other than work.

Julie hoped Claire would get pregnant easily. After everything that had happened, she deserved a baby of her own. Even though Claire had been a grown woman when the fires orphaned her, it didn't lessen the reality that she no longer had anyone from her family in her corner. Mind you, based on Sophie's retelling of her mother's recent visit, sometimes in-laws were a better bet than biological parents. But Julie had known Matt's mother for forty years and Louise could be a difficult nut to crack. A baby would give Claire a family member she could call her own and a way to pave the rocky road Julie felt certain still existed between the two women.

"The first item on the agenda is the fun run and—" Bec glared at Claire. "Craft group is next week, remember? Alternate meetings."

Claire's fingers didn't pause in their work on the square. "I'm more than capable of crocheting and being part of this meeting."

Erica opened her laptop and a bright and appealing webpage with a watermarked background of mountain ash declared: Myrtle's Tall Trees Fun Run and Stroll. "I had one of those golden weeks when the kids were healthy and happy and Nathan was home, so I mocked up a website. Nothing's set in stone and I can change anything we don't like and add in things we want. Oh, and I've been in contact with an online company that can handle the registrations. There's a small fee involved but it will be totally worth it."

"Erica! That's sensational." Claire leaned in closer. "I love the trees."

"Wow." Bec looked slightly stunned. "Thank you. Can we add Petrovic Family Homes as a sponsor? Adam's donating the T-shirts and $2,000, which means we have a budget and some wriggle room."

"We better open a bank account then," Claire said. "I've got a meeting in Colac on Thursday. Sophie, can you meet me at the Bendigo Bank at one o'clock?"

"We need three signatories," Bec said. "I'll meet you there too."

"Great!" Sophie's fingers flew across her iPad screen, taking the minutes. "Perhaps we could have lunch after?"

Claire's gaze returned to her square.

Bec consulted her agenda. "I've spoken to Gary at DELWP about the route. He was enthusiastic and supportive so I've followed up with an official request. We should hear by Friday. So, how are we going to advertise this?"

"We can get listed on fun-run calendar websites," Erica said. "As soon as we've settled on our website's colors and the banner, I'll set up social media accounts. But for them to work, all of us need to post. I plan to Insta my training. We need to keep it real and post photos of us looking sweaty and out of breath, running with kids in the jogger stroller, stuff like that. We can use fun hashtags. We want to encourage all age groups to come."

"We're organizing it so we can't actually run on the day," Bec said authoritatively.

"I'm substituting Nathan for me while I'm running," Erica said firmly. "I promise you I'll be on deck before and after, but I need to do this run."

The next agenda item was the market and Layla brought up the topic of food trucks. "My cousin's business is gözleme."

"What's that?" Bec asked.

"It's Turkish tradition maybe like English pie but better. In villages, they fill pastry with cheese and spinach and cook over a fire. Here my cousin also fills with beef and chicken and roast vegetables."

"They're yummy. When we lived in Melbourne I used to buy one when I shopped at the Queen Vic Market," Sophie said. "Would your cousin bring his truck to our market?"

"He and his family visit in January. He will bring if you want."

"The daytime CWA ladies are on board for the Devonshire tea tent," Julie said. "But I like the idea of food from around the world. It ties in with putting Myrtle on the map. What about inviting some of the Otway Harvest Trail businesses?"

"I'll send out letters," Sophie said.

Claire's crocheting fell into her lap. "You know what might work? As well as the market, what if we showcase Myrtle with some old-fashioned but fun country things, like cow milking and wool spinning, bee keeping and ... I don't know, whip making? Matt's made some beautiful whips."

"That sounds like you're advertising Oakvale Park," Bec said.

Claire glared. "Well, this entire event is advertising Petrovic Family Homes."

Erica sighed. "Do you think we could have *one* meeting where the two of you didn't snipe at each other?"

Go Erica. Julie's initial reservations about the woman's foot-in-mouth disease had faded. Surprisingly, both Claire and Bec had the grace to look chastened.

"I think Claire's idea is great," Erica continued. "I love Oakvale Park's café and gift shop. It's where I take my bemused and often critical city visitors, not just for the view but because Tamara's cooking's fabulous. Perhaps Oakvale Park might be interested in providing some sponsorship? Of course, if Tamara chose to have a market stall, she'd have to pay the same fee as any other vendor."

"The Men's Shed will happily get involved," Julie added. "They can pre-cut little wooden boats and tool boxes and then help the kiddies build them on the day. I'll ask Phil, Sophie. Save you an email?"

"Thanks, Julie."

"So, just to confirm, we're committing to a fun run followed by a market and a family fun day?" Bec said. "We've only got a few months to pull it together, so it's going to be tight."

"Nathan's got contacts with a race-timing company. They set up the gantries and provide the wristbands so we can pass off all the technical aspects of the run to him."

"The family fun stuff is easy," Claire said. "It's not much different from what we did at Christmas and Easter before the fires. Matt and I will reach out to everyone and we'll ask the CFA to run a duck race along the creek. It's always fun and a good money spinner."

"Slow down," Sophie said. "I have to minute all of this."

"We'll need more hands. I'll liaise with the other CWA," Bec said.

"What about inviting other women to become involved in Nightlights?" Julie suggested. She hoped she sounded casual—that she'd hidden her urgent desire for this evening CWA group to thrive and become the tour de force Myrtle needed. "You could put notices up at the school, playgroup, preschool. Perhaps everyone could invite a friend?"

"Would Tamara like to come, Claire?" Bec asked.

Claire matched Bec's gaze. "I can ask her."

Julie closed her eyes and tried not to audibly sigh. Bec's question was another shot across the bows in the Bec and Claire battle. Tamara's close and continuing friendship with Taylor Norris had dented any chance of the de facto sisters-in-law ever being close.

Sophie read out what she'd recorded in the minutes to confirm it was correct. When everyone was clear on their allotted tasks, Bec closed the meeting with the CWA motto.

"Thank God. I'm starving." Claire dived onto the food.

Erica laughed. "I was like that too when I was pregnant."

Claire's hand stalled on an asparagus roll. "I'm *not* pregnant. Why on earth would you say that?"

Two red spots glowed on Erica's cheeks. "I...it's just Tamara mentioned you're trying and I've been hoping like crazy for you. Plus, you're always so hungry, so I just assumed. Sorry."

"I'd appreciate it if you didn't discuss me or my reproductive system with Tamara—or anyone else for that matter," Claire said stonily.

"At least that's one thing I don't have to worry about," Sophie muttered, picking up a chocolate ball.

Erica threw her a grateful smile. "Have you and Josh done something permanent?"

"No, but you have to have sex to get pregnant."

"God, I remember being so tired that sex was the last thing I could think about." Erica patted Sophie's hand. "The kids get older and things get better."

"It's not me who doesn't want sex." Sophie's eyes suddenly widened. "Oh, God. I can't believe I just said that."

"Maybe you need to," Layla said.

Sophie kept her gaze fixed on the chocolate wrapper. "I think it's my fault that Josh isn't attracted to me anymore. I should have lost this baby weight ages ago, but since going back to work, all I do is eat chocolate."

"Don't be so hard on yourself," Claire said firmly. "Your lack of sex probably has nothing to do with your weight."

"What do you mean?"

"Despite popular opinion, guys aren't immune to losing their libido. Especially when they're under a great deal of stress."

"I don't think it's stress. Not now Josh is working again." Sophie looked up and turned to Bec as if seeking confirmation. "Did Adam ... I mean with his burns and everything he's been through ... Did he ... Do you still have sex?"

Bec stiffened as if she'd sat on a red-hot poker. "I really don't feel comfortable talking about sex."

Sophie bit her bottom lip. "Sorry."

Claire laughed. "Oh my God, Rebecca. When did you get so freaking precious? Have you conveniently reinvented history? You were the first of our year level to lose your virginity and you were so damn proud of it. All you did was talk about sex. We couldn't shut you up."

Layla dropped her gaze to her lap. Erica stayed unusually silent.

Bec's chin shot up, her eyes glittering. "Not that it's any of your business, Claire, but Adam and I have a perfectly normal and healthy sex life. And we've made two beautiful daughters, which is more than you've managed."

"Anyone for a cup of tea?" Julie said briskly, frustrated she had to step in yet again. She felt for Claire, sensing her hurt and disappointment at not being pregnant, but honestly! How hard was it for Bec and Claire to be civil to each other for an hour a week? Most of all, she despaired that her plans for this group would ever come to fruition, because every time they functioned as a team, they fractured all too soon.

CHAPTER FOURTEEN

BEFORE THE FIRES

Claire breathed in the warm summer evening air, perfumed with stephanotis, and let out a long and relaxing sigh. That evening's rehearsal dinner at Oakvale Park for the bridal party, extended family and out-of-town guests had not only gone off without a hitch, it had been so much fun. After the formal part of the night had finished—a sit-down dinner for twenty in the wood-paneled dining room—people drifted out onto the sprawling lawn or lounged in the white cane chairs scattered in clusters along the veranda.

Someone had produced a bottle of cognac and, as many of the guests were staying at the homestead, no one seemed in a hurry to call it a night. Claire was spending her last night as a single woman with her bridesmaid, Olivia, a friend from Melbourne. They'd booked into the Queen Anne B & B in Myrtle and Claire had signed up for the full pre-wedding luxury bridal package.

"Are you absolutely sure you want to stay at the B & B tonight?" Heather asked one more time as she and Ron prepared to leave Oakvale Park. "It's not too late to change your mind."

"Mom, please. We've been through this. The hairdresser and

makeup artist won't drive out to your place. Besides, with tomorrow's predicted heat, the less distance I travel, the better."

"Promise me you won't get dressed without me."

"I don't need to promise. Of course I won't get dressed without you."

Claire kissed her parents goodbye and walked slowly back along the drive to the homestead and the guests. The off-white house glowed peach in the summer twilight and the fairy lights in the dozen oaks closest to the house made the trees shimmer like excited brides. She could relate—she'd been excited for days. After all the months of planning, this time tomorrow, she and Matt would be married. Husband and wife! It was hard to believe it was only fifty-one weeks since they'd met. Then again, time was irrelevant for soul mates—it seemed like she'd known him forever.

She crossed the lawn, looking for Matt, but couldn't spy him so she scanned the veranda, checking the groups. She saw Bill and Matt's uncles and cousins but no groom. Luck was on her side and she managed to sneak inside the house without being intercepted by tipsy relatives, but after checking the main living areas and the kitchen, she still hadn't found him. She decided to use the bathroom before returning outside. As she walked past the library, its door slightly ajar, she heard the quiet rumble of voices. Through the crack, Claire saw Louise sitting on the dark green chesterfield, her body turned as if facing someone. Her future mother-in-law's face was intensely earnest.

"Dad and I are just concerned you're rushing into this marriage without fully thinking things through. We want you to be absolutely certain that Claire's the one. If you've got any doubts at all, it's much easier to back out now rather than later."

Claire's heart stuttered in her chest and her brain fought the words. Surely, she'd misheard? Of course, she knew the timing of her and Matt meeting had caused the Cartwrights angst. Tamara had been openly hostile and Louise's coolness only had occasional moments of warming. Claire had despaired the situation would never improve but the run-up to the wedding had been a turning point.

Tamara had organized a girls' night, Louise had thrown her an old-fashioned but very enjoyable shower tea and Bill had insisted the Cartwrights host the rehearsal dinner. Initially, Claire was worried this would upset her parents but they appeared untroubled. In fact, they'd urged her to accept the offer, viewing it as the Cartwrights welcoming her to the family. These recent events had been enough to convince Claire that when Matt said, "My parents love you," he spoke the truth.

"It would be different if Claire was just marrying you." Louise laced her fingers tightly in her lap. "But she's not. She's marrying into the farm. Into our business. She has to fit in."

Claire strained to hear Matt's reply, but his voice was an indistinct rumble.

"She's not Taylor though, is she." The sadness in Louise's voice was matched by the downturn of her lips. "Claire's an only child and I'm yet to meet one who isn't self-centered. Our family works as a team. I know I'm right when I say Claire's not a team player."

Claire flashed hot and cold and her feet twitched. Every part of her wanted to storm into the library and tell Louise that her career was based around teamwork. That she loved Matt and would happily be part of Team Cartwright if Louise or Tamara opened the door to give her chance. But Heather's sage advice of never getting between a son and his mother stayed her feet. Getting into an argument with her future mother-in-law on the eve of her wedding would not only be idiotic, it would cause damage she might never be able to fully repair.

No, it was best not to act hastily. After all, she was marrying Matt, not his mother or his sister. She was in this for the long haul. She had years up her sleeve and plenty of time to consult her mother on the best ways to show Louise she was very much a team player. Decades to demonstrate she loved Matt as much as Louise loved him. And she'd give Louise grandchildren to dote on and stake her claim in the Cartwright family tree.

Even so, she wasn't keen for Matt and Louise to continue their conversation unfettered.

Carefully taking four noiseless steps back down the hall, she called out in a bright and breezy voice, "Matt? Are you down here?"

THE PRESENT

"You look amazing." Matt's eyes appreciatively skimmed Claire's long black tunic, leggings and boots.

"Are you sure? I'm just trying to wear something I can trampoline in and not look old."

"I hate to break it to you, Postie, but it's a disco for teenagers. At thirty, you're already way old."

"Thanks a lot!"

"Hey, I'm not complaining."

He flicked his tongue against her ear and the familiar spark of desire flared. She sank against him and kissed him before reluctantly pulling back. "We'll be late."

"You're always late so no one will notice. Besides, you're mid cycle, right? It's prime time."

Her gut cramped. The fact that he knew her cycle haunted her. "Having sex later will work better than having sex now before I go jumping on a trampoline." She reassured herself that she was telling him the truth, because if she'd wanted to get pregnant, she'd have followed that advice.

"Right, good point. We better get going."

As the disco was a work event, Claire drove the health center's car. After the long months of winter, it felt both unusual and liberating to be heading out at 6:00 P.M. in daylight. The oak trees dripped with catkins and spring was in the air.

"We should go to the nursery this weekend," Claire suggested. "I want to plant a crab apple, a crepe myrtle and a weeping cherry."

"Blossom addict." Matt put his hand on her thigh. "And talking about planting, it's been almost four months since I started trying to plant a baby in you. Just to rule out any problems my end, I saw Colin."

Claire's hand's tightened on the steering wheel. She couldn't believe he'd gone to see their GP without telling her.

Seriously? Think about what you're not telling him.

She moved her thoughts well away from that tricky problem. "And Colin told you to relax because it's early days, right?"

"Yeah. But seeing I was there, he got me to jack off into a jar. Said it was the easiest test to rule out any problems."

Oddly, she wanted to know the results. "And?"

He grinned. "Good news. My swimmers are in peak condition and ready to do the fifteen hundred."

Something akin to disappointment twisted in her gut. "Yay!" She hoped Matt didn't hear the hollowness in her voice.

"Colin suggested you make an appointment for a blood test next time you're in Colac."

Her heart sank. "Did he suggest it off his own bat or did you ask him if he thought it was a good idea?"

"Yeah, you got me. I asked, but he said as we're both over thirty, it's best not to waste any time."

"Okay, but the time to have the test is just after my period starts."

He squeezed her thigh. "Hopefully by then, my buff swimmers will have done the job."

"Hopefully."

They would not have done their job, because a tiny mix of estrogen and progesterone was tricking her body into thinking it was already pregnant. But with Matt obsessing about babies, she could no longer put off having the test. Thinking about it, she realized it wasn't a total disaster.

"Matt?"

"Yeah?"

"If I do the blood test and everything's in the normal range, do you promise me you'll sit back and relax until we've been trying for a year?"

"Promise."

As she could order blood tests and had online access to the results, it would be easy enough to do a cut and paste and alter the hormone levels before showing Matt. It would give her some breathing space. Eight precious months of breathing space.

THE TRAMPOLINE ROOM in the indoor sports center was unrecognizable—the difference a few colored lights, a smoke machine and music could make was mind blowing. Twenty teenagers were taking it in turns to "trampce" and while they waited, they danced on the floor.

"The DJ's got the right touch," Shane yelled into Claire's ear.

She nodded. "He's worth every cent."

"Trampoline volleyball next time?"

"Good idea. And a quiet area for them to chill and just hang out."

"Dad!" Shane's daughter Lucy appeared, her face flushed. "Everyone wants the adults to trampce."

"So you can laugh at us?"

"Yeah. Course. And to say thanks."

"What did your mom say?"

Lucy pointed to Sally and Matt, who were kicking off their shoes. "I even asked the DJ to play you something old."

Abba's "Dancing Queen" boomed from the speakers.

Shane laughed. "Righto, let me show you how the oldies can rock it."

Four minutes later, Claire was breathless and sweating. "Oh God, I'm dying."

"You need to get out with me in the fields and chase a few pigs. This job of yours and the hours you're putting in are slowly killing your fitness." Matt tucked damp tendrils of hair behind her ear. "It's another reason why I'm looking forward to having you barefoot and pregnant. We can work together. Life will be simpler."

Flashes of pregnancy, of being a mother, of life on the farm with her days spent in the critical company of Louise and Tamara assaulted her. Panic settled in a hard lump in her stomach. She pulled at her tunic. "Melting. Need fresh air."

Claire pushed open the door and stepped outside, welcoming the cold blast of night air. Tilting her head back, she closed her eyes and spread her arms wide, concentrating on breathing deeply.

When she opened her eyes, Matt was standing next to her.

"Milky Way's stunning tonight."

"I love that we have this sky."

"Yeah." He slipped his hand into hers. "And I love you. When does this gig finish?"

"The kids leave in half an hour and then there's pack-up so we should be able—" Claire turned at the sound of someone vomiting. "Can I borrow your cell phone?"

Matt handed it to her with the flashlight app lit. They rounded the side of the building and heard running feet. Matt set off after them. Claire crossed the garden bed and found a boy lying face down in the dirt, reeking of alcohol and vomit. The girl sitting next to him didn't look to be in much better condition.

"I'm Claire." She dropped down next to the boy and tried pulling him into a sitting position so he didn't aspirate the vomit. He flopped like a rag doll. "What's his name?"

The girl rocked back and forth and didn't reply.

Claire put her hand on her shoulder. "What's your name?"

"I feel sick."

"I can help you. What's your name?"

The girl raised her head. "Beth'ny."

"Okay, Bethany. Who's your friend?"

"Brock."

"Brock." Claire spoke loudly. The boy couldn't hold himself up so she lay him on his side in the recovery position. He barely managed a moan. She texted Shane her location and *COME NOW!*

"Brock's pretty sick, Bethany. What's he taken?"

The girl stared at her feet and Claire held onto a sigh.

"I'm a nurse. I'm not judging you. I want to help but I need to know what he's taken. What you've taken."

Matt jogged back holding two bottles and with a couple of teenagers in tow. "Vodka."

A bottle of vodka could render a teen unconscious with alcohol poisoning but something made her ask, "Have you taken anything else with the vodka?"

She noticed the boys shuffle their feet.

Bethany suddenly starting pointing, screaming and dry retching.

"Matt, get the first-aid kit out of the car."

"On it." He ran.

"And you," she pointed to one of the boys, "keep Bethany upright and tell her to breathe slowly."

The boy knelt beside Bethany. "Are they going to be okay?"

"I hope so, but to treat them I need to know what they took." Claire didn't recognize any of the teenagers from the disco but that didn't mean they hadn't been inside earlier in the evening. Had they taken MDMA? These days it was pretty cheap and easily available. "Did they take Ecstasy?"

"Nah."

It was like pulling teeth. "I'll do my best to protect you, but Brock's your friend and he's unconscious. Tell me what he's taken before it gets really dangerous."

"It's nothing dangerous." His voice broke on "dangerous," immediately declaring his age. "They just smoked some weed."

Just. The kid had no idea. "Your friends are greening out."

The boys looked at her blankly.

"It happens when you smoke dope after drinking a lot of booze. Bethany's hallucinating. Her body wants to get rid of the alcohol but the weed's stopping her from vomiting. Brock's so out of it he's in danger of choking. Did you drink and smoke dope too?"

"No. Just vodka."

Shane and Matt's shadows fell over them and the boys visibly shrank. Matt shoved the large first-aid backpack at Claire with unnecessary force and she almost toppled backwards.

Whipping it open, she grabbed the torch and handed it to him. "Hold this while I insert an IV. Shane, call an ambulance and track down Brock's and Bethany's parents."

"Will do," the policeman said. "Boys, come with me."

Claire tightened the tourniquet around Brock's arm and, blessedly, a healthy young vein popped up. Sliding the cannula into it, she withdrew the trocar and connected the IV. "He probably needs his stomach pumped but at least I can give them both fluids."

An hour later, Brock and Bethany were in an ambulance and on their way to Colac. Shane and Claire had spoken to all the teenagers at the disco before making sure each was picked up by an adult. Three young people had planned to walk home so Matt drove them, leaving Claire and Shane to tidy up and debrief.

"Where do you think they got the cannabis from?"

Shane was leaning against the kitchen sink, his big hands dwarfing a coffee mug. "There's always been a bit of cannabis in Myrtle. I've long suspected some of the tree-huggers have a plant at home for their personal use but unless they're driving under the influence, out on the street stoned or selling it, there's not much I can do. It's almost a tacit agreement between us that it stays at home and away from the kids."

"Are Brock Gillis's parents tree-huggers?"

"No. Neither are the parents of the other kids. It's unlikely he got it from home but never say never. I'll talk to the parents tomorrow. My gut tells me it's come in from outside town. I'll talk to the boys in Colac and the school principal. See what I can find out."

"This will put the wind up the community. I think I should run an information forum about drugs and alcohol for the teens."

"You should do one for the parents too. There's a lot of drinking going on out there." He sighed and set down his mug. "Since the fires, I've been called out to a lot of domestics."

"More than before?"

"Yeah. It's mostly angry blokes, but not always."

"The Uber's back." Matt stood in the doorway.

Shane clapped him on the shoulder. "Thanks for dropping those kids home, mate."

"Too easy." Matt looked at Claire, his gaze intense. "I'm heading home. You coming?"

She laughed. "Of course, I'm coming. How else would I get home?"

"For all I know, you and Shane are having a planning meeting to create even more work for yourselves." Matt's tone was unreasonably tight, like he was spoiling for a fight.

"Already done that, Matt," Shane said genially. "She's all yours."

"Is she? Good to know."

"You go, Claire," Shane said. "I'll lock up. Thanks for your help tonight."

"If you're sure ..."

"Bloody hell, Claire," Matt muttered. "You heard the man. Let's go."

She said goodnight, picked up her bag and walked silently with Matt to the parking lot. He handed her the car keys before swinging into the passenger seat.

The moment she'd steered the car onto the road and pointed it towards home, she said, "Did something happen when you were dropping off the kids?"

"Nope."

"You sure? You seem a bit out of sorts."

"Just tired."

She squeezed his thigh. "Thanks for being here tonight."

He turned on music before leaning his head back and shutting his eyes.

WHEN SHE CAME out of the master bathroom, their bedroom was unexpectedly dark. Not only had Matt turned off his bedside lamp, he hadn't lit hers like he usually did. She negotiated the room by memory and slipped under the covers before snuggling into his familiar warmth. As she kissed his exposed shoulder, she cheekily rested her cold feet on his calves.

"What a night."

She expected him to roll over and wrap his arms around her like he'd been doing since their first night together on the beach. Even during the traumatic and dark weeks straight after the fires, when they'd been existing in a haze of shock, he'd done it, although then he'd clung to her in desperation as if she might vanish at any moment. She'd done the same to him. Tonight though, he stayed facing away from her, his body eerily still.

"Matt?" Her hand crept over his hip. "You changed your mind about prime time?"

His hand swooped, fingers closing around her wrist and stalling her progress. He threw her arm away from him and sat up. Light flooded the room.

She blinked rapidly, forcing her pupils to adjust to the brightness. When Matt came into focus, his face was chiseled from stone.

"What's wrong? Do you feel sick?"

"Yeah, I do."

Matt was rarely ill. She sat up and pulled on her nightie, preparing to get what he needed from the medicine cabinet. "Throw-up sick or temperature sick?"

"Heart sick."

"It's heartbreaking that kids are writing themselves off like that. That's why it's important we—"

"That's *not* what's upsetting me."

Surprise trickled through her. "What then?"

"You."

"Me?" She recalled how short he'd been with her and Shane at the end of the night and his snarky remark about work. She sighed. "I'm sorry we got home ninety minutes later than we planned. I promise you've got my complete and undivided attention right now." She leaned in to kiss him.

His hands pressed firmly against her shoulders, holding her away from him. "Don't."

The unfamiliar growl in the word rumbled through her, climbing apprehensively along the length of her spine. "Tell me what's wrong."

"Like you don't know."

"I don't know and I don't read minds. Tell me."

"Fine." He crossed his arms. "Tonight, when I saw that kid on the ground and you told me to get the first-aid kit, I heard the worry in your voice. Not much bothers you and it rattled me. I wasn't thinking straight and when I got to the car, I did what I do in a farm vehicle: I opened the glove box to grab the kit. Thing is, I didn't find a first-aid kit. I found your birth control pills."

A tingling whoosh engulfed Claire's body. Her stomach contents rose to the back of her throat. Her blood drained to her feet. "I—"

"No! It's not your turn yet. At first I thought the pills must be your old ones but I couldn't work out why they'd be in the car. You always kept them next to the toothpaste so you remembered to take them. Then I turned the packet over. Today's pill was missing. And yesterday's pill and the last three weeks' worth, going by the broken foil. No wonder you're not freaking pregnant!"

Claire recoiled. If she'd been standing, the velocity of his hurt and anger would have knocked her off her feet. "I'm sorry."

"You're *sorry*? For what? That you're still on the pill? Or that I found out?"

Her hand tangled in the bedsheet as guilt and shame circled her determination not to get pregnant. "I'm sorry you found out this way."

"Hell, Claire. *That's* what you're sorry for?" His hands tore through his hair. "What about the fact you've been lying to me for months?"

"I didn't lie to you."

"And how do you figure that?"

"You never asked me if I'd stopped taking the pill."

"Oh, so you're lying by omission? That's even worse!"

"It's the same way you lied to me the night we met."

"It's nothing like it! And we dealt with that."

Claire stared unseeingly at her nightie-covered knees and said quietly and truthfully, "More than anything, I didn't want to upset you."

"Well, you got that wrong. Upset doesn't even come close to how I'm feeling. Try furious. No, try betrayed." His voice trembled. "I don't understand what the hell's going on. We agreed it was time to have a baby but you're actively making sure it doesn't happen."

This was the discussion she'd never wanted to have. She shouldn't be having it now—he never drove the clinic car so she'd thought it the ideal storage place.

"We didn't agree, Matt. You decided." Her tongue was thick and her mouth dry, making speech difficult.

"That's bullshit."

"It isn't. You didn't ask me if I was ready. You told me you were."

"I didn't need to ask. Kids have always been part of our five-year plan. You once told me that a wedding followed by babies was your idea of bliss. What the hell happened?"

His anguished confusion tore a corner of her heart. She gripped the bedsheet tighter. "I ... I've changed my mind."

"You've changed your mind? Why doesn't that surprise me? First, you changed your mind about getting married. I'm not thrilled about it but I respected your decision, because marriage is just a piece of paper. But now you don't want kids? What are you really saying, Claire? That we're over? That you're leaving me?"

"No! God, no. I love you." She reached for him frantically.

He blocked her touch. "I'm not sure I believe you."

"I love you. How can you doubt that? You know I fell in love with you the moment I met you."

"Well, you've got a hell of a way of showing it. What do they say? Actions speak louder than words."

If he needed action, she could give him action. "Let's get married."

"*Now* you want to get married?"

The thought of losing him made her light-headed. "Yes! You've always said anywhere, any time. All I had to do was say the word, so the word is yes. We'll need a new marriage license but if we apply tomorrow, we can get married in a month."

He stared at her, his face a sea of roiling emotions. "The thing is, Claire, if you don't want to have children, I don't think I want to marry you."

"What? Why?" Sharp pain pierced her and she hugged her knees. Anger followed. "Am I just a baby machine to you?"

With a jerk, he threw off the covers and pulled on his jeans. "I don't know what you are to me. Right now, I don't even recognize you."

"I'm the same person you fell in love with."

He stood at the foot of the bed shaking his head so hard his curls bounced. "No, you're not. My Claire wants babies. A family."

Just the thought sent panic spiraling through her. "We've got a good life, Matt. Fulfilling jobs. We're involved in our community, we're organizing Myrtle's family fun day. Can't that be enough?"

For a moment his face was as blank as if he'd had the sense knocked out of him. Then his face twisted in disgust. "God, I'm such a moron. This is about your bloody job, isn't it?"

It wasn't. But as she couldn't separate the complex strands that were her feelings about children, how could she even start to try to explain them to Matt? Over time, the threads had formed a hard lump inside her and nothing she did or tried shrank or shifted it. If anything, it continued to grow, sending out ominous tendrils that clawed at her until they twisted so tightly it was difficult to stand straight. She'd learned to ignore it, because if she ever actively thought about the snarling mess, she broke out in a cold sweat. It was easier for Matt to think it was her job.

"Despite what everyone's saying, Myrtle's still struggling. You were there tonight and that's just one example. I can't walk away when people need me."

His hands closed around the iron bed end, the skin white across his work-scarred knuckles. "You know, I was in awe of how you go out of your way to help people, but now, I don't know. Do people need this much help or do you need to help them? And if you do, where the hell does that leave me?"

"It doesn't leave you anywhere, Matt. I'm already yours."

"That's bullshit. You didn't even tell me you'd changed your mind about having kids."

"I wanted to tell you but I knew if I did you—"

"Wouldn't understand? You got that right." Not once since they'd met had he ever looked at her with such an unforgiving expression. "I need the truth, Claire. Are you saying you don't want kids until X date or you don't want kids at all?"

Dread bubbled in her chest, urging her to fudge the truth. "Matt, we love each other. Isn't that what counts?"

"You can't have love without trust. Right now, I'm not sure I can trust you, let alone your answer to my question. That's if you actually give me one."

"I'm just asking you to think about a new way of being together. Please."

"A new way?" His brow furrowed the way it did when he was confronted by a difficult problem. "We don't have kids now, so how will this be a new way? Hell, Claire. I've never thought of you as selfish before but perhaps Mom's right."

Matt's invocation of his mother sent Claire's stomach heaving. Bubbles of buried memories rose quickly and furiously to the surface— the night before their wedding.

In the twenty-one months since, Claire hadn't told anyone about the conversation she'd overheard between Matt and his mother. She'd never gotten the opportunity to tell her own mother and seek her advice, so she'd stayed silent. After the fires, when she and Matt had lived in the big house, he'd gone to great lengths to reassure her that his family *was* her family and around the time of her parents' funeral, she'd even believed it herself. It hadn't lasted. Matt, however, continued to tell her that Bill and Louise loved her like a daughter.

Except now Matt was quoting his mother at her.

"Mom's right. You're living your life without any consideration of me, the farm or the family."

"I'm not sure your mother's correct on that point. Think about it. We've come through the post-fire hell. Other couples didn't make it, but we did. We're still together. How could we have done that if I wasn't considerate of you, the farm and the family?"

"I think we've got a different definition of considerate."

"No, we don't. Matt, I love you. You love me. We belong together, you know we do." She crawled up the bed toward him. "We can be happy without children."

He was silent for five or six beats, his cheeks hollow. "That's where we differ. I don't think we can be happy without kids." He uncurled his fingers from the bed end and turned to the door.

"Where are you going?"

"Out."

Sheer terror engulfed her and the room spun. Matt was the one who always wanted to stay and talk things out when she just wanted time alone to think. Not once had he ever walked away from her.

"But you're coming back?"

His back stiffened but he didn't reply, nor did he stop walking. Stunned, she watched him and the dogs disappear from the room. It was only the sound of the front door slamming that converted his threat into reality.

"Banjo! Paterson!"

But there was no familiar clacking of nails on the floor. Matt had taken the dogs with him. The stifling silence of the new house pressed in on her and hot tears splashed down her face and soaked into the bedsheet.

This was why she'd never told him that she'd changed her mind about children.

CHAPTER FIFTEEN

THE DAY OF THE FIRES

Under a hot and blue December sky on the beach at Lorne, Bec was full of joyful anticipation. The surf rolled in gently and the girls were busy building a sand castle with a moat. Bec was trying to enjoy the latest blockbuster novel but she'd read the same page three times. She was too excited to concentrate.

The familiar sound of an arriving text gave her a tingle and made her fingers itch to swipe. Checking that the girls were still occupied, she hungrily read the words. *I love you. I will always love you, no matter what.*

Giddy with the happiness of being cherished and fizzing with exhilaration at the new chapter of her life that was about to begin, it wasn't until a news alert lit up her cell phone that the true and devastating meaning of "no matter what" hit her. *Please, God, no! No!* Her hand slapped her mouth, holding back the scream that assaulted her lips. Her knees jerked to her chest. Agony rocked her; the pain eviscerating.

The ABC news declared an out-of-control wildfire—an inferno— had engulfed Myrtle. Grave fears were held for property, livestock and people's safety. Beside herself with fear, Bec made frantic call after frantic call but none connected. When her cell phone finally rang, her shaking fingers almost disconnected the incoming call from Matt Holsworthy.

The CFA captain's voice was hoarse. "I'm sorry, Bec. It's not good news."

Adam was neither dead nor very alive.

It wasn't the news she wanted. In that moment, Bec's life changed in ways her own actions could never have precipitated.

BEC COULDN'T REMEMBER EXACTLY how or when she'd arrived at the hospital and she didn't care. There'd been road blocks and police cars and changing arrangements but none of it mattered. Nothing mattered when a nightmare of unfathomable dimensions had caught her up in its web.

After listening to the doctors outline the extent of Adam's brutal injuries, Bec sat alone in the relatives' waiting room. The debilitating pain that had struck her on the beach the previous afternoon had changed to numbness. She welcomed the way it dulled the full ramifications of the tragedy: she was still Adam's wife.

Adam was a hero and the wife of a hero had a duty to stay by his side when he was fighting for his life. The mother of his children had a duty to stay and show strength—reassure them that some of the familiar anchors in their lives were still holding fast despite almost everything else going to hell around them. She understood she must do everything in her power not to betray her daughters or risk losing their love and trust.

The medical staff, the media, Adam's family, the girls—everyone was looking to her for decisions. She craved to be left alone, to curl up into a ball and grieve, but her needs and wants had been annulled.

When Scotty arrived at the hospital, he'd badgered the staff until they'd allowed him to see her. To see Adam. Scotty's usually healthy glow was replaced by a pallor tinged with bilious yellow. His chest rose and fell fast, his breathing as ragged as if he'd just run up a steep hill instead of walking down a flat corridor. Raising his big hands to the glass, he peered and squinted, trying to find Adam's prone and charred body amid the state-of-the-art medical equipment.

He swore softly. "How is he still alive?"

"Adam hates to lose."

"Yeah." Scotty turned away before slumping into a chair and burying his face in his hands. His normally square shoulders slouched and his work-toned body shrank in on itself, as though the flames had shriveled him. Patches of his skin glowed pink, as if the sunscreen had missed those areas. The sight cracked the numbness inside Bec. She reached out and rested her hand on his shoulder, needing to touch him. Needing to be touched in return. She squeezed, her fingers barely denting the firm muscle under his T-shirt.

"It should have been me." His hands muffled his voice. "He should have been at Lorne with you."

"No." It was an automatic response but Bec recognized the truth in both his statements. "You know Adam never comes to Lorne if there's outstanding jobs and he expects the same from his employees."

Scotty raised his head, his face stricken. "It's so screwed up."

"I know."

"Thank God you and the girls weren't in town."

Her mouth dried with a cocktail of guilt and relief. Why had she been spared when others were so badly injured? *Dead.*

"I owe him everything, Bec."

The idea of Scotty owing Adam anything crushed her. "No, Scotty. You don't."

"I do. He risked his life to save me and Trav."

"What I don't understand is why you were even at the vineyard? That wasn't part of the plan."

He grimaced. "The weather changed everything. Our golf game was canceled when Adam got the callout from the CFA. You know he left the truck to rescue us? I screamed at him to leave. He said he was coming. I thought he was right behind us." His shoulders shook. "I should've checked. I should have gone back."

"Shh," she soothed, despite knowing it was useless. "This isn't your fault. It's not mine and it's not yours. It's no one's fault."

"I don't believe that."

"I do." The lie fell easily, taking its place on top of the pile of deceptions she'd been telling for months.

"All I know is, I can't leave now."

Her heart flung itself against her ribcage. Surely one of them got to stick to the original plan and get what they wanted? "You can. You must."

"I owe the bugger."

"No!" She heard her fear and worked to speak calmly. "You don't."

He looked at her, his clear blue gaze filming with unshed tears. "Yeah, I do. Can't you see? Think about it. You know this has changed everything. I've gotta stay. Run the business so he's got something to come back to."

A wail of lost dreams caught in her throat. Trapped—like her.

THE PRESENT

Bec's work for the CWA and her Thursdays kept her sane. Her love for Thursday was new but that didn't lessen her affection for it. Thursday meant freedom—it was the only day of the week she had the house to herself. More importantly, she could leave it whenever she wished as long as her absence fell between the hours of nine and three. She'd learned to bank the exuberance that filled her, knowing she needed to eke it out and make it last a full seven days. But as she re-read the email on her cell phone, all traces of happiness rapidly drained out of her, replaced by the stinging needle pricks of anxiety.

As we discussed at parent-teacher conference, Ivy has become increasingly withdrawn in class and in the playground. Over the last few months, I've asked her often if there is anything bothering her at home or at school. She insists she's "all good." I disagree. I'm concerned about Ivy and feel she would benefit from seeing a psychologist. Although she could see the visiting school psychologist, there is long a waiting list. I have attached the names of some recommended child psychologists in Colac and Geelong ...

Bec pressed the button on her cell phone, locking the screen, as if the action would banish the problem. Part of her was pleased the teacher was validating her worries about Ivy, but another part didn't want to have to deal with it. Although Adam thrived on challenges at work, he wanted everything problem-free and picture perfect at home. Perhaps the solution was to take Ivy to the psychologist and not mention it to Adam?

Logistics streamed through her mind. School hours on a Thursday were the only time she could easily leave Myrtle so traveling to Geelong was out. She hoped there was a psychologist in Colac who worked on Thursdays. At least if Adam asked where she was going she could tell him she was visiting her mother. A jab of pain caught her under the ribs. Damn it! To cover that lie, she'd have to tell her mother and these days she avoided telling her mother anything other than a fabricated version of her life.

Just your mother?

Bec batted away the thought. Even before the fires, if she'd ever complained to her mother about Adam or criticized him, she'd been lashed by disapproval. Now, with Adam's hero status set in stone—there was even talk of erecting a small statue of him in the park—Bec didn't risk saying anything negative. If she did, it incited one of her mother's rants, and no matter how hard Bec tried to ignore the invective, it invariably landed a blow that left her bleeding.

"When your father abandoned us, I struggled to put food on the table but you ..." A red-painted fingernail would point accusingly at Bec. "Your husband is a rich and generous man. He bought me this house. He visits me without being asked. You, my own daughter, don't do this. Adam worships you and the girls. He gives you everything your heart desires, but are you happy? No! You sit here and complain he won't let you stand up all day and cut people's hair. Pah! Why do you want to work instead of supporting his business that gives you everything? You're spoilt and ungrateful. This nonsense must stop."

At least this psychologist plan meant her mother would appreciate her visits. *Hah!* Her mother preferred Adam's visits over Bec's because he always came bearing gifts. It occurred to Bec that for the plan to work, she'd have to ask Ivy not to mention to Adam she was missing school on Thursdays. Was that a problem? No. Unlike Gracie, Ivy generally tried to avoid upsetting her father.

Oh God! If she asked Ivy to fudge the truth about missing school on Thursdays, she'd have to involve Gracie in the lie as well and Gracie was a loose cannon with secrets. Bec's temples throbbed at the mounting details required to execute the deception just so her daughter could see a counselor. Given the way Ivy had been behaving lately, she might refuse to go.

Hot tears stung Bec's eyes. Once subterfuge and planning had been exhilarating. Now, like so much of her life, it was just another task that dragged at her. That and this endless fatigue. She should probably have a check-up.

A loud thump startled her and she jumped. Had Adam forgotten something? Worse—did he need her to do something? Usually on a Thursday she dropped the girls off at school and then kept going, avoiding returning to the house until after lunch, but that morning Adam had unexpectedly offered to do the school run.

"Relax, babe. Enjoy your Thursday," he'd said before squeezing her butt and kissing her cheek. "You deserve it."

Had that been code for, "I'm coming back"? That he'd want sex? Since his lingerie gift, he'd been keen on lunchtime matinees. She reminded herself it was only 9.15. Still, the day before she'd seen him holding a plain box not dissimilar to the one the lingerie had arrived in. When she'd asked him about it, his good eye had twinkled at her. "Don't go spoiling the surprise."

Surprises no longer gave her any joy or delight.

She heard another thump and glanced down at her spring capri pants and plain white blouse. Her heart rate sped up. Thursday was her one dress-free day of the week. Well, it was between the hours of eight and four when Adam was guaranteed to be out of the house. This was when she wore her favorite clothes—the few articles she'd chosen for herself. Before the fires, Adam had always preferred her in a dress but he'd tolerated trousers. Since the fires, he hated her in pants, including functional panties.

If Adam saw her dressed like this there was a risk his temper would ignite. She sucked in a deep breath—she'd pretend she wasn't home.

You nong! Your car's in the garage.

Slipping off her shoes, she ran across the plush carpet, slowing at the stairs to carefully but quietly make her way to her walk-in closet. She stripped with speed, her clothes falling in a heap at her feet, and grabbed the new bra and panties set Adam had bought her the week before, after he'd decided her bras were too boring. Then she slipped a long-sleeved dress over her head. She checked her watch. It had taken her less than three minutes and in that time the intercom hadn't buzzed. Perhaps Adam really had just called in to grab something before leaving again.

Her hammering heart slowed. Catching sight of herself in the mirror, she saw her irises were almost obliterated by huge black discs and her cheeks glowed pink. How the hell did anxiety make her look this good? Shoving her feet into heels, she walked downstairs and straight to the office. She stopped short in the doorway. Scotty stood in front of a filing cabinet, his long fingers rifling through the files. He glanced up, his eyes soft and warm and then he gave the smile he'd been giving her since Adam came home from the hospital. Cautious. Tinged with regret.

It represented with excruciating accuracy everything the fires had stolen from them.

"Bloody hell, Scotty!"

"Hi, Bec. You okay? You look a bit steamed."

"That's because I am. You just gave me a fright."

"Sorry. How?"

"It's Thursday!"

"Yeah." He rolled the filing cabinet closed and rested a hip on the corner of the desk. "Help me out with the significance of that?"

All the adrenaline that had been whizzing around her body since she'd heard the noise in the office made her dizzy. As she sat down, fatigue rushed her, dousing her anger. Foolishness immediately followed.

"Adam doesn't use the office on Thursdays."

He laughed. "Surely you didn't think I was an intruder? This is Myrtle."

Bec wasn't going to admit to him that she'd thought he was Adam. "I don't know what I thought, but I was scared. If you call in without Adam, start using the intercom, okay?"

"Sure." He sounded his normal and accommodating self but a flash of something akin to hurt flickered in his eyes.

Bec couldn't worry about it. She couldn't add it to her increasing stack of concerns or she might collapse under the weight.

Scotty sat down next to her. "How are things?"

"Good." Lying came easily these days.

"I reckon this Putting Myrtle on the Map project must almost be a full-time job. It'd be great if we got a couple more shops out of it. What do you reckon about a book store and a gift shop?"

She suddenly saw him through a red haze. "Perfect. Seeing as you sold me down the river on the hair salon, why don't you suggest to Adam I run a gift shop instead?" It was an unfair crack directed at the wrong man, but she couldn't find a way to say sorry.

His mouth twisted but he didn't look away. "How are the girls?"

Ivy's struggling and I don't know why. Gracie's stubbornness is wearing me out. "Fine."

"It's me, Bec."

She glared at him. The gap the fire had burned through their lives was widened by her frustration with him for turning his back on his chance to leave Myrtle. She'd stopped asking him months ago why he'd become a business partner and shackled himself to Adam instead of taking his chance to free himself when her husband had returned to full-time work.

Why couldn't he see that his care and growth of the business while Adam was in the hospital was enough to repay his debt? Only, she knew the answer. One glimpse of Adam's disfiguring scars would render all her arguments void. Instead, they played this restrained game of polite chit-chat.

"How are things with you, Scotty?"

"Good."

"Loving your work, are you?"

"Don't, Bec. Please. We did what we had to do. Besides, business is booming. Adam's happy. There are worse things ..."

Are there? She blinked rapidly, not wanting to cry because it changed nothing. All it did was thin her unravelling resilience to threadbare, leaving her vulnerable and less able to cope with Adam. With the girls. Her post-fire life.

She changed the subject to something safer. "Thanks for creating a job for Josh Doherty."

Scotty's tense demeanor relaxed and he shot her a smile. "No worries. He's a top bloke."

"When I asked Adam if he could find Josh a job, he said he didn't need a bloke whose experience was factory work and logging pine trees."

"I got him in to do a few jobs for me. Now Adam's gone and poached him for a special project."

Scotty sounded pissed off with Adam, which both surprised and heartened her. It was about time. "What special project?"

"You know the rules. Adam loves the grand gesture and the big announcement. I'm not raining on his parade."

"I promise I'll fake surprise."

"Just in case you don't, I'm not telling you." Scotty stood. "Any chance of a coffee? I ran out yesterday and forgot to buy some."

The last time Scotty had asked her for coffee had been the day before Adam was discharged from the rehabilitation hospital. At the time, she hadn't realized it would be his last coffee invitation or the last time they'd be alone together.

His request caught her off guard but good memories won out over a flash of spite. "Come into the kitchen and I'll make us both one."

While she brewed him an espresso, Scotty chatted easily as if he sat at her counter every day. He told her about the house plans he'd had drawn up.

"I've built enough houses for other people to know what I do and don't want."

"In a house," she muttered.

He let out a long breath, his exasperation clinging to it. "Yes, Bec. In a *house*."

"Is this why we don't talk anymore?" she teased, hoping to reverse her mistake and return to keeping things light. But his smile dimmed and suddenly she didn't want to hear his reply. "Show me the plans."

He brought them up on his cell phone and she envied the simplicity and functionality of the design. Scotty was building the sort of home she'd once dreamed of living in. "Wow! With those fully retractable frameless glass doors, you'll bring the outside in."

"That's the plan."

"What's the plan?"

Startled, they looked up to see Adam standing in the kitchen. Scotty straightened, leaving his cell phone on the counter.

"I'm showing Bec the latest design for Woollambah."

"You're just in time for coffee." She didn't comment on his unexpected arrival.

Adam's gaze took in the two empty coffee cups and his eyes narrowed. "Looks like I'm just a bit late."

"No, mate," Scotty said easily. "Bang on time. By the way, you were right about the Luxton figures. They don't add up."

Bec wanted to ask, "What about the Luxton figures?", but she knew if she did Adam would just tell her to let him worry about the business, so she stuck to the topic of Scotty's house plans. "I think the design you guys came up with for Woollambah is fantastic. Will the glass doors be a challenge to install?"

Scotty laughed. "They'll be more of a challenge for my bank balance."

Adam threw him a loaded look. "You can afford them. We're set for another record-breaking quarter."

Scotty dropped his gaze to his cell phone. "I'll be happier when we rent all the Myrtle shops."

"My clever wife's on the job with Put Myrtle on the Map, aren't you, babe?"

Bec smiled, appreciating the praise. "That reminds me, I need you to approve the Petrovic Family Homes banner Erica's designed for the website."

"Show me in half an hour. First I'm looking over the Luxton figures. Those bastards. Did they really think they could put one over me?"

"They'd be fools to try it again," Scotty said, following Adam to the office.

BEC OPENED the laptop on the kitchen counter with the internet browser ready on the mocked-up website. So much for Adam's promise of her relaxing Thursday—she was yet to leave the house, taking longer than half an hour with Scotty. As the clock ticked toward eleven, she was hedging her bets and preparing lunch just in case Adam decided to eat before doing his site visits. She'd just plated a slice of chocolate cake when she heard voices, the click of a door and then the diesel throb of Scotty's ute.

Adam walked into the kitchen and rested his hip against the curve of the kitchen counter before reaching for an apple from the fruit bowl. He tossed it into the air like a cricket ball then caught it. He'd spent hours doing something similar with a stress ball as part of the occupational therapy for his hands.

"Got it sorted?" she asked.

"You could say that."

"Great. I'll show you the banner." She rested her forearms on the counter and touched the laptop's trackpad.

"You weren't expecting me to come home, were you?"

Intent on the screen and concentrating on moving the mouse into position, she said absently, "You don't usually on a Thursday."

"Is that when Scotty visits?"

A warning prickle raced across her skin. She looked him straight in the eye. "Apart from today, Scotty's never in the office when you're not here."

"I don't believe you."

"I don't have any reason to lie."

"Is that so." He pushed off the counter. "When I was in the hospital, Scotty ran the business. He was in the office then."

"And I was with you in Melbourne."

"Not every day. You looked pretty cozy leaning over his cell phone with your tits at eye level. Hoping to get lucky, were you?"

A spark of indignant anger flared. "No! And if my cleavage was showing, it's your fault. Every dress you bought has a neckline like this."

"Yeah, I bought them for me, not him." He moved in behind her and whipped up her full skirt.

"Adam!" Her hands clawed at the material, trying to pull it back down. "What are you doing?"

"Looky here. You're wearing your fuck-me underwear." He pressed her body between the counter and his torso, his breath hot on her ear. "Well, Scotty's gone but as you're obviously gagging for it, let me help you out."

"I'm not gagging for it at eleven in the morning! And I'm only wearing this underwear because you want me to." She tried to turn and face him but as her shoulders lifted, they hit his chest. He'd pinned her with no room to turn. Stuck facing forward, she said as calmly as she could, "Adam, I don't want to have sex with Scotty. Ever."

"Good. That's what I wanted to hear."

Her anxiety let go in a long whoosh. "Can I show you the banner now? As soon as you've approved it, the website can go live."

Adam didn't step away—he moved in closer. The rounded edge of the granite now pressed painfully into her belly and she heard the metallic sound of his fly opening. Then his erect penis was pressing hard between her legs.

"What are you doing?"

"What do you think?"

She squirmed, trying to shift away from his persistent efforts. "Adam, don't."

"That's the way. Play hard to get."

"I don't want to play anything."

"Come on, Bec. Don't be a spoilsport."

Was she being a spoilsport? As she wrestled with the thought, his hands grabbed her breasts. Normally this wasn't a problem but today hot pain twisted through her and she flinched so violently the momentum threw her back against him, grinding her behind into his crotch.

"That's more like it. Keep going, pretend you don't want it."

"I'm not pretending, Adam. I don't want it."

"Cock tease."

"I'm begging you to stop."

"Keep begging." His breath grazed her ear.

"Adam, please!"

"Good, you're getting into it." He gripped her neck and pushed her down, bending her over the counter. "Just remember, you're mine."

With her cheek pressed hard against the cold granite, her gaze locked on the computer screen and the red and white Petrovic Family Homes banner.

Family values. Family-friendly prices. Family first.

She closed her eyes.

CHAPTER SIXTEEN

JOSH TOOK A BITE OUT OF HIS PEANUT BUTTER ROLL AS SCOTTY'S ute pulled up in a spray of gravel. He gave the builder a wave as he approached.

"Hey, Josh. What are you doing here? Shouldn't you be working on the Beckwith site?"

"Adam texted and said he needed me here."

Scotty frowned as he joined Josh on the bench. "Right... Is this late break or early lunch?"

"Bit of both. I missed breakfast." Josh didn't tell him that Sophie had left early for a breakfast meeting and the change in the morning routine had thrown the kids, making them particularly difficult. Both had balked at going to daycare. Liam's initial truculence and refusal to walk into preschool had developed into chest-heaving sobbing, setting off Trixie. By the time the teacher had levered Liam off Josh's legs and the childcare worker had lifted Trixie out of his arms, sweat was trickling down his neck despite the cold.

"Breakfast's the most important meal of the day, mate." Scotty pulled a packet of cigarettes out of his pocket and offered him one.

Josh shook his head, feeling the grip of cravings. "I gave 'em up when Liam was born. Figured I owed the kid not to get sick."

"Wise move." Scotty shoved the pack back in his pocket. "I've tried giving up a few times."

"Yeah. Me too. What about the patches?"

"Seems weak."

"Nah, mate. Nicotine's a bastard. Harder to give up than dope."

"You don't want to get into that," Scotty said.

"It can be good." It had stopped the terrifying images of fire and flames. It had quieted the noise in his head taking it from shrieking terror to a dull roar of unease. "After the fires, it helped me sleep. Then Sophie found my stash and went ballistic. Made me promise I wouldn't use it."

Scotty scratched the back of his hand. "Women, eh? Can't live with 'em, can't live without 'em. You got much left to do here?"

"Two hours, tops." Josh glanced behind him at the long, white-plastic-covered greenhouse and finally asked the question that had been begging to be voiced from the moment he'd started this job. "Why are builders growing tomatoes?"

"This is Adam's baby, not mine. Now the vineyard's gone, this is his new plan while he waits for the rezoning. The way he tells it, the tomatoes are a combination of utilizing assets and helping Myrtle."

"I don't get it."

"Tomatoes are a fast crop and they'll be a shot in the arm for the summer farmers market and the Put Myrtle on the Map gig."

"Does he know anything about growing tomatoes?"

"Travis is the man."

"Travis? You've gotta be kidding?" Josh thought Travis was a sandwich short of a picnic.

Scotty laughed. "He's no rocket scientist but he knows plants."

"Fair enough."

Scotty fell silent and stared out across the plowed under vineyard. The old stand of Monterey pines that had provided shelter from the wind and privacy from the road hadn't survived the fires. Cut down and with the roots grubbed out, they'd been replaced by three rows of gums and a pittosporum hedge that did a fair job of blocking the wind and the view of the quiet gravel road.

The story of how Adam had risked his own life to save his employees was entrenched in Myrtle folklore. Josh wondered if being on the property ever bothered Scotty or Adam. Lately, Josh hated being on his block of land. It wasn't just the specter of the naked slab taunting him about his inability to provide a home for his family, it was also those moments when, despite the air being crisp, clean and cold, the acrid smell of smoke filled his nostrils and the roar of the fire throbbed in his ears.

The raucous laugh of a kookaburra shattered the silence. Scotty sighed. "Better get back to work. As soon as you're done here, I need you on the Beckwith job until further notice. Okay?"

"More than okay, mate." Josh preferred working for Scotty over Adam, although he couldn't exactly put his finger on why. Mind you, given what he'd put up with over the last three days, it might have something to do with working with Travis rather than working for Adam.

As if Adam knew Josh was thinking about him, the man walked out of the massive greenhouse and came toward them with a wave.

Scotty slid to his feet. "G'day, Adam."

"Scotty-boy. What brings you out here?"

"Just telling Josh we need him at the Beckwith site by two."

"No can do. I need Josh here."

A muscle twitched in Scotty's cheek. "I need him over there."

Adam shook his head. "Take the new apprentice."

"We agreed he wasn't ready."

Josh glanced between the two men, wondering at the tension, but enjoying the sensation of not only being needed but being argued over. "Can I do both jobs?"

"Listen to him." Adam laughed and slapped Josh on the back. "This is why you're our best worker and why I've decided to erect the frame on your house pro bono."

Josh stared blankly at Adam. "Are you serious?"

"Scotty, tell Josh I never joke about business."

The builder looked at his boots and shoved his hands into his pockets. "If Adam's offering to frame your house, he's serious."

"Damn straight," Adam said. "You pay for the materials, work with us to erect the frame and chuck in some beers for the boys. Sound like a deal?"

"Hell, yeah!" It sounded like a miracle.

"Good. Go ahead and order the frame and then sort out a build date with Scotty."

Josh was horrified to feel the prickle of tears—confused to feel them—and he blinked rapidly. Damn it! This was good news. Awesome news. He should be laughing and punching the air, not freaking sniffling like a girl.

Adam glanced at his watch then looked at Scotty. "Haven't you got that meeting about the Beckwith slab?"

"About that ..." Scotty glanced at Josh and then back at Adam. "It'd be—"

"You better get moving or I'll have Louis haranguing me about bloody tradesmen with no sense of time."

"Yeah." Scotty still hesitated, rocking on his feet and looking like he wanted to say something more. Eventually, he turned and jogged to the ute.

Pure excitement poured through Josh, steamrolling his previous rush of emotion. He shoved out his hand. "Thanks, Adam. Jeez, thanks doesn't sound enough. Thanks for the work. For this. For everything."

Adam accepted the handshake. "No worries. You're a handy bloke to have around. In fact, you're handier than I thought. Travis tells me you're an electrician. Why the hell didn't you mention it?"

Josh shrugged. "I'm not certified. I only told Travis because he was about to cut a live wire with the circular saw."

"Two bricks short of a load that one, but his heart's in the right place. Lucky you were there to stop him frying himself. Did you finish your apprenticeship?"

"I did all the technical college stuff. Just didn't finish my time."

"Right. But you can install the greenhouse lighting?"

"Yeah, but you'd have to get one of the other electricians to sign off on it."

"Not a problem. Start on it now and as soon as you've finished the wiring you can give Travis a hand planting the seedlings."

"Too easy." He knew absolutely nothing about planting anything but if Travis could do it, he'd pick it up fast enough.

"Good, and none of those half-assed four-hour days Scotty's had you doing. I need you working full time."

"Sure. No problem." Josh wasn't about to say no to the man who'd just offered to frame the house for free. He'd worry about childcare later.

SOPHIE THREW her arms around Josh's neck. "Oh my God, I can't believe it. It's almost too good to be true."

"I know, right?" Josh grinned widely, looking happier than she'd seen him in months.

Excitement leaped and twirled in her belly. "Do you think it might continue? Not just the job but the free build? I mean if it does, we could have a house by this time next year." *I could give up work and have another baby.*

"If it does, the house will be finished earlier than that," Josh said.

She ran on the spot, squealing. "If there's ongoing electrical work, you should ask if you can finish your apprenticeship with Petrovic Family Homes."

His mouth tightened. "Don't get ahead of yourself. This is just an emergency job cos the other sparkies are busy."

She couldn't understand why Josh was so pessimistic all the time. Petrovic Family Homes had kept the odd jobs coming consistently for three months. Why was he expecting them to stop now? Especially when Adam was increasing his hours. "Please be happy."

"I am happy." Josh twisted the top off a beer and tossed it into the trash with the same skill he'd used to shoot baskets. "Want one of your girly drinks?"

"Sorry, I have to run. CWA meeting."

He grunted and took a long drink.

She eyed the beer. Now money wasn't quite as tight, Josh had taken to drinking a few beers each night after work before crashing into a fitful sleep. "Don't celebrate too much without me," she said, aiming for light and breezy. Then she cupped his face with both hands and kissed him long and deep, welcoming the thick throb of desire pumping around her body.

Josh tensed against her. "I thought you were going out."

Trying her best to be sultry and sexy, she said softly, "That was just a promise. We'll celebrate properly when I get home."

He stepped back fast, as if she'd scorched him, then he turned on the TV. "It's been a big day. I'll probably be asleep when you get home."

It would have stung less if he'd slapped her. Parts of her curled up, wanting to hide, but others came out punching, desperate to conceal the pain of rejection. How dare he do this to her now, when for the first time in close to two years they had something to celebrate?

She picked up her iPad, hugging it close to her chest like a shield. "Zoom your mom and dad. They'll want to know the good news."

He didn't respond and she tapped her foot. "Josh? Did you hear me?"

"Yeah." He didn't turn away from the TV. "Zoom."

"And put the bloody bottles in the bin before you go to bed." She stomped out of the shed and gunned the car to the CWA.

With her mind still racing and her stomach churning, Sophie walked into the meeting room early.

"Hi, Sophie."

"Oh! Claire. Hi." She hadn't expected anyone else to have arrived, let alone Claire. The nurse looked different, but Sophie couldn't quite put a finger on why. It was probably something to do with her hair. Or maybe it was eye makeup?

Claire frowned. "Are you okay? You sound a bit flat."

"Oh, you know. It's always a rush to get here. My head's still at home."

"How's Josh?"

Sophie's cheeks burned. Why had she told the group about their sex life—or to be precise, their lack of a sex life? Especially Claire, who seemed to have a hyper-alertness for detecting everyone's problems even when she was off duty. Despite Bec telling Sophie that Adam's burns hadn't impacted their sex life, Sophie had been hoping that Claire's comment about stress being a possible reason for Josh's lack of interest might actually have merit.

Unfortunately, what had happened at home earlier had categorically destroyed that theory. Sophie's breath caught on the unassailable truth. Even with great news to celebrate, Josh wasn't attracted to her.Not wanting to acknowledge that fact and desperately needing a temporary escape from everything she hated about her life, she remembered something she'd read online: how a fake smile could generate happy feelings. She twitched her lips up, feeling the tight stretch, and answered Claire.

"Actually, we got some great news today. The frame's going up on the house."

"That's fantastic!"

"What's fantastic?" Erica tumbled through the door minus her usual red woolen coat. The evening was almost balmy compared with winter's raw and bitter bite. "Tell me! I love good news."

"Josh is working more hours now and even though I still have to sort out extra childcare, the huge news is we've ordered the frame for the house."

"Woo-hoo!" Erica high-fived her. "That's awesome. I'm sure between Layla and me, we can help with the kids until you find something more permanent." She turned to Layla, who'd come in behind her. "Right, Layla?"

"Yes. Malik loves playdates."

Sophie chewed her lip, feeling a little overwhelmed by their enthusiasm and generosity. "Are you sure? It's a big ask."

"I can help too," Julie offered, giving Sophie a congratulatory shoulder squeeze. "We'll draw up a roster to cover you until you've sorted things out."

"I think I'm going to cry."

"No need for that." Erica hugged her. "Oh! Nathan was given a box of champagne last week, the real stuff. Promise me you'll call the moment the frame's up. I'll bring a couple of bottles over to celebrate."

Long embarrassed by her living conditions, Sophie hadn't invited any of the women to the shed. But for some reason the idea of them visiting to celebrate the frame was suddenly very appealing. "That would be amazing. Thank you."

"In lieu of booze, this calls for a cup of tea right now." Claire flicked teabags into cups.

Bec's eyes flashed like police lights. "We do supper at the end of the meeting."

"Live a little, Rebecca." Claire whipped plastic wrap off a plate and offered everyone a piece of lemon slice. "I baked! I must have known we'd be celebrating."

"You never cook," Bec said tartly. "What seismic shift took place in your life?"

Sophie expected Claire to do her usual dramatic eye roll at the comment, but she caught a momentary flicker of something cross the nurse's face. Distress? No. That didn't make any sense. Even in her own straitened financial circumstances, she'd cheerfully risk money betting that Claire got a buzz out of sparring with Bec and went out of her way to deliberately bait her.

Claire's chin rose. "Of course, I cook. I just don't compete."

Bec mumbled something about being an expert competitor in the game of disregarding the rules before refusing a square of slice. Tonight, their president was as beautifully dressed as ever but despite the cheery bright watermelon pink of her dress, she looked pale. Not even her carefully applied makeup could completely hide the angry red dot of a pimple, and black shadows smudged the delicate skin under her eyes.

Her face seemed puffy. Actually, all of Bec looked a little bloated and her dress fitted just a little too snugly. Sophie couldn't help the fizz of schadenfreude that bubbled happily through her. She was all too familiar with the monthly pre-period liter of hateful fluid. It was almost comforting to know that beautiful women with close to perfect lives got it too.

Sophie sat next to Bec. "Before we start, I want to thank you."

"Thank me? What for?"

Sophie laughed, embarrassed, but appreciating the joke of Bec feigning ignorance about something so monumentally significant to her and Josh. "You know why. For the free framing of our house. It's only happening because of you." She squeezed her hand. "I don't know how we're ever going to thank you enough."

Bec gave her a slightly confused look before her forehead smoothed and she smiled. "Nonsense. Adam and I feel it's important to give back to the community especially—"

Bec glanced over at the other women, her face tight.

Claire was laughing a little too loudly at something Erica had said and her eyes looked dark and large in her flushed face. If it had been anyone else, Sophie would have said they'd downed a couple of drinks before the meeting.

Bec looked back at Sophie. "Your support as secretary means a lot."

"I didn't expect to enjoy doing this job on top of work and the kids and—" *All the crap with Josh.* "—and everything, but I love it. I'll wrangle this lot into order so we can start."

"Thanks." Bec straightened her agenda papers, laid her pen horizontal to the piece of A4 and then shifted her glass of water so it lined up with the right-hand edge of the paper.

"I know some people think I'm too focused on protocol but if Put Myrtle on the Map is going to be a success and not an unmitigated disaster, we've got a lot to get through. If everyone thought the rules didn't apply to them, we'd have anarchy."

When the meeting started, Layla outlined the food-truck vendors who'd applied to attend. "Our theme is street food from around the world. We have Turkish. There is pizza and curry and Korean twisted potato on a stick. I don't know this potato but my husband says it's delicious."

"Do we need a vegetarian option that isn't deep-fried potato?" Bec asked.

"Curry can be vegetarian," Erica said.

"There's a vegetarian restaurant in Geelong. I think they have a van." Claire's fingers flew across her cell phone's screen. "I've sent you the details, Layla. Also, what about inviting the Timboon ice-cream van? Everyone loves ice cream."

"Good idea," Julie said. "Did the Nguyens talk to you about a coffee cart? I hope they can manage to get one, because we need the few businesses we have in town benefitting from the day."

"If they can't, it's not a huge walk from the park to the bakery. We can put up signs with directions." Sophie added sandwich boards to her equipment list.

Bec tapped her pen. "Claire, you've got a big job. Are you and Matt on top of all the family fun activities?"

"Yes!" Claire snapped. "Why wouldn't we be? When I say I'll do something, Rebecca, I get the job done."

"In that case, I'll take your rude reply as a no to what was an offer of help."

"Oh! That reminds me," Erica said, slapping her palm against her forehead. "I knew there was something I was going to text Claire about. I know you're keen to do the plastic duck race in the creek, but a friend in the UK told me about her village's teddy-bear drop. I thought it might be something different."

"Unlike other people—" Claire's eyes flashed at Bec "—I'm open to new and different ideas. What's a teddy-bear drop and how does it work?"

"People make and decorate a parachute and attach it to their bear. Then the teddies are dropped off the church's bell tower and the bear that lands closest to the target wins."

"Erica." Claire's voice was unusually soft but it sliced through the air with terrifying menace. "Have you failed to notice that all the churches in town burned to the ground?"

"Of course not! I was thinking we could use the fire tower."

Claire flinched and looked away. "Right ..."

Erica's cheeks flamed pink and she gripped the edge of the table tightly as if that would keep her seated. "I get that when we first met I waded in feet first, but you know what? Over these last few months, I've listened and learned. I resent your inference that I'm so thoughtless!

"Of course I've noticed the burnt-out churches. When I walk the girls to school, we pass the corner where All Saints stood. Every time I see the pile of blue-stone rubble, I ache. It was such a pretty church."

Claire was staring intently at her hands as if they were something new and surprising to her. "It had beautiful stained glass windows. They were donated by the Pendergasts in memory of their sons. They both died in the Great War, blown up by mines," she said almost absently. "The windows would have shattered first. Then the fire would have licked the pews, and consumed the cross-stitched cushions before storming the altar."

A sound erupted from her—a noise that no one who knew her well could mistake for a laugh. "And to think we'd all been worried about the damage termites were causing to the rood screen."

"You're right. It was a very pretty church," Julie said hurriedly, throwing a concerned look at Claire. "I got married there and so did my daughter."

Erica's face lit up with interest. "What about you, Bec?"

Bec shook her head. "No, we're neither Anglican or Catholic. I got married in Geelong."

"I got married in Melbourne but not in a church," Sophie added quickly, deliberately colluding with Julie to take the focus off Claire.

"What about you, Claire?"

Sophie opened her mouth to divert the question by asking Erica where she and Nathan got married but Claire spoke first.

"Matt and I aren't married."

"What? But ..." Confusion rushed across Erica's round face. "You wear a wedding ring."

"It's my mother's wedding ring." Claire twisted it along with her engagement ring. "She died in the fires."

"I'm so sorry," Erica said. "That must have been hard."

"Yeah." The word sailed out on a long sigh. "Still is."

"Is that why you and Matt haven't got married yet?"

Claire jerked in her chair, turning sharply toward Bec. She tapped her pen hard and fast on the table, the staccato sound drilling into the heavy air of the room. "Earth to Madam Chair. Isn't it time you pulled this meeting back on track?"

Sophie braced herself for yet another terse exchange, but when Bec spoke her tone was light.

"Oh, so now you want to invoke the rules?"

At first, Sophie thought Claire was blinking in surprise at Bec's unexpected teasing but when it continued, she realized the nurse was fighting back tears.

"You know me, Rebecca. I'm all about disruption whether it's inside or outside the rules," she finally said in an unsteady voice.

"Erica, good ideas are always welcome and thanks for the suggestion about the teddy-bear drop," Bec said smoothly. "The problem is, the fire tower isn't exactly close to the park whereas the creek conveniently runs straight through it, making the duck race ideal. Also, anyone can slap down a two-dollar coin and buy a duck but the teddy-bear drop needs people to come prepared. It's something to consider in the future but this time I think we should stick with the duck race. All those in favor?"

"PENNY FOR THEM?"

Julie startled at Phil's voice. It wrenched her away from the unwanted thoughts of the now broad bean–sized lump in her breast. Why had she allowed her fingers to stray there that morning? For weeks, she'd studiously avoided the area. After all, if she couldn't touch the lump then it wasn't there, digging in with its malignant roots and staking a deep and devastating claim on her body. But in the shower, she'd stupidly touched it. Felt its mass and insidious form. Now she couldn't shift its ominous presence from her mind.

She'd been around the block of life many times in her sixty-seven years and she knew without a shadow of a doubt that life wasn't fair. But why couldn't it at least mete out trauma in measured doses instead of dumping it on the same people over and over again? Death wasn't something she feared for herself—in an odd sort of way it was comforting to know she'd see Hugo, Heather, Ron and her parents again. No, it was the thought of Phil and Penny's grief she feared. The agony of watching them witness her slowly wasting away—dying—as they fought their own rage, sorrow and impotence. They'd endured enough losing Hugo.

"I turned off the TV for port and talk but you've hardly said a word since you got in. Everything okay?" Phil's free hand tousled Charger's velvet ears as the puppy slept in his basket next to the chair.

It was time to get a grip. She didn't want Phil sensing she was worried. Since Hugo's death, his blood pressure had been all over the map and the last thing she needed was him stressing over her. "Sorry, darling. I'm a bit distracted by Claire. She was in a funny mood tonight, laughing too loudly and generally being overly enthusiastic. Gushy, almost."

"That doesn't sound like Claire."

"I know. I mean, she can be stubborn when she gets the bit between her teeth but that's what makes her a great community leader. She gets the job done. Excluding her childish behavior with Bec, she's usually the calm one."

"How did she bait Bec tonight?"

"She started the meeting with supper to celebrate Sophie and Josh's good news about the house."

"Surely Bec was okay with that?"

"If it had been anyone else's idea, she probably would have been fine, but it was Claire's, so of course she was going to sulk. But later in the meeting she surprised me. I'm tempted to believe she actually protected Claire after the conversation strayed to All Saints."

Julie stared into the red velvet port, remembering Claire's pinched face. "Erica asked Claire where she got married."

"Geez." Phil's hands stalled in his stroking of Charger and the puppy whimpered in his sleep. "But to be fair, it's not all Erica's fault."

"I know. Part of me thinks Erica's right when she says that by not knowing everyone's fire stories it's like walking through a field seeded with land mines. What she doesn't understand is that, fire or no fire, we all have stories. They're ours to tell or not and that decision can change minute by minute depending on who we're talking to."

"At the Men's Shed, if anyone opens up, it's always survivors talking to other survivors. I do it. I only talk about Hugo to the blokes who knew him."

Julie drained the port, welcoming the liquid warmth streaming through her veins and fuzzing her mind. "Because they give us Hugo stories in return."

"Yep."

She sighed. "I'm wondering if Claire needs some Heather stories."

"You up for it?"

"I think I have to be."

JULIE PULLED up in front of Claire and Matt's new house on Saturday afternoon hoping to catch Claire at home. The flush of green —all weeds—that crawled over the now hardened imprints of truck tires created during construction surprised her. Julie had expected to see retaining walls, flower beds, newly planted fruit trees and raised boxes primed with compost ready to welcome seedlings that would yield summer vegetables.

Weeks earlier, Claire had sought her advice on landscaping, wanting to have clear plans before Bill arrived with the bobcat and cheerfully did his own thing in his gung-ho way. They'd walked around the property, sketching out a design and discussing plantings. But apart from one area of freshly turned soil, no progress had been made.

Slinging a carry bag onto her shoulder, she got out of the car, opened the hatch and scooped up the puppy. "Let's go, Charger."

Walking around the veranda to the back door, she noticed a lack of boots and the distinct absence of welcoming dogs. Bother. Perhaps she should have called ahead. Peering through the glass, she saw the comfortable leather couches but no sign of humans or animals. Charger wriggled and squirmed in her arms, desperate to get down. "Hang on, buddy."

She slid open the veranda door and stepped inside. Even though the house was unlocked, Julie knew it didn't mean anyone was home. This far off the main road, it wasn't necessary to lock anything. "Coo-eee. It's Julie."

She lowered Charger to the floor and kept a firm grip on his lead. The puppy strained excitably, desperate to explore all the delicious doggy scents.

"Claire? Matt?"

Charger barked his high-pitched puppy yelp.

"Sorry, buddy. I think you're going to be disappointed."

But she let him direct the play anyway. He romped fast across the wooden floors and skated on the rugs as they slipped under him. The kitchen and laundry were unoccupied, as was the office.

"I think we've missed them."

"In here, Julie."

She followed the croaky sound and found Claire getting out of bed. "Stay."

Both Charger and Claire stilled.

"Are you talking to me or to that gorgeous puppy?" Claire reached her hand toward Charger. The puppy leaped forward, licking it with gusto.

"Both. If you're in bed at two in the afternoon, you must be sick."

Claire didn't volunteer her ailment but as half the town was down with a spring cold and her nose was red and her face blotchy, it wasn't much of a stretch.

"Hello, beautiful," Claire said to the puppy. "Where did you come from?"

Julie perched herself on the end of the bed. "He's the son of one of Turbo's litters."

Claire looked at Julie properly then. "Hugo's Turbo?"

"Yes."

"No wonder you're gorgeous." She scooped the wriggling puppy into her arms. "Is this Ami-Louise's puppy? I thought Phil said Penny was getting her a miniature schnauzer."

"He's mine." Julie shrugged at Claire's astonished look. "I know. Phil's always been the dog person, not me, but Charger makes the hole Hugo's left in my life a little bit smaller. Keeps him close."

She slipped the bag off her shoulder and carefully removed an object wrapped in a tea-towel. "And talking about keeping people close, I was looking for my grandmother's vase to give to Penny and I found this."

Claire released Charger and unwrapped the tea towel. She stared at the item in her lap. "Mom's antique Coalport china plate."

"She must have left it at our place after the CWA Christmas breakup or someone thought it was mine and put it away. I'm just sorry I didn't find it sooner, but we haven't been entertaining so I had no need to open the sideboard."

Claire's finger slowly traced the scalloped pattern of the rectangular sandwich plate. "Asparagus rolls and Anzacs cookies."

Julie smiled. "Her signature bring-a-plate foods."

"She said there was no point competing with your scones, yo-yos or lamingtons." Claire's voice wobbled. "Oh, Julie. I miss her so much. And Dad."

Julie's heart cramped and she squeezed Claire's hand. "I know you miss them terribly. I miss her too."

Heather's voice tumbled into her head. For Pete's sake. Just go and see Colin and get checked out.

"I still have times when I think, "Mom will get a kick out of this," or "Dad will want to know that," and I go to call them. That's when I realize they're not here anymore. It's always a surprise and it wallops me. Then everything rushes back, turning the anticipation and joy of sharing something fun into this awful gnawing hollowness that throbs and aches. I end up hating the good stuff that I wanted to share with them."

Tears ran down Claire's cheeks and Julie glanced around for a box of tissues. Who didn't keep tissues in their bedroom? As she dug in her handbag for a travel pack, Charger jumped at Claire, his pink tongue licking her salty cheeks.

It took a beat before Julie realized Claire wasn't laughing or giggling or even swatting the puppy away. Instead she was rocking and keening—an agonizing wailing, gulping sound. It tore through Julie like the cut of a blunt saw. Not even during the catastrophic hours, days or weeks after the fire, when everyone was one breath away from losing control of their emotions, had Claire fallen apart like this. Not in plain sight, anyway.

Julie wrapped her arms around the younger woman who she'd cuddled as a baby, and tried not to let her own grief swamp her too. "Oh, Claire. I didn't think the plate would upset you so much. I know you have so few things of hers. I wanted it to be a good thing."

"It ... is." Her sobs increased. "It's ... l-like ... t-treasure. Thank you."

"You'll have to make some Anzac cookies."

Claire dragged in a wet and noisy sniff. "I..d-don't h-have anyone to t-talk to about M-Mom and D-Dad."

"Of course you do. You've got me and Phil. You've got Matt."

"H-he d-didn't h-have enough t-time to g-get to know them to m-miss them."

"I'm sure that's not true. He and your dad got on well. Remember their fishing trip? Claire, Matt worships the ground you walk on and he only wants you to be happy. Of course he'll listen to you talk about Heather and Ron."

Claire's sobs escalated and Julie stroked her hair. She was all too familiar with the way grief sucked people back to that unfair, uncertain place of dank and haunting halls. How it trapped them there for a minute, an hour, a day—sometimes longer—ripping the scab off a healing wound and resetting the clock.

Julie held Claire until her shaking shoulders steadied and she'd inelegantly wiped her snotty face on the top bedsheet.

She shot Julie a sheepish look. "Sorry."

"It's me, remember. No need for sorry. Mind you, I can hear Heather reading you the riot act about using a bedsheet as a hankie."

Claire's weak gurgle approximated a laugh. "Yeah. You're right. It's pretty gross."

Charger bounced around, sticking his muzzle between them, trying to get to Claire. Julie grabbed him by the scruff of the neck and put her hand on his rump.

"Sit, Charger. When he gets too annoying for old Taffy, she biffs him like an Italian nonna keeping her grown son in line. He needs the rough and tumble of playtime with some younger dogs. When will Matt be home with your two?"

Claire threw back the covers and pulled on a polar fleece. "I'll just splash my face. You put the kettle on."

"Okay." Julie made her way back to the kitchen and switched on the kettle before taking the puppy out for a toilet break. While she waited for him to do his business, she automatically pulled the dry laundry off the clothesline, folding it neatly just as her mother had taught her sixty years earlier. As she coupled together the last pair of socks, she was struck by the fact that every item of clothing was Claire's. That wouldn't have been unusual if the clothes were delicates but it was a mix of darks and lights, work and casual gear. Where were Matt's things?

"Come on, Charger. Inside." The puppy tore back to the veranda and bounded through the open door straight to Claire, who was sitting with two steaming mugs of tea. Julie followed, placing the basket of clean laundry on the kitchen table well out of puppy harm's way. "Is Matt away?"

"Hmm."

"Did he stay on in Hamilton after the sheep sales?"

Claire ducked her head and it seemed to Julie she'd ducked the question. Claire scooped Charger onto her lap and the puppy barked, lifting his paws onto her chest and licking her face.

"I could eat you up." Claire cupped his face between her palms and kissed his nose. "Yes, I could."

The uncharacteristic gushy baby talk made the hairs on the back of Julie's neck rise. "Claire, what's going on? Where's Matt?"

Claire ruffled the puppy's ears before returning him to the floor. He whimpered at the loss of adoration. "He and the dogs have moved into the big house."

"No! Why?"

Claire eventually raised her head and Julie immediately understood her red-rimmed eyes had nothing to do with a spring cold, allergies or hay fever.

"We had an argument. He's been gone a week."

Once Julie had wondered if Claire and Matt's initial starry-eyed relationship would last three months but the fire and its aftermath had welded them together. "It must have been a hell of a disagreement. Have you talked since?"

"Not really. He comes back here when I'm at work but he's always gone when I get home."

"But you *are* going to talk to him. You can't fix a problem passively, Claire. You must take action."

She heard Heather's unwelcome voice drift into her head. *Take your own advice.*

Shut up, H. You're already dead. You're not here to let anyone else down. "Marriage is a marathon. You can't let the first hurdle fell you."

"We're not married."

Julie threw out an arm in exasperation. "You know what I mean. You've survived more in the last two and a half years than most couples experience in a lifetime. When you love each other, nothing's insurmountable."

Claire flinched. "I think some things are."

Julie thought of the lump in her breast. Of Phil and Penny. She drank her tea.

CHAPTER SEVENTEEN

As soon as Julie and Charger left, Claire forced herself into the shower. She blow dried her hair before rummaging around in her makeup bag, looking for rarely used concealer. She needed all the help she could get to hide the ravages a week of crying and too much wine had wrought on her skin.

It had been a week punctuated by moments of fast-rising fury. How dare Matt move out! His behavior was juvenile—running home to his mommy and his childhood bedroom a decade after he'd officially stated his independence by moving into the manager's house. Initially, she'd taken satisfaction in knowing how uncomfortable he'd be in the single bed but then she realized Louise would insist he sleep in one of the many guest rooms with their generous queen-sized beds.

Her blood-pumping outrage was always followed by a swift descent into misery. The fact that he'd moved out was inconceivable and yet, in the deepest corners of her soul, she knew from the moment she'd decided not to have children his leaving would be inevitable. She'd selfishly hoped to have a lot more time with him but the truth had escaped quickly and cruelly.

Now he hated her.

She hated herself.

Surveying her reflection, she ran her fingers around the chain of the triple-heart necklace her parents had given her when she'd graduated the first time.

"We're so proud of you, darling. We know you're excited about going to far-flung places and helping people. Your mother and I thought this was the perfect gift to remind you to think of us occasionally," her father had teased.

As she'd opened the jewelry box, her mother had added, "I'm the gold heart, your dad's the white gold and you're the rose gold cuddled in the middle."

"Oh, Dad. I think of you and Mom all the time."

No matter where she'd lived and worked, her parents' love and support had been tangible. But their deaths had destroyed that, leaving only the memory of them. She didn't need a necklace for that.

Well-meaning people had offered her platitudes like "take comfort in the memories," and sometimes she was able to do that, but memories didn't write to you each week like her parents had done when she was working in Papua New Guinea. Emails she'd eagerly downloaded when she'd returned to Wewak from the dense jungle of the Sepik. Memories didn't call you at odd hours because they'd miscalculated the time difference, nor did they collapse in laughter when the bouncing delay on the line made the conversation more like a game of Mad Libs.

Memories didn't drop by with a couple of casseroles saying, "I know between work, training the puppies and planning the wedding, you're probably not cooking. Matt's always ravenous so I thought this would help."

"Damn it." The tears that constantly hovered rose again. She blinked fast, trying to avoid them streaking her makeup and ruining her facade. The process of putting herself together each day had become like constructing a paper doll, carefully folding the clothing tabs over the cardboard body. She'd been doing it every morning to hide her real self from Myrtle. Any chink in her armor would bring questions. And she lacked answers.

"All set?" she asked the mirror. "You just have to walk to the big house and talk to Matt."

Just? She barely had enough emotional fortitude to face Matt. There'd be nothing left over to deal with Louise and Bill, who she felt sure wouldn't be shy in giving their opinions. She'd spent the week on tenterhooks, expecting Louise and Bill to walk in at any minute and berate her. They hadn't. It defied their usual modus operandi but the irony of their staying away now wasn't lost on her.

Her cell phone rang. Hope and anticipation carried her to the kitchen. She turned over her cell and read the caller ID. Disappointment struck.

"Hi, Shane."

"Hope it's okay to call you on a Saturday afternoon but it's the first chance I've had to follow up on last Friday night."

"Of course. No problem." After completely losing her self-control with Julie, it was a surprise to hear her voice sounding firm. "The hospital sent me discharge summaries for Brock and Bethany. They were lucky."

"Yeah, they were. I've spoken to all the kids involved and to their parents. The good news is, the cannabis isn't local. Dylan Fells bought it from a kid who got it from, and I quote, 'an old stoner in Anglesea.' Of course he doesn't have a name or an address for the bloke. The Colac boys tell me they haven't seen much cannabis about since they raided a property with a hundred plants out near Lake Corangamite. If anything, there's a shortage of dope and ice is the problem. Thankfully, I haven't seen any here." Shane sighed. "Yet."

"I guess it's a relief that your gut feeling about the cannabis coming from out of town was right."

"I think it's still worth doing those drug and alcohol talks."

"Absolutely. Formal for the parents and informal for the youth group."

"Sounds like a plan. I better practice my basketball-shooting skills. Lucy told me they sucked."

Claire laughed. "You're doing better than me. Mine don't even exist. See you next Friday."

When she ended the call, she stared at her cell phone. Perhaps a text might be better than walking up to the big house. Bringing up a new message, she chewed her lip before typing with unsteady fingers, *Hi, Matt. Could you please come over and bring the dogs? Cx.*

She read it again and her thumb hovered over the back button, wondering if she should remove the last two letters. *Why? You always sign off that way.*

The fact she loved Matt wasn't their problem. She hit send and waited. It was the first piece of communication between them in over a week.

CLAIRE FACED Matt across the living room and tried not to sink under his unforgiving look.

He'd arrived fifteen minutes after she'd sent the text but he didn't look happy. Banjo and Paterson had gone berserk when they saw her, racing around in circles and vying for her attention. It had taken monumental effort not to sink to her knees and cry into their coats. Instead, she'd ruffled their ears, scratched their bellies and told them how much she'd missed them. They'd been too overexcited to obey instructions for longer than a minute so Matt had put them outside. Now they pressed their noses against the glass door, whimpering to come in.

Claire wanted to capitulate. She'd do almost anything to distract herself from the restrained anger on Matt's face, which left bewilderment stark in its wake. She caught a flash of Max on his face— the same injured look her nephew gave Piper when she teased him.

Matt stood in his socks with his hands shoved deep in his pockets. Their relationship might be floundering on the jagged rocks of a fundamental difference, but a well-raised country boy never wore his muddy boots inside the house.

She forced herself to break the silence. "How are you?"

"How do you think?"

"I don't know. It's why I asked."

His top lip curled. "Forgetting the fact you've kicked me in the balls, I'm freaking fantastic."

"I'm sorry."

"Yeah, so you said."

"Believe me. I'd fix this if I could."

He frowned so hard his eyes almost disappeared under his chocolate brows. He rubbed his face and when he dropped his hands away, his eyes implored. "You *can* fix this, Postie. It's not hard. Please your mind about having kids."

Her throat tightened and she swallowed around the choking lump. "What if we die?"

"What?"

"I'm an orphan. My parents died. What if we die too?"

"Aren't you too old to be an orphan? Anyway, the odds of us dying when our kids are young are pretty slim."

"As slim as another wildfire?"

"You know as well as I do we've all learned heaps since the fires. The new emergency management setup means there's better communication. If there was another fire, we'd evacuate. It's already in our fire plan. I'd never risk your or the kids' lives."

The kids. Her heart rate rocketed and words tumbled out fast. "You say that but how can you promise anything? We live in the country. It's where most of the accidents happen. There's floods, fires, head-on collisions, cars slamming into trees, tractors rolling, quad bike crashes, lightning strikes—"

"Hey!" Matt was instantly by her side, wrapping his arms around her and pulling her in close. "Shh, now. Deep breaths."

Sobbing, she fell into him, pressing her face to his chest. She'd missed him so much and this was like coming home. His calm voice washed over her and she followed his instructions, sucking in slow, fortifying breaths. Breathing him in.

His scent jolted her. Her nostrils tingled and her eyes felt as if someone had just hurled sand. He didn't smell anything like her Matt, but of the overpowering perfume of Louise's laundry powder and fabric softener. Two products Claire was allergic to and never used. She stepped back from him, sneezing in triplicate.

"Sorry." He shot her a baleful look. "Claire, what's going on? You don't catastrophize. You're practical and pragmatic. None of those awful things you're stressing will happen. But if it makes you feel better, of course we'll make living wills and talk to the family."

"I don't have any family."

"Don't be silly."

It was as if he'd reached inside her chest and pulled out her heart. "How am I being silly?"

"You're overflowing with family. Between Mom and Dad and Tamara, the aunts, uncles and cousins, our kids will be loved."

"But they're n—"

"And, in the statistically unlikely event something happens to us, they'll adopt our children just like they've adopted you."

Her eyes burned but she knew it wasn't just from the effects of his perfumed shirt. It was his quick and easy solutions—ones that totally dismissed her worries and the loss of her parents as inconsequential. That and the fact that he was totally blinkered about his parents' relationship with her. The frost of old anger thawed, warmed by her ire.

"Your family haven't adopted me. They barely tolerate me!"

"That's nonsense."

"No. It's not."

He threw up his arms. "They've turned themselves inside out to involve you in the family and the farm but you don't make it easy. You resist invitations. When you accept, you're always late. You never take kindly to well-meant advice and you're hardly on the farm because you're always bloody working. Even when you're physically present, your head's elsewhere. Everyone in Myrtle takes precedence over us."

Us. The Cartwrights. It had only taken eight short days for Matt to go from considering Louise's doctrine a slight possibility to it being set in stone. "That's so far from the truth, I'm not even going to discuss it!"

"Well, that's your new thing, isn't it? Not discussing things. First it was changing your mind about having kids and not telling me. Now it's a point-blank refusal of my family's loving care. All they want is to help you achieve what you've always said you wanted." He ploughed his hands though his hair, pushing the strands up into wild spikes. "What the hell is wrong with you? You're ruining our lives."

His dearth of understanding shocked her. Her kind and considerate Matt had vanished. There was no point asking him why he was pinning all of this on her, his reply would only be a further litany of her faults. Matt and her parents had always been her allies but now she'd lost both.

A crushing loneliness pressed down on her and she gripped the edge of the bookshelf to stop herself from sinking to the floor. The idea of spending another night in the house alone was more than she could bear. "I'd like to have the dogs tonight, please."

"I need them."

"On a Saturday night?"

"I'm helping Dad move sheep tomorrow."

"It's hardly out of your way to collect them in the morning."

"It is actually. We're working in the west fields."

She stared at him—this man who looked like her Matt yet sounded nothing like him. The edges of her civility frayed. "You've had them all week."

"Of course I have. They're working dogs."

"You know they're more than that. They're *our* dogs. Yours and mine." She couldn't stop her voice from rising. "It's only fair I get to spend some time with them too."

His jaw tensed. "I'm surprised you care that much about them."

The creul words crashed into her with the stunning blow of falling bricks, rendering her momentarily speechless. The arrival of the puppies had been one of their happiest moments and Matt knew that. This was about invoking tit for tat: you hurt me so I'll hurt you.

"You're surprised?" she finally managed to splutter. "How is that even possible?"

"Put it this way. I find it difficult to fathom that a woman who doesn't want to love and nurture a child wants joint custody of dogs."

"That's unfair."

"Is it?"

"Yes! Just because I don't want children doesn't mean I don't love anymore. I love you and I love the dogs."

"You've got a hell of a way of showing it."

"I'm not the one who walked out on us."

"You may as well have."

"Matt." Her voice broke at his intransigence and she hauled in a deep breath. "I don't want custody of the dogs. I want you and the dogs living back here with me."

"Well, if you want that, you know what you have to do."

And they'd reached the impasse again, only this time it felt wider than it had eight days earlier. The dogs' whining reached fever pitch. She and Matt turned to them, watching the animals' paws scratching the glass. Two sets of mournful brown eyes stared back at them.

Matt's shoulders slumped and he jerkily grabbed his hat off the table. "Mom and Dad are going to church in the morning. Bring the dogs up to the big house after that then."

"Thank you."

He grunted and walked out without another word.

"I THOUGHT we were going to watch *Dance Divas*." Ivy wandered into the kitchen, her face mutinous.

Bec stopped wiping the outside of the fridge and bumped Ivy with her hip. "Out of the way." She sprayed the granite with liquid cleaner before rubbing it furiously with a cloth.

"You're nuts, Mom. It's already clean, remember? You wiped it after dinner just before you said, 'Go turn on the TV and I'll be there in a minute.' That was half an hour ago. You've missed it."

Bec felt bad but it wasn't enough to slow her frantic rubbing. "Sorry, darling. I'll watch it with you tomorrow night."

"That's what you said last night and then you cleaned the kitchen like a crazy person. It's not even dirty. You never let it get dirty. You need a real job, Mom."

A hysterical laugh echoed in her head. Even before she'd received the bolt-from-the-blue news, a job wasn't something she'd ever managed to successfully navigate with Adam. Now it was totally out of the question.

After dropping Ivy off at counseling the day before, she'd used her free hour to have her annual medical check-up. She'd almost considered it a treat, because she could legitimately turn off her cell phone for sixty minutes. Receiving bad news had never crossed her mind and she'd been reeling ever since. She hadn't managed to tell Adam or her mother. She hadn't told anyone.

There'd been a couple of minutes when she'd considered phoning Sophie or Erica, but just the thought of saying the words out loud made her cry. The news kept spinning in her mind, and coming up with plans on how to break it to Adam had preoccupied her all day. Now she'd missed couch time with Ivy. Again.

"I'm really sorry, Ives. I guess the start of daylight savings has energized me to spring clean. I'll do better tomorrow night. Promise."

"You better." Resigned, Ivy kissed her cheek. "Night, Mom."

"Don't read past eight thirty, okay?"

Ivy glanced at her feet.

"Ives, I mean it. It's the track and field carnival tomorrow."

Ivy muttered something that was probably "track sucks" or "whatever."

"Even if it wasn't the track carnival, you know lights out is eight thirty."

Ivy's sigh rolled out, long and put-upon. "*Okay.*"

"Say goodnight to Daddy. He's in the office."

"I will. I *always* do."

"And I'll come up and tuck you in."

"If you remember..." Ivy stalked out of the kitchen in high dudgeon, the dramatic effect lessened somewhat by her pink unicorn pajamas.

Bec half-expected Ivy to create an illness overnight to avoid the athletics carnival, whereas Gracie would be wide awake before the sun, excited and planning how many ribbons she was going to win—all first-place blue, of course. With Ivy's general withdrawal from everything she'd previously enjoyed, it had been a relief when she hadn't objected to seeing the counselor. Not that Bec had noticed much of a difference since the sessions had started—Ivy still had her nose permanently buried in a book.

The counselor—Jane—was yet to identify anything specific as troubling her elder daughter but she'd told Bec, "Ivy has a general heightened anxiety."

Bec had wanted to respond with, "Who doesn't?", but instead had said, "Surely if Ivy was going to be anxious, it would have been when her father was so sick and she was living with my mother? Not now when everything's back to normal."

"After a long period of stress our body isn't always able to turn off the stress response even when normal returns. Ivy missed a lot of school and girls can be harsh. She may be finding it difficult to re-enter her friendship group."

"Reading all the time doesn't help! Neither does giving up all her activities."

"And we've talked about that. Give Ivy some time. She'll get there. Perhaps throw her a birthday party to help her reconnect with her friends?"

Bec had latched onto that idea like a drowning woman clutching a lifebuoy. "A sleepover?"

"It's best to discuss it with Ivy and see what she wants."

Too easy! Bec had finished the interview with Jane feeling buoyant. She loved throwing parties and up until last year the girls always had themed birthdays from princesses to ponies and Minions to mermaids. She'd planned on bringing up the topic of Ivy's party with her that same afternoon, but when Ivy had uncharacteristically failed to put her lunchbox on the sink for washing, Bec had gone looking for it. At the bottom of Ivy's school bag she'd found two crumpled birthday-party invitations that Ivy had never shown her. The dates had already passed.

Her stomach had churned with frustration at her daughter and indignation at the mothers of the birthday girls. It wasn't like Bec didn't know them. Why hadn't they mentioned the invitations at the school gate and checked with her that Ivy was coming? Granted, these days she dropped the girls off at school and immediately drove home instead of lingering to chat, but even so, they could have called. But few people called her anymore and she'd fallen out of the habit of calling them.

If it wasn't for Sophie, Layla and Erica, she wouldn't speak to another woman all week. The urge to clean rushed back and she picked up the spray bottle, pressing the trigger. Instead of a long, strong stream, only a dribble came out. Damn. She didn't have a spare. As she stowed it under the sink, she said, "Okay, Google. Add Spray and Wipe to my shopping list."

It was Adam's latest toy and he'd been urging her to use it.

"Okay, I've added Spray and Wipe to your shopping list," Google Home's voice cheerfully replied.

Adam walked into the kitchen. She hadn't seen a lot of him during the last couple of days. He and Scotty were busy with contract negotiations for the eco-tourism development and there'd been a flap on with one of the houses, something to do with the delivery of the wrong kitchen cabinets. Between the girls, her committee work for Put

Myrtle on the Map and her general fatigue, she'd only been half-listening to him for weeks. She made sure she murmured in the appropriate places and asked enough questions to sound like she was taking an interest but it was hard to get enthusiastic when he blocked her from any real business involvement. That was probably why she couldn't remember him telling her he was framing the Dohertys' house, although she couldn't believe she would have forgotten that.

"Okay, Google, dim the lights," Adam said. The lighting immediately lowered to nightlight level and he grinned. "Okay, Google, romantic music."

"Okay, check out this romantic music on YouTube," replied the Google voice.

A ripple of unease wove through Bec but she quelled it. His request for romantic music combined with the fact that the girls were at home reassured her that Adam wouldn't be suggesting a repeat of the "playing hard to get" sex game from a couple weeks earlier. Not that he'd tried to play it again, thank God. He'd seemed genuinely shocked when, after a stiff drink, she'd told him she hadn't enjoyed it. He'd apologized, telling her he'd thought she'd been playing along just like she had in the office, the spa and the lounge room.

Occasionally, in the middle of the night, she dreamt she was trapped. When that happened, she'd lunge up from the nightmare in a cold sweat, waking as the word "rape" dissolved behind her eyelids. Of course it dissolved—it wasn't true. What had happened in the kitchen wasn't rape—it was a misunderstanding. Despite Adam's mood swings and his battle with pain, he was her husband. He loved her. She'd never been in doubt of that fact. Sometimes she wondered if he loved her too much.

He hadn't been the one to look outside of their marriage.

Since she'd told him how she'd felt about that morning in the kitchen, Adam had initiated what he coined Bec's Vanilla Special—sex in bed with the lights off after he'd given her a massage. Whenever she thought about their sex life, she tried to focus on those pleasant memories. But the kitchen episode seemed determined to shove its unwanted way back into her consciousness, always bringing with it a racing heart and a dry mouth.

"Do you want a cup of tea? Hot chocolate?" she asked Adam.

"No." He slipped his arms around her waist and swayed them to the music. "All I want is you. Seeing the girls are in bed, I thought we could play another game."

She tensed and her pulse quickened. "I'm so tired, Adam, I can barely stand up."

"That's the beauty of this game. No standing required."

"The moment I lie down I'll just zonk out." She gave a light laugh. "Surely, you don't want to have sex with a woman who's asleep?"

"I'm game if you are."

"Adam!"

"Flaming hell, Bec, where's your sense of humor? Listen." His arm pulled her in more tightly against him. "I've been giving you the vanilla special for a couple of weeks so now it's your turn to give back. Besides, I thought we could try these." From his pocket, he pulled out a string of purple silicone beads of various sizes.

A tingle of anxiety prickled her skin. "Wh-what are they?"

"Butt beads. My present to you."

She recoiled so fast she tasted dinner in the back of her throat. "No, Adam. Just no."

He stiffened and backed her up against the gleaming stainless steel fridge. "You know what? You're turning into a selfish bitch."

"I'm not. I'm pregnant." The words rushed out before she could stop them.

Stupid! Stupid! Stupid! She'd planned on telling him in public on Saturday night at his favorite restaurant, despite the fact that it was in Lorne. She hated going to the seaside town now—it reminded her of the life she'd gotten so close to having, then lost. But telling Adam the news in Lorne was the self-flagellation she needed. The past was over and no amount of grieving would change it. She'd accepted her future during one terrifying telephone call and now she had little choice but to find a way to make it work.

Adam was staring at her, his face impassive except for the constant watering of his bad eye. "You can't be pregnant. You've got that thing ..."

"That's what I thought, but when I saw Colin yesterday for a check-up, he couldn't find it. Apparently, sometimes IUDs can fall out during a heavy period ... Anyway, he insisted on doing a test before inserting a new one—" she made quote marks with her fingers "—'to rule out a pregnancy' only it didn't rule it out. I can't believe it. Adam, I'm two months gone."

After Gracie was born, he'd told her they needed to focus on building the business and more children would only distract them. She'd obliged him without too much regret although a part of her would have liked a third child. What worried her now was that since the fires, his patience with her and the girls was thinner than it had been. Truth be told, it had never really been all that thick.

His ominous silence tightened around her like a lasso and she heard her continued gabbling: "I know it's a shock. I can't get my head around it either. I know you didn't want any more kids but—"

"A baby? It's mine, right?"

"Of course it's yours! It's all that sex."

"Babe, I'm kidding! God, I'd forgotten how being pregnant made you touchy." His mouth pulled into the rictus smile the scar tissue allowed and his good eye sparkled. She glimpsed the Adam who'd arrived at her door in his sports car thirteen years earlier to whisk her away from her humdrum small-town life.

"You—you don't mind?"

"Mind? Hell no. Business is booming and a third kid shows everyone I'm well and truly back to form. We can easily afford three kids. Four even." He swung her around. "It's the perfect surprise."

Relief sagged her knees. She leaned against him so she didn't slide to the floor. "I wasn't sure you'd be happy."

He nuzzled her neck. "Seriously, woman, you worry me sometimes. I love kids. This one might be our boy."

"I was thinking that too. You always wanted a son."

"Hmm." His mouth had moved down her throat and onto her décolletage. "I always loved your pregnant knockers." Pushing her dress off her shoulder, he tugged at her bra and closed his mouth around her nipple, sucking it.

Needle-sharp pain shot through her and she squealed.

He raised his head. "Shh, you'll wake the girls."

"It hurts, Adam. Remember, my boobs get tender for a few months. And I get that horrible metallic taste in my mouth, go off coffee and get so tired I have to nap."

"Hell. I'd forgotten all that." His disappointed grimace slowly converted to a smile. "But I do remember how horny you get after the first three months. I guess I just have to be patient for a few weeks. Meanwhile there are other things we can—"

"Mommy, are you okay?"

Bec looked over Adam's shoulder and saw Ivy, her blue eyes wide with fright. She frantically pulled at her dress, covering herself. "Of course I'm okay, sweetheart. Why?"

"I heard you screaming."

"It was more of an excited squeal, sweet pea." Adam dropped an arm from Bec's waist and opened it up to his daughter for a hug. "You're going to be a big sister again."

"You're having a baby?" Ivy's gaze narrowed into thin slits as the full significance of how Bec had got pregnant sank in. "That's just gross!"

"It's not gross, Ives. It's a wonderful thing."

Only Bec wasn't certain who she was reassuring more—Ivy or herself.

CHAPTER EIGHTEEN

On framing Friday, as Sophie was calling it, she took the day off work. "It's too momentous an occasion to miss."

Josh agreed.

As Sophie watched the blue steel struts rise and be bolted into position on the concrete slab, she felt the pressing weight of the long months of worry—fear that this day would never come—rise from her toes and vanish out through the top of her head. This was hope. This was vindication. This was the change in fortune they not only needed but deserved. All day, she'd found herself bursting into spontaneous laughter. It wasn't just from observing the progress of the frame but from watching Liam and Josh.

Caught up in his parents' excitement, Liam had insisted on wearing his toy hard hat and tool belt from the moment he'd tumbled out of bed. Scotty made a fuss of him, calling him his right-hand man and high-fiving him whenever he walked past. At one point, Scotty lifted her son up into the cab of the crane to touch the levers. Later, Liam cried in disappointment when the crane drove away.

Like his son, Josh had worn a smile from ear to ear all day. Hours later, he was still smiling. It made her heart sing.

When the builders declared the job done, Josh grabbed her and danced them around the uprights like they were in a fifties musical. She'd barely caught her breath when Erica arrived with French champagne and her husband.

"This is Nathan."

"Pleased to meet you, Sophie. I can tell from your face that Erica's told you all about my many and varied domestic disasters. She never lets the truth get in the way of a good story, but sadly, they're mostly accurate."

Sophie laughed. Based on Erica's anecdotes, she'd sketched an image of Nathan in her mind. But this lanky, sandy-haired and self-deprecating man looked more like a surfer than a successful stock trader and business advisor. "My favorite story's the Thermomix."

"Nathan used it to whip up some dips for the party." Erica set down a platter on the waiting trestle table.

"Sorry, Josh, but it was a matter of honor," Nathan deadpanned. "Champagne or beer? I chucked in some Prickly Moses just in case."

As Nathan finished pouring their drinks, Layla and Osman arrived bearing a tray of Turkish meatballs. Sophie and Josh had only just greeted them when Bec, Adam and their daughters pulled up in their SUV. The girls wore dresses in the same shade of blue as their mother and a perfect match to the teal uprights. Gracie, the youngest, rushed her hellos before racing over to the trampoline. Ivy hung back, standing quietly between her parents.

"Ivy can mind the kids." Adam slung his arm over his elder daughter's shoulder. "She's great with littlies, aren't you, sweet pea?"

"Maybe," Ivy muttered, gazing at her feet.

Sophie could see Liam, Rafi and Malik busily driving toy trucks through the sand pile and Scarlett and Trixie were playing close to the slab. She remembered being Ivy's age. It had been an awkward time when part of her had wanted to be a kid but another part was desperate to hang out with the adults. "There's no pressure, Ivy. Right now, the kids look pretty happy."

"Off you go, Ives." Adam gave her a gentle push on the behind before turning to Nathan, who'd appointed himself bartender. "G'day, mate. I'll skip the girly bubbles and have a beer, thanks."

Sophie noticed fine fatigue lines on Bec's face as her friend presented her with a large platter groaning with tastefully arranged antipasto. "I hope this is okay."

"Are you kidding? It's amazing." Sophie caught sight of Julie and Phil climbing over the stile. "Bec, have you met Layla's husband? Osman, this is Bec ..."

Leaving Bec in conversation with the Buluts, Sophie ran toward the older couple. "Look! Can you believe it!"

Julie kissed her. "It's a very pretty blue."

"That's what I think."

Phil wrapped his arms around her in a bear hug. "It's worth celebrating, that's for sure. Where's Josh? I haven't seen him in ages. It'll be good to have a chat."

Sophie scanned the growing crowd but she couldn't spot her husband. "He's around somewhere. Maybe he's setting up the barbecue. Come and have a drink."

"Sophie!" Erica stood in the middle of the slab with Layla and Bec, waving a champagne bottle at her. "You're lagging behind. It's time for a refill."

Sophie waved and after introducing Julie and Phil to Nathan, she was making a beeline for the women when Adam Petrovic caught her arm.

"Sophie. Great party. Thanks for inviting us."

His appreciation momentarily threw her. This was the man whose largesse had fast-tracked their house and saved them tens of thousands of dollars. "Are you serious? We're the ones supposed to be thanking you. Without your generosity, we'd still be a good six months away from framing."

"It's my pleasure. Your husband's a good worker and we reward reliability."

He sipped his beer and Sophie tried not to stare at the two missing digits on his left hand. Tried not to think about the paralyzing terror he must have experienced before the fire burned him. Adam had selflessly put his life on the line to save others. Did he ever resent the fact that the men he'd saved had escaped with minor burns? That he'd spent months in the hospital and now lived with the debilitating effects of his injuries? Given his generosity to her and Josh, she decided it was unlikely he held any ill will toward anyone. Adam Petrovic was a true hero—a quiet achiever who just got on with things, putting his family and his community ahead of himself.

"There's more work coming through with this eco-tourism resort. You never know, Sophie, you might have external walls and a roof sooner than you think."

"Oh my God! I think I have to hug you."

Adam laughed. "My wife might have something to say about that." But he leaned in anyway.

She gave him a quick kiss on the cheek, feeling the uneven skin of his face under her lips. Giddy from a flute of champagne and emboldened by his hint of further help, she asked the question she hoped was the solution to their immediate problems.

"With this eco-tourism resort, will there be enough work for Josh to finish his apprenticeship?"

Adam wiped his watering eye with a white handkerchief monogrammed with AP. "If that's what he wants, of course we'll take him on as an apprentice electrician."

Her hands flew to her lips, her palms pressing together. "Thank you, Adam. Thank you so much."

It was impossible to believe that after almost two years of struggle, they were finally closing the book on the worst chapter of their lives. What a day! She couldn't wait to tell Josh the good news.

❦

CLAIRE PULLED UP AT THE DOHERTYS' open gate at exactly 5:35 P.M.. It was five minutes after the stated time on the texted invitation, which meant Claire was politely on time just as her mother had taught her. She saw the taillights of the Petrovics' distinctive red and white SUV disappear around the bend of the drive and she drummed her fingers on the steering wheel. Was she mad coming to this party? Who put their hand up to attend a social gathering of young families when they had neither a husband or children?

She impulsively backed up a couple of hundred yards before braking hard. Too many thoughts spun and twirled in her mind and she dropped her forehead to the steering wheel as if the act would still everything and give her peace. The first thought to rise out of the melee was that she should return to the Dohertys'.

"We wouldn't miss it," she'd assured Sophie earlier. If she didn't go, her non-attendance would spark more questions from this group of women than the fact that she was arriving without Matt. She'd already planned exactly what she'd say to explain his absence—there was a break in the fence and they couldn't risk prize sheep getting onto the road. Their eyes would predictably glaze over at the mention of sheep, effectively killing any more inquiries. After that, Claire was skilled enough to keep the conversation well away from herself by asking them questions about their kids.

Decision made, she lifted her head. It took her a moment but she realized she'd pulled over at the school bus stop. For months after the fires, she'd experienced this sort of delayed recognition, because so many identifying markers—both natural and manmade—had vanished. This was where Hugo's creation of a 44-gallon drum painted to look like a Holstein had once stood. It had worked like a charm, pulling tourists in for a photo of the decorative mailbox and making them notice the garden produce for sale along with bags of horse poo.

Hugo. A pang of desolation caught her under the ribs. Instead of pulling back onto the blacktop, she put the car into first and thudded over the cattle grid. It was surreal to be following the same track down the hill but experiencing a smooth ride. It wasn't the only change. Gone was the weathered corrugated-iron milking parlor with cows filling its yard. The air was free of the sounds of blaring music blasting from speakers accompanied by Hugo's enthusiastic but off-key singing. The track suddenly stopped where the sheds once stood. She turned off the ignition and sat staring into the blank space, struggling to sketch the missing buildings and trees in her mind.

Giving up, she got out of the car and walked toward a flat and grassy rectangle—the only evidence that a house had once graced the space. In the mild evening, it was as if it never existed and sadness rolled through her like damp Myrtle fog. Squatting, she pressed her palm against the moist ground.

"I miss you, Hugo, darling. You always made me laugh. More importantly, you always gave me sensible advice."

Disconsolately, she wondered what Hugo would have suggested about the current situation with Matt. She pushed herself to her feet and walked around what had been Hugo's garden, trying to find the nook where Matt had told her he'd broken up with Taylor. When he'd asked her if she wanted to explore the attraction that arced between them. But nothing looked the same. Nothing hinted at its position, and why would it? Nothing between her and Matt was the same anymore either.

Hugo had been so supportive of them. Given his shock death, she now regretted how self-indulgently happy she'd been back then. Blissed out on new love, she hadn't given much thought to how Hugo's new relationship was progressing. Before she'd moved back to Myrtle, Hugo had requested they swap houses for a few weekends. She'd happily acquiesced, thanking him for his thoughtfulness at giving her precious time with Matt, but at the same time teasing him about the perils of falling for a city woman.

"Are things easier where you are, Hugo, darling?"

The closest she got to a reply was a low bellow from Mick Albanini's bull.

Her cell beeped with a text. *I'm desperate for the salty hit of chips.*

Are you far away? Erica. It was accompanied by a smiley-face emoji with a tongue hanging out.

Claire recognized the text as a hand of friendship. She also knew she wasn't very good at reaching out and grasping those hands. She glanced up at the sky, seeking her best mate.

"You telling me something, Hugo, darling? You do realize there'll be husbands and kids there, the full catastrophe?"

The strident squawks of corellas filled the air.

"Okay, fine! I'll go. I could do with a drink and I'll have one for you, shall I?"

With fingers flying, she texted a reply. Hang in there, E. The chips are five minutes away.

JOSH TWISTED the top off another beer. He was standing on the edge of the slab watching everyone jostling around the trestle table. It was groaning with food, most of which the guests had brought with them to help them celebrate the frame. Today was a good day. A hell of a good day in fact. He just wasn't sure about this party. The conversation at these things irritated the hell out of him.

He'd got stuck in a conversation with Nathan about cricket. Even after he'd clearly told him that watching grass grow was more entertaining, the bloke had put the hard word on him to join the club. If that wasn't bad enough, ten minutes later, Nathan and Adam were talking about investment portfolios. He'd walked away seconds before he'd lost it. For God's's sake, after he and Sophie paid the mortgage, bought food and fuel, and put money in the house fund, there was just enough left over for a few beers.

And then there was Phil. His neighbor had bided his time before cornering Josh at the barbecue.

"Why not come along to the early-morning men's exercise group? They meet Mondays, Wednesdays and Fridays."

Josh had felt pressure building up inside him—the same sort of tension that had exploded out of him when Sophie's moronic sister had visited. This time, he'd managed to slow it down and keep it inside.

"You've probably forgotten what early mornings are like with little kids."

The retired dairyman had laughed before clapping him on the shoulder. "Glad to see you haven't lost your sense of humor. If you change your mind, just turn up. Be good to see you there."

Yeah, like that was going to happen.

At least the Turkish guy was quiet. All he'd asked of Josh was to explain the controversial umpiring decision in the previous week's Australian Football League's grand final. Josh had managed that.

"Josh! Come eat dessert."

Sophie was waving a bowl at him, her smile wide, eyes sparkling and cheeks flushed with excitement and expensive champagne. She looked exactly as she had the night they'd met, except then her glow had come from a couple of cans of alcopop. He'd gotten hard just listening to her laugh. Now he struggled to get hard even when she offered to go down on him, but he couldn't blame her. Hell, he couldn't even get hard watching porn.

Adam appeared next to him. "Josh, you got a minute?"

He wasn't going to say no to the man who'd absorbed the installation costs of the frame. "Sure."

"Let's walk and talk."

Josh followed Adam behind the shed to the water tank. The sun was a vivid red ball dropping fast and sending out fingers of orange and peach across the cloud-streaked sky. He knew it was pretty. Knew he should enjoy it. But he couldn't look at those colors without flinching.

Did pretty sunsets make Adam's heart rate jump wildly? In the fading light, Josh looked for a sheen of sweat on Adam's top lip, faster breathing and a reddening of his face—although that was hard given it was permanently pink. But the builder looked cool and calm in his neat, casual clothes.

"I've always had a soft spot for this bit of land. You bought yourself a good view." Adam gazed out toward the horizon.

"Yeah." It was all Josh could manage as he worked on slowing his pulse.

"I was telling your lovely wife earlier, Petrovic Family Homes needs to keep reliable and dependable workers. It makes our life easier and you're a good worker, Josh. That's why we helped you out with the framing. It doesn't matter whether we're asking you to clean up after the bricklayers or rig up a complicated hydroponic system, we appreciate the way you always get the job done and done well."

The warm words of praise steadied him. "I really appreciate the work and your faith in me. Your help with the build, man, it was totally unexpected. I'm happy to do odd jobs. Hell, I'm just happy to be working. Being unemployed sucked."

"Would have been tough."

"Yeah."

"I get it," Adam mused. "A bloke's gotta work. The good news is, there's plenty more of that if you want it."

Since Josh had installed the LED lighting in the greenhouse and planted a shed-load of tomato seedlings a few weeks earlier, he'd been back doing odd jobs for Scotty. Josh enjoyed the diversity of the work and the pay—cash and plenty of it. Up until now, he'd been content with being a temp worker but the week before he'd overheard Scotty and Adam discussing the eco-tourism resort. It sounded like it was close to getting off the ground and a project like that could be a game changer for him.

Josh bit the bullet. "Are you offering me a full-time job on the books?"

Adam took a thoughtful sip of his beer. "At this point, do you want that? It'd mean you earn a lot less."

Josh's father had been a factory-floor union rep throughout his career as a fabricator and fitter and Josh had grown up surrounded by conversations about the importance of workers' rights. Many evening meals had been spent listening to his father discussing safe work environments, sick leave, vacation pay and retirement funds.

Always remember, son, working cash-in-hand only benefits the bosses.

Then again, his father had never lost everything he'd ever owned in a fire then been laid off. The last twenty-two months had taken Josh's well-entrenched views of security—both at home and work—and rendered them unrecognizable. Even so ...

Adam seemed to sense Josh's hesitation. "I'm only thinking of what's best for you, Sophie and the kiddies right now. And that's getting you out of this bastard shed and into the home you deserve. For that you're gonna need as much moolah as you can get your hands on so cash works best. Doesn't mean we can't formalize arrangements down the track. You're young and fit. Plenty of time to load up your retirement account after the house is built, eh?"

Adam's reassurance quieted the memory of his father's insistent edicts, lessening Josh's feelings that he was somehow a traitor to the union cause. "Yeah. Good idea."

"I'm glad we're on the same page. Listen, Josh, I've got a bit of a favor. There's a job needs doing on Monday."

"Something at your place?" Given Adam's reduced finger dexterity, Josh assumed it was a job that required fine motor skills.

"No. Back at the vineyard."

Josh stomach churned. "Did your sparky pick up a problem with my wiring?"

"No, all good. Excellent, in fact. You impressed Ricky and that's hard to do. This problem's a bit complicated. You know how the supplier was late delivering the tomato plants? It's put us right up against it, time wise. Trav's running the lights 24/7 to fast-track the crop. Watching that freaking electricity meter whirl makes me dizzy. I may as well be throwing hundred-dollar bills into the creek."

Josh knew exactly how much electricity cost. It was one of their most expensive household bills. "I bet."

"I should charge the nursery a late fee to cover the costs." Adam sipped his beer. "Don't get me wrong, Josh. God knows, I'm all about helping my community. Growing the tomatoes seemed like a good idea at the time but at this rate, getting them ripe and ready for the farmers markets and Put Myrtle on the Map day is going to send me broke. That's where you come in."

Josh didn't follow. "I don't know anything about tomatoes."

"But you know electricity. I need you to install a bypass for me. Just for this crop."

A tingling whoosh shot along Josh's spine. "A bypass is illegal."

Adam nodded. "Sure. And I hate asking you. Under normal circumstances I'd never do it but I'm not telling you anything you don't already know. The fires killed Myrtle's economy. No one in the State Administration gives a stuff about us. As far as they're concerned, they've done their bit by throwing buildings at us and saddling us with a maintenance debt that's currently bigger than the shire's budget.

"It's up to us to kickstart the town and get the money flowing again. If we don't, she's gonna die. I don't know about you, but I'm not prepared to have that happen on my watch and sometimes ..." He shrugged. "... Well sometimes, needs must."

Josh's brain was struggling to compute under the assault of alcohol and adrenaline but he heard Adam's reasonable tone and accurate words. Josh couldn't argue that Myrtle's economy barely had a pulse and the government didn't care. It was Adam's solution that slipped and slid against everything Josh believed to be right and true.

"Surely there's another way to fix the problem. One that doesn't involve stealing electricity?"

"Stealing's a bit strong, mate. It's more of an interest-free loan just to get this first crop over the line. Believe me, I've thought about it every which way from Sunday but if we reduce the hours we run the lights, plant growth slows. That means we'll miss the peak tourist period and if that happens, I'm screwed. If I'm screwed, then Myrtle's screwed, because I'll be strapped for cash and it'll put a filthy black cloud over the eco-tourism project. If that happens, there goes a whole heap of jobs, including yours."

Josh's scalp itched and he rubbed his head hard. "What about taking on another partner for the tomatoes?"

"Partners expect profits. This project's a labor of love for Myrtle, but even love's got to break even, right? You see my dilemma?" Adam's gaze moved from the horizon to Josh. "Our dilemma, really."

Josh swallowed around a fast-closing throat. Installing a bypass wasn't just illegal—if it was discovered he was the electrician who'd done the job, he'd be charged with a criminal offense. "If the tomatoes are charity, can't you get a grant to cover the power costs?"

"A good idea, mate but again, no time." Adam sighed. "I can see I've made you uncomfortable."

"Yeah."

"Thing is, Josh, I want to see you right. You, Sophie and the kids deserve to be comfortable and installed in your house as soon as possible. If you want that, I can help make it happen. All I need from you is a show of good faith. Install the bypass and remove it in January. I'll keep you off the books so there's no paper trail leading back to you. No one else needs to know. Too easy."

Too easy? Was he serious? Josh's left leg trembled uncontrollably. "What about Scotty?"

"This is nothing to do with Scotty. If you do this for me, you're not only cementing your place as an esteemed friend of Petrovic Family Homes, you're committing to Myrtle."

His scarred hand clapped Josh's shoulder. "And I don't know about you, Josh, but I didn't survive that fire to lose the town two years later. Did you?"

The faint roar that had taken up residence in Josh's head on the day of the fires kicked up a couple of notches. He'd lost a house and a job to that fire. It had saddled him with a mountain of debt, made him renege on his promise to Sophie that she could stay at home with the kids and it kept him tied to a town that was barely functioning. And now, just as everything seemed to be coming together for him and Sophie, it was all turning to hell again.

The buzzing in his head intensified and the choking scent of smoke in his nostrils dried his mouth. Fear threatened to drop him to his knees. He'd fought this fire so many times already, he'd be damned if he was going to let it win again. The bypass was just a job.

One job.

"I'll do it tomorrow."

"Good man." Adam clinked his beer bottle against Josh's. "That's the spirit we need to put Myrtle on the map."

CHAPTER NINETEEN

CLAIRE LOCKED THE CLINIC AND WALKED TO THE CWA ROOMS
with her laptop and her dinner—leftovers from the night before. There
was no point rushing home to eat and chat with Matt before the
meeting anymore. Over the last couple of weeks, eating dinner was
something she dreaded.

During the day when she was busy at work she could pretend that
her relationship hadn't hit the wall. But in the evenings it was
impossible to ignore. She'd taken to standing in the kitchen and bolting
food, although there were more nights than she cared to admit when
dinner consisted of ice cream or a bag of salt and vinegar chips. The
evenings the dogs stayed for company were easier. Unlike her appetite,
theirs were completely unaffected by the split.

Phil always unlocked the CWA rooms for them before leaving the
Men's Shed so Claire walked straight to the kitchen. She planned to
eat while she paid some bills and prepared her treasurer's report. She
was looking forward to presenting it at the meeting along with hard
copies. The act would suck the disapproving air from the protocol
queen's lungs and Claire couldn't deny she'd enjoy watching Bec's
pained face.

She'd forced down half the chili con carne and had almost completed the treasurer's report when she heard the main door click shut. Damn. Was it meeting time already? She'd been so busy balancing figures she hadn't gotten around to mentally preparing for the girl chat that opened the evenings. Although she had no difficulties talking with patients, her off-duty self struggled with breezy chatter. She always wanted to cut to the chase, but in groups of women, chatter was elevated to gold status. And when wine wasn't on offer, she needed to psych herself up for it.

Glancing at the time on her computer, she saw she still had enough time to type the final figures and do some deep breathing before Commandant Bec started the meeting.

"Why are you here?"

Claire gritted her teeth both at the lack of hello and the question. She didn't look up from the screen. "Solving world peace, Rebecca."

"Well, I hope it involves paying the deposit to the timing company."

"Already done." Claire glanced up and did a double take. Bec's hair was a mass of wild spikes and flat curls reminiscent of bed hair and stale hairspray. Her face was pale, puffy and devoid of makeup.

Claire hadn't seen Bec's natural complexion since they were fourteen, when the gangly teen had metamorphosed into a curvaceous young woman who never stepped out of her house without blow dried hair and a full face of makeup, including expertly applied eyeliner.

The eyeliner had impressed Claire then, and in a funny way, it still did. She was far too impatient to spend the time required to master liquid eyeliner. In an odd charitable teenage moment, she'd conceded that the vacuous girl had a gritty determination even if it was misdirected.

Back in the day Bec lacked the funds to dress well, but since her marriage she was Myrtle's fashionista, even if her look was more brassy than refined elegance. But not today. She was wearing a long black cardigan that had the lines to be elegant if it hadn't been wrapped over a dress that strained at every seam. Claire wasn't at work, so she didn't censor her surprise.

"You look like crap."

"So do you. Believe me, that's saying something."

Claire's laugh bubbled up and out, tinged with an edge of hysteria. "I'll give you that. There's no point denying that I do indeed look like crap."

Bec's flinty glare faded and her stiff stance softened. She unexpectedly pulled out a chair and slumped onto it.

Claire closed her laptop. "I thought you'd come to rush me into the meeting room so we'd start on time."

"No point." Bec's voice was tired, matching her general demeanor. "Erica just texted. She and Layla went to Geelong to check out marquees and they've been delayed. Sophie's kids are vomiting and Julie's sick."

"Julie's never sick."

"Fine. Don't believe me."

"Spare me. What I mean is, she doesn't normally succumb to the viruses that flatten everyone else. Is she okay? Does she need a meal dropped round?"

"This is all I know ..." Bec picked up her cell phone. "Sorry, Bec. Minded the grandkids yesterday and now feeling like death warmed up. Please accept my apologies and have a good meeting." God, I hope my girls don't get this bug and give it to me. I'm throwing up enough already."

Suddenly, all the out-of-place pieces came together. Something deep inside Claire ached. "You're pregnant?"

Bec's hand swept from her breasts to her belly. "You think I'd look like this if I wasn't? I don't remember feeling like this last time. My mouth tastes disgusting, my legs are lead weights and all I want to do is sleep."

"You're older."

"And your sympathy's astounding. No wonder your patients love you."

Strangely weary of their usual point scoring, Claire held up her hands in a gesture of surrender. "I didn't say you were old. God, we're the same age. It's just you're not twenty-one anymore and—"

She cut off her spiel. Bec wasn't a patient. This was just a conversation between two women who barely tolerated each other. All she had to do was offer up the expected social niceties. She mustered up the words in her mind but her throat burned. She was unsure if the problem was her relationship with Bec or the pregnancy.

"Anyway ... congratulations!"

Bec didn't respond. She was no longer looking at Claire but vigorously rubbing a mark on the table with her forefinger. She lurched to her feet, briskly opened the cabinet under the sink, plucked out the Spray and Wipe and a cloth and returned to attack the barely visible food stain.

Red flags ran up Claire's professional pole. "I take it the pregnancy was a surprise?"

Bec kept rubbing. "Adam and I are thrilled."

"Of course."

The frantic rubbing stopped and Bec's mouth thinned. "You always have to take a shot at me, don't you?"

Exasperation broke over her like a rash. "How is agreeing with you taking a shot? I was being sincere."

"Of course." Bec's cleaning strayed to the rest of the table.

"Hey!" Claire moved her laptop out of the firing line as Bec sprayed frenetically, at complete odds with her usually controlled actions. "I get we have a history of snark but, hand to God, Rebec—Bec. I'm trying to be empathetic. Work with me."

"You're kidding, right? We've only ever worked against each other."

"Obviously, you've got a huge case of pregnancy brain if you've forgotten we're currently on a committee together organizing Myrtle's biggest ever event."

"And you fight me on everything."

"You fight me back."

Bec straightened the laptop so there was a perfect half-inch gap between it and the edge of the table. Then she reached for the dirty dinner plate.

Claire impulsively put her hand over Bec's, desperate to still it. "Rebec—Bec. Being thrilled about the baby doesn't mean the shock and surprise of the pregnancy hasn't left you reeling."

For a moment Bec stared at Claire's hand, then she made a strangled sound and sat down hard. "I shouldn't be pregnant. This wasn't supposed to happen. I had an IUD. But I'm having a baby next May whether I want to or not!"

The situation was familiar work territory for Claire—distressed woman dealing with unexpected news. She flicked into counseling mode, treading carefully. "What do you want to do?"

"I don't know!"

"You've got options."

"Options?" Bec stared blankly at Claire.

"Choices. About the pregnancy."

Bec's eyes widened into shimmering Pacific blue lagoons before quickly darkening to navy. A ragged sound split the air. "You think I've got choices? That's hilarious."

Claire stuck to the point. "Do you want to be pregnant?"

"It doesn't matter what I want."

"Of course it matters."

"Claire." Bec shot her a withering look. "Adam knows I'm pregnant. He wants the baby."

"Yes, but what do you—"

"There are no buts. Think about it. If you got pregnant and Matt knew, would you have a termination? No, because if he found out he'd ... it would end your relationship."

"That already happened when he found out I was doing everything I could to avoid getting pregnant."

The words slipped out so effortlessly it wasn't until she saw the astonishment on Bec's face that Claire realized what she'd said. Dear God, what the hell was wrong with her? If she'd wanted to tell someone the truth, she should have told Julie. But she'd been too scared, not wanting to risk even more censure dumping on top of Matt's rigid condemnation. So what had she gone and done instead? Spilled her guts to a woman she didn't trust. A woman who, three years earlier, had gleefully broken the news about her and Matt to a judgemental Myrtle.

"Sh—wow." Bec sounded like her younger self. "I thought you were just being competitive so you looked as bad or worse than I do."

"Well, that's what we do when we're within fifty yards of each other, isn't it? Try to win."

Bec's mouth tweaked up slightly at the edges. "You know, when I was a kid, all I wanted was to grow up and leave home. No one tells you being an adult sucks. I miss the simple moments of being a kid. Like when we were devastated at losing the Camp Otway Cup. Back then we thought that was as bad as things could possibly get."

"Only you were devastated."

Bec rolled her eyes. "Sure. And you never kept us up half the night cursing and crying that the Apollo Bay girls cheated at orienteering."

"Did I?" Claire searched her memory. "I honestly can't remember."

"Well, you did. You hated them for stealing your best event."

"I was pretty good at orienteering." She laughed. "Maybe it was so traumatic I've suppressed it."

It was supposed to be a funny line but it hung there between them, loud and lingering. Neither of them said a word.

Bec finally broke the silence. "Your mom was great. She picked us up, drove to Anglesea and bought everyone milkshakes to cheer us up. She talked about being the better woman and the importance of fair play."

"That sounds like Mom."

"I liked your mom. She had this way of being kind, caring and practical, but fun too. Unlike my mother, she always made me feel I could do just about anything. You must really miss her."

Claire had forgotten that Bec had known her mother. How

Heather had regularly driven her and Bec to and from Girl Scouts and pony club until Claire dropped out of both in favor of school-based activities and study. Apart from Julie, Bec was the first person since the funerals to voice how Claire felt about Heather. She didn't want to feel gratitude but it pricked the backs of her eyes with tears anyway.

"I do miss her. A lot. I didn't realize how much I depended on her until she wasn't here anymore."

"And Louise is hardly your biggest fan."

"You've noticed?"

"I'm not blind."

Matt is.

Bec's cell phone beeped and she read the text. "Layla and Erica are a few minutes away."

Grateful for the interruption, Claire pushed back looming tears and pulled a lipstick holder with a small mirror out of her handbag. "Guess it's time to put on our game faces." She peered into the mirror. "Lipstick alone won't cut it. I think I need foam filler under my eyes."

Bec produced the biggest makeup bag Claire had ever seen and passed the concealer. "So, are you and Matt over?"

Claire didn't want to answer the question but there was something oddly soothing about the fragile détente that she and Bec had just reached. If she said she didn't want to talk about it, she'd shatter a precious link to her mother. But even with Matt's ultimatum ringing loudly in her ears, she was loath to tell Bec the truth. That was too real.

"I don't know."

"I get that you have a career you love, but I always thought you'd have kids too."

The tangled knot of emotions inside Claire tightened with a jerk. She pressed her fist to her sternum. "Things change."

"I know."

The way Bec said the simple words—soft yet harsh—made Claire study her. But the woman she knew all too well was back, her previous distress deftly hidden under a layer of foundation, blush and powder. She'd discarded the cardigan and must have tugged on her dress, as it was sitting better on her frame, accentuating her new pregnancy curves.

"Sorry we're late!" Erica rushed into the kitchen with Layla trailing behind her.

"We bring sorry cakes," Layla said, putting down a box. "Will I make coffee?"

A slight shudder rippled across Bec's shoulders but as she straightened them, her breasts lifted, followed by her chin. "That's a lovely idea, Layla, but right now just the smell of coffee makes me want to throw up."

Erica's hand paused, hovering over a decadently iced cupcake. "Oh my God! Are you up the duff?"

Bec beamed a smile that belonged to someone who was not only content with their lot but was a tiny bit smug about it. "Yes! I'm knocked up. Preggers. And I couldn't be more excited. Adam and I always wanted three and after everything ..." she regally waved her hand, minimizing the horrendous trauma the fires had inflicted on her husband and herself, "... it's such a gift."

It was as if the woman she'd been fifteen minutes before had never existed and Claire was left wondering if she'd imagined their conversation. The gushing and girly Bec Petrovic was back, striding across the stage of life just as she'd been doing for years.

An unexpected ball of sadness lodged in Claire's chest, adding to an old collection.

JULIE HEARD PHIL SAY, "I don't think she's contagious," before he appeared in their bedroom doorway. "Jules, you up for a visitor? Bec's here."

"Give me a minute." Julie flicked the cover over the photo album.

As she hauled herself high onto a pile of pillows, she tried to use the height to outrun her guilt. She hadn't picked up stomach flu from the kids—she'd given in to an overwhelming desire to curl up in bed and hide. It had been a bad couple of days. The worst in months, but this time it wasn't just the desperate and aching chasm inside her that was the space Hugo had once filled. It was also the new and added weight of the breast lump. There were times when drawing in a deep breath seemed too difficult.

Despite resorting to despised sleeping pills, she'd slept fitfully. When she'd managed to sleep, her dreams were vivid 3D. One minute she was hugging Hugo, feeling his bulk filling her arms and his warmth and vitality seeping into her. The next minute she was flung to the nightmare of her future funeral. Under dark damp skies she watched the slumped and stricken figures of Phil and Penny and the confused and bewildered faces of little Ami-Louise and Ethan from a distance. Then she'd wake with a start, her nightie sopping with sweat and the bedsheets tight and tangled.

Poor Phil. He hadn't questioned her assertion that she had a bug. Instead, he'd given her the full invalid treatment—changing her bed and bringing her lemonade and dry crackers before graduating her to steamed chicken and rice. She'd drunk and eaten everything before retreating under the cover and dozing. Today, after forty-eight hours of nursing her, she read on his face the hope that she'd recovered enough to get back on deck.

Penny had telephoned with profuse apologies, reiterating how bad she felt and how she'd honestly thought the children had been well and truly past the infectious stage. Neither Penny nor Phil coped very well when Julie was sick, probably because she was rarely ill. They did their best but they still constantly turned to her for advice and guidance. But the guilt that her lie was causing Penny's distress didn't even make a dent in her resolve to keep her own counsel. Not even Charger's pathetic hang-dog looks were enough to propel her from bed and take him for a walk.

Phil reappeared with a hesitant Bec, who held a bunch of yellow gerberas.

"Look who's here," Phil said.

The claws of guilt dug in more deeply and Julie's desire to pull the covers over her head intensified. "Hello, Bec."

"I saw these and I thought they might cheer you up." Bec handed her the flowers before standing awkwardly, as if she didn't know how to be in someone else's bedroom.

Julie stared at the bright posy. A muscle in her back tensed so sharply it made pain throb under her shoulder blade. An image swamped her—a parade of women visiting and all of them bearing flowers. Bec's visit was a perfect example of what would happen when the news of her cancer spread. Kind and well-intentioned people would come and stand uncomfortably in this room, their auras stained with sympathy, but with relief in their eyes that it was she who was dying and not them.

"Jules?" Phil's voice jerked her out of her reverie. "I'll pop these in water for you. Cup of tea, Bec? Coffee?"

Bec shook her head. "I can't stay long."

"Quick cup of tea at least," Phil said, heading back to the kitchen.

"This is the first time I've ever visited you at home. I hope I'm not intruding."

"Not at all," Julie said automatically, patting the bed. "Please sit down."

Bec lowered herself gingerly as if Julie were a fragile piece of china.

"Thank you for the flowers. It's very kind of you although not at all necessary. I'm much better. I'll be back in the swing of things tomorrow." Perhaps if she kept telling herself that, it might be enough to trick her body into waking up in the morning lump free and with her energy and enthusiasm restored. "I feel bad that you've wasted your time."

"Not at all. It's nice to be able to do something for you when you're always looking after people."

"Nonsense."

"It's not nonsense." Bec wrung her hands, her large diamond

engagement ring and wedding ring spinning loose on her finger. "You invited me to craft group."

"That was for rather selfish reasons."

"I doubt that."

"I handpicked the five of you to kickstart a new guard. Myrtle needs young blood to relieve the load from old shoulders."

"You're not old! Adam said you and Phil did a phenomenal job on the rebuilding committee and he's impossible to impress. Besides, I read the other day that old is eighty. You're a long way from that."

Julie couldn't stifle her sigh. "It only took five hours to age me five years."

Bec flinched. "The fires aged everyone."

Julie knew she should reach out and pat Bec's hand but she lacked the energy to do it. Was reassurance and support a well that ran dry?

"You're right. The fires exacted a harsh toll, but when you're thirty years younger, you're more robust. I'm weary, Bec. I'm ready to stop."

"That's just the stomach flu talking. It wrings all the energy out of you and messes with your mind," Bec said resolutely. "I know when I get sick ... everything seems pointless. It's like the virus throws a party and only invites sadness."

Julie thought about the misery and pain Charger had tempered for a few weeks before a new black cloud rolled in.

"I'm sure you'll be feeling your normal energized self again soon." Bec adjusted her position on the bed. "Ouch. Oh! Sorry. I didn't mean to sit on this."

Julie's hand shot out to the small photo album but Bec had already picked it up. It fell open to a photo of Hugo taken on the garden tour day before the fires. He was wearing a green and white checked shirt, moleskins, an Akubra hat and a broad smile. With his hand resting on Turbo's head, the photo was quintessentially Hugo.

"It's my favorite photo. He's where he belonged, with the people and animals he loved. The only thing missing is a cow."

"He looks happy."

"He was happy. When the dreadful Amber stomped on his heart, he wasn't in a good place for a long time. By the time this photo was taken, he'd recovered. I know it's silly, but it helps to think of him now with someone who cherishes him in the way he deserved to be loved."

"Was he seeing someone when he ..." Bec's voice trailed off in the way so many people's did when they realized if they kept talking they'd have to say the word "died."

"No."

Bec studied the photo a little longer before handing the album back to her. "He was always very kind to the girls. When they were desperate for a puppy, he let them play with his."

Julie traced the outline of her beloved son. "That's my Hugo. He adored children." Her voice broke. "I hate that he lost the chance to have some of his own."

"Oh God." Panic vibrated in Bec's voice. "I'm so sorry, Julie. I didn't mean to upset you. Here. Have some water."

Julie accepted the glass. She took a sip, not because she was thirsty, but because on top of everything else, the agonized look on Bec's face was more than she could bear.

"Better?" Bec asked. "Oh, what a stupid thing to say. I know water doesn't make things better. What I meant was—"

"It's fine," Julie fudged. "Really."

Bec's ring spinning intensified. "Layla took the minutes last night and she'll email them to you, but the good news is people have actually signed up and paid to run. It's starting to feel very real. But there are some CWA things that are confusing me. Please don't step back now when I—we need your wisdom and expertise. We need you."

Once, Julie had not only thrived on that need, she'd welcomed it. As young married women, she and Heather had been a force in the town. They'd organized, baked and fundraised their way through the construction of a new preschool, the replacement of the elementary school's play equipment and the resurfacing of the netball courts. They'd petitioned the government's roads department for improved signage and visibility at a notorious intersection that had claimed five lives, and they'd served on both the CWA and the agricultural fair committees. In the years between Myrtle losing its doctor and gaining a nurse practitioner, they'd been there for the women in the district who'd needed a listening ear and occasionally a bed.

Despite her and Phil's devastating loss of Hugo, the animals and dear friends, after the fires people had instinctively looked to them for guidance and direction. Neither of them had questioned the community's need—they'd been involved all their lives so they'd just got on with listening, running community meetings and helping a shocked and traumatized Myrtle plan for its future. They'd stood like sentinels trying to protect the town against over-enthusiastic outsiders keen to help and the clueless bureaucrats who'd tried treating Myrtle as an urban community, not a country town with its own history.

Julie didn't regret any of it but each time she thought the job was done, something else was asked of her. It was unceasing. She didn't have wisdom. She had a hole in her heart and a lump in her breast. All she wanted to do was close her eyes and sleep.

CHAPTER TWENTY

"Come on, boys," Claire called the dogs. They came racing up to her, anticipation shining in their eyes. "Time to go to the big house."

Since Claire's first request for the dogs to stay over, she and Matt had fallen into an unspoken pattern of the animals spending every other night with her. Tonight was her night. It was also youth group so she'd come home early from work and taken them for a run along the creek before feeding them. Technically, they could stay on their beds on the veranda but as she was going to be out it seemed petty not to return them to the homestead where there was company.

She hadn't seen or spoken to her in-laws since Matt ... *Left you.* She shied away from the words. The two times she'd dropped the dogs off, the elder Cartwrights had been out. But it was Friday night so they'd be home and she was mentally prepared for if she ran into them. They would be the ones dealing with a surprise. Bundling the dogs into the car, she drove the short distance along the oak-lined road, remembering as she often did the last time she'd seen and hugged her parents. She tried to feel their tight embraces and their love circling her. Tried to avoid her sadness.

Pulling up close to the house, she gave the dogs strict and stern instructions to heel. It was more to do with moral support for her than good behavior from them. Flanked by the dogs, she walked along the veranda until she reached the kitchen door. Despite having walked through it thousands of times, she hesitated to pull open the screen door. Did she still have the right to enter unannounced?

But if she knocked, she was acknowledging that she and Matt were estranged. That was far too much power to give the Cartwrights. Blowing out a long breath, she opened both doors and allowed the dogs to run in first. She followed.

Bill turned, a coffee plunger in his hand and surprise on his face. "Claire."

"Hello, Bill."

The door to the dining room swung open. "Bill, we're waiting for coff—Claire." Louise said her name with the chill of an icicle. Claire had hurt her son and clearly, the gloves were well and truly off. The restrained politeness Louise had always practiced was no longer required. "This is unexpected."

The strain of maintaining good manners despite years of lukewarm welcomes suddenly collided with Matt's abandonment of her. In the process, her own bloody-mindedness kicked in. "Unexpected? Really? It's Friday night and I'm often here for dinner."

"And you're often late. This time you've missed dinner completely."

"I won't detain you, Louise. I'll just have a quick word with Matt."

"He's occupied."

"I'm sure he'll spare me two minutes."

She heard her confident words and prayed they were true. Without waiting for a reply, she brushed past Louise and walked into the dining room. Tamara, Lachlan and the children were in their usual positions down one side of the table and Matt was sitting opposite Tamara as he always did. But the chair next to him—her chair—wasn't empty. It was occupied by a woman with short blond hair whose head was tilted close to Matt's as if she was hard of hearing.

The conversation in the room ceased abruptly and all eyes turned to Claire. Blood roared in her ears.

"Claire." Tamara broke the silence. "You've never met Taylor, have you?"

Taylor remained silent but her combative brown gaze was fixed unflinchingly on Claire. The message was crystal clear: *I'm here. You're not.*

"Shut up, Tam." Matt threw down his napkin and rose to his feet.

Claire plunged deep, trying to force her mouth to work so she could greet the woman professionally—as if Taylor was a client instead of Matt's ex-girlfriend—but her body was frozen and unyielding. She was suddenly conscious of Matt's hand under her elbow and the pressure as he steered her and her barely cooperating legs out through the French doors and onto the veranda.

The cooling evening air penetrated her shock. Gulping deep breaths, she walked fast into the garden.

Matt followed, his hand rubbing the back of his neck. "Are you okay?"

She had no idea what she was, but she nodded anyway.

Relief lifted his worried face. "I'm sorry."

"Sorry?"

"Yeah. What Tamara said. She was out of line."

Claire wanted to scream, "Tamara isn't the only one out of line!" But she reined it in. Miraculously, she managed to ask relatively calmly, "Why is Taylor Norris sitting in the dining room?" *In my chair!*

"She and Tamara have been friends for years," Matt said as if that explained everything.

"Yes, but she doesn't normally eat at Oakvale Park."

"She's spending the weekend at Tamara's. Guess it made sense for her to come to Friday-night dinner."

Sense? "Surely if Tamara's got a weekend house guest, she'd miss Friday-night dinner."

"Mom invited her."

Claire's stomach cramped. Of course Louise had invited Taylor. If

Claire were a betting woman, she'd go for odds-on favorite that this entire visit had been stage-managed by the Cartwright women.

She swallowed, trying to keep her voice steady. "Did you know she was coming?"

Say no, Matt. Please say dinner was an ambush.

"Mom mentioned it when I got in last night."

Calm vaporized and Claire heard herself yelling. "You knew she was coming and you didn't object?"

His conciliatory face reshaped itself to mutinous. "Hell, Claire. It's not my house. My parents have the right to invite whoever they want to dinner."

"And you have the right to refuse to join them. But no. Not only didn't you object, you went to dinner."

"It's almost three years since I saw Taylor. To be honest, after everything, I'm surprised she wanted to come."

Her arms flew into the air. "You sat next to her!"

"I sat where I always sit." He swore softly. "This isn't my fault. If you weren't behaving like a crazy woman, you would have been sitting next to me and Taylor would have sat somewhere else."

"You honestly believe your ex-lover would have been invited to dinner if I was there?"

He gave it a moment's consideration. "Probably not."

Her frustration ebbed and relief trickled in. Finally, he understood. "Th—"

"Mom wouldn't have wanted you to feel uncomfortable."

His words pierced like a sniper's bullet and white lights exploded behind her eyes. She knew better than to criticize Matt's family; her mother had advised against it and for almost three year she'd held fast to that mantra because she loved him and he loved her back. What did it matter if his parents didn't love her? But now everything had gone to hell and they stood on either side of a great divide.

"Matt, how can you be so freaking blind? Your mother and sister have never forgiven me for not being Taylor."

He crossed his arms. "God, not this again! You're being ridiculous."

"Am I? When you broke up with Taylor, your mother and sister kept in touch and what do you know? At the first sign of trouble between us, they invite her here. Given you broke her heart so badly, she should have refused their invitation, but she didn't. She came and they're cheering."

Claire wrapped her arms around her waist, trying to stop herself from trembling. "And let me guess. Tonight, over pre-dinner drinks, Taylor told you how sorry she is to hear we're having problems. As you pulled out her chair for her to sit, she whispered about how devastated and hurt you must be. When Bill was opening the second bottle of wine, she let it drop that only a heartless bitch would change her mind about having children and then string you along."

"Would she be wrong?"

She refused to be side-tracked. "And after coffee and dessert, your mother and sister will arrange for the two of you to be alone. Then they'll listen through the door and high-five each other when Taylor suggests you call her any time you feel the need to talk."

"Just to set your story straight, Taylor made that offer to me this morning when we met for coffee in Colac. Mom and Tamara were here at the farm."

Her blood ran so cold it burned. "You bastard!"

"You don't get to call me names."

"We've barely separated and you're turning to your ex-girlfriend? The one you told me you didn't love enough to marry? Not only are you a bastard, you're a cliché!"

"Take some responsibility."

"Oh my God!" Suddenly it all made sense. "You're a serial monogamist. When the going gets tough at two years, you just walk away, only this time you're walking backwards!"

Matt stiffened. Right then she knew she'd lost him and she almost cried out from the pain.

"Way to go, Claire. Now you've added paranoid to the list of your bizarre behaviors. You've completely lost the plot. For God's sake, please get some help before we try and talk again."

SOPHIE STUDIED the kitchen and bathroom tile samples she'd brought home from the store in Colac. The kids were in bed and Josh sat nursing a beer.

"What do you think?" she asked.

"We made all these decisions when we built the first house. Why reinvent the wheel?"

"Because this is a totally different house. Last time it was a traditional brick homestead. This time, because of the Colorbond siding, the look is sleek and modern. It demands different tiles."

Josh swore under his breath. "We don't even have walls yet."

"Remember last time how we suddenly had to make all the decisions about fittings in a rush? This time I'm getting in early to avoid the stress."

"Fine." He pointed the neck of the beer bottle at one of the tiles. "That one."

"Really? Are you sure?"

"Hell, Soph! Why ask my opinion if you don't want it?"

"I do want it, but you chose without even looking at them. Do you even know if it's a bathroom or kitchen tile?"

He grunted. "You know you get off on this stuff way more than me."

Sophie wanted to disagree—it wasn't how she remembered things at all. When they were building the first house, Scotty had called unexpectedly saying the job was being fast-tracked due to another client pulling out. This meant he needed a list of their preferred flooring and fixtures ASAP. Josh had immediately rung his parents, asking them to mind Liam. Then he'd towed her around kitchen and bathroom showrooms all weekend. Pregnant and prone to fatigue, she'd had a mini-meltdown over the stovetop decision. Josh had sat her down in a café and fed her tea and cake while he read a stack of brochures.

Indefatigable, Josh was the one who'd found the bathroom tiles she'd loved so much. It was Josh who'd scoured websites reading appliance reviews and chosen the oven and the sink. On the Sunday afternoon, when they'd finally completed the list with an hour to spare before Liam was dropped home, Josh had tumbled her into bed to celebrate. Now she couldn't even get him to look at one tile.

She swallowed a sigh and changed topics. "How was work?"

"Yeah."

"What are you doing at the moment?"

"You know. The usual. Fill-in stuff."

"But that'll change once work starts on the eco-tourism site, right?"

Josh ran his nail under the beer label, peeling it back in strips. In the weeks since the framing party, she'd been waiting for him to report back on his conversation with Adam. But like everything with Josh at the moment, it was a balancing act. He either accused her of being too pushy about his work or being more interested in Put Myrtle on the Map than him.

"Josh?"

"What?"

"You've asked Adam about finishing your apprenticeship?"

"Didn't have to. He brought it up."

Yes! She was glad she'd been proactive and mentioned it to Adam at the party. Adam offering Josh the position was better than Josh asking for it. Josh hated asking anyone for anything. "When do you sign the papers?"

"I don't."

"What? Why?" Anxiety scuttled through her. She wanted him to have job security.

"I said no."

"What the hell, Josh! We discussed it. We agreed."

"It's crap money."

"For one year!"

"Yeah, well you want this house built quick, so we need more money, not less."

"But we need to plan for our future. Qualifying will give you job security." She could hardly believe she was the one talking about the future when it had always been Josh's mantra.

He snorted. "Security's BS. Anyone can turn around and sack you."

Aggravation simmered at his negativity and she wanted to shake him. "You lost one job, Josh. One! And it wasn't because you sucked at it or were a bad employee who was unreliable or took too much time off. It was because of the fires. Adam told me how much he respects you. He's not going to sack you."

Josh took a long drink. "He says that now, but there are no guarantees."

"There are! He told me the eco-tourism project will take at least eighteen months to complete. Even if there's no work after that, by then you'd be a qualified electrician. That will make getting another job easier."

His leg jigged up and down. "What don't you get about me hating wiring?"

"What don't you get about us needing you to have a secure and well-paying job?"

"I've got a freakin' job!" He lurched to his feet, knocking the table as he stormed away.

The chosen tile tumbled off the edge, hitting the concrete floor and smashing into six jagged pieces.

"SORRY FOR THE NEEDY GROUP TEXT." Sophie nursed a glass of wine. "Sorry for gate-crashing your evening."

"Don't be sorry," Erica said. "I'm glad you reached out. Sometimes we need to have a cathartic whine about our darling husbands. Don't tell Nathan I said that, though. He sent the wine and he took over the bedtime rituals. Honesty, Scarlett manages to invent a new one every week."

"I'm sorry I couldn't host," Bec said. "Adam's frantic at the moment with the eco-tourism project. He needed a quiet house."

"I'm sorry your day is difficult," Layla offered.

"Do we all have to apologize for something?" Claire asked, clearly bemused by the round of apologies. "Normally I'd default to being sorry for being late but as you've all come to my place ..."

"You have to apologize for the house being a mess and for only having chips instead of homemade dips," Bec said without malice.

"Chips are totes fine with me." Erica greedily filled her palm.

"And your house isn't messy. It's lovely." Sophie tried not to think about the smashed tile on the shed floor and Josh sitting rigidly on the couch with his headphones jammed over his ears. When he'd refused to look at her, let alone talk to her, she'd been so upset that she'd used the Put Myrtle on the Map's WhatsApp account to ask if anyone could meet her.

Claire's response had been instant, suggesting Sophie come to her place. The fast reply hadn't surprised her. Claire never seemed able to fully switch off being at work. It made talking to her a very different experience from a cozy chat with a girlfriend. Claire was either cracking jokes or suddenly turning serious and making the conversation like a counseling session. Sometimes Sophie didn't want solutions, she just wanted to drink wine and vent.

Sitting on Claire's couch with the scent of new leather curling seductively around her, Sophie realized these women were no longer just a random group of knitters or a reluctant committee. Over the last six months, and without her really noticing, they'd become her friends. She wished Julie was here so she could thank her for starting craft group but she hadn't responded to her message. Then again, Julie wasn't as glued to her cell phone as the rest of them.

Sophie took another sip of the fruity pinot gris. "Have we driven Matt away? I guess we should apologize to him too for invading his house."

Claire drained her wineglass and refilled it.

"Have I said the wrong thing?"

"At least I'm off the hook this time," Erica quipped.

"Our visit probably gave Matt the excuse he wanted to escape to his workshop," Bec said. "Right, Claire?"

Claire's head jerked back as if she'd been smacked on the chin. "It's okay, Bec. There's no point keeping it a secret anymore." Her head dipped and her hands gripped her wineglass so tightly her knuckles gleamed. "So the news is, despite me not wanting him to leave, Matt's moved out. The way things stand at the moment, he's not returning any time soon."

Shocked silence dripped down the walls. Sophie didn't know what stunned her more—that Bec had known about the situation and was trying to protect Claire or that Matt Cartwright had moved out. Matt and Claire were the poster couple with the relationship everyone aspired to. If Sophie was honest, she'd envied them their easy way of being together, especially when she and Josh currently spent more time arguing than not.

Her skin prickled with sudden apprehension. If Matt and Claire's relationship could fail, where the hell did that leave her and Josh?

Claire suddenly sat up and leaned forward. "But you didn't come here to talk about me. We're here to help Sophie. What happened?"

"Claire!" Sophie's premonition of doom vanished under a streak of incredulity. "Matt's left you. That's far more important to talk about than my silly fight with Josh."

"I doubt it was silly. Silly wouldn't have made you text us."

"Sophie's right, Claire," Erica said. "It's time to drop the counseling shtick and just be Claire McKenzie, wronged woman. You get drunk while we trash the rat bastard."

"Thanks for the offer but it's not necessary. It might be a shock to you but I've had twenty-odd days to get used to it."

"And not everyone feels comfortable discussing their personal life in a group," Bec added.

"Or at all," Claire muttered. She raised her wineglass to Bec.

"And the shocks just keep coming," Erica said. "That's twice in five minutes Bec and Claire have been nice to each other. I'm buying us a Lotto ticket."

Layla, who'd kept quiet, put her hand on Claire's shoulder. "I don't think your Matt is really a bastard."

Sophie waited for Claire's curt rebuttal but it didn't come. Instead, she watched as the woman she'd always thought of in terms of calm, composed and capable fell crying into Layla's arms.

Layla gave the others a frantic look as she patted Claire's back. Sophie found a box of tissues in the kitchen. Erica offered Claire wine, water, tea and, in desperation, shots. But nothing dented Claire's crying jag. If anything, it worsened, her body shaking with sobs.

"Claire's usually the one helping us. How we can help her?"

When no one said anything, Sophie looked straight at Bec. The pregnant woman was sitting rigidly in her chair staring at Claire's heaving back as if the sight was both mesmerizing and frightening.

"Bec?"

Bec snapped out of her reverie and picked up her cell phone. "I'm calling Julie. She's known Claire all her life."

"Claire, you make yourself sick." Layla sounded close to tears herself.

Sophie tried thrusting tissues at Claire, but her face was buried on Layla's chest.

"Come on, Claire, get a grip," Erica said firmly. "You're getting snot all over Layla's pretty blouse."

"Erica! That's not helpful." Sophie couldn't believe her insensitivity.

But the volume of Claire's wailing diminished. She gave a series of almighty sniffs and took some wet, crackly breaths before finally raising her head. Accepting Sophie's tissues, she wiped her face.

"Thanks, Erica. I needed a jolt."

Erica gave a wry smile. "You're welcome. Sometimes when we're totally losing it, a bit of humor's a circuit breaker. It occasionally worked for me for me during the dark days."

"And I've made a huge mess of your blouse, Layla. Sorry." Claire offered her the face cloth Sophie had dampened.

"It's no problem. Are you feeling better?"

A harsh bark of laughter filled the room. "I feel like crap. And foolish."

"You're not foolish. You're hurting," Sophie said.

"Have you talked to anyone about whatever it is that's going on between you and Matt?" Erica asked.

Claire gulped wine.

"I'm taking that as a no."

"Believe me, talking won't fix it. Each time we try, things get worse."

Erica seated herself on the coffee table and faced Claire. "When I had PND, I didn't want to talk to anyone either but in the end, it was the talking that helped more than the drugs."

"I'm not sick!"

Erica didn't flinch at the hurtful accusation. "But you're not well either, are you? If you were, you wouldn't have said that to me."

Claire looked at her lap.

Sophie glanced around uneasily for Bec. This sort of fraught situation was too much for fledgling friends. They needed Julie.

"Matt says I'm crazy." Claire didn't sound as if she completely disagreed.

Erica snorted. "And as a farmer, he's eminently qualified to diagnose."

"I'm sure he doesn't really think you're crazy," Sophie offered. "Anyone can see that he loves you to death."

Claire moaned. "He *loved* me. He stopped the moment I told him I don't want children."

"You don't want children?" Layla looked bewildered. "But you are great with kids."

"It's usually the other way around," Sophie mused.

She'd read an article about married men who didn't want children and the women who had to decide to either put the relationship ahead of their need for a child or walk away. Why on earth wouldn't Claire want to have a baby with a bloke who loved her? And if Matt wanted kids and Claire didn't, Sophie struggled to see where there was room for compromise to reach an agreement. The only way for them to survive this impasse was if one of them did a complete backflip.

Erica glared at Sophie and Layla while slashing the air in front of her throat with her fingers. "Claire, love doesn't just stop. Matt's probably angry and hurt and a whole heap of other things. When we're angry we don't listen without an agenda. We only hear what we want to hear.

"When I got sick and I couldn't be the mother to Rafi that I desperately wanted to be, I hated myself so much. Angry was my default setting and I pushed everyone away. Counseling's the only reason Nathan and I survived that time and I'm so thankful for it. When we're stuck in a spiral of hate, an impartial person sees the things we're blind to."

Claire closed her eyes as if she wanted to block out Erica, but Erica wasn't put off by the lack of eye contact.

"Claire, you spend your days helping people, but you know what? Sometimes the helpers need help and that's not a crime. What would you say to a couple whose long-term relationship had just broken down?"

Claire kept her eyes shut. "There's no point suggesting to Matt we go to couples counseling. He says the problem's all mine. He refuses to talk to me until I get some help."

The image of Claire on the television news the night of the fires rose again in Sophie's mind, only this time it wasn't accompanied by a heart-thumping jolt of anxiety. For almost two years she'd held a vague and unsettling thought that the fires had forged Claire and Matt into different people and *that* was the reason they'd never married. It had bothered her so much, she'd sought reassurances from Josh that the fires hadn't altered him.

"I was never in danger," was his standard reply until one night he'd lost his temper. "Stop asking questions you already know the answers to!"

Not long after, Josh lost his job. That event had caused him far more angst than the fires. If tonight was anything to go by, it still did. Although Josh was currently driving her bonkers, it was just temporary house stress and it would soon be over. Unlike Claire and Matt, they weren't faced with wanting very different things.

Sophie didn't understand women who didn't want children—it made her uncomfortable. Now that Trixie was approaching two, her need to have another baby was firing on all cylinders. She was back to glancing in prams and she'd been spending quiet moments at work daydreaming about another baby. She had it all planned. The moment they moved into the new house, she'd get pregnant and work until she was thirty weeks. This was another reason she wanted Josh to start the final year of his electrical apprenticeship now—it meant he'd be qualified when her maternity leave finished and she could stay at home with the kids.

Despite knowing that Josh hated it when she got in his face, tonight she'd let her dissatisfaction with his job situation get the better of her. Stupid! It was time to take a new approach. Josh's parents were due back in a month and when his father learned Josh was not only giving up important workplace benefits, but a chance to qualify as an electrician, he'd talk some sense into him. Josh always listened to Craig.

All things considered, she was in a far better position than Claire.

Sophie realized Erica was still talking. "Maybe you can't get Matt to go to counseling, but what would you say to a woman who'd collapsed in a crying jag a few weeks after her partner left her?"

It took a moment but Claire eventually opened one eye before huffing out a long breath. "I'd recommend counseling."

"I rest my case."

"I don't want to go!" Claire's fingers fiddled with a hole in her jeans enlarging it. "What does it say about me when the health professional has to get help?"

"It says you're normal. No one's bullet proof, Claire. And no one, except perhaps a masochist, cheerfully puts their hand up for therapy. It's confronting. Doesn't mean you don't do it. Right now, you have two choices. Counseling or a breakdown. I know which I'd prefer."

Claire shook her head as if she couldn't quite believe what she was hearing. "And to think the first time I met you, Ericia, I thought you were flaky."

Erica laughed. "That's my secret power. I suck you in with my bumbling ways and then when you least expect it, I hit you with my smarts."

"Listen to Erica. She talks sense." Layla gave Claire a shy smile. "You don't have time for a breakdown. We have too many jobs to put Myrtle on the map."

"Good point, Layla," Erica said. "So, Claire, what's it to be?"

Bec finally stepped back into the room and Sophie hurried over to her. "Is Julie on her way?"

Bec shook her head. "She's not picking up her home phone or her cell. Claire—"

Claire rocked to her feet, her face twisted with fury. "Do *not* talk about me as if I'm not in the room!"

"I see you've recovered," Bec shot back. "And we're not talking about you, we're talking about Julie."

"What about Julie?"

"When you were so upset and none of us could get through to you, I called her. I thought you might like her here."

"Oh." Claire had the grace to look contrite. "Um ... thank you. That was very thoughtful, especially since Mom ..."

Bec shrugged. "But she's not answering. Have she and Phil gone away?"

"Phil's gone fishing for a couple of days but I saw Julie at the gate this morning," Sophie said.

"Maybe she went to a friend's place for dinner?"

"She told me that, as she had the TV to herself, she was going to watch *Call the Midwife*."

"A box of tissues, a glass of wine and *Call the Midwife* is my idea of bliss," Erica said. "It's my weekly therapeutic cry."

"Perhaps she thinks I'm calling to ask her about CWA stuff and she doesn't want to be interrupted," Bec mused.

"That doesn't sound like Julie though, does it?" Sophie said. "I mean, she's the mom of this group, isn't she?"

"She is very kind to me when we move here," Layla said.

"And she got the five of us working together," Erica said. "That's no mean feat."

"Claire, you ring. If Julie's going to answer anyone, it will be you," Bec suggested.

"Good idea. She'll probably text to tell me to call tomorrow."

Watching Claire's transformation from overwrought and distraught to focused and practical gave Sophie whiplash. But then again, the nurse was used to dealing with other people's problems.

Claire swiped her cell phone and pressed the screen a couple of times before raising it to her ear. "Voice mail. I'll try her cell." She walked while she waited. "It's rung out. Okay, Phil's out of town and Julie's home alone and not answering her telephone. Bec, you're sober. Can you drive me to Beechside?"

"Of course."

"We'll all come." Sophie was starting to worry.

"Maybe just Bec and Claire," Layla said. "All of us is too many."

"I'm sure we're worrying over nothing," Claire said, "but please, stay here and eat ice cream. We'll call when we get there, okay?"

"Okay." But the plan didn't reassure Sophie, who couldn't shift the concern on Claire's face out of her mind.

CHAPTER TWENTY-ONE

"There's going to be a perfectly logical explanation, right?"

Bec slowed to take the tight bend, surprised by Claire asking her opinion. "I hope so. They don't need any more heartache. They've been through enough—"

"We've all been through enough. Sometimes I wonder if it's ever going to stop."

Bec wanted to agree but she was worried her voice would give too much away. At least it was dark and Claire couldn't see her face. She braked. "Will you get the gate?"

"Is the Pope Catholic?"

The last vestiges of the dusky apricot light lit up the whitewashed wood and Bec watched Claire handle the gate with competent ease, just like she handled most things.

Growing up, Bec had resented the way Claire glided through life seemingly unaware of how lucky she was to be blessed with loving and supportive parents and the choice of a career. Not that Bec hadn't eventually enjoyed hairdressing but she would have liked the choice to have stayed at school longer. Perhaps studied to be a preschool teacher.

Instead she'd come home on a very ordinary Wednesday afternoon ready to tackle her homework and her mother had informed her that everything was arranged—Bec was starting an apprenticeship the following Monday.

There'd been a fleeting thought of disobeying the edict, but it had been nuked by the very real possibility her refusal would get her kicked out of home. So, she'd done what she was told and set out to become the best apprentice Carol's Cuts N Colors had ever employed. It seemed a lifetime ago now.

Claire swung up into her seat just as Bec's cell phone rang. Adam's name lit up on the dashboard and her stomach cramped. If it wasn't a committee meeting, Adam didn't like her going out at night, so she'd told him this was a special meeting to troubleshoot a problem with the fun-run trail. As Adam was currently obsessed with covering his costs for the tomato crop—and that was largely dependent on the day drawing a decent crowd—he'd almost pushed her out the door. Even so, this call would be him checking when she'd be home. Bec didn't want to talk to Adam with Claire in the car so she foolishly pressed the red button hoping he wouldn't call back. The cell immediately rang again. Her heart thumped as she pressed the green button.

"Hi, I'm in the car with Claire McKenzie," she said quickly, before he could say a word.

There was a brief silence. "That's a new one, babe."

Bec's hand tightened on the wheel, her mind racing, trying to pick words that would avoid him saying something she didn't want Claire to hear.

"Believe me, I'm as surprised as you are, Adam." Claire sounded like she meant it. "By the way, I've assigned a marquee at the family fun day especially for your tomatoes and I'm following up with the other CWA about making tomato sauce. Bec says you're worried about ripening times so I thought green tomato pickle might work too."

"Excellent idea, Claire." He said her name with the same smoothness he always used with other people. "And what are you two up to tonight? You're not leading my wife astray, are you?"

"Absolutely," Claire said. "It's what I do."

He laughed. "Just remember, she's carrying precious cargo."

"That's why she's the designated driver."

Bec interrupted the banter, her stomach tight with worry that the conversation would blow her lie. She told him what he'd rung to hear. "I won't be too much longer."

"No rush. You girls enjoy yourselves." The line went dead.

The moon was rising and between its light and the car's there were long shadows dancing across the farm road. "Stop!" Claire pointed. "Roo!"

The large marsupial suddenly appeared in the middle of the road dazzled by the lights. Bec braked hard, her mouth dry. "Thanks. You can't have drunk that much wine. I didn't even see it."

"I know this stretch of road like the back of my hand. There's a break in the trees and it's a popular place for them to cross. Besides, Hugo and I totaled a farm ute here once and you never forget that. I reckon this old man kangaroo is probably a relative of the one we hit."

Bec suddenly wanted an answer to a question that had always intrigued Myrtle. "Did you and he ever ...?"

"No way!"

The roo moved off and Bec pressed her foot on the accelerator. "You make it sound like he was freakishly unattractive."

Claire laughed. "Spoken like someone who never milked with him and only saw him in town clothes. No, Hugo darling and I were definitely in the friend zone. Why?"

"Oh, there were rumors."

"There's always rumors in Myrtle. Mind you, Mom and Julie probably started the ones about Hugo and me. Right, we're here."

Claire hopped out and strode toward the house only to suddenly stop, pivot on her booted heels and walk back to the car. She pulled open Bec's door. "What are you doing?"

"She'll want to see you, not me. I'll wait here."

Claire's face flickered with familiar irritation and Bec braced herself for the verbal sting but it didn't come. "Come with me. Please?"

Surprised by the request, Bec grabbed her keys. By the time she got out of the car, Claire was almost at the veranda. So much for wanting company. Bec heard the indignant bark of the Lang's old dog and Claire murmuring to him. When Bec reached the light of the veranda, Claire turned to face her with a puppy in her arms.

"Meet Charger. He won't hurt you. If anything, he'll lick you to death. Julie's besotted with him. He reminds her of Hugo and his dog." Still holding the puppy, Claire pushed open the front door. "Julie? It's Claire."

Bec gave her a gentle push. "Thanks a lot."

"And Bec."

They walked into the kitchen, which displayed the happy wear and tear of a well-used and well-loved room. Family photos adorned the sideboard and the old radio blared loudly. A newspaper lay open at the crossword and a cold cup of tea and an empty plate with a few strands of lettuce, a speck of tomato and a crust sat next to it on the kitchen table.

"This looks more like the remains of lunch than dinner."

Claire turned off the radio. "Julie loves doing the crossword at lunchtime."

Bec rummaged among the papers. "Here's her cell phone. It's open on a dictionary app."

Charger whined and squirmed and Claire set him down. His nose quivered and he shot out of the room straight down the hall, his little legs sliding and skating on the bare boards. He whined at the bathroom door.

Claire strode after him, knocking loudly. "Julie? It's Claire and Bec. You in there?"

The puppy barked and jumped, scratching at the door.

Bec tried the handle. It turned but the door wouldn't open past a crack. "Julie?"

Whining, the puppy shoved his nose into the space. He went quiet just long enough for them to hear Julie saying faintly, "Can't ... move."

Claire's eyes reflected fear. "I'll go outside and see if I can climb in through the window. You stay here and keep talking to her."

Bec pressed her mouth to the door. "Julie, it's Bec. Can you hear me?"

"Yes." Julie's voice sounded a little stronger.

The puppy was frantic and making such a racket that Bec picked him up, hoping the touch would quieten him. He snuggled into her, licking her face. Tears instantly threatened. Bloody pregnancy hormones. They were like the bulldozers that had rumbled into Myrtle after the fires and razed the burnt-out shells of barely standing buildings: they flattened years of protective defenses with ease, leaving her exposed and vulnerable. She cleared her throat, trying to pull herself together.

"Your puppy's adorable. Just as well Ivy hasn't met him or she'd have kidnapped him. She loved your—" *Use his name. Julie always uses his name.* "Loved Hugo's puppies."

"I ... remember."

Relieved Julie was responding, she kept talking. "I wanted to buy one of Hugo's puppies but Adam was adamant." She laughed at the word play—years of practice made it easy. "Arguing over that puppy was as close as we ever came to getting a divorce."

Adam had made the same joke the year before the fires. Back then, she supposed there was a slim chance Adam may have divorced her if he'd known about her plans. But not now. The fires had forged her and Adam together forever—his disfigurement, her guilt and grief, their shared pain.

"Hang in there, Julie," Claire said. "Won't be long."

"Don't get a fright when you see Claire's big bum coming through the window."

"I heard that!" Claire's voice sounded closer now. "My bum's got more of a chance of squeezing through this gap than your boobs."

"Spoken like a flat-chested woman."

Julie groaned. "Girls ..."

Bec heard a dull thud followed by Claire swearing and then, "Oh hell, Julie!"

"Claire? What's going on?"

"Give us a tick."

Bec couldn't make out what either of the women were saying, but she heard groaning. Then the door opened just enough for Bec to squeeze into the room. A chair lay on its side, Julie lay on the floor and Claire was kneeling beside her.

"Oh, Julie! What happened?"

"I was dust—I fell off the chair." She closed her eyes as if explaining took too much energy.

"Bec, grab a couple of towels and put them under her head. Okay, Julie, look at me."

The bossy nurse was in charge and in this instance, Bec was happy to let Claire run the show.

Claire opened the flashlight app on her cell phone and whipped it over Julie's eyes. "Your pupils are normal and reacting so that's one less thing to worry about. Did you black out?"

"I don't know. I've been here for hours." Julie grabbed their hands. "Bless you both. I thought I'd have to spend the night here. What made you come?"

"We were having a special CWA meeting—"

"We were having a wine and whine." Claire rolled her eyes at Bec. "Sophie needed to vent. When you didn't answer either phone and we knew Phil was away, we came over to make sure you were okay. What hurts?"

"Ankle and hip."

Claire ran her hands along the length of Julie's legs. "You haven't broken or dislocated either hip so that's a win although you're going to have some pretty spectacular bruising. Your left ankle's swollen like a balloon."

"I'll tie up Charger and get some ice," Bec offered, happy to have a job.

When she returned from the kitchen with a tea towel and a bag of frozen peas, a very pale Julie was propped up against the bath. Claire had wrapped a bandage from Julie's toes to above her knee.

"Thanks." Claire accepted the tea towel–wrapped peas with an appreciative smile before placing the bag over Julie's ankle. She sat back on her haunches. "Feeling dizzy?"

"Dizzy, no. Stupid, yes." Julie sighed. "I've been lying here cold and uncomfortable for hours and thinking how cross Heather would be with me."

Claire laughed. "For climbing onto a rickety chair instead of a sturdy step stool?"

"No. For not telling anyone about the lump in my breast that's been growing there for months."

Bec saw the anxiety on Julie's face and lowered herself down next to her to take her hand. "A lump isn't automatically cancer."

"Exactly." Claire nodded her agreement. "It could be—"

"I'm sixty-seven, Claire. You know the odds are stacked in cancer's favor."

"I know that nothing's conclusive until the test results are in."

"I don't want tests."

"Julie! If Mom was here she'd tell you you're being ridiculous."

"If your mother was still here, Hugo would still be here and me having cancer wouldn't be the straw that breaks Phil and Penny."

Bec got an inkling of understanding. "Have you been ignoring the lump to protect them?"

"Julie, that's bonkers," Claire snapped.

"How is it different from you making yourself sick over Matt and refusing to try to work things out?"

Despite the heat in their voices and the pulsating frustration that filled the small space, Bec heard the love the women shared. Her own mother's love for her was tied to her marriage to Adam and the money he provided so she could live a comfortable life, rather than happiness for Bec. Claire had lost a loving mother and Bec was sorry, but despite that awful loss, Claire still had a woman in her life who loved and cared for her.

A bud of jealousy glowed green and opened inside her, twisting round her heart. "Actually, Julie, Claire had a spectacular meltdown tonight. After her wails scared the sheep and her tears had soaked Layla's blouse, she's agreed to get some help."

Claire's eyes flashed. "I don't think I actually said that."

"But you want Julie to see a doctor?"

"Yes! Unlike Matt and me, cancer can be cured!"

"In that case, the solution's obvious. Julie has the tests and you talk to a counselor."

"Who crowned you Solomon?"

Bec crossed her arms. "Go ahead. Be snarky. I really don't care. All I want is for Julie to get the help she needs. If that involves you throwing yourself on a pyre, so be it."

"Jeez, Rebecca. You're all heart."

"She is and when you get off your high horse, Claire, you'll see that." Julie glanced between them, her mouth flat and sad. "I suppose now you both know about the lump, I'm not going to get a moment's peace unless I agree to tests."

"No," they chorused.

"Well, I've got rules," Julie said reclaiming some control. "I'll have the tests but Phil and Penny aren't to know."

"But—"

"No buts, Claire. We do it my way or not at all."

"Bec, tell her it's a bad idea."

"What if Julie takes it one step at a time so it's not so overwhelming for her?"

"Thank you."

Bec felt Julie's gratitude in the squeeze of her hand and in the accompanying squeeze of her heart. "You're welcome."

"Okay, but I want it noted I'm not happy." Claire sighed. "I think you've broken your ankle. I suppose you can have the tests while you're in the hospital and Penny and Phil will be none the wiser. But afterwards, no matter the results, you must tell them."

Bec tried imagining herself in Julie's situation. "I don't think you should be on your own when you get the results."

"I want both of you there with me."

"Bec and I together in the same room and well behaved?" Claire laughed. "Challenge accepted!"

Julie fixed her with a grimace. "And as I'm putting myself through this, I want proof tomorrow that you've made an appointment to see a counselor."

Claire's gaze slid away. "Okay."

The ring of the home telephone drifted down the hall. "That will be Phil."

Bec scrambled to her feet. "I'll tell him about your ankle and that you're going to the hospital for X-rays. Then you can call him from there and fill him in on all the procedures so when he finally arrives back, he won't question any of the tests."

"Wow! For someone who's anal about most everything, you're amazingly quick at subterfuge and obfuscation," Claire teased.

Bec forced herself to laugh. Claire had no idea. And if Bec had anything to do with it, she never would.

"WHO WANTS ICE CREAM?" Sophie asked after the sound of Bec's car melted into the quiet night.

"I think I need Turkish tea."

"What's that?"

"Black with lots of sugar." Layla adjusted her head scarf. "All this news gives me a bad surprise."

"A shock," Sophie said. Then, at Layla's questioning look, elaborated, "A bad surprise is a shock."

"Why does Claire say no to children?"

"I don't think it's that unusual." Erica switched on the kettle.

"It might not be in inner Melbourne but out here, it's pretty uncommon," Sophie said. "I work with a girl who just got married and the moment she got back from her honeymoon, people started asking her when she was going to have kids. They joke and say stuff like, 'Come on, Myrtle needs more football players,' but it's still pressure."

"I've had friends who are hell-bent on their careers and adamant they don't want kids," Erica said. "They think that because I've got kids I'll judge them for their decision, which I don't. But the friendships suffered. It isn't just that they don't want children, they don't want to be around them either."

"But Claire likes children," Layla said. "At the barbecue, she plays in the sandpit with Malik and Rafi. None of us did."

"She was probably taking a breather from us." Erica poured boiling water over the tea bags. "That night there were kids everywhere. We were all obnoxiously playing happy families. If we're honest, we do talk about the kids a lot. That night was probably worse because it wasn't a meeting."

Layla spooned sugar into her tea. "We didn't know about Matt. It's hard for her."

A surge of indignation shot through Sophie. "So why didn't she tell us weeks ago? We could have made sure we didn't inadvertently hurt her feelings. I mean, it's not like we've all just met. We're friends now, aren't we? We share stuff. Sometimes I think Claire doesn't know how to be one of the girls. Like tonight—instead of being my friend, she was busy being the health professional."

"Natural helpers find it hard not to help," Erica said.

"In that case, we need to teach her how to be a friend, otherwise one day, I might just deck her."

"But why no children?" Layla repeated, still clearly bewildered. "Children are a gift. Family is precious."

"And they're bloody hard work, too, Layla," Erica said. "If we wrote down the pros and cons of having kids, none of us would do it. Think about it. The first couple of years are a slog. No sleep, no time for yourself, no time for your husband, lackluster sex if you can muster the energy to try, mountains of washing, cold cups of tea, dealing with more bodily fluids than you ever thought possible and worse than any of that, the heart-stopping terror when they get sick."

Sophie handed out bowls of ice cream. "When I got pregnant with Liam it was a total accident. Josh had this whole timeline planned for us and kids didn't feature until we'd been married five years and bought our first house. When the family planning nurse gave me the news, she said more than fifty per cent of pregnancies are unplanned. Claire just needs to get knocked up. The hormones take over fast and it's goodbye logic and hello baby."

"Given Matt's moved out, that's an unlikely scenario." Erica glanced at the kitchen clock. "We should have heard by now. Not that I'm not concerned for Claire, but I'm worried about Julie." She suddenly started pulling open drawers and rummaging through them.

"What are you doing?" Layla asked askance. "This is Claire's house."

"I'm looking for pens and paper. If Claire's like me, she's picked up a notepad and pen from every hotel or conference she's ever attended and put them in a drawer for shopping lists and things."

Drawing a blank in the kitchen, Erica moved purposely to a wooden side table with two thin drawers. She pulled open the left one and held up a handful of pads and three pens. "Bingo!"

"Why do you want paper and pens?"

The cell phone rang and they all jumped. Sophie leaped on it. "Hello?"

"It's me," Bec said.

"Hang on, I'll put you on speaker." She pressed the button and lay the cell on the coffee table. "How's Julie?"

"Lucky we came. She fell in the bathroom and she's broken her ankle."

"But's she's okay otherwise?" There was an extended silence. "Bec, spill," Erica commanded.

Bec sighed. "None of you can say a word to anyone, okay? Not even the guys."

They murmured their agreement.

"She's worried about a lump in her breast."

"Oh, God." Sophie grabbed Erica and Layla's hands. "That's so scary."

"It is, but it's more complicated than that," Bec continued. "She's been agonizing for weeks, not telling anyone, because after Hugo, she doesn't think Phil or Penny can cope with any more bad news."

"Poor Julie," Layla said.

"Send her our love," Erica said.

"I will." Bec rang off.

"We should send her flowers," Sophie said. "I'll organize them in the morning."

Erica pushed pads and pens toward them. "Words last longer than flowers. How about we write and tell her how much she means to us?"

Sophie thought sending flowers was a lot easier but reluctantly accepted a pen and pad. Taking herself over to a comfy chair, she gazed through the floor-to-ceiling windows into the night. These days, the inky darkness was surprisingly unintimidating, and she sought inspiration from the silver pricks of light weaving a mat across the sky. What did she want to say to Julie?

After scrunching up three pieces of paper, she said, "This is too hard."

"Make a list of everything Julie's ever done for you and see if that helps," Erica suggested.

Sophie chewed the pen and slowly wrote all the random acts of kindness that Julie had bestowed upon her since she'd moved to Myrtle. She valued all of them but she especially treasured the invitation to join the craft group. It had widened her small world and introduced her to this eclectic but caring group of women. Slowly, words started to flow but while she wrote, uninvited thoughts about her mother dogged her. Since the unsuccessful visit in late August, she'd had little contact with Aileen other than the occasional frosty telephone call. With Christmas six weeks away, she was dreading the next call. It would come, as it did every year, with its usual festive season demands and inflexibility.

Sophie asked herself what she would write if she had to pen a similar letter to her mother. I love you but I don't like you? I'm sad you don't support me and Josh? I'm angry and hurt that you judge me for wanting the same things as Kylie as if I'm not entitled to them. I'm furious that you blame me for my house burning down.

What was that all really saying? You can choose your friends but not your relatives? Whoever coined that phrase knew something she'd never suspected until now. She'd choose accepting and kind Julie over critical Aileen every time.

WHEN BEC ARRIVED home from the hospital, Adam was waiting for her on the couch—arms crossed and wearing a skeptical look. "Since when are you and Claire McKenzie best friends?"

Bec ignored the lack of a greeting and bent down and kissed him on the cheek. "Sorry, I'm late and we're not best friends. We're not even friends, but we're learning to be civil for the sake of Put Myrtle on the Map."

"Fair enough. That idea of hers about green tomato chutney is a good one."

"It's my idea but I'm so tired at the moment, I'm delegating jobs."

"Poor baby. Sit." He patted the couch. "Put your feet up and I'll make you tea. Peppermint? Chamomile?"

Since she'd told Adam about the pregnancy, he'd been making little gestures like this. She reminded herself there was much about him to appreciate and be grateful for. "Peppermint would be lovely, thank you."

"Coming right up."

Bec leaned back and closed her eyes and the evening rushed back. What if Claire hadn't had a meltdown and she hadn't called Julie? She shuddered at the thought of Julie spending the night on the cold bathroom floor.

"Here you go."

She opened her eyes and accepted the proffered mug. "You're the best."

Adam grinned. "Damn straight."

He sat next to her drinking a Coke. Her tea smelt fresh and reviving but it didn't taste quite like she remembered. Then again, nothing tasted normal thanks to her body turning her off anything it thought might harm the baby. She understood the scent and taste of coffee making her feel ill, because caffeine wasn't healthy, but peppermint tea? It didn't make a lot of sense.

Despite the bitter coppery taste, she drank it, because Adam making the effort to get her a drink was like Adam giving her a gift—he needed her appreciation. The last thing she wanted was for him to get snarky and say, "Why did you say yes to tea if you're not going to drink it?" Then tell her she was selfish.

His palm rested gently on her thigh. "I thought your meeting was at the CWA?"

A low-grade warning trickled through her. Before the fires, he'd never called her to ask where she was or what she was doing, but now he called if she wasn't home five minutes after her stated time. Sometimes, like tonight, he called earlier. This change in him didn't make a lot of sense to her. She could have understood it if she and the girls had been trapped by the fire and he'd been the one in horrendous limbo wondering if they were dead or alive, but he'd always known they were safe in Lorne.

In the early hospital days after he'd been weaned off the respirator, she'd often looked up from reading the paper or a magazine to find him studying her from beneath his bandages.

"I tried calling you five times that day. Who the hell were you talking to?" He'd asked her the same question half-a-dozen times in as many weeks.

"No one," she'd always said calmly despite her thundering heart. "The network was jammed and then it failed completely. No one could get through to anyone. All calls got the busy signal."

Was it the memory of trying to call her on that day that was making him call so often now? Was this her fault?

"Earth to Bec?"

"We were at the CWA when we got a call from Julie. Phil's out of town and she'd fallen over and hurt herself."

"Claire's the nurse. Why did you need to go?"

Bec knew the questions would keep coming and with each answer, she risked him finding out there hadn't been a CWA meeting. The perfect way to distract him came to her and she weathered a momentary stab of guilt that Claire didn't really deserve to be thrown under the bus.

"Claire had been drinking so she wasn't safe to drive. She and Matt have split up."

"You serious?" Adam's eyes lit up with the glee of gossip. "Who's she screwing around with then?"

"Why do you automatically think it's her and not him?"

"Babe. I know you don't like her, but bottom line, she's a very fuckable woman. That's if you like her type, which, for the record, I don't."

Bec had gotten used to Adam's dissertations on who was hot and who was not a long time ago. She was far more interested in the second part of his statement. "What do you mean by 'type'?"

"Claire McKenzie's a ball buster. Matt's been blinded by her body from the moment he laid eyes on her and she's had him by the balls ever since. He doesn't give a damn how weak that makes him, but what can you expect? His father's the same. Louise Cartwright wears the pants in that family and everyone toes her line."

Bec got a momentary reprieve from her guilt—at least she hadn't said Matt left Claire. "I never thought about it that way."

"So apart from Claire being drunk, how's Julie?"

"Broken ankle."

"That'll slow her down a bit."

"Yeah." Bec yawned. "Sorry. It's been a big night."

His fingers stroked her inner thigh. "Bedtime then?"

She barely had enough energy to walk to the bedroom let alone have sex. "Adam, I'm exhausted."

"I know, babe. All you need to do is snuggle your naked body up next to mine and talk dirty while I take care of myself."

When she thought about the months of sex games he'd wanted her to play and the things he'd asked her to do before she got pregnant, this request was both tame and easy. "I can do that."

He stood up and pulled her to her feet before swinging her into his arms. "I'll even save you the walk."

Laughing, she kissed him. Loving this version of Adam was easy.

"... DIGITAL PHOTOGRAPHY."

Clare glanced up from her sandwich, suddenly aware that Shane had stopped talking. Unfortunately, her mind was so full of other things she had no idea what he'd been saying. "Sounds interesting. Tell me more."

Shane had suggested a working lunch to debrief on the previous youth group and plan the next one. He picked up his milkshake. "How about we eat first? You look like you could murder that sandwich."

She'd been staring intently at the overfilled baguette, but it wasn't because she was hungry. Lately, she'd found herself focusing on all sorts of inanimate objects as if they might offer the solutions she needed to fix her crumbling personal world, which seemed to race further away from her control every day.

"Is everything okay, Claire?"

She flicked out strands of purple and white from her lunch. "I should have told Minh no onions."

"I meant is everything okay with you."

Claire wasn't up to rehashing everything. It was bad enough that the CWA women had watched her hit rock bottom. She wasn't exposing herself to the risk of falling apart like that again, especially not in the bakery café. Right now she needed Shane to be her colleague and for this meeting to only be about work. "All good here. You?"

"Not bad." Shane cleared his throat and tugged on his collar. "Are you sure you're okay?"

"Absolutely." She bit into the baguette and tried not to think about her morning.

The day after Julie broke her ankle, Claire had rung a psychologist to schedule an appointment so she could show she was keeping her word. If someone had questioned Claire on her choice of counselor, she'd have justified it by saying Alissa came highly recommended by the medical community and she'd heard good reports from some of her patients. Truthfully, she'd called her because she knew the woman had a minimum four-week wait before seeing new clients. As an extra precaution, Claire had deliberately phoned well before office hours so the call would go to voice mail. Problem was, Alissa had picked up.

"It's your lucky day, Claire. I've got a cancellation appointment at 9:00 tomorrow morning."

Lucky? The temptation to hang up had been so strong it was only the fact that Alissa had her number that stayed her hand. In the twenty-four hours since accepting the timeslot, Claire had almost canceled a dozen times, but that morning she'd forced herself up and out the door, and driven to Colac. She'd sat in a room obviously decorated to make people feel safe—right down to the frothy maidenhair fern, the glass of water and the strategically placed box of tissues. But she didn't feel safe; just exposed and vulnerable. She'd cried for an hour before being released back onto the street feeling worse than before she'd gone in. If that was counseling, it totally sucked.

Shane shifted in his seat. "I want to believe you when you say you're good, but at the last youth group, you weren't yourself. And it wasn't just me who noticed, it was Lucy and her friends. She said you've always been—" he made air quotes with his fingers " 'a legend' and 'not judgy,' but that night they got a different vibe. So did I."

He leaned forward, his face contorted like so many other Myrtle residents when they remembered. "The fires ... we both heard, saw and did stuff that day. Things only a soldier understands. Afterwards, I hit the ground running, trying to help, trying to ease some of the pain. I was manic, working all hours, but when I achieved something it didn't feel like it because there was always more that needed doing.

"I was barely sleeping, hardly eating and nine weeks later it hit me like a ton of bricks. All I could think about were the people I didn't save. Thank God for Sally. Without her pushing me to get some help, I don't know where I'd be. No one's immune, Claire. In the last six months, we've lost a couple of good CFA men to the black dog of depression. Myrtle can't lose any more carers. It can strike at any time. Has it hit you now?"

Anguish, gratefulness and a soupçon of guilt clogged her throat and she sucked in her lips to trap all of it. This big-hearted policeman had just tried to help her by baring his soul. The honor of what he'd done almost undid her and she breathed in sharply, trying to steady herself.

"Thank you for caring, Shane. I'm not great but I promise you, I don't have PTSD."

His bushy eyebrows drew down. "You sure?"

Hell's bells! He wasn't giving up. The only way to make him believe her was to wade back into the mess. "It's nothing to do with the fires. It's Matt. We're ..." Her heart sped up and her gut twisted. God, even the condensed version threatened to undo her. "It's complicated."

"Aw, damn." Embarrassment pinked his cheeks. "Sorry. I shouldn't have pried."

"No! You didn't pry. You did the right thing and I appreciate it." She rallied a sad smile. "Full marks for using the skills we learned in mental-health first aid. Never stop. I'm the one who should be apologizing. I'm sorry I've been distracted. That Friday was a particularly bad night and I should have canceled, but sensible thinking was beyond me. I just hope I haven't wrecked the trust we're building."

"Of course you haven't. You didn't go ballistic, yell or throw anything. You just looked really sad. Everyone was worried about you."

"The last thing they need to be is worrying about me. Some of them have parents who can be quite irrational at times."

Shane huffed out a breath. "Some of them have parents who are nuts."

She nodded. "The fires changed their family dynamics forever. In the normal world, children trust their parents implicitly. They don't start questioning or thinking their folks are fallible until their mid-teens. But on the day of the fires when they turned to their parents for help, instead of getting the reassurance they craved that everything was going to be alright, they saw their own fear and terror reflected back at them.

"Now they're feeling let down, angry and scared. They don't know who to trust anymore. And some have parents who are struggling so much that the kids are parenting them. One girl told me she's sneaking antidepressants to her mother. It's horrifying and terrifying all at the same time. It's why we need the drop-in nights."

"So you're still up for being involved?"

"Hell, yes!" She needed to throw herself into work more than ever. "Fill me in on this digital photography plan."

"Other communities have used art as part of their recovery process and I reckon for non-sporty kids this might help. Not that I'm excluding anyone." He outlined his ideas for a digital photography exhibition using photos taken and chosen by the teenagers. "The fire didn't just change the bush, it changed us. I reckon that could be the theme."

"So, we'd display their photos on screens in the stadium using the data projector?"

"Yep. And invite the community. Might even be able to rustle up some prize money."

"I love it. And if the teenagers are occupied taking and editing photos, hopefully it means less time available for them to write themselves off in other ways."

"That's the plan. And on the drug front, I've requested support from Highway Patrol for random drug testing. I've also upped my breathalyzer and roadworthiness tests on the main road in and out of town. Sometimes you get lucky. Like that country copper in the northeast who pulled over a truck and found ice and two million in cash."

Claire got an image of Shane standing in the middle of the road, arms crossed and legs wide. "Did you ever see that old cowboy movie about the gunslinger called Shane?"

"Ain't no one coming into my town unless I say so." He laughed. "I better get back. The paperwork's not doing itself."

"And I've got new mother's group."

"Thank God for babies, eh? Disasters come and go but there's something about a new baby that lifts us up and reassures us that everything's going to be okay."

A prickle of goosebumps whooshed fast and painfully across Claire's skin but she didn't disabuse him. What was the point?

CHAPTER TWENTY-TWO

JULIE HATED THE WHEELCHAIR AND SHE HATED WAITING. TODAY she was waiting for Bec, who was rarely late. And for the results she knew would confirm her gut instincts and validate the look on her doctor's face when she'd examined her breast. Waiting to tell Phil that as much as she'd tried to protect him from any more hurt and pain, she'd failed.

"Where the hell is Rebecca and why isn't she answering her telephone?" Claire asked. "I don't get why she didn't drive up with us."

"We've got a couple more minutes."

"I'll take one last look on the street."

Julie watched Claire's long legs make short work of the distance and was struck by how much she moved like Heather. They shared more than just a walk, but unfortunately, Claire had inherited Ron's stubbornness—once her mind was made up, she didn't change it easily. Her opinion of Bec was a case in point.

The rumble of a diesel engine made Julie turn. A ute with Scotty Ferguson at the wheel pulled to a stop right in front of her. Bec slid out of the passenger seat, her hair tangled and wild at the back. Julie couldn't remember the last time she'd seen Bec with messy hair or wearing trousers and muted colors. The elegant outfit suited her and her pregnancy curves.

Scotty leaned over. "Hey, Julie." He gave her a wave before saying to Bec, "Text me when you're done?"

Bec nodded, smoothing down her hair.

When Scotty drove off, Julie said, "We were getting worried."

"Sorry. We had to run an errand for Adam and it took longer than expected."

Claire hurried over, hands on hips. "Why is your cell phone switched off?"

"Flat battery. I forgot to charge it."

"You never forget anything."

Julie shot Bec an understanding smile. "Pregnancy hormones play havoc with the most organized mind."

Claire reached abruptly behind Bec. "So, this is why you're late." She held a sales tag aloft. "Been having too much fun shopping?"

Bec's cheeks flamed red as she grabbed the tag. "None of my clothes fit, okay? Happy now?"

"Not particularly." Claire bent and released the brakes on the wheelchair and when she glanced up, she said, "You look good, Bec. Those colors suit you."

Bec glanced down at her clothes as if seeing them for the first time. "Thanks."

Julie smiled to herself, sensing a thaw in the permafrost of the younger women's relationship. "Come on, you two. You're going to have to leg it."

They rode the elevator in silence to the fourth floor. Julie appreciated that neither woman asked her how she was feeling, which saved her from saying, "Nauseous. Nervous. Resigned. Heartsick. Scared. Numb." She was also thankful they were avoiding inane comments like "no news is good news" or "I'm sure you're worrying over nothing."

The waiting room was quiet and Julie transferred out of the detestable wheelchair into a regular chair. Bec sat with her while

Claire spoke to the receptionist and the nurse. Julie knew Claire would be gathering information so she could answer not just her questions, but the ones Phil and Penny would ask once their shock wore off. Questions about surgery and long months of chemotherapy. Just thinking about her family made Julie want to flee the room. Was this why the universe had engineered her fall and given her a fractured ankle—so she couldn't run? God, she could barely hobble.

"Mrs. Lang. Doctor will see you now," the receptionist said.

"I guess this is it." But Julie stayed seated.

Claire, bless her, gave her a few moments before passing her the elbow crutches. "Am I right in thinking you want to walk in?"

"Yes." Walking felt defiant. Unaccepting.

It was also slow but she was soon seated between Claire and Bec around a low table. Liz, her doctor, slid into the empty seat as if joining them for coffee and a cozy chat. Julie got a nostalgic pang for the old-fashioned big oak desks that doctors used to sit behind. At least its presence prepared people for bad news, unlike this interior-designed faux-casual setup that made her glance around for a waitress to take her order. Liz's demeanor was professional and calm and Julie wondered how many times over her career she'd delivered bad news like she was about to now.

"Julie, as you know, given the size of the lesion, the skin retraction and how it appeared on the mammogram, we were fairly convinced it was cancer."

The words slid into place without fuss—like reinforcements to a retaining wall that had been in position for a long time.

Bec gave a soft "Oh." Claire looked like she had a dozen questions loaded and ready to fire. Questions that would include words like "stage" and "prognosis."

"But diagnosis is always dependent on the pathology, which is why the biopsy is so important." Liz reached into a folder and pulled out a sheet of paper. "Sometimes, the results are unexpected and in this instance, I'm thrilled to tell you our suspicions were wrong."

A buzzing filled Julie's ears. "Are you saying ..." Her tongue thickened and stuck to the roof of her mouth. She swallowed and tried again but she could barely hear herself speak. "Are you saying I don't have breast cancer?"

Liz nodded. "That's correct. You have what's called a granular cell tumor. They're very rare. With their irregular margins and the way they adhere to other structures, they mimic breast cancer both on physical examination and on the mammogram. The good news is, your tumor's benign. No cancer. The bad news is, you need surgery to remove it. I'm afraid it will be extensive as it's attached itself to the adjacent muscles. Granular cell tumors tend to reoccur so to reduce the risk we need to get nice clear margins. I can operate on Friday.

"I realize this is a lot of information to absorb so I'm going to give you a few minutes with your friends and then my nurse and I will pop back in to discuss everything and answer your questions."

Liz rose and handed a copy of the pathology report to Julie. "I know most of it probably reads like gobbledygook but I thought you might like to have the proof. I've highlighted the word 'benign'."

The fluorescent yellow word jumped out, its message clear: a future free of a sinister and choking malignancy. She burst into tears.

"Oh, Julie! Thank God, thank God." Bec hugged her tightly.

Claire handed her a tissue and hugged her too. "You've put yourself through weeks of hell for no good reason. Promise me you'll never sit on anything like this again."

"Promise." Julie held their hands "I can't thank you enough for being here. I'm sorry I've put you both in a difficult position. The secrets stop today. I'm going to tell Phil and Penny."

"They'll understand why you were scared," Bec said. "They love you."

"Love's just another word for hurt, disappointment and pain," Claire muttered.

No one corrected her.

BEC REACHED into the back seat for her water bottle and was momentarily dazzled by the late-afternoon sunshine bouncing off the row of brightly colored shopping bags. Ivy's birthday presents.

"You right?" Scotty asked, his eyes hidden behind black sunglasses. "I can pull over."

She rose slightly, giving her arm a longer stretch until her fingers gripped the bottle. "Thanks, but I've got it."

He shot her his trademark grin and despite her thorny and complex feelings for the man, she smiled back.

"And thanks again for today, Scotty. I really don't know what I would have done without your help."

"No problem. Hopefully your keys will turn up."

They were on their way home from Geelong, and Bec was still pinching herself at how a fraught and difficult day had turned into a golden one full of unexpected surprises. She'd woken up that morning, not anticipating any problems, having meticulously planned earlier in the week how she could keep Julie's secret and give Adam a valid reason to spend the day in Geelong.

"Colin says I have to have some extra tests for the baby, because I'm older. They can only be done in Geelong, so I'm going up on Wednesday."

"I'll drive you."

Hot and cold flashes raked her skin. "I can't ask you to give up a day of work sitting around while I have blood taken and drink some horrible stuff and have blood taken again."

"You're not asking, babe. I'm offering. Besides, I'm the boss and I can do what I want. We can have lunch and do a bit of shopping. Make a day of it."

"Great."

But later that afternoon, luck had fallen her way. "Sorry, babe. I've got to go to Melbourne on Wednesday. How about you reschedule those tests?"

"Colin wants me to have them this week."

"There are still two days after Wednesday."

"You're right." She'd kissed him. "I'll do my best."

She sent up grateful thanks that Adam's dawn departure and late return from Melbourne would give her plenty of time to get to and from Geelong. The girls were excited about catching the bus to school and Layla had offered to pick them up at the end of the day. But all Bec's carefully laid plans collapsed like a house of cards when she was leaving the house and her fingers touched empty metal on the row of key hooks. Where were her car keys? She'd upended every handbag, checked the pockets of her jackets, looked in drawers and, despite knowing it was impossible to lock the keys in the car, had peered inside anyway.

Nausea churned her stomach. She'd promised Julie.

Despairing, she checked the clock. Claire would have already left. The home telephone rang, making her jump, and she recognized Scotty's number. Since he'd given her a fright by arriving unannounced in the office, he'd taken to calling her first. Wearily, she picked up the telephone.

"Hey, Bec. I'm on my way to Geelong. Is it okay if I call by and pick up something from the office on my way past?"

She grabbed the unexpected lifeline. "Can you give me a ride?"

"Of course."

For the first ten minutes of the journey, she'd been tense and on edge, ready to obfuscate when Scotty asked her why she needed a ride. But although he'd asked her some questions—was the air-conditioning level okay, did she want the radio or music—he didn't ask her about Geelong. He'd chatted easily about Woollambah—how the shire had finally approved the plans for his house and that building would start in the new year. Then he'd told her about his sister, who she knew now lived in Melbourne, and his young nephew, who was cricket mad. By then she'd relaxed into his conversation.

"You should take him to the cricket during the Boxing Day match."

"Hopefully. But work could be busy then."

"How? The building industry shuts down until early January."

"Yeah, but this year Adam's got those bloody tomatoes. I might be picking."

"Doing your bit for Putting Myrtle on the Map?"

"Yeah. Something like that."

He'd switched on some music then and she must have fallen asleep because the next thing she knew he was saying, "Where to, Bec?"

She'd opened her eyes to see they'd hit the traffic in the suburbs of Geelong. He hadn't even questioned her request to dash into a maternity-wear shop before visiting the hospital.

Later, when he'd picked her up, he'd told her he'd been busy and had missed lunch. Did she mind if they grabbed something to eat before driving home? High on Julie's good news and realizing she was ravenous, she'd happily agreed. The late lunch had been followed by shopping for Ivy. Although Scotty was there, the experience had been so dissimilar to shopping with Adam it had felt like she was shopping alone. She'd reveled in making her own decisions until she was almost giddy with the freedom of it.

She glanced again at the brightly colored shopping bags. "I think I went a bit overboard with Ivy's presents."

Scotty laughed. "What tween girl doesn't like pretty things?"

Bec faced the front, watching fields dotted with black Angus cattle flash past. "Mine. She's only interested in books."

"You make it sound like reading's a bad thing."

"When reading's all she does, then it's not good. It's antisocial." Whether it was the result of being the recipient of Scotty's silent support all day or just the need to tell someone, she found herself saying, "Ivy's being difficult about everything at the moment. She's even refusing to have a birthday party."

"Is she?" He sounded surprised. "Adam said the girls are great and excited about the baby."

"Adam and Gracie are excited about the baby. Ivy's furious with me for getting pregnant."

"Ah!"

"What?"

"When I was Ivy's age, Mom got pregnant with Paul and I was sick with embarrassment. Every time I looked at Mom, I got an image of her having sex with my father so I stopped looking at her completely. But once Paul was born, those horrifying images vanished and everything went back to normal. Ivy'll get over it. You know how great she is with little kids. She'll love the baby to bits."

"I hope so. It isn't like I did it deliberately to hurt her."

But the idea that Ivy was angry with Bec, and had been even before she got pregnant, needled her yet again.

The relaxed and comfortable air in the cab changed, although Bec wasn't able to identify its new feel. As each mile clicked past bringing them closer to Myrtle, she felt the calm of the day seeping out of her, replaced by tension with spiked edges.

"So ..." Scotty finally broke the silence. "... you and Adam ...? The baby ... it wasn't planned?"

"No." She stared out the window at dry fields and dirty sheep. "But it's going to be good for us." If she said it often enough it would become the truth.

Scotty didn't say anything until he'd pulled in from overtaking a cattle truck. "Well, you're looking great. Especially today. Those new clothes suit you."

"Thanks." Bec fiddled with the hem of her new top, knowing that when she got home she'd have to take it off along with the new pants and hide them in the back of her closet. Adam would hate them. Adam would hate that she'd spent hours alone in a car with Scotty. Her stomach twisted.

"I'm glad you lost your keys."

"Why?"

"Today's been like it used to be." Scotty ran his hand over his head. "I've missed our conversations, Bec. Missed the coffee and the café meetings when Adam was in rehab."

Fury bloomed like an octopus' inky stain. "That's not my fault—it's yours! We could still be working together, still having coffee, still—" She realized she was yelling and she dropped her volume. "If you'd stood up for me when Adam came back to work. If you'd insisted I stay on in the business then everything could have been the same."

"That's unfair and untrue. I stood up for you. Hell, I told him what a great asset you were to the company and how much we needed you."

"And then you sided with him and hung me out to dry."

"No! I pushed it until he told me in no uncertain terms that you were his wife and to back the hell off. This isn't all on me, Bec. I'm only thirty per cent of the company. Adam's still the boss."

"And let's not forget he saved your life," she said bitterly. *And then he took mine.*

Scotty thumped the steering wheel. "Yes, he saved my life. It's not something I can just conveniently forget. If it wasn't for him, I'd be dead."

"But you're not."

"And neither are you."

"No."

But she wished Scotty could forget and walk away. Wished he'd grab the life he'd wanted so badly before the legacy of Adam's disfiguring injuries had tied them both to him forever.

Sadness enveloped her like a gray damp cloud, bringing with it a resurgence of the private grief she'd hidden for so long. This was why she and Scotty avoided each other. Being together was like looking in a mirror and facing regrets. It was just too hard.

Wretchedness and contrition pinched her. "Scotty ..."

"Yeah?"

"Thanks for the ride."

"Any time."

"About the car keys ... I feel really silly."

"Don't worry." He tapped his nose. "I won't tell a soul. I'm good at keeping secrets."

So am I.

· · ·

DESPITE THE MISERY that had chased Bec to sleep, the next morning she woke feeling brighter and more focused than she had in weeks. Her first thought was that her car keys were still missing. Osman had kindly driven the girls home the previous night but unless she found the keys before the school run, she was going to have to confess to Adam. She really didn't want to do that.

Adam was snoring gently next to her and she carefully slid her left leg out of bed.

He immediately rolled over and threw an arm across her chest. "Good morning. How did you sleep?"

She smiled at him. "I had the best sleep I've had in ages."

"That's good." He dropped his head in close, kissing her deeply while his hand slipped under her negligee.

She recognized the prelude and slid her mouth away. "The girls will be up in a minute."

"You should have thought of that last night when you went to bed instead of waiting up for me."

Despite his conversational tone, unease ran up her spine. This Adam—critical and needy—had been absent for weeks. "I'm sorry. I was exhausted."

"Why? I was the one who drove to Melbourne and back and dealt with asshole bureaucrats who've got no concept of profit margins. The least you could have done was stay up to ask me about my day and make me a relaxing cup of tea like I've been making you."

"You're right. I was thoughtless." She cupped his face, determined to appease him. "Let me make it up to you with a cooked breakfast. I feel so great this morning, I can even face bacon."

"I'm not wasting your new-found energy on breakfast. We've got some time before the girls wake up."

She heard the faint flush of a toilet. "Too late. They're already up."

"Lucky I locked the bedroom door then."

"HURRY UP, Ivy or we'll be late for school."

Ivy was using her spoon to chase corn flakes around a pond of milk. "It's not my fault. I was up early."

The pointed comment was aimed squarely at Bec. She'd been very late to start breakfast. Adam hadn't rushed things and when the girls had rattled the door, he'd just grinned and said, "We'll be out in a minute."

"Why was your door locked?" Gracie asked. "I wanted to read you and Daddy my reader."

"Because they were having S.E.X.," Ivy said.

"Ivy!" Bec didn't know if she was outraged, embarrassed or both.

"Well, you were. I heard you. It's gross."

"What's S.E.X.?" Gracie spied her father walking into the kitchen. "Daddy!"

"How are my girls?" Adam dropped a kiss on each of their heads. "Did you miss me last night?"

Gracie smiled up at him. "No. We played with Malik and then Osman drove us home."

Bec's toast lurched to the back of her throat. She hadn't thought to tell Gracie that was a secret.

Ivy's cereal bowl flipped and milk poured across the table. Adam jumped back to avoid the liquid dripping onto his pants. Bec dropped paper towel on the debris and waited for Adam's roar. He hated the girls making a mess.

Instead he ruffled Grace's hair. "Why were you playing at the Buluts'?"

"Because Mommy—"

"I've lost the car keys." Bec looked straight at Adam. "I was too embarrassed to tell you."

He made a tsking sound. "Just as well you rescheduled those tests then."

Panic dried her mouth. *Think!* "Actually, that was why I was so tired last night. After the drama of losing the keys, the hospital rang, insisting I come in. Claire McKenzie was great and she drove me to Geelong." She held her breath.

"And we caught the bus to school," Gracie added.

Ivy kicked her sister under the table.

"Ouch!"

"You did have a big adventure." Adam squatted down in front of Gracie. "Are you sure you didn't hide Mommy's keys just so you could catch the bus?"

"No," Gracie said indignantly. "I wouldn't do that."

He rose to his feet with a sigh. "Are you sure, Gracie? Because I just saw them hanging on the hook."

"What?" Bec rushed into the laundry and Adam followed. There, hanging in their rightful place, were her car keys. Her mind had been so clear when she'd woken up, but now it scrambled through memories of her frantic hunt for the keys. "I—I don't understand. They weren't there yesterday. They just weren't."

Adam rested his chin on her shoulder. "I think they've probably been there the whole time, babe."

"No." But she sounded as bewildered and as unsure as she felt.

"You can't deny how vague you've been lately." Adam patted her belly indulgently. "Hey, little one. I hope your mommy's got it all together by the time you get here."

Bec unhooked the keys. "So do I."

JOSH TUCKED the sheet around his sleeping son. With his curls spilling onto the pillow, Liam looked like a cherub instead of a tearaway kid. Peaceful and innocent. Trusting. Josh's heart cramped. Sometimes the responsibility of being a father freaked him out and he wanted to run and hide for a bit. Spend time in a space where it was impossible to let anyone down.

Tonight, Liam had pestered Josh to "build" with him in the concrete sand. The last thing Josh wanted to do was play "building the house." The reality of the build was hard enough. He no longer associated the blue steel and the recently installed Colorbond walls with happiness. Truth was, whenever he looked at their partially completed home all he saw was the illegal electrical bypass. A necessary line he'd crossed to give his family the security they deserved.

It churned his gut.

Since installing the bypass, he'd deliberately tried not to think about it. Whenever thoughts wormed their way back, he reminded himself that no one else knew about the bypass and that Adam was keeping his side of the bargain, so it was worth the stress. Once the bypass was removed and he'd shifted Sophie and the kids out of the shed, *then* he'd enjoy their new home. But right now, he avoided looking at the house as much as possible.

Josh walked into the living area and Sophie glanced up from the laptop screen. "Did you read him *The Little Yellow Digger?*"

"Yeah. Twice. He loves that little bulldozer, but I'm sick of reading it. When's he going to get sick of hearing it?"

"Probably not until the house is finished. He's so excited about getting his own room that all he wants are stories about building things."

"You want something to drink?" Josh strode to the fridge and grabbed a beer, wanting to kick back, relax and banish all thoughts of the build.

"Hot chocolate would be nice."

"Why? It's not cold."

She looked straight at him. "It's not alcohol."

Josh's jaw tightened. "Don't start, okay? I worked a ten-hour day lugging bags of cement and shoveling sand. I can have two beers." He pointed at the computer. "What are you doing?"

"Updating the build spreadsheet. Why did you stop filling it in?"

"Because most nights I'm too knackered and on the weekends we're busy with the kids."

Those weren't the reasons. He hated the bloody build and filling in the spreadsheet reminded him of the deal he'd done with Adam. "Anyway, it's pointless now. We've never earned this much money before and we're easily living off your wage. Mine's double what it was at Sustainable and it's going straight into the house."

Sophie's head tilted. Josh couldn't tell if it was from surprise at his attitude flip on the spreadsheet or if she was contemplating the healthy balance of the house fund.

Her fingers clicked on the keys, adding more numbers. "After we've moved into the house, will you reconsider the apprenticeship?"

He murmured his assent and drank more beer. It was easier than trying to explain why he hated being an electrician. Easier than telling her he'd be looking for another job as soon as their house was complete. Easier than having a row.

Sophie gave him a wide smile. "By the way, with all the chaos of dinner and bedtime, I forgot to tell you. Adam rang me at work today. He said the window guys have an opening in two weeks and can come to us."

Josh's leg jigged up and down of its own accord. He pressed his palm to his thigh to still it. "Adam shouldn't be bothering with stuff like that."

"He said he tried calling you but you were out of range."

"I'll order the windows tomorrow."

"It's already done. Adam said he had a supplier who was cheaper than Great Glass. In fact he suggested we let Petrovic order everything as they get volume discounts. Even though we're owner builders, should we do that instead?"

"Whatever you reckon." Anything to get the house built. Anything to minimize conversations like this.

"It will make it easier for both of us. I'll drop the money off on Friday." She closed the laptop. "Erica and Nathan invited us to lunch on Sunday."

The Solomons had been issuing a lot of invitations lately. So far he'd avoided them by working late and pleading exhaustion. "Yeah, nah."

"Why not?"

Josh's chest tightened. He wasn't about to tell Sophie that the last couple of times they'd been in a group of people, he'd come out in a cold sweat. "I don't want to go. They're not our type of people."

"Of course they're our type of people."

He snorted. "They're rich wankers."

"They're not!" Sophie's indignation bounced off the iron walls. "Erica and Nathan are some of the kindest and most generous people I know. Look at the party they threw us."

"Yeah, well, we're not a charity case to make them feel better."

Memories of the framing party hammered him—Nathan and Adam talking share portfolios. Adam asking for the bypass. Suddenly his T-shirt stuck to his back, glued there by sweat. The walls of the shed closed in on him and his chest was working hard to move air. He needed space. Lurching to his feet, he strode outside.

A left turn would take him to the new house. A right turn to the water tank. Straight ahead led to the creek.

His body froze, his legs stiff and leaden.

Unable to move, he stared up at the night sky and wondered if there was peace among the stars.

CHAPTER TWENTY-THREE

"OH! MINCE PIES! WHO'S THE HONEY WHO BROUGHT THEM?" Erica whipped the cling wrap off the plate and dived on one of the fruit-and-pastry delights.

Sophie laughed at Erica's enthusiasm. "Me. You look like you haven't eaten one since last year."

"I haven't." Erica licked her sugary fingers. "I have a self-imposed rule not to buy them until December or else I'd end up the size of a house. But it's so hard. For weeks they call to me in the bakery and the supermarket."

"You can afford to break early this year. You're looking great by the way. All that training for the fun run's paying off."

"Thanks. You too. The Insta account's getting more and more love. When people sign up they're following and posting their own training pics. Why don't you run with me one morning?"

"I'm driving to work before you even head out the door."

"What about after work? Josh could bring the kids over and supervise Nathan at the barbecue while we run?"

This was Erica's fourth invitation since the framing party. Sophie's initial excitement that they were finally getting a social life beyond the occasional evenings with Julie and Phil had been tempered by her inability to get Josh to accept. He'd never been the life of the party but he'd always been happy enough to share a beer with the blokes while she chatted to her girlfriends. He'd been the one to tell her country people were friendly, yet now when they were making friends, he was resisting joining in. She put it down to exhaustion.

"I really appreciate the invitation but can we take a raincheck? Right now with the house and Josh working really long hours—"

"Oh, I totally get it. It's a frantic time for you. Just let us know whenever you're ready. After all, we're not going anywhere."

"Oh! Mince pies." Claire walked into the kitchen but she didn't pick up one of the treats. "Come on, you two. You're holding up proceedings."

"We're hardly late. It's seven thirty-one."

"I know, but if we don't start, Bec will keep busy by lining up Layla's and my papers perpendicular to the edge of the table and organizing our pens in color-wheel order. That will give me an overwhelming urge to swipe the lot into one big mess."

Erica laughed. "You'd enjoy that."

Claire's mouth pulled down. "This time I'd regret it."

Since the night Claire and Bec had raced over to Julie's house, there'd been a shift in hostilities. Sophie sensed they were both working on a peacekeeping mission, however fragile. She followed Claire and Erica into the meeting room and poured everyone a glass of water. She pushed one toward Bec.

"Thanks." The word was imbued with gratitude beyond what the act deserved.

Bec had recently "popped out" and was looking pregnant. It was particularly obvious in the ruched and clingy jersey dress she was wearing, which made the baby bump look like a small volleyball. Sophie wondered if Adam had chosen the dress. Personally, she'd always preferred maternity wear that flowed around her, hiding more than it revealed, but then again she didn't have the same figure as Bec.

Plus, Adam adored her and this baby. If he wanted to tell the world exactly that, then this dress did the job, and then some.

When Sophie had dropped by the Petrovic office to pay the deposit for the kitchen cabinetry, she'd found Bec sitting on Adam's lap. His face was pressed into her breasts and his hand was stroking her belly. Bec's face had flushed when she'd seen Sophie and she'd scrambled to her feet, apologizing profusely. Adam had laughed and swatted Bec on the bum.

"Sophie's not embarrassed, are you, Soph? In my book, there's nothing sexier than a pregnant woman, especially my pregnant woman."

Oddly enough, Sophie hadn't felt awkward stumbling in on an intimate and affectionate scene. She'd thought it was sweet that after more than a decade of marriage, Adam idolized his wife and marveled at her pregnant body. She couldn't remember ever feeling that Josh had idolized her pregnant form. He certainly didn't idolize her now. Despite her finally losing some unwanted pounds, he barely touched her.

Bec drained her water glass and refilled it. "All I seem to do is drink. I'm constantly thirsty."

"When do you have your glucose tolerance test?" Claire asked.

"Claire!" Sophie warned. "You're off duty."

Layla smiled encouragingly. "Tonight, you're CWA Claire."

Claire flinched and her mouth whitened around the edges. "I was only trying to help. If Bec's thirsty—"

"She'll tell her midwife, won't you, Bec?" Erica said.

"Let's make a start." Bec tapped her pen. "Julie's an apology but she sends her love. She's recovering from breast surgery and she's graduated to an air boot for her ankle. She's hoping to ditch the crutches soon. Phil's whisked her off to Robe for a few days with the family."

Everyone murmured their approval. Bec's pen moved to the third point on the agenda. "Layla, have you completed your food-handling course?"

Sophie leaned close to Bec. "First we have to accept the minutes of the previous meeting."

"Oh! Yes, of course." Bec's laugh was strained. "Even when it's written down in front of me I'm forgetting. God, some days I swear I'm losing my mind. The day I lost the car keys, I turned the house upside down looking for them and the next morning they were hanging on their hook. I still have no idea how that happened. It doesn't make any sense."

"Pregnancy brain!" Erica, Layla and Sophie said simultaneously and laughed.

"I don't suppose I'm allowed to ask if you're getting enough sleep?" Claire said.

"I'm sleeping like a log but I wake up feeling more tired than when I went to bed. I'm hanging out for the energy blast I always get in the middle of my pregnancies. Okay, I need someone to move a motion to accept the minutes of the previous meeting."

"I'll move them," Claire said.

"I second," Layla said.

"And we have another first," Erica teased. "Claire and Layla embracing meeting protocol."

"I finished the food-handling course. I want to make jars of spicy Turkish tomato sauce with the tomatoes."

"That's a great idea. I've got the paperwork from the shire that approves this kitchen for commercial cooking ..." Bec rifled through three folders before sighing. "At least I thought I'd printed it out."

"You asked me to do it." Sophie pulled out the certificate she'd laminated at the office.

"No, I didn't."

Sophie laughed. "Yes, you did. Remember? The other night when you called me about the agenda items. It's just another example of—"

"Don't say pregnancy brain!"

"I wouldn't dare," Sophie mumbled, shoving the certificate under some papers and sharing a look with Erica.

"Claire," Bec said briskly. "Have you spoken to the other CWA about helping us make the tomato sauce?"

"I have."

"And?"

"It's tricky. They're happy to support us with the Devonshire tea tent on the day but they reminded me their group is busy with their own projects. More than once I was told we needed to build up our group. I agreed, but I did point out that Put Myrtle on the Map is everyone's priority. To cut a long story short, I managed to negotiate that if we match woman for woman on sauce and chutney-making day then we'll repay in kind for a project of their choice next year. And to show good faith, we're having a CWA tent next to the Devonshire tea marquee to try to snag some new members."

"And who's going to staff that?" Bec snapped. "There's only five of us. We're spread thin as it is and Erica, don't even think about offering Nathan. He's not a woman!"

"Yeah, but he'd give it his best shot."

Claire doodled on the margin of her agenda. "Sally Radley's offered to help so I've signed her up and inked her name on the roster. We've already delegated a lot of the work on the day. The timing company's coordinating the fun run and Nathan and Erica are the contacts on the ground. The blokes from the Men's Shed are on traffic control, crowd direction and the drinks stations set-up.

"I've got a commitment from a group of teens led by Lucy Radley to staff the drinks stations. Sophie, Layla and I are at the oval from cockcrow looking after the market and I'm on call for the community groups. After you and Adam have presented the winning runners with their medals, there's nothing else required of you except to kick back, put your feet up, sell a few bottles of tomato sauce and strong-arm any potential new members."

"And troubleshoot problems."

"Exactly." Claire smiled. "You and your walkie-talkie can run the show from the CWA tent. The rest of us will base ourselves there when we're not required elsewhere. Of course, if you can't see this working, I'm open to other suggestions."

Bec's face was a combination of surprise, irritation and respect. "You've really thought it through."

"I have my moments."

"Thanks, Claire," Sophie said. "I'll minute that."

"It's exactly what I would have suggested if this baby hadn't stolen all my concentration," Bec said grumpily. "So, back to tomato sauce day. The date will depend on ripening. Adam says it's looking likely they'll be able to pick for the December farmers market."

"Because Claire and Sophie work, we should cook on first or second weekend of December," Layla suggested.

Everyone's eyes drifted to their cell phones, consulting their calendars. Sophie saw the little gift icon and a pink entry for Trixie's birthday. "Not the second weekend."

"Too close to Christmas?" Layla asked.

"No." Bec looked straight at Claire. "Too close to the second anniversary."

CLAIRE CALLED the dogs and forced herself to stride across the field. She'd seen Matt's ute climbing gut-buster hill a few minutes earlier, which meant he was going to check on the hives. What she didn't know was whether he was alone or had company. If Matt had taken Taylor to see the bees, it would not break her heart in two, it would smash it into a thousand tiny pieces.

Over the previous few weeks, Claire had endured three counseling sessions, finding it increasingly difficult to return after each one. The day before, Alissa had finished the hour by saying, "If what you say is true and you do want to try to salvage your relationship with Matt, talk to him about couples counseling."

Alissa's easily spoken suggestion didn't match the herculean effort required of Claire. She hadn't spoken to Matt since the night Taylor had sat in her chair at the big house. The night he'd accused her of being paranoid. Their communication was now reduced to curt texts and emails about mortgage repayments and bill paying. He no longer came inside when he dropped off the dogs—they just appeared at the glass doors with their bright eyes, lolling tongues and canine smiles. So, over the last twenty-four hours, she'd agonized over the best way to ask Matt about counseling. She associated texts and emails with anger rather than conciliation so she didn't want to use that medium. If she telephoned, he could hang up on her. At least in person, if he tried to walk away she could follow.

The sun beat down and despite her hat and the liberal application of sunscreen, Claire felt her skin tightening. Summer was here, arriving in a rush of hot days that were perfect for hay cutting. Perfect for fires. She breathed in deeply, kidding herself she was filling her lungs with fresh air after hiking up the steep climb. As her nostrils twitched, seeking scents, she knew she was checking for smoke. Would be for the next five months until fire season was well and truly over for another year.

That's if you're still living here.

Blocking the thought, she crested the hill and the dogs barked. Tearing off, they headed straight to Matt. Claire saw him turn. She raised her hand, not waving, but holding it still as if asking, "May I approach?"

He walked to her and as he got closer she noticed his clothes hung more loosely on his frame, his face was drawn and deep lines bracketed his mouth. He didn't smile but she was prepared for that. It was the extinguished light in his eyes—the complete absence of the love that had glowed there just for her—that sent pain ripping through her. She almost doubled over from the loss. *Oh, honey. How did we get here?*

"How are the bees?"

"Now you're interested?"

His animosity jostled her. Part of her shriveled. "I didn't come to argue with you, Matt. The last time we talked—"

"Is that what you're calling it?"

Claire swallowed, working at not giving in to his antagonism. "Last time you told me to get some help before I talked to you again."

His stiff body relaxed just enough for a ripple of conciliation to soften his demeanor. She glimpsed a tiny part of the man who'd loved her.

"And have you?"

"I've been seeing a counselor. It's ... hard."

"Is it helping?"

"Maybe."

"Has it changed your mind about having kids?"

"Alissa said it would be a good idea if you came too."

He pulled his hat off and wiped his brow on his sleeve before jamming the hat back on his flat curls. "Thing is, Claire, I'm not the one with the problem."

She'd prepared for this. "If I'd broken my leg or been diagnosed with cancer and I asked you to come with me to see the doctor, would you come?"

"This situation's nothing like that."

"How is it different?"

"It just is."

"It's not."

"Yeah, it is."

The urge to yell bubbled up and she forced herself to stay calm. "I'm doing what you asked, Matt. I'm getting help but I need yours too. Not all of our problems are mine."

"We didn't have any problems until you decided you didn't want kids." His voice cracked. "You took an amazing thing and trashed it."

"I'm not an island."

"Funny. You've been acting like one for a long time."

She crossed her arms to hold herself together and changed topics. "The anniversary's coming up."

"Yeah." He looked down and scuffed the dirt with the toe of his boot. "Thank God there's no big memorial service this year. I mean, hell, it's sad and awful but we can't keep looking back."

Claire didn't have the energy to revisit previous arguments that it was important to take time to remember the dead. "People are doing private things. I'm going to the cemetery. I'll probably see Julie and Phil there."

He nodded and she sensed his discomfort.

"So, you won't come?"

"To the cemetery or counseling?"

"Either or."

"I don't see the point."

Any lingering hope that they might survive as a couple vanished under the weight of his words. "What if we don't call it counseling but an assisted opportunity to say goodbye? Alissa suggested ten o'clock on Monday."

Incredulity crossed his face. "You're suggesting we officially call it quits on the day we were supposed to get married?"

"It's already a day associated with so much pain and heartache, why taint another one?"

He didn't say a word.

"HELLS BELLS!" A hand hit Josh's shoulder and fright made his fingers release his lunch bag. A sandwich and a can of beer spilled onto the footpath.

Phil scooped them up, his brows drawing down under the brim of his hat. "Sorry, Josh. Didn't mean to startle you. I called out twice but you were miles away. Busy time of year, eh? Lots to think about."

"Yeah." Josh wasn't about to tell Phil that lately the only thing he'd been thinking about was the electrical bypass.

"Great news about the house. Sophie called in yesterday, all excited and waving the key. After all this time, you must be pinching yourselves that it's finally at lock-up."

"Yeah."

Phil slid Josh's lunch back into the bag. "Everything okay?"

Everything's fucked. "Everything's fantastic. Kitchen's going in next week."

"Sophie won't know herself. I bet she's planning Christmas dinner."

Josh had no idea. She'd probably told him but Sophie, work, the kids—everything—was just background noise compared with the buzzing in his head that was louder than the bypass stealing electricity. He took back his lunch. "I have to get back to work."

"Before you go ..." Phil cleared his throat. "Julie and I are having a small gathering on Monday with Claire, Mick and Shane. Thought you might like to come?"

The buzzing in Josh's head morphed into a roar and his heart sped up. He spent enough of his time trying not to think about that freaking awful day, let alone deliberately stopping to acknowledge it. "I'm working Monday."

"Are you sure? It's just I saw Adam yesterday and I got the impression he was giving his staff the day off. I know he's going to the CFA service."

"I don't know about any of that. I have to go or I'll be late back."

Josh strode to the car and burned rubber down main street. He drove without really knowing where he was going, so ten minutes later it was a surprise to realize he was on one of the original logging tracks. He pulled over, parking under a stand of tall old-growth trees. Beech myrtles—the town's namesake. Over 300 years old, they were now dead—cooked beyond redemption when their rainforest habitat ignited in a hell fire never seen before. His boss at Sustainable Timber had told him that mountain ash and beech myrtle weren't like eucalypts that shot after a blaze. The big trees survived light fire but not the inferno that tore through their beloved home.

He wasn't sure the town that shared their name was surviving either.

Grabbing the beer from the bag on the passenger seat, he tugged on the ring pull. The popping sound and whoosh released a ratchet of tension before he took a sip. He downed the contents between bites of the sandwich, tasting neither. He hadn't enjoyed food or drink for a long time.

No way in hell was he going to the Langs' on Monday. He got that Hugo's death had hit them hard, especially Julie, but why did they want to invite the people who'd survived and force them to remember? Make them feel guilty for living? His hand tightened on the empty can and it collapsed with a loud scrunch. He wasn't sitting around doing nothing on Monday while Sophie was at work and the kids were at daycare. It wasn't a freaking federal holiday. He'd talk to Scotty that afternoon.

He suddenly remembered the builder saying something about a meeting in Geelong. Fine. He'd talk to Adam. In person. Josh wasn't going to let the boss fob him off over the telephone. No matter what, he was working Monday. Decision made, he negotiated a three-point turn on the narrow road and took a left toward the Petrovics'.

On the way he passed the old vineyard. The previous Wednesday, Scotty had been pissed off when Adam was late turning up for a site meeting. He'd mumbled something about Adam wasting time talking to his bloody tomatoes. If Adam was at the vineyard, it would save Josh six miles. He slowed and turned right.

He hadn't been there in weeks—not since he'd installed the bypass. True to his word, Adam hadn't got him back to do any more work there, which suited Josh. He didn't want to see the evidence of his illegal handwork. He saw enough of it in his mind, right up until his first beer of the day. He was surprised to find the gate closed and he hopped out to open it. His fingers encountered a padlock. Damn. He'd be driving to the office after all.

A screeching sound made him look up and a flock of black cockatoos streaked across the sky, their tail feathers a flash of vibrant yellow. As he dropped his gaze to the empty parking lot, he looked beyond to the greenhouse and saw the shadow of a person through the white polypropylene. Josh vaulted the gate.

Travis's Doberman appeared from behind the hedge, baring its teeth.

Josh flinched. He hated that bloody dog. "Beast! Stay!"

The dog's head jerked as he recognized Josh's voice. The barking stopped and the animal lost interest in him, loping back toward the pittosporum hedge. That's when Josh noticed a glint of silver. He followed Beast and found Travis's and Adam's cars parked behind the hedge under the shade of trees. Josh slid open the heavy door of the greenhouse.

Heat poured out to meet him and he stared, stunned at the size of the plants. The small tomato seedlings he'd carefully planted into the grow wool were now over three feet high and all of them had cascading vines full of vivid red and green tomatoes—the colors of Christmas.

A skitter of something that bore a distinct similarity to relief washed through him. At least the lights were doing their job and the crop was ready to do its job for Myrtle.

It made his uncomfortable role with the bypass worth it. Just one more month and he could whip the damn thing out and forget about it. One more month and the house would be finished. One more month and he could forget the last two years had ever happened and concentrate on the future.

As he walked down the middle of the greenhouse to the workbenches, red, green and black fruit flashed in his peripheral vision. He'd helped Travis build the benches—"help" being a relative term. Josh had built them while Travis assisted by almost killing himself with the saw, not to mention banging his thumb with the hammer. Josh had written him off as useless but going by the lush foliage of the tomatoes, Scotty was right. The guy knew plants.

Through the back wall of the greenhouse, Josh made out the shape of a shed. It hadn't existed the last time he'd been there. It was built so close to the greenhouse, the doors must line up. The radio was on and steam curled from a coffee mug. The workbenches were covered in crap—string, pruning shears, bits of plastic tubing, feeder sticks, an ashtray filled with butts—but it was the ziplock bag of herbs that caught his eye.

Suddenly a lot of Travis's behavior fell into place. He wasn't necessarily a dickhead, just a stoner. Though given he'd left his stash in full view where his boss could see it, he was still a dickhead. Josh picked up the bag, intending to hide it, but found himself smelling the contents.

The musky aroma took him back to the weeks after the fires when he'd smoked to forget.

Until Sophie had discovered his stash and flushed it down the toilet. He hadn't wanted to give it up but it was fractionally easier than dealing with Sophie's questions about why he was smoking it in the first place. Running his thumb along the yellow and blue strip, he sealed the bag and shoved it under a pile of papers. Out of sight. Out of temptation.

The back door of the greenhouse scraped its metal on metal sound and opened a third of the way. Travis stopped short. "Josh. What are you doing here?"

"Looking for Adam."

"He's not here."

"His SUV is."

"Is it? I haven't seen him." Travis's gaze shifted uneasily from the roof to the plants and then to the counter.

"Don't worry. I haven't nicked your stash. I just shoved it under the tomato catalogues so Adam doesn't see it."

Travis grinned. "It's good stuff. I can get you some if you want."

"Why would I want it?"

"Monday." A shudder rocked Travis's thin body, making his tattoos dance. "It's gonna be a shit day."

"Yeah. That's why I want to talk to Adam."

"Like I said, he's not here."

Instead of stepping into the greenhouse, Travis remained standing in the partially opened door. When they'd been planting and Josh had done the same thing, Travis had always said, "Born in a tent, mate? Shut the door, you're letting the heat out."

Josh looked beyond him to the shed. Travis's eyes darted again. Josh would bet his last dollar Travis didn't want him entering the shed.

Well, screw that. Adam was somewhere on the property and the shed was the next place to look.

He pushed past the slight man and blinked rapidly, unable to see after walking from the bright light of the greenhouse into the dim shed. "Adam?"

"He's not here." Travis's hand closed around Josh's arm. "Come back to the greenhouse and call him."

Josh threw off the smaller man's grip and strode forward, walking into something that clogged his mouth and nose and scratched his eyes. His hands flew up to swipe it away and he realized he was touching leaves. He stepped back. A shaft of sunshine streaming through a hole in the iron provided just enough light so he could distinguish racks of plants hanging upside down to dry. He knew enough to know they weren't tomatoes.

"What the hell are you up to?"

"Josh!" Scotty's breathless voice sounded behind him. "Mate. You shouldn't be in here."

Josh spun around. Scotty was panting, bent over with his palms pressed to his thighs. Josh stared at the man he both liked and respected, trying to fathom what the hell was going on. His brain felt encased in lead and nothing made sense. He finally managed to say, "I came to see Adam."

"Best you don't talk to him here. Come on." Scotty jerked his thumb in the direction of the door. "Follow me back to my place and we'll grab a beer."

Josh couldn't get his feet to move.

"Hello, Josh. No one told me you were here." Adam materialized from the dim recesses of the shed. "This is a pleasant surprise."

"I'm just taking Josh back to my place for a beer," Scotty said.

"You're too busy to be taking a beer break. Besides, I heard Josh say he came to see me. You and Trav need to give us a minute."

Travis immediately walked away but Scotty lingered, one hand scratching the back of the other, his gaze firmly on Adam, who silently inclined his head. Scotty hesitated then turned slowly. The clang of the door shutting behind him kickstarted Josh's brain.

"You're growing—"

"Tomatoes."

"The bypass—"

"Immensely helpful. All that light's given us ripe, plump tomatoes in time for the farmers market."

"Fuck the tomatoes, Adam. You lied to me."

"No, I didn't. Those tomatoes are doing double duty. They're helping Myrtle and they're the perfect cover for the real crop. Companion planting, I like to call it. We've got some lovely cannabis plants nestled in between the Romas and the Black Russians. They're growing a hell of a lot better than our other crop."

Other crop? "Jesus, Adam. You're breaking the law."

"Then I'm in good company. That bypass you installed hardly qualifies as legal."

Josh's hands tore at his hair as his own blind stupidity hit him. He should have guessed something was up. Adam's largesse to the community, to him and Sophie—it was too good to be true. And yet all of it had sounded feasible. Looked real. Was real. The tomatoes existed —he'd planted the suckers. The farmers market was real. Hell, Sophie was ordering dozens of bottles and jars to fill with tomato sauce and chutney for Put Myrtle on the Map day.

Josh's mind suddenly cleared. He jerked around.

"Where are you going?"

"To rip out the bypass."

"I don't think that's a wise idea."

"I don't give a rat's ass what you think."

Adam folded his arms across his broad chest. "I think you might be interested, especially when you hear how much money you owe me."

"I don't owe you a cent."

"Ah, Josh. That's where we differ. I've got a sheaf of unpaid invoices for building supplies."

"That's bullshit! We've paid for everything."

"Have you? Since the frame went up, the office has done the ordering and Sophie's been paying cash. I've been a bit distracted with the tomatoes and she's never asked for a receipt. That's the thing about cash, Josh. It lacks a paper trail. It'd be a shame if I set the debt collectors on you for failure to pay."

The ground shifted beneath Josh's feet and every hair on his body rose painfully. That bypass was like a toxic cloud; its presence tainted his job and the new house. He'd let Sophie take over coordinating the build, because every time he looked at the place or thought about it, all he saw was the deal he'd done with Adam.

Now it appeared he hadn't made a deal at all. He'd walked straight into a trap.

He stared down the man everyone in town venerated. "You can't repossess anything if you're in jail."

"That's not going to happen. This crop's worth too much to Myrtle and besides, I've got friends in the boys in blue."

Josh didn't believe him. "Shane Radley would bust you in a heartbeat."

Adam laughed. "Why do you think he's joined forces with Claire McKenzie running those drug and alcohol information nights? Why he's doing random vehicle checks? Shane's got a mighty talent for looking like he's on the job when really he's been looking the other way for years. It won't be me facing charges, Joshy-boy. It'll be you for installing the electrical bypass."

"You prick."

"I'll let that pass because I know you're upset. Fortunately, there's an easy solution to this mess you're in. As long as you don't touch the bypass and you keep your trap shut, everything's sweet. If you do anything stupid then being homeless will be the least of your problems." Adam rocked back on his heels. "I'd hate to see those beautiful kiddies of yours suffering because of your lack of judgement."

The cloying sweet air of the shed pressed in on Josh. It was suddenly hard to breathe. Helping Adam was supposed to have secured the house and the block, not risked everything. He closed his eyes, and Sophie's and the kids' trusting faces floated in front of him. He'd brought them to this bloody town for a job and a house—neither of which existed. Now, just when he thought the road was clear, he was mired in a crime.

Adam slapped him on the back and propelled him into the greenhouse. "And there are perks, mate. You get your own personal supply of the good stuff." He shoved a bulging ziplock bag of weed into Josh's shirt pocket. "Not only will it help you sleep at night, it'll make you see you've made the right decision."

Josh wanted to fling the bag back at the smug bastard. Tell him he didn't want his stinking drugs. Tell him he sure as hell didn't need them. But his hands stayed by his side.

He hated that he couldn't do it.

CHAPTER TWENTY-FOUR

BEC OPENED HER EYES AND IMMEDIATELY SHUT THEM TIGHT against the bright morning as pain drilled into her head. Her tongue felt thick and dry and she reached blindly for the water bottle on the bedside table. Fearing the vice-like pain, she kept her eyes closed and slowly raised her head, lifting the bottle. Water slopped into her mouth and ran down her chin. She fell back onto the pillow, the effort exhausting her.

"Hello, sleepyhead."

The bed moved and she cracked her eyes open in the smallest possible squint. Adam was sitting next to her, his head bent low and his brown eyes so close she could see the chocolate flecks. A sudden flash of heat tore across her skin and her body stiffened, pressing rigidly into the mattress.

"Sorry, babe. Didn't mean to give you a fright. I've taken the girls to school and I've made you cup of tea. How are you feeling?"

"I want to say better ..."

"Death warmed up, eh?"

She would have nodded but it hurt to move. It wasn't morning sickness. Thankfully that had passed, but the energy she'd craved and had recently enjoyed was short lived. First, she'd gotten a urinary tract infection—her first ever—and it had been humiliating having to pee in a jar with a nurse hovering to make sure she didn't contaminate the specimen. Then—oh the joy—the antibiotics gave her thrush. As soon as she'd gotten over that, she'd got this virus. She'd wake in the mornings fuzzy headed and heavy limbed. By the afternoon, she felt more like herself but by the time morning came around again, she woke with a dry mouth and a runny nose.

"You look like you've got hay fever. Take an antihistamine and see if it helps."

"I guess it's worth a shot."

He laughed. "I think so. You were snoring to beat the band last night. If it helps with that, it'd be good."

"Sorry. Did I keep you awake?"

"Little bit. I closed your mouth at one point."

She vaguely remembered that. "Did you give me some water too?"

"Yeah. You were out of it but you mumbled, "Thirsty." Mouth breathing does that." He stroked strands of hair off her face. "Drink your tea and take things slowly. Will you be okay to pick up the girls?"

"Yes. 2:00 till 9:00 is my best time of day."

"And you're all set for the CFA crew?"

The CFA? Her mind scrolled, reaching for details like flicking through a cell phone. Hazy thoughts about Put Myrtle on the Map curled like vapor, unable to be hooked. Christmas existed as an entity but was devoid of any details and after that she reached black space. Had Adam told her about the CFA? Did she have a list for it? God, she had so many lists, but even when they were in front of her she struggled to remember what was on them. "Easy. Beer and more beer," she bluffed.

His mouth jerked down. "You think Monday's something to joke about?"

Oh God. The anniversary. Her heart pounded. How could she have forgotten that? "No. I'm sorry. It's the virus talking."

"Everything has to be perfect. If you're not up to it, get your mother to do it."

The thought of her mother in the house on Monday was worse than the thought of being hostess on a day when all she wanted to do was pull down the blinds, hide in the dark and cry. "I'll be fine."

"Good. I have to go. Scotty's let Louis Beckwith get away with murder so I'm meeting the bugger to sort out the mess."

He leaned in for a kiss and her body did another one of those crazy involuntary flinches. The movement spun pain through her, winding up her stiff and sore neck before settling in the back of her head. Maybe she really did have allergies.

He glowered at her. "Is there a problem kissing your husband goodbye?"

She struggled onto her elbows and kissed him. "Have a good day."

"Always."

He strode out of the room full of the purpose and energy she envied. She lay listening to the rumble of the garage door and the gradual fading of the car's engine. The bedside clock told her it was closer to ten than nine. Agitation fluttered in her chest and belly. There were things she needed to do but she couldn't remember what they all were. She moved to get up and gasped at the red-hot ache in her arms and knees and noticed she had bruises on her thighs.

That didn't surprise her—in her dozy state, her coordination wasn't fabulous. The weekend before, at the tomato-sauce day, she'd walked into the corner of the long stainless-steel bench. Claire had sat her down with an icepack next to Julie, who was sorting tomatoes. Bec had appreciated the excuse to sit quietly with her. Although the deep grief lines on Julie's face remained as they ever would, she looked different. Relaxed? No, it wasn't that, but she was certainly less strained.

"I feel a thousand pounds lighter," Julie said softly. "I should have had more faith in Phil and Penny and told them earlier. Thing is, Heather and I always confided in each other about how to deal with the big things and, without her, I was floundering." Her gaze flicked to Claire then back to Bec. "How are things with you?"

Bec pressed the icepack on the forming bruise, welcoming the distraction of the pain. She couldn't tell Julie about Ivy's anger and increasing isolation, her own non-specific illness, of not being on top of anything and her inability to remember two things without a list. That the CWA was her only respite from home and how she'd fallen in love with tomatoes because they increasingly took Adam out of the house. Guilt immediately twisted its snake-like way through her. That wasn't fair. Although Adam's need to have her constantly close hadn't changed, since her pregnancy his behavior had. Instead of getting frustrated with her general malaise, he was mostly solicitous.

But as she couldn't say any of it, she went for the town's current default setting. "It's not an easy time of year."

Julie nodded. "It makes the rush and stress of Christmas look like a walk in the park. I think of Hugo every day but I don't like to think of him on the anniversary."

Bec didn't understand, especially as she'd overheard Julie inviting Claire to Beechside on Monday for what was obviously a time to remember. She'd fought feelings of hurt and disappointment that the invitation didn't extend to her, despite knowing there was no reason why it should. Unlike Claire, she wasn't a close family friend. Besides, like the rest of Myrtle, Julie would expect Bec to be a supportive wife and spend the day by Adam's side.

"Why don't you like to think of Hugo then?"

"I hate the idea of him dying alone."

That day entire families had perished but Julie's words conjured up a completely different image. Bec pressed even harder on the cold pack until the burning chill drove the image away. She tried to make amends for asking a question that had forced Julie to speak the harrowing words.

"You once told me he had his dog with him. I know a dog's not a person but in some ways, maybe it was better? A dog would have snuggled in ..."

Julie reached out and caught Bec's hand. "That's a lovely way of looking at it. Thank you. Oh, look, there's Adam. He's looking worried." She let go of Bec's hand and waved to him.

A wave of loss rolled through Bec. It had stayed with her for the rest of the afternoon after Adam had insisted she come home early because Gracie was complaining of a stomach ache.

Now, in her bedroom and thinking about Julie again, another wave of loneliness rolled in. Bec fought it with the tattered energy she had, knowing the worst thing was to succumb to the void. Like so many of the district's residents, she just had to hang on and get through Monday. Adam had said the CFA members were coming. That meant baking sausage rolls, pin wheels, a sponge cake, pavlova with cream and fruit ...

The thought almost made her lie down again. What was today? Friday? She checked her cell phone. Friday. Thank God. She hadn't totally lost it. Okay, she could do this. To be ready for Monday, the weekend would be consumed by cooking and cleaning. If she shopped today, she could involve Ivy in the cooking. Surely a sullen Ivy helping her in the kitchen was better than a sullen Ivy alone in her room?

Her fingers flicked screens on her cell phone, digging down through a complicated series of folders until she found the one photo she'd kept, taken during those precious months before the fires. In the first weeks after the blaze she'd taunted herself by looking at it every day. Initially, gazing at it had bathed her in precious memories and given her solace, but as time passed, anger dominated, a raging fury at the pointless futility of it all. One random act of lightning on drought-stricken land in a raging-hot wind had not only killed people, it had stolen the lives of the living.

When Adam was discharged home, she'd tried to withstand the need to look at the photo. She had enough challenges each day without reminding herself what should have been. That part of her life was over. Finished. Choices and decisions had been made, forced upon her and accepted. The last time she'd looked at the photo was the night Scotty drove her back from Geelong. She traced the face of the man she loved and couldn't have. A tear splashed onto the screen, distorting the image. "I wish ..."

But there was no point wishing. Wishing was for fools.

Bec swiped the photo closed and got up. There was a menu to be planned, groceries to buy and flowers to be arranged. None of it would happen unless she did it.

JULIE WAS LYING on her belly in the grass, pulling out weeds with her non-impacted arm when Phil's shadow fell over her. She glanced up into his worried face. "Stop looking at me like that. I'm fine."

"You've said that before."

She rolled over and sat up, trying hard to keep her shame from digging in. "I've also said I'm sorry a hundred times."

Phil sat down next to her and picked up her hand. "In a crazy way, I sort of get why you didn't want to tell me. When I had that funny turn six months after the fires and we thought I'd had a stroke, all I could think about was how I didn't want to be a burden to you."

"You would never be that."

"Neither would you."

"I should have told you about the lump."

"Next time." He cleared his throat. "Anyway, I wasn't thinking about any of that. I came out here because you've been on your belly doing yardwork long enough."

"Hugo loved the garden. I want it to be perfect for Monday."

"Hugo never worried about a few weeds and neither should you."

"Talking about weeds, can you take me to the cemetery this afternoon? I want to supervise you tidying it up."

"I swung by and it looks like Claire's beaten you to it."

"Did you see her?"

"No, but Heather's and Ron's graves have received the same treatment."

"She's keeping busy, which means things aren't good. I should call her."

"After lunch and a nap."

"I don't need a nap!"

"I do." His eyes twinkled. "You can keep me company on the bed."

She laughed and elbowed him gently in the ribs, pleased to feel a flutter of desire after weeks of emptiness. "Still using the same old line after forty years."

"Well, if it ain't broke ..."

"Oh, I meant to tell you, Penny rang. She says she's got the food organized for Monday. She tried banning me from doing any baking. I told her people would bring a plate and that I was making Hugo's pavlova."

"Fair enough." He picked a blade of grass and spun it in his fingers. "Did I tell you I invited Josh?"

"No, but that's a good idea."

"Yeah. I ran into him at lunchtime yesterday. He had a sandwich and a can of beer."

"Tradie tradition."

"That's a beer at the end of the day, love. Not lunchtime. Has Sophie said anything?"

"No and neither has anyone else. They're all sticking to safe topics while I'm convalescing. When I'm out of this boot, I'm putting a stop to it."

"I can't shake the feeling something's up with Josh. I've been inviting him to stuff for months but he never comes."

"Darling, he's a young man."

"We've got some young bucks at the Men's Shed," Phil said defensively. "They're the ones doing Flab Busters and they're all competing in the fun run."

"It's not like when Josh lost his job. He's not alone all day with the kids anymore. He's got company at work. When you add in Sophie's working full time, the kids and building the house, that's probably enough for him. Besides, Sophie's always been more outgoing than Josh."

"That's true. Although remember when they first arrived and how keen they were to get involved? Josh talked about joining the CFA."

"Then life as we knew it changed forever."

"Yeah." He concertinaed the grass. "But don't you think after what he went through, he'd want to join now more than ever?"

"There's plenty of people in this town who've never joined the fire brigade. I think some of them look at Adam Petrovic and change their minds."

Phil grunted. "If Adam hadn't broken rank and left his crew, Scotty and Travis would be dead."

Julie fought down old anger and grief that someone hadn't broken rank for her son. That a tanker hadn't managed to make it down the rutted road to Hugo. But thoughts like that were a one-way journey to despair. Instead, she concentrated on the good men and women who'd done their best under the worst conditions of their fire-fighting careers, risking their lives in the process. If they'd been able to save Hugo, they would have.

That they hadn't was a grief they carried too.

CHAPTER TWENTY-FIVE

The Inferno

Claire and her bridesmaid, Olivia, a friend from Melbourne, joke, laugh and sip champagne as Karen does their hair and Jasmine applies their makeup. The air conditioner's working flat out trying to keep the inside temperature tolerable while outside the mercury is rising so fast it's threatening to hit 109 by one o'clock.

As they walk the short distance back to the B & B, Claire says, "Just as well we're getting married in a church. It's always cool inside All Saints."

"As long as the drinks are cold, nothing else matters. Although they wouldn't dare be anything else if your future mother-in-law has anything to do with it. She's forthright, isn't she?"

Claire doesn't respond. Today is her day and she's not thinking about Louise. As she steps inside their room, her cell phone rings and her heart soars. "Hi, honey."

"Hey, Postie."

"Isn't it bad luck to talk to the bride on the wedding day?"

Matt laughs. "I think that's seeing the bride before the wedding and I won't be doing that."

Something about the way he says it makes her ask, "Is there a problem?"

"Not really. Just a grass fire on the Lorkin's place. I'm on the truck heading over there now."

"You're on a CFA call-out on our wedding day?"

"They're shorthanded. Don't stress. It's nothing to worry about. Captain Matt's my best man so he'll make sure we both make it. But if I'm a bit late, don't panic. I promise you, I'll be there. Nothing's getting in the way of me marrying you today."

"The bride's the one who's supposed to be late. You just want to make a grand entrance because you know you look drop-dead gorgeous in that tux."

She hears a man's voice in the background, calling out instructions.

"I've gotta go." Matt says. "Love you, Postie. Can't wait to see you."

"Everything okay?" Olivia asks.

"Looks like I'm having a traditional country wedding after all."

Olivia gives her a confused look.

"Hugo was late for his wedding to Amber because he was delivering a calf. Matt's father was late for his wedding because of lambing and Matt might be late because he's fighting a grass fire."

"That wouldn't happen in Melbourne. More champagne?"

An hour later, Heidi, the B & B owner, knocks on the door. "Sorry to interrupt, Claire, but I've got the radio on and there's a watch and act—"

"At the Lorkin's. I know, Matt called." Claire's mind is delightfully fuzzy with champagne.

"There are a couple of other fires, including one at Sheepwash."

"Perhaps I better tell the reverend Matt will definitely be late."

"Sheepwash is twenty miles away from Oakvale Park, so I'm sure you don't have anything to worry about."

Claire glances out the window and her buzz vanishes. The blue sky is now eerily gray. "Where are the other fires?"

"I only remember Sheepwash, because I was thinking of the reception."

Claire's cell phone rings and Heidi closes the door as she leaves the room. Claire reads the name on the screen. It's Heather.

"Hello, darling."

"Hi, Mom. Have you been listening to the radio?"

"Yes. Relax. I've just been talking to Louise and the fires are too far away to be a threat. But you were right to stay last night in town. That wind! Just horrible. I'm worried your bouquet will wilt before the photos. I can't wait to see you in your dress. Oh, your father's calling. I better go. Love you, sweetheart. See you soon."

Heather hangs up in her usual abrupt way. Claire is watching the sky and listening to the old Queen Anne house creaking in the wind.

CLAIRE DRINKS water and listens to the radio. Olivia suggests she eat some of the food Heidi's prepared. "It's been ages since breakfast. You don't want to faint at the altar."

Claire's gut is churning. Food is the last thing she wants. She's been calling Matt and leaving messages but he isn't calling back. Both CFA tankers sped out of town a couple of hours ago with sirens blaring and haven't returned. The bloke on the radio drones on about fire fronts and an imminent cool change. The sky is gunmetal. Claire can't tell if the color is smoke or rain.

"You might be lucky with that cool change," Oliva comments. "A thirty-degree drop in temperature means we can dance all night without melting."

Heather rings. "We're just leaving now."

"Mom!" Claire wails, frustrated for the first time with the McKenzie failing of always running just that little bit late. "I'm supposed to be dressed by now."

"Sorry, darling. Pop your dress on and relax. You're going to be a beautiful bride. I'll be there soon."

Claire stops herself from saying, "How is forty-five minutes soon?" and says instead, "Love you, Mom."

Oliva helps her into her dress, tells her to close her eyes and then turns her around to face the mirror. "Now."

Claire opens her eyes and stares. Is that beautiful bride really her? Her hands rise to her mouth as excitement skips and jumps and twirls inside her. "Oh my God. I'm really getting married."

"Yep." Oliva raises her wineglass. "That Matt Cartwright is one lucky bloke."

"I'm one lucky woman."

Nick the photographer arrives. "Hell of a day! The trees are bent double and anything not nailed down is flying down main street. I know you wanted to walk to the church but that veil of yours won't last two minutes."

Surely he's exaggerating? While Nick sets up his equipment, Claire runs downstairs, surprised that the hall lights are on. She opens the front door. The heat hits her like an entity. Thick smoke and grit swirls in the air and her forearm rises instinctively to protect her face and eyes from sandblasting. She struggles to close the door. The first frisson of fear flitters through her.

"Heidi!" she calls. "Has anyone mentioned anything about Myrtle?"

The woman appears from the front room, the sound of the television following her.

"They're evacuating Deans Marsh but we're fine. There's nothing on the radio, TV or the internet about fires near us."

"Then why does the sky look like that?" Claire points out the window to the enormous billowing cloud backlit by an orange glow that's coming from the direction of Oakvale Park. She rings the emergency number. She gets the busy signal. She tries Matt. She gets the busy signal. She calls the police station. Busy signal.

Slow-cooked fear bursts into panic. "All of this feels wrong."

"Ring the CFA?" Heidi suggests.

Jacqui Datsun answers the call.

"What do you know?" Claire asks.

"Both tankers are out supporting Sheepwash. We've radioed for them to come back just in case."

The lights in the hall snap off and the voices on the television abruptly cease. "We just lost power."

"Us too. Likely the whole town's out."

Claire's heart thumps. "No power and no tankers. If the fire hits town, we've got no protection."

"It's still a good twelve miles away."

A rumbling noise sounds in the distance. Thunder? Relief sinks into her like a refreshing shower. "I think the cool change just arrived."

Claire hears an expletive down the line and men shouting. The CFA siren suddenly shrieks its penetrating blare.

"Claire, you still there?" Jacqui asks, agitation and alarm vivid in her voice.

"Yes."

"Come to the shed. Now!"

Claire drops Heidi's telephone onto its cradle and lifts her skirts. Running up the stairs, she yells to the B & B owner to get water and blankets. She rushes into the bedroom. Olivia's flirting with the photographer.

"We have to go."

"But your parents aren't here."

"I mean we have to leave. Evacuate. Hear the siren? It's not safe. The fire's coming."

"But towns don't burn down."

Claire rips the blanket off the bridal bed and throws it at Olivia. "I'm not prepared to risk it."

Outside, it's dark. The wind deafens them. Its maniacal strength buffets them and it takes real effort to stay upright. In the distance, Myrtle's welcoming avenue of trees glows orange. Flames leap and arc skywards. The air cracks and crackles around them and they pile into Nick's van. Claire insists on driving.

"I know the way."

She closes the vents to block the smoke and hopes the seals in the van are tight.

As she throws the car into reverse, there's an almighty explosion. The van rocks and Olivia screams. Despite her dread, Claire forces herself to look in the rear-view mirror. Flames shoot a hundred and fifty feet into the air.

"I think the service station just blew up."

A terrified silence greets her. The radiant heat pummels them. Smoke curls under the door. She drives slowly, barely able to see beyond the end of the hood, praying desperately that she'll make it to the CFA shed without colliding with anything. Her mind races, counting streets, calculating distances, studiously avoiding thinking about the fact that she's not wearing any protective clothing. That a fire ball is racing fast toward them and coming from the opposite direction of the known fires. That it's coming from the direction of her parents' home. That Matt's out there somewhere in this apocalypse without her.

Embers fall like red and black rain and the windshield wipers melt into a rubbery mess. She takes a left, praying she hasn't missed a street, and strains to hear the CFA siren over the wind. She hits something, hopes like hell it's another car. "Sorry."

"Don't worry. You got us here." Nick points to the distinctive red and white CFA logo barely visible through the smoke. He pulls open the door.

"Get down low." Eyes and throat stinging, Claire throws her skirts over her arm, grabs Olivia's and Heidi's hands and runs.

The CFA shed creaks and groans in the cyclonic wind. The ground feels like it's shaking under her feet. Claire hears the voices of firefighters and the thrumming whir of the pumps but she can't see a thing in the smoke. Ted Gregson opens the shed door halfway and hurries them inside. About a hundred pairs of terrified eyes stare at them.

"Mommy, it's a princess," a little girl says.

Laughter momentarily breaks the tension. It's silenced by the boom of another explosion. People keep arriving. Everyone squeezes up. Someone Claire doesn't know complains, saying there's no more room.

Three people say, "Shut up. There's room."

Shane Radley ushers in a family. Shock is etched on their faces. On his. The policeman catches Claire's eye and tilts his head toward the children. She sees burns on their skin.

"I need a first-aid kit. Water."

Jacqui Datsun directs her to the back room. Olivia, Heidi and Nick follow.

"Tell us what to do."

"Clear a space."

They push tables to the walls and bring in chairs. While the others hand out face masks and water, Claire irrigates eyes, cools burns with wet strips of fabric ripped from her wedding dress, lies fainters on the tables until they've rallied, dispenses Ventolin for people struggling to breathe and fights a battle with her own lungs in the thick smoky air.

The fire rages around them. Claire has no idea of time. She hates that there's a window in the room and she tries not to look at the vivid red glow on the other side of the glass. It's like looking through an oven door, only from the wrong side. Will they roast inside this tin shed? Will she die on her wedding day? In a momentary lull and desperate to talk to Matt and her parents, she pulls her cell phone from the pocket the dressmaker specially made for it and her hankie. There are no bars.

"I'll be back in a minute." She goes to the office. "Jacqui, can you get Matt on the radio?"

The woman looks stricken. "Myrtle Tanker just radioed. They've been caught. They're preparing for a burnover."

Claire's knees sag and she swears her heart stops. Vivid in her mind is the night she met Matt. How they sat in Bert and he closed the Thermaguard curtains, cocooning them in a private space. She hears him saying, "Hopefully a fire will never burn over the truck and we won't have to use these."

She has no idea how long she stands gripping the doorway to hold herself up and reading the same fear on Jacqui's face.

The radio crackles and Captain Matt Holsworthy's voice fills the room. "Myrtle Station, this is Myrtle Tanker. All safe."

"Matt!" Claire yells, reaching for the radio.

"Captain, can the bride hear the groom's voice?" Jacqui asks.

There's another crackle. "Postie, I'm okay. I love you."

"I love you too. I don't know where Mom and Dad are."

Jacqui throws her an apologetic look as she asks for the captain. "Holsworthy, make your way back to Myrtle ASAP. We're fighting a fire without a tanker."

"We're doing our best but it's a warzone out here."

"It's no different here."

"Has Adam Petrovic made contact?"

"Isn't he with you?"

"He was. It was too dangerous to take the tanker down Duck Pond Road and risk getting trapped. He insisted against advice and legged it across the fields to rescue his workers from the old vineyard."

Claire knows firefighters are volunteers and sometimes they choose to stay and defend their own property instead of going on a call-out but to leave the team mid-active duty? It doesn't sound normal. Then again, there's absolutely nothing normal about today.

She leaves Jacqui talking on comms and walks into the main room. She is struck by the change—she can hear conversations. The rocket sound of exploding gas bottles has ceased and the noise of the wind has lessened. Ted Gregson steps inside, covered in a layer of ash and barely recognizable in his CFA uniform.

"That was the longest hour of my life," he rasps, voice scratchy from heat and smoke. "The good news is the front's passed. The bad news is the town's gone. Prepare yourselves. It looks like Armageddon."

Claire goes outside with Shane Radley. The police station's on fire. The health center's a pile of rubble, blown apart by an exploding gas cylinder. Houses are ablaze. A charred kangaroo limps past. Dead birds lie on the road where they've fallen from the sky, killed by the radiant heat. Through the veil of smoke, people stagger toward Claire —some with blankets around them, some with melted footwear, some being carried. Then she sees tanker two and hears the call, "We've got injured people."

She snaps out of her stupor. "We need ambulances," she tells Shane. "Radio for ambulances."

"I already have but everything's still burning. I watched those bloody beautiful trees fall like stunned giants." He flinches. "They're still falling. It's not safe. They won't allow ambulances through."

"But they're sending strike teams, right? They're clearing the road? Shane?" New panic surges. "We need ambulances or people will die." She tries not to think about the likelihood that some people were already dead.

"We might have to take the worst ones out ourselves." Shane spins around and faces the shocked crowd behind him. "Anyone whose truck isn't torched and has a chainsaw on board report to me at the tanker." He hurries over to talk to the CFA crew.

"Claire." Ted Gregson touches her shoulder. "They need you back there."

She nods and walks inside.

A thousand triage decisions later—verdicts she won't allow herself to second guess—she's saved some lives and lost others. A tiny part of her is on constant alert waiting for her parents to walk into the shed and find her. For Matt to find her.

FIVE HOURS after the conflagration engulfs Myrtle, arms wrap around Claire's waist. She turns and looks up into familiar but red, raw eyes.

"Oh, honey." Her hands fly to his singed curls, his grimy cheeks, his jacketed shoulders and then his chest. "You're really here."

He strokes fallen strands of her hair—her wedding 'do half intact— and then holds her gently away from him, taking in the filthy lace bodice of her dress and the remains of the full skirt she's hacked at to make bandages. "You look amazing."

"If you think that, your eyes need irrigating."

He kisses her. "Can they spare you for a bit?"

She glances at her eclectic first-aid team, all of whom have taken breaks on her insistence. Olivia and Nick nod at her. Matt takes her hand and leads her outside. It's dark—true dark now, not fire dark. Stars blink through the smoke haze. All around them tongues of flames lick blue and orange—Myrtle is a giant campfire of glowing embers. Exhausted fire fighters keep up the good fight, extinguishing spot fires to keep their tiny refuge safe. Claire thinks about what she's seen and wonders what Matt has encountered.

"It came from nowhere," she says.

He nods. "It was the wind change. It sucked up the flames and blasted fire balls in every direction. It was hotter than anything we've ever experienced. And fast. So fast. It leaped fire breaks. Embers got blown six miles. Some poor buggers didn't have a hope in hell of getting out alive. Mom and Dad are safe and so's the homestead. But we've lost our place and all the wedding presents. Sorry."

She shakes her head and hugs him hard, needing to feel him. "I don't care about the presents. When I heard you were in a burnover, I thought I'd lost you."

"Thank God for Bert and all that training."

She kisses him, tasting smoke, ash and blessed relief. Matt pulls away, clearing his throat.

"Do you need water?"

He rubs his jaw and an agonized look crosses his face. "Postie, we found three burnt out cars on Cardine Road."

Claire's stomach goes into free-fall.

"I'm really sorry. Heather and Ron didn't make it out."

Matt's confirmation coalesces her hours of abject fear. Sobbing, she sinks into him.

CHAPTER TWENTY-SIX

THE PRESENT

After telling Alissa about her conversation with Matt, Claire fidgeted on the counselor's couch. "He's always on time so I doubt he's coming. Perhaps I should have made an appointment with an attorney instead."

"Perhaps the date's too confronting for him?"

"It seems appropriate to me."

The doorbell buzzed and every muscle in Claire's body jerked.

"Excuse me." Alissa rose gracefully and walked out of the room.

Claire heard the murmur of voices and then Alissa returned, followed by Matt. Her gut cramped painfully and she wondered if she'd have to excuse herself and rush to the toilet.

"You came."

"Yeah." Matt sat on the couch, positioning himself as far away from Claire as possible. He crossed his arms, looking miserable.

"Thanks for coming, Matt," Alissa said before Claire could. "I appreciate it may not be easy for you being here."

Matt made a huffing sound. "What's not easy is Claire putting a bullet into our relationship for no good reason."

"In my experience, there's always a reason, but it's not always obvious to those in the middle of it," Alissa said smoothly. "How did Claire's decision not to have children make you feel?"

Matt stared at Alissa as if she were an alien. "How do you think it made me feel?"

"I don't know. That's why I'm asking."

Matt glared at Claire. "Surely you told her?"

She nodded but Alissa said, "I want to hear it from you, Matt."

"Gutted." He poured himself a glass of water and drank it slowly. "And angry. I've never felt this angry in my life. It's like a slow burn inside of me. Every time I think about it, the embers flare and I rage again. I can't believe she's done this to me. To us. God! If I hadn't found those pills, how long would she have strung me along? I've been telling people we're trying to start a family and she's been making me look like a fool."

Matt's hurt battered Claire and she wanted to hug him, but she'd lost that right weeks ago.

"Did you mean to make Matt feel foolish, Claire?"

"No. Never. I love him. I wanted to tell him, but I couldn't. I knew if I did, he'd leave me and the thought of that ... it was worse than waiting for death inside the CFA shed."

"Is Claire's fear of you leaving her a fair assessment of your reaction, Matt?" Alissa asked.

"Yeah. But, damn it, Claire. You ripped out my heart." He stared at his knees. "During those awful weeks after the fires, when I closed my eyes and could only see scorched earth and blackened sheep, besides you, the only thing that got me through was planning our future. Dreaming of kids. Now when we've finally got our lives back on track, I don't understand why you've done a 180?"

Tears pooled behind Claire's eyes but all the things she'd learned about herself over these last long weeks suddenly solidified. For the first time, she told Matt the truth. "That's the thing. We're not back on track."

"We were until you lost the plot."

"Matt," Alissa said calmly. Firmly. "Problems in a relationship are rarely one-sided. It's helpful if we can avoid the blame game."

He threw up his arms. "Fine. Sorry. The thing is, yes, the farm was a mess for a year. Yes, we had to rebuild the house. But even when everything around us was crap, Claire and I have only ever been tight."

"And that's my fault," Claire said. "I let you believe that."

"No! You're not that good an actress." Matt turned to Alissa. "Since the fires, I've seen a heap of marriages go to the wall. The blokes always say there was no sex, just arguing. We've never argued until all this blew up and that included building a house. Our sex life was good. Great. We were a team. We've been a team from the moment we met."

"Would you say your relationship faced some challenges before the fires?" Alissa asked.

"No." Matt rubbed his palms on his moleskin-clad thighs. "Well, there was the initial misunderstanding about Taylor, but we sorted that out fast. We've been good ever since."

"Would you agree with that, Claire?"

"I think we believed it. We fell in love the moment we met and it was exhilarating. For months we lived in a blissful bubble of happiness. In the early weeks when Matt visited me in Melbourne, it was easy to pretend no one was upset or hurt that we'd got together. Six months before the wedding, we moved our bubble to the cottage. I think during that first year we ignored the call of the real world. Then it came at us like a speeding train."

"The fire was hardly real-world stuff," Matt said grimly. "Most people never experience anything like it, thank God."

"I'm not talking about the fires," Claire said.

Alissa wrote something down on her notepad. "Matt, how did your family react to the news about your breakup with Taylor?"

"That doesn't have anything to do with Claire and me," he said tersely. "I broke up with Taylor and I chose Claire. They accepted my decision."

"If they did, they weren't happy about it," Claire said, emboldened by Alissa's mediating presence. "And I think somewhere deep in your heart you know that too. But you love them and you loved me so it's been hard for you to acknowledge there's a problem."

Matt stiffened. "My parents loved and welcomed her. This is Claire's problem."

Claire laced her fingers, needing the painful reinforcement of bone on bone to hold her resolve. To go against her mother's relationship advice.

"The night before our wedding, I overheard your mother urging you not to marry me."

Matt's head swung toward her fast, his eyes wide with shock. "You misunderstood. Mom was just checking I was sure you were the one."

"It didn't sound like that."

"And in two years, you've never once thought to mention it or ask me about it?"

"No."

"Why?"

"Lots of reasons."

She gazed at her engagement ring and Heather's aged wedding band. "Initially, the fires drove it out of my head. Later, when we were living with your parents, you kept telling me how lucky we were to have their support. I didn't want to argue with you and give them a chance to tell you they'd been right all along. And I followed Mom's advice of never getting between a mother and her son. She'd told me if I loved you long and strong, if I was polite and considerate of your family, they'd eventually truly welcome me. Then Mom died."

"And my parents stepped up and organized the funerals for you."

"I'm not saying your parents don't give us practical support—they do—but it comes with a weary and resigned tolerance of me. No matter what I do, Louise, Bill and Tamara find me wanting. I know you say it's because I don't try hard enough but, Matt, I tried hard for over a year and nothing changed.

"I don't think you noticed how hard I was working to find a role on the farm until I stopped trying. That's when I threw myself back into my job, because it was easier. But I guess the big reason I never told you any of this was because you love your parents. I didn't want to be the difficult person complaining and causing problems. But I've ended up being that person anyway. I can't win."

She raised her head and met his eyes. "As far as your family's concerned, me not being Taylor *is* the problem."

"That's not true."

"Oh, Matt!" Exasperation broke its leash. "Over the last three years, Tamara's found a million ways to drop Taylor's name into the conversation. When she does, Louise picks up the ball and runs with it. Not once have you asked them not to talk about Taylor in front of me. In fact, every time they mention her, you go silent."

"You make it sound like they talk about her all the time."

"Matt," Alissa said, "when your family mentions Taylor in front of you and Claire, how does it make you feel?"

"Claire's exaggerating. It doesn't happen that often."

Alissa didn't respond. Matt picked at a loose thread on the couch. "Fine! I don't like it."

Alissa ignored his belligerence. "Why do you think you feel that way?"

Claire watched his face twist and her heart tore a little. She wanted to tell him she understood exactly how hard it was to acknowledge and face difficult feelings. She'd been doing it for weeks.

"I dunno." He rubbed his jaw. "Look, all I've ever wanted is for everyone to get along and be one big, happy family. Is that too much to ask?"

"It's a noble aim but sadly we can't control other people's feelings," Alissa said. "Would I be right in saying your family loved Taylor and considered her to be part of the family?"

Matt let out a long sigh. "Taylor's my sister's best friend. We all grew up together, and yes, after we'd been dating for two years, the family expected us to get married. But I didn't love her enough. I told them that. I told them I'd been thinking about breaking up with her for weeks and that Claire had nothing to do with it. Why are we even talking about this? Hell, Taylor and I broke up three years ago. Three years!"

"Yet you had coffee with her a few weeks ago!" Jealousy hung off Claire's words.

"And that was stupid. I get that now and I'm sorry. My only defense is that your bombshell about not wanting kids gutted me. I wish I'd never met up with her and if it helps, it only took one coffee and that dinner for me to remember exactly why I broke up with her. Why I don't love her. Why I love you."

His face implored Claire to understand. "Taylor's got *nothing* to do with us. I don't even know why we're talking about her."

"This isn't actually about you, Matt," Alissa said succinctly. "It's about your family's feelings. It sounds like your family considered Taylor part of the family for years, so when you broke up with her, they experienced a shock. Before they'd had time to absorb the news and grieve for their loss, you introduced Claire. Even though you initiated the breakup with Taylor, the speed at which everything happened made it easy for your family not to welcome Claire. There may even be some misplaced blame."

Matt frowned. "Hang on. Are you saying they found it easier to blame Claire for the breakup than me?"

"Absolutely. They know and love you. Claire was a relative stranger who took the place of a woman they knew and loved."

"Maybe I can concede that might have happened at the start, but we've been together three years! Apart from these last few weeks there's never been any reason for my family to think that Claire and I aren't a couple. We're engaged, for God's sake. It's not my fault we're not married."

"Again, this isn't about your feelings."

Claire envied the counselor's sangfroid but unlike Claire, she had the advantage of detachment. Every time Claire thought about the mess with Matt's family, she wanted to cry.

"If my feelings don't count, why the hell did you insist on me being here?" Matt asked grumpily.

"Your feelings do count," Alissa said gently. "But right now we're unpacking your family's feelings because they're negatively impacting on your relationship with Claire. Let me try to explain. There's a reason for the expression "love is blind." Before the fires, you and Claire were flying high on new love. Studies have proven that during this intense time, body chemistry changes so there are a lot of chemicals flying around. Some of them are protective of the new relationship.

"It's the bubble Claire mentioned before. Back then, even if you'd noticed your parents weren't as enthusiastic about your new relationship as you were, the chemicals blocked it from real consideration. Claire noticed the coolness from your family but it didn't bother her because she had you and her parents' love and support to buffer your family's hurt and disappointment. The fires changed those dynamics."

Alissa turned to Claire. "Tell Matt how you feel when his family mentions Taylor."

"I feel devalued. I want Matt to tell his mother and sister not to talk about her in front of us."

"Seriously?" Matt stared at her, surprise wide in his eyes. "You're hardly a fragile flower. You run the healthcare center. If you felt this strongly about it, why didn't you tell them?"

"And give them another reason to resent me? If I'd told them, we'd have argued about it like we're doing now. Like we do whenever I try to explain I feel like an outsider in the family. Or you'd have brushed me off, saying there isn't a problem, that your parents love me and I just need to lighten up."

Matt stared furiously at the blue painting on the wall, his jaw working.

Alissa glanced between them. "Matt, Claire tells me you're currently living with your parents."

"Yeah." He sounded suspicious.

"Have your parents passed comment on your separation?"

"They're angry with Claire but they don't have a monopoly on that."

"How does their anger make you feel?"

"Hell! Is that the only question you ever ask?" He ploughed his hands through his hair. "There's been times their anger's gotten under my skin. And before you ask me why, even though I hate what Claire's done to me and how she did it, they were being harsh about other stuff."

"Did you tell them how that made you feel?"

He barked out a vicious laugh. "Yeah, right, and then we hugged. Look, I live in the real world with a regular family. I did what I've been doing since I was a teen. I went for a fast gallop. My mother's a strong woman. I love and respect her, but she's not always easy."

Claire swallowed a gasp. It was the first time she'd ever heard Matt say anything negative about Louise.

"If you don't always find your mother easy, can you appreciate that Claire might experience similar feelings?"

He sat perfectly still for a few seconds and then he turned to face Claire, his handsome face haggard. "Two years ago today when I broke the news to you that Heather and Ron were dead, you sank into me like a child. You're always so strong, but you fell apart and it terrified me.

"We'd lost the cottage, the wedding presents, everything we owned and even though you kept going, kept working, you folded in on yourself for a bit. I didn't know what to do. I just knew I wanted to make you happy again. It made sense to me to offer you my family, because you'd lost yours. I wanted something good to come out of something bad. I honestly believed that living at the homestead would do the trick. Bring everyone closer and merge us into one big happy family."

"Just wanting it isn't enough."

"No. I'm starting to get that."

Claire's body ached with the unique pain love inflicts. "I appreciate that you wanted to help. But even if Louise and Bill had learned to love me, and Tamara and I became friends, a lot of the time I feel like you've forgotten Mom and Dad ever existed.

"You talk about looking forward but it's important to remember too. I have so few physical reminders of my parents and I need to talk about them to keep them close. I loved them. I miss them every single day. I'm sorry that makes you uncomfortable, but it really shouldn't. My love for them doesn't lessen my love for you."

Matt shifted on the couch. "The reason I don't talk about Heather and Ron isn't because I doubt your love for me or because I don't miss them. It's because I thought it would upset you. Guess I got that wrong. I'm starting to think I've gotten a lot of things wrong. As for the family, I honestly thought we were immune from the occasional barbed comment. I didn't think it was worth saying anything to them and risking a major row that would make things worse. I'm sorry."

Claire's heart rolled. Was there hope? Probably not. The issue of children still lay between them like a heavily fortified border crossing.

Matt glanced at Alissa. "I've been too busy trying to keep the peace, haven't I?'

"You've been trying to make Claire happy and keep your mother happy too."

"Yeah, and failing miserably at both." He shook his head as if ordering his thoughts. "I thought loving Claire was enough. You got any tips on how I can dig myself out of this mess?"

"That depends on what your priority is. If it's your relationship with Claire, then your responsibility lies with supporting her. Claire needs to know she comes first in your life. Your family, but especially your mother, needs to know and understand this too. It means facing up to those hard calls you've been dodging. There are difficult conversations ahead with your family."

Matt turned to Claire, his brow furrowed. "Is my mother the reason you don't want to get married now? To have kids?"

She wrung her hands. "It's not that simple. It's hard to explain. I'm not totally sure myself."

"Try me. Start with the wedding. After overhearing Mom, were you even going to marry me that day?"

"Of course I was!" She leaned toward him. "You saw me in the dress—or what was left of it. You're the only man I've ever wanted to marry."

"So, you wanted to marry me BF but not AF?"

"Can you explain the terms?" Alissa asked.

"Before the fires and after the fires," they said in unison.

"Right."

Claire looked straight into Matt's troubled gaze. "I love you. I love you more now than I did then. But when the fire raged around the CFA shed, there was an hour when I thought I might die. I had no idea if you were safe or fighting just as hard as me to stay alive. Or worse. I lived through eight agonizing minutes after the mayday call, thinking you'd died in the burnover. I could hardly stand up. I couldn't picture my life without you in it."

He shuddered. "The whole time the fire buffeted the truck all I could think about was you. That being with you was the only thing that made any sense. I promised myself if I got out alive, I was marrying you the moment we'd mopped up and making a honeymoon baby just like we'd planned. Only, we drove back into town and there was nothing left. After that, everything went to hell. When we finally came out of the fog of funerals, sifting through the remains of the cottage and shooting the sheep, you said it was too soon to get married. There was too much going on to organize a wedding."

He looked at Alissa. "It didn't have to be a big wedding. Hell, all we needed to do was go to the registry office, but every time I suggested it, Claire had a reason to delay. The night I discovered the pills, suddenly she wanted to get married. I don't understand any of it."

"Claire, can you talk to this?"

Again? Pain rocked her. She'd told Alissa in an earlier session and it had wrung her out for days. But if she and Matt were to have a chance at staying together, she had to dive back into the darkness. "After the fire front went through and I knew you were safe, I waited for Mom and Dad to walk into the shed. With every passing hour and with every story I heard from people coming in from all over the district, I hoped against hope they would walk in next."

Her voice broke. "Matt, they died driving to our wedding! Driving to *me*. If they hadn't gotten into the car to come into town, there's a chance they might still be alive. And on the few occasions I can bear to think about their deaths, the terror they must have gone through and the excruciating pain they must have experienced ... it kills me. I feel so guilty they died."

She reached for the tissues. "I'm ... s-sorry, but whenever I think about our w-wedding day then, or in the f-future, instead of picturing us all happy and excited ..." She swiped away tears but it was useless. They cascaded over her lower lids and down her cheeks like water tumbling over Myrtle Falls. "All I ever s-see are Mom and Dad's burnt bodies."

"Oh, Postie." He pulled her into his arms and stroked her hair.

Claire pressed herself into him, breathing him in, not caring that she was only making things harder for herself when he let her go. She buried her face in his shoulder and knew she was on borrowed time. Too soon, her eyes would start burning from Louise's laundry powder.

She hauled in another breath and realized there was no perfumed scent tingling her nostrils. She raised her head, peering at him through watery eyes. "Are you doing your own washing?"

"No." He gave an embarrassed smile. "I grabbed this shirt from the house."

His thoughtfulness pierced her clean through. She had no reserves left to withstand it and her body shuddered, aching and crying for what they'd lost. Why was the distance between love and hate such a minuscule margin and yet a wide and barren plain?

"I can understand about the wedding," Matt said. "But I'm at a loss about the kids."

"I can't do it ... on my own."

She tried to explain further but the words stuck in her throat, snagged by snot, tears and fear. Matt made soothing sounds. He was probably hoping it was enough to calm her but she felt everything collapse inside her.

"Postie, please. You're scaring me. Alissa, why is she saying she's on her own? I mean, I get she's been on her own for a few weeks but not before that. And don't ask me how I feel or what I think. I don't bloody know, which is why I'm asking you."

"After the fires and the loss of her parents, Claire's had your love, but as you've conceded, not your support to help her cope with your family. All of it's left her feeling vulnerable and alone. Add in a near-death experience that turned everything she believed about her life and her security on its head, her work that's daily proof many children and families are struggling emotionally, and suddenly the idea of having children and protecting them from harm is a terrifying prospect."

Claire hiccupped. "She's nailed it."

Matt rubbed his face. "I thought I was helping. I thought looking forward and making the future we'd always planned for was the answer. I didn't realize it was making you feel so alone. That it meant you didn't trust me or yourself to have children."

He suddenly sagged, falling against her like he'd done in the early weeks after the fires. His voice thickened. "I've been a selfish prick. I've made it all about what I wanted and told myself it's what you wanted too. I'm sorry. I'm so, so sorry."

Relief that he finally understood slid in under Claire's grief. She cupped his damp cheeks. "Thank you."

"I love you, Postie. So very much."

Once she'd thought loving and being loved by Matt was enough to guarantee their survival as a couple. The fires had obliterated that notion. Today, he'd finally heard her and she appreciated how hard it was for him to face the revelations. But she doubted it was going to be enough to save them. His need for children was almost as strong as his need to breathe and she didn't feel the same way. The thought of motherhood scared her rigid. More than anything in the world, she didn't want to stomp on his heart again, but she couldn't see any way around it.

"I love you too, honey. You give my life meaning but—" Her heart raced and she had to push the words she needed to say to the front of her mouth. "It's just ... right now I can't promise you I'll change my mind about having kids."

He closed his eyes. She anticipated that when he opened them, she'd see sadness and regret in their rainforest depths and know their relationship was truly over.

"How about we put kids on the back burner for now and work on the more immediate things?" he said.

Shock made her blink. "You're prepared to do that?"

"I think I owe it to you. Are you up to working with me?"

A voice inside her screamed, *Yes*. But she said, "We're going to need some help."

He gave a wry smile. "I reckon Alissa will be happy to grill us on how we feel about stuff, right, Alissa?"

The counselor stood. "Another session can be arranged. Your hour is up."

"We'll be in touch." Matt ripped a heap of tissues from the box, grabbed Claire firmly by the hand and walked them outside into the rippling summer heat. He gazed down at her, his look pleading. "Please, can I come home?"

CHAPTER TWENTY-SEVEN

THE INFERNO

Josh strides up from the creek. Sweat sticks his shirt to his back. He'll take summer heat over winter damp but today's more than hot—it's a scorcher. He pauses under the shade of a rough-barked gum to catch his breath and take in the view of the house—the pitched terracotta roof, the timber sash windows, the turned veranda posts and the gingerbread fretwork. Their house. Pride and excitement shoots through him as it does every time he looks at it. They did it. They finally got their own place in a piece of paradise. He can't wait to show it off to his parents when they arrive on Christmas Eve.

He walks over to Liam's paddling pool and splashes his face with water. Refreshed, he considers the best place to erect the swing set. Sophie reckons it should go on the brown grass just beyond the house but Josh has plans for that rectangle. If the promotion the boss mentioned yesterday comes through, this time next year they might have an in-ground pool. They'll definitely have a baby. He checks his cell phone and does a mental calculation. Sophie should be arriving at her mother's about now. He's cross Aileen and Kylie refused their Christmas invitation. He doesn't think Sophie should be driving so far at thirty-seven weeks pregnant or that her mother expects her to do it. He'd told her as much.

"If you're worried, you can drive me," Sophie had said.

For a moment, Josh thought Sophie was serious and then her eyes twinkled.

"Kidding! It's bad enough I'm giving up a day to go to Melbourne to listen to my mother and sister talk about shiny things without inflicting it on you."

"Tell them you've got a platypus in the creek for Christmas."

Sophie laughed—the sound rueful. "No point. They don't get it. While I'm in Melbourne, can you please knock some things off the list? Oh, and remember to bring in the baby clothes off the line. They won't take long to dry."

The wind kicks up and he suddenly remembers the washing but a small willy-willy distracts him. Sophie's in full-on nesting mode and she'll kill him if she comes home to a house full of dust. He races inside and starts closing windows. As he eats lunch, he turns on the radio. There's something about a fire at Sheepwash. It's a long way from Myrtle but it's not far from plantation five. He's suddenly relieved he hasn't completed his fire training otherwise he'd be called in on his precious day off. He reads Sophie's job list and chooses "assemble crib and change table," excited about the coming baby.

He opens the back door and the wind blows smoke into his face. Coughing, he looks up. He doesn't know the names of clouds but there's a bloody enormous one in the distance that looks different from usual. He goes back inside and rings the Langs for some advice. The call goes straight to voice mail. He checks the CFA website. No fires near Myrtle, but that cloud's bothering him. He reads advice on preparing for a wildfire.

Pulling on a long-sleeved shirt and his work boots, he connects the new garden hose to the tap. At least there are no worries about trees being too close to the house or needing to clean out gutters—the garden's not planted and the gutters haven't had time to collect leaf debris. Mind you, in this wind, they could easily fill. He shivers. He hates blustering hot northerlies and the air's swirling, full of topsoil from the nearby fields.

He reflects on the years when he smoked. How that first drag on a cigarette filled his lungs, instantly relaxing him. This smoke has the opposite effect. He's jittery and on edge. He lugs the ladder from the shed and fills the gutters with some of their precious tank water.

Back inside, he realizes he hasn't heard from Sophie. Normally, she reports her every move to him whether he's interested or not. The non-specific dread he damped down by filling the gutters with water spins its agitation through him. He texts Sophie.

Guessing you arrived safe?

Her reply is instant. Yes! Sorry! You know what Mom and Kylie are like. Going to leave by 5pm, no matter what. Hopefully Liam will sleep on the way home. Love you. Xx

Josh checks the CFA website again. All reports say the only fire causing concern is the one at Sheepwash. It must be the brutal wind that's blowing smoke over Myrtle. The sun glows red like the moon during a lunar eclipse, battling to push its rays through the smoke. He thinks of his workmates—poor bastards. He doesn't fancy being out in that. It's dim inside now and he flicks on a light.

Nothing happens. It takes him a second to realize it's not a blown globe and that the lights on the oven and microwave are off too. Probably too many buggers using their air-conditioners and the grid's packed it in. He checks his cell phone for the obligatory power-company text. Nothing. That's when he notices "Emergency only" where the reception bars should be. Great. No power and no cell phone. It's going to be a long, hot afternoon. At least he has cold beer and the battery-powered radio to listen to the cricket.

A noise comes at him like the thundering roar of a hundred fighter jets. *Why the hell are the Roulettes doing training flights out here?* He races outside into the wind and smoke. Everything looks the same as it did before until he turns around. His brain refuses to decode what he's seeing—it looks like his uncle's photos of napalm bombing in Vietnam.

The tops of the mighty trees at the bottom of the creek ignite like a match struck on dynamite. Burning ribbons of bark fly through the air. The chairs near the paddling pool explode in white light. Fear immobilizes him. Heat sears him. The wind sucks every drop of sweat from his skin and dries his lungs. The fire consumes all the light, replacing it with vicious blackness. Then panic whips him into action. He races inside. Dials the emergency code, ready to shout, "Fire!" Hears an automated voice telling him, "You have been put on hold."

Christ almighty. He's on hold for death.

The closed windows fight the smoke but it curls in under the doors. The smoke alarms shriek. He's back outside with the hose but there's no power. Without power there's no way to pump water from the tank. He must leave. He looks at the car just in time to see it go up in flames. He retreats inside. He uses some of the water he has to wet towels and then rolls them against the base of the doors. Within moments the fire is licking the veranda posts—squinting yellow, terrifyingly orange—lighting up the windows. Relentless heat presses in on all sides. The air's too thick to breathe.

The skylight in the kitchen melts.

Flames dive into the house. He screams at them. Throws water onto them. They hiss and retreat before flaring again, providing the only light he has. He's stamping flames. He's bagging with blankets. He's losing. He'll die here. Survival forces him out of the kitchen. He runs into walls, uses his hands to find doorways and closes doors behind him until he reaches the study. It's the middle of the house. He prays the house will last until the raging inferno blasts its way to its next destination. Prays he can escape.

Before today, Josh has only thought about death as something that happens to old codgers. A slipping away after a long life lived well. Quiet. Peaceful. Not this clawing fear with a deafening soundtrack. The thought of flames backing him into a corner and burning him to death tempts him to kill himself first. Before he can figure out a way to do it, the roof peels back like the lid on a sardine can. Suddenly, he's looking up into a box of fireworks. His face stings. His throat aches. His lungs burn. He runs outside anyway.

He doesn't know where he's going. Nothing's familiar. Everything's on fire. He breathes through a wet blanket, desperately seeking air in the smoke. The earth heats the soles of his feet through his heavy work boots. He recognizes the fence. He scrambles through, the wire burning his hand, and he stumbles onto the road. There's a slither of relief before an almighty crack echoes around him and a tree falls in front of him. He leaps back.

Town. He needs to get to town. To safety. To sanity. He trudges down what he thinks is the middle of the road. Cows press on fences, dead and dying. Their shocked eyes plead with him. He knows they see the same emotion reflected in his.

A CFA tanker appears out of the smoke and he shakes his fist at it. "You're too fucking late."

"Sorry, mate." A man he doesn't know puts his hand on his shoulder. "So f-ing sorry."

They take him to the CFA shed. A woman wearing a frothy floral dress and a shocked face asks Claire McKenzie about his burned hand. It takes him a moment to realize Clare's wearing the remains of a wedding dress.

Someone makes him a cup of tea but his hand is shaking so much he can hardly raise it to his mouth. Voices swirl around him.

"It broke every rule in the book."

"They never told us it was coming."

"How can you fight a fire you don't know about?"

"That fire was unfightable. I don't want to think about the ones who didn't get out."

Josh lurches to his feet, hit with his first cogent thought in hours.

"You alright, mate?" someone asks.

"I need a cell phone. My wife. She'll be petrified. I've gotta tell her I'm safe."

"Give your name to Jacqui. She's got the manifest and she'll radio the Red Cross. Best we can do until the roads are safe and we can get out."

In the small hours of the morning, Jacqui Datsun calls out, "Is there a Josh Doherty here?"

"That's me."

Her worried face lightens. "Congratulations, Josh. You're a dad. Your wife's just had a baby girl."

A cheer goes up around the shed.

Josh weeps.

CHAPTER TWENTY-EIGHT

THE PRESENT

Just after lunch on Monday, Sophie was cursing her work computer when her boss stuck his head into her office.

"G'day, Sophie. Thought you were taking today off."

"No. I had a day off for the framing so I thought ... To be honest, I feel a bit weird about today. Last year we went to the big memorial service but this year, it's all a bit different. Unlike a lot of people, we only lost the house."

"That's still a big thing."

"Yes, but we were all safe. I was up in Melbourne and the shock of seeing the footage of the fires on the news sent me into labor. Trixie was born the next day. And Josh was never in danger."

"So, Tornado Trixie joins the terrible twos tomorrow? That's when the fun starts. You've probably got a list of things you want to do for the birthday girl, so why not take the afternoon off?"

Sophie respected Glen, liked him even, but he wasn't one for generous offers like this. "Are you sure?"

"Absolutely. And don't worry about making it up. My treat. See you tomorrow."

"Thanks, Glen!"

Sophie switched off her computer, grabbed her bag and ran out to the car, the sound of freedom and opportunity ringing in her ears. Josh had a day off and they had three hours before the kids needed to be collected from daycare. She planned to take advantage of every minute. This was the gift of time they needed and she was seizing it with both hands and a big dash of forgiveness.

The night before, she'd gone to bed early and slept soundly, only vaguely aware of Josh staggering into bed after midnight. The beer bottles that had greeted her in the kitchen that morning told her why he'd been so hard to rouse when the alarm went off. Why he'd groaned and pulled the blankets over his head instead of helping her with the morning chaos. She'd been pretty snippy with him, especially as she'd had to drop the kids at daycare. But now, with the afternoon off, she was in a forgiving mood.

Sophie had a feeling—needed to believe the feeling—that without the kids sleeping one flimsy partition away, she could finally coax Josh into having sex. All the self-help articles said men needed sex to feel close. Hell, she needed sex to feel close to Josh, because right now all they seemed to do was argue. She hated it. With them both working full time and the new house only weeks away from being completed, they needed some couple time to break the dry spell. After that, everything would fall into place.

She decided not to text Josh, because that would ruin the surprise. She was ninety-nine per cent certain he'd be home—when she'd asked him if he was going to the Langs', he'd said, "No way."

The day was warm and sunny but without the dangerous north wind that had helped cause so much devastation two years earlier. The wet winter and soggy spring lent a lush green to everything and the first days of summer hadn't been extreme enough to steal it. The tree ferns down by the creek were back, with their wide green boughs creating a cool canopy, and the damp chocolate earth was the perfect place to sit by the creek, dangle their legs, and revel in the rush of cool water against hot skin. They'd have a picnic.

Sophie usually made calls to the CWA committee on the drive home, and she checked in with Erica and Layla, but she left her questions for Claire and Bec for the next day. She knew Claire would be at Julie's and although Bec hadn't said anything, she'd heard from a daycare mother that the Petrovics were hosting a CFA function. That was another community group Josh had resisted joining. The moment they were installed in the new house and Josh could no longer hide behind its construction as an excuse not to participate, she'd work on getting him connected.

As she pulled up behind Josh's car, she hugged herself with excitement. Between the afternoon's gift of time alone together and the next day's surprise arrival of Josh's parents for Trixie's birthday, her husband was in for a great twenty-four hours. Hopefully, it would be enough to put a smile on his dial and keep it there.

"Surprise!" Sophie called out as she walked into the shed.

It took one look to determine the place was empty. Josh's cell phone was plugged in and charging. Ignoring the dishes in the sink and the unmade beds, she quickly changed into her swimsuit and sarong. Then she packed picnic supplies into a backpack, slung it over her shoulder and went looking for Josh.

It took her a little longer to work out he wasn't inside the new house either. It wasn't just that there were more rooms to check, but she'd developed a ritual dance of joy each time she walked into a room. This house was completely different from their first one. Two years earlier, she couldn't have imagined herself living in anything this modern, but given all they'd been through to get it, she appreciated this house far more that the first. Running her hands along the newly installed glass backsplash in the kitchen, she squealed. This Christmas she'd have an oven.

Exiting through the empty space that would become the laundry, she walked to the spot where Josh often stood gazing down toward the creek. Cupping her hands around her mouth, she called, "Josh!"

The only reply was the squawk of rosellas. Where was he? His cell phone was in the shed so he couldn't be far away. A flicker of white caught her gaze and she noticed her plastic star-gazing chair under a tree. As she approached, she saw three empty beer bottles underneath it. That Josh was drinking on a day off didn't bother her as much as the lack of a second chair. She bent down to pick up the bottles and found a box of matches, cigarette papers and bag of plant matter. A shiver went through her.

Please let it be tobacco.

But she knew that was wishful thinking even before she scooped up the bag. Tobacco would be in a blue or red pouch, not a ziplock baggie. She smelt it anyway.

Fury burned through her. No wonder he'd been hard to wake that morning. Vague for weeks. Moody. He'd promised her he'd stopped smoking dope and she'd believed him. Had he lied to her? Clutching the bag, she screamed his name.

She ran down to the creek but there was no sign of him so she hiked back up the slope to the shed. Remembering her mother and sister's infamous visit, she checked his car but it was empty. A curl of apprehension flattened her anger. Had Scotty picked him up for a job?

She rang the builder. When he answered, she heard the buzz of chatter in the background and Adam's booming laugh.

"We gave everyone the day off, Sophie. He probably changed his mind and went to a gathering."

"Thanks."

She called the Langs. "Is Josh with you?"

"No, love. Everything okay?" Phil said.

She looked at the bag of weed in her hand. She was being ridiculous. Sure, marijuana was an illegal drug but it wasn't a dangerous one. When Josh smoked it, he just got sleepy and hungry. It was the lingering effects the morning after that she objected to—he found it hard to get going and she was left feeling like a nagging wife.

"I'm sure everything's fine. It's just I came home early from work to surprise him and I can't find him anywhere. His car and cell phone are here but he isn't."

"I'll come straight over."

She remembered the day and instantly felt selfish. The Langs had guests in honor of Hugo. "No. Phil, really it's—"

"I'm on my way." The line went dead.

Phil's concern scurried under her own and suddenly she was frightened. Surely if Josh had hurt himself and was lying injured somewhere, he'd have answered her calls. Unless he was unconscious. Or worse. Oh God! They'd seen the first tiger snake of the season a couple of weeks earlier. She wanted to run around the block again but she waited for Phil, willing him to clamber over the stile right this second even though she knew it was a good seven-minute walk.

The thrum of a diesel engine made her turn and the Myrtle Health Center car drove toward her, pulling up with a small spray of gravel. Phil, Claire and Matt Cartwright got out.

Matt? Sophie didn't have time to wonder about his presence because Phil was saying, "I brought some help."

Claire wrapped her in an unexpected hug. "You okay?"

"I was. Now I'm starting to freak out. He's not at work and his cell phone and car are here. He said he was spending the day at home. What if he's been bitten by a snake?"

"He can't be too far away," Matt said. "We'll fan out to find him. Sophie, you go with Claire and start at the creek and walk back from there. Phil and I will search the northern section of the block." He pulled out his cell phone. "Reception's not bad, so whoever finds him calls the other, okay?"

They agreed and the men strode to the northern boundary, calling out Josh's name as they walked.

Claire looked at Sophie's sarong and the flip-flops on her feet. "Put on your boots."

Sophie obeyed and added shorts and a T-shirt before they walked down to the creek. "We used to picnic here all the time before the fires."

"It's all grown back." Claire fingered the tip of a tree fern. "It must do your head in knowing such a pretty and tranquil place threw up the fireball that took out your house."

Sophie shivered. "I'm just glad none of us were here."

A frown line appeared on the bridge of Claire's nose. "Josh was here."

"No. He was in town when the fire hit. You were probably too busy treating people to notice."

"No, I remember. He arrived on tanker two after the fire front. He'd gotten trapped out here and was inside the house when it caught fire. He was lucky to make it out."

"You must be confusing him with someone else."

"I'm not. We treated the burn on his hand, irrigated his eyes and kept a close eye on him for smoke inhalation. When they opened the road, I put him on the hospital bus because of his breathing."

No! Sophie stared at Claire, shaking her head.

Claire touched her arm. "I'm sorry. I thought you knew."

Much of the twenty-four hours following the fires were a blur to Sophie, but some things were sharp and vivid. The television images of the fires. Claire's tattered wedding dress and devastated look. Men weeping. Her fast labor. Josh managing a call at 3:00 in the morning to reassure her he was fine.

"Relax, Soph. I was never in danger. I'm really sorry, but the house has gone."

When Josh had finally walked into the maternity ward the following day, it had taken her a moment to recognize him. Apart from his work boots, none of his clothing was familiar. He'd hugged her long and hard before scooping a sleeping Trixie into his arms. He hadn't let her go for an hour.

When she'd asked him about his bandaged hand, he'd said, "I was stupid. Touched some hot wire. It's nothing to worry about." Then he'd kissed her and said, "I hate that I missed the birth. That I wasn't here for you. Tell me everything."

He'd coughed on and off for weeks.

Thoughts thundered through her: Josh standing by the tanks staring toward the creek; all the reasons he'd given her to avoid going down there. Her gut twisted sharply. "He's told me over and over that he was never in danger. That he was in town early and the CFA was the safest place to be. Now you're telling me he was out here alone and he nearly died! Why would he lie to me?"

"I don't know. I've learned some stuff about men lately. Sometimes, despite their best intentions, they do dumb things. Josh loves you. You'd just given birth and you had a baby to worry about. He probably thought he was protecting you. That because he'd survived and was safe, you didn't need to know."

"But that's crazy! I had a baby. I didn't come close to dying."

"It's faulty thinking, but he was traumatized. We all were. None of us were thinking straight for weeks. Some of us still struggle."

"But the fire ... he must have been petrified." She suddenly gagged. "Is this why you're always asking me how he is? Why Phil came straight over when I couldn't find him? Oh God. He's been drinking and I found some dope. You don't think he might have—" But she veered violently away from the thought, unable to say the words.

Claire's cell phone rang and she answered it on speaker. "Matt?"

"We've found him. We need you and the first-aid kit."

"Is he okay?" Sophie asked, almost knocking the cell out of Claire's hands.

"Is he conscious?" Claire asked.

"Yes. Just come."

Sophie ran as if her life depended on it, beating Claire back to the house. Matt was waiting outside alone. "Where is he?" she panted.

Matt put his hand gently on her arm. "Phil's with him."

"Yes, but where?"

"He's safe but he's not very well. Let Claire see him first."

"No! I'm sick of people not telling me things."

Claire took her hand. "Let's go together."

An anguished look crossed Matt's face but he reluctantly walked them over to the water tanks. Phil was squatting, talking quietly. Sophie peered around him and gasped. Josh was curled up in the small gap between the tanks, his arms around his knees and his head tucked low in brace position. His dark hair stuck to his scalp, drenched in sweat. A chill walked over Sophie's skin.

"Josh!"

His head shot up, eyes wild. "Where are the kids? Get the kids!"

"They're at daycare."

But he didn't seem to hear her. "It's my fault. This fuckin' fire. We're gonna die."

"No, Josh. No. There's no fire. We're okay."

"Are you deaf? Listen!" Josh tried to grab her.

She stepped back and swung around to see three anxious faces watching them. Tears stung her eyes. "What's wrong with him?"

"I think he's having a post-traumatic stress incident." Claire pulled out her cell phone. "He's confusing today with the past."

"It's that bloody weed, isn't it? I told him not to smoke it."

Phil put his hand on her shoulder. "It's probably a whole lot of things, Sophie. Fire trauma, losing the house, losing his job ..."

"But things have been going great." Even as she spoke, she heard how hollow the words sounded.

She remembered his mood swings. Yelling at her sister. His irritability. His general detachment from her, the kids and his parents. Their lack of intimacy. How had she failed to realize his behavior over the last six months was different from the grumpy and stubborn days he'd experienced on and off ever since she'd met him? She'd put all of it down to him losing the house and his job, not almost losing his life.

She was suddenly screaming. "You should have told me! All of you should have told me!"

"Don't tell anyone," Josh ranted, reaching up again to pull her into the gap. "You can't trust Shane. No one can save us."

Fear squashed her anger. "What's he talking about? He's not making any sense. He looks like Josh, but he's nothing like Josh."

Claire finished her call. "I've spoken to the psychiatric intern. I'm going to try and give him a sedative. It should stop him seeing and hearing the fire. Is that okay with you, Sophie?"

"I suppose ..."

"He'll have to spend some time in the hospital."

Sophie's body shook and she couldn't stop it. "Oh God, you don't mean the normal hospital do you? You mean a mental hospital."

Phil wrapped an arm around her. "He's sick. He needs treatment just like he would if he'd been bitten by snake."

"I think I'd have preferred that."

Sophie couldn't think clearly for all the random thoughts charging around her head. Layla or Erica could pick up the kids but she'd have to call daycare to give permission. If she texted Bec, she'd tell Adam and Scotty that Josh wouldn't be at work tomorrow. She wouldn't even have to ask Claire to come to the hospital with her—she knew the nurse would be there ready to explain all the confusing medical stuff. And Phil would do anything she asked him. Matt too, she supposed, going by his kindness so far. Should she call her mother and ask her to meet her at the hospital? She jettisoned the thought. She needed support, not criticism. Her mother would blame Josh's condition on their desire to own their own home.

She needed to do the best thing for Josh. "I need to call Josh's parents."

"What's their number?" Matt, asked, cell phone in hand.

She told him, surprised she could recall it. He dialed before folding her shaking fingers around the cell phone and lifting it to her ear.

Janet answered it in two rings. "Hello, Janet Doherty."

"Mom. It's Soph."

"Hello, sweetheart. Do you have a new number?"

Janet's familiar and caring voice was too much for her. She broke down sobbing. "We need you."

"THANK YOU SO MUCH FOR COMING," Bec said for the umpteenth time as she and Adam farewelled the last of their guests.

It was almost five o'clock. Bec had been smiling and chatting for hours, playing the perfect hostess. While Adam needed praise and adoration from her, he deflected it from people outside of the family. She'd lost count of how many times today she'd heard him say, "I did what anyone else would have done in the circumstances." But when people asked to see his Star of Courage, he always popped open the box.

The girls had gotten sick of being on show and retreated to watch a movie. Bec wished she could be let off from the drawn-out goodbyes, especially when there were always half-a-dozen people who stayed until the very end. Some had tried to leave earlier but Adam had insisted on them staying for "one more beer." They'd complied. Although he'd always been a big personality, fewer people said no to him since the fires.

As she'd wafted from group to group offering food, people had told her with warmth and sincerity how much they admired Adam. Not just for his heroic actions two years earlier but for all he'd achieved since. For two years, she'd tried desperately to view Adam through the lens of the town. It had been easier since her pregnancy, because the man who brought her tea and rubbed her feet was that man.

She'd murmured her appreciation and buried all the signs she wanted to be elsewhere and with someone else. Hid how the fires had ripped through her life, wresting away the chance of change and leaving only ashes and duty.

"That went well, babe." Adam closed the front door. "Everyone turned up except Matt Cartwright. Who'd be a farmer, eh? Bloody pigs and sheep. Beer time, I reckon, Scotty."

"I should get going," Scotty said.

"Not yet." Adam bent down and pulled two bottles from the ice bucket.

Bec couldn't see Adam's face but she heard the edge to his voice. It was the one he used with her and the girls when his patience was thinning. She tried to read Scotty's expression but she was out of practice.

Adam tossed a beer bottle straight at Scotty, who caught it. Adam didn't look drunk but she'd been so busy she hadn't had time to count his drinks. Maybe some more food would help soak up any stray alcohol in his system. "Would you like something to eat with that beer?"

"Yeah, babe. That'd be good. We'll take a plate to the office."

"You're working? *Now?*"

"No rest for wicked, eh, Scotty?"

"Too right." But Scotty barely cracked a smile.

Bec had just finished loading a platter with sausage rolls and pizza squares when her cell phone rang. Claire's name lit up the screen and surprise penetrated her weariness. Claire never rang. Her thoughts immediately slid to Julie and her heart sped up. As she answered, she heard a distorted PA announcement. "Claire? What's wrong?"

"It's Josh Doherty."

Bec found herself seeking a seat as she listened to Claire briefly outline how they'd found Josh and now he was in the hospital. "Layla's picked up the kids and Matt and I drove Sophie to Geelong. We're here until her in-laws arrive from Melbourne."

Bec didn't know which bit of news shocked her more—Josh or Matt. "You and Matt?"

"Focus, Bec!" But Claire's voice lacked severity. If anything, there was a lilt of hope and definitely relief. "Can you set up a private message group for Erica, Layla, you and me? I don't know if Julie's up to it, but that's not my call. Phil will have told her what happened. Maybe go see her? Actually, Phil should be in the group too. Sophie's going to need childcare, meals, maintenance help—you know the drill. And she's in shock, so she's not up to talking to anyone today. Can you tell Adam and Scotty that Josh is off work until further notice?"

"Of course. Oh God, poor Sophie. Send her my love."

"Will do. And Bec?"

"Yes?"

"Thanks."

"You're welcome." She experienced a flush of goodwill toward Claire. This time she didn't fight it.

As Bec walked to the office, she heard the low rumble of voices. It stopped when she walked in.

"That looks great, Bec," Scotty lifted the platter out of her hands. "Thanks."

"I've got bad news. Josh Doherty's had some sort of breakdown and he's in the hospital."

Scotty paled. "Is he okay? Dumb question. I mean, he didn't try anything stupid, did he?"

"I don't think so. Claire said he was reliving the fire as though it was happening today."

"What sort of stuff was he saying?" Adam asked.

"I don't know."

"Jeez, the last thing we need is a nutcase," Adam muttered.

"Adam!"

"Kidding, babe. I'll go and see him tomorrow. Tell him we'll look after the family while he's off sick."

"Thank you, but check with the hospital first. I don't know if he's up to visitors."

Scotty was staring out the window. "Bloody hell! This is our fault."

"Don't be stupid," Adam said sharply.

"This wouldn't have happened if he'd worked on the Beckwith site."

"That's bullshit and you know it."

"What do you mean?" Bec sensed an unusual tension between them.

"Nothing. Scotty's talking through his ass. Go and call Sophie. Tell her we'll pay Josh sick leave."

"I'll do it," Scotty said.

"No. Bec will do it. Right, babe?"

She didn't understand what was going on but she heard the warning in Adam's voice. "Claire said Sophie wasn't up to talking to anyone today."

"Yeah, but this is good news. She needs to know that money is one less thing she has to worry about."

"Adam!" Scotty spun around from the window. "Let's do this right. Josh doesn't—"

"Shut up, Scotty," Adam growled. "Go home and cool down."

"Perhaps Scotty's—"

"This has got nothing to do with you, Bec. Go and call Sophie."

She backed out of the office. The door slammed behind her, muffling their raised voices. What the hell was going on? Scotty hadn't disagreed, let alone argued, with Adam in two years. Worried the girls might hear the yelling, she went to check on them. She was relieved the sound didn't carry as far as the TV room.

"Mommy!" Gracie jumped up. "Ivy's reading and she won't play with me."

Ivy didn't look up from her book. "Is Daddy still downstairs being a hero?"

"Ivy!" Bec was shocked and a little bit scared by the sarcasm in her daughter's voice. "Today's a difficult day for Daddy."

Ivy glared at her, blue eyes flashing. "No, it's not. It's difficult for you."

The unexpected words hit with terrifying accuracy and she tried to cover her shock. "Being a hostess at a party is tiring but you helped me with the cooking and that part was fun."

Ivy didn't say anything and eventually dropped her gaze, returning to her book.

"I'll go and start dinner. I'll call you when it's time to set the table."

First, she had to make a phone call. She walked into her bedroom and sat on the bed before bringing up Sophie's number. Her finger hesitated on the call button, and then she called Claire instead. At the end of their discussion it was decided that Claire would pass on the message about paid sick leave immediately and Bec would follow up with a text the next day so Sophie had the offer in writing. Just as Bec ended the call, her cell phone rang.

"Scotty? Where are you?"

"I'm at the gate. Are you okay?"

"Yes. Why wouldn't I be?"

He sighed. "This news about Josh ... Adam's drunk a lot and he's in a filthy mood. He just threw me out and I wondered ... You know, if you were worried ..."

"Why would I be worried?" The words shot out crisp and snappy as appreciation and anger mixed uneasily.

"I dunno. Just if you were ... You and the girls could come to my place."

She heard a hysterical laugh and realized it was coming from her. "He'd go ballistic, Scotty."

"Someone else's place then?"

Scotty had no idea the lengths involved for her to leave the property without being grilled by sober Adam let alone drunk Adam, and she didn't want to scare the girls. Anxiety made her lash out. "What's gotten into you today, anyway, Scotty? Regret finally catching up with you? Maybe Adam's right. You need to go home, cool down and think straight."

"Bec." It was a plea.

She cut the call and closed her eyes, wishing this day would end. Wishing tomorrow morning would arrive in record time. She heard Adam's tread on the stairs and opened her eyes just as he walked in holding a mug of tea. She relaxed. Adam in a filthy mood would no more make her tea than fly to the moon. Drunk Adam wouldn't do it either. Maybe Scotty was the one who was drunk.

"Here." Adam sat down next to her.

"That's thoughtful. Thanks."

"Did you call Sophie?"

"Yes."

"What did she say?"

"That you're a godsend on an awful day." It wasn't strictly a lie. She could imagine Sophie saying it.

"Good."

She put her hand on his thigh. "I really appreciate it too."

"Ring her every day and get a report. The moment he's allowed visitors, I'll drive up to Geelong. He's a good worker."

"You've always said that." There was no benefit in reminding Adam that he'd called Josh a nutcase when he'd first heard the news.

"Mommy! Daddy!" Gracie ran into the room and bounced on the bed. "I'm hungry."

Adam caught a squealing Gracie around the waist and tucked her under his arm. "I'll get you some dinner. Leave Mommy to rest."

"I've got enough energy to heat up some leftovers."

"No, you've had a huge day. Stay there and enjoy your tea. The girls and I will be fine."

Bec lay back on the pillows, already feeling lightheaded and sleepy, but knowing that napping at seven was crazy. She'd just close her eyes for a few minutes.

IT WAS dark when Bec tried to open her eyes. They felt like lead weights and it took her a couple of attempts to force them open. Adam was lying on his back, snoring. Her body felt like it did many mornings these days—heavy and aching—but today her skin was cold, as if the sheet had fallen off her. It hadn't—she could feel it against her. The clock said 4.59 and it took her sluggish mind a moment to realize she'd slept ten hours. It took another few seconds to work out why she was cold. She was naked.

Why was she naked?

She remembered closing her eyes fully dressed. Adam must have undressed her when he came to bed and thought it was too hard to put her nightie on her. Why couldn't she remember being undressed? Her body jerked and she got a flash of her arms being pulled up above her head. Heard Adam telling her to turn over.

Her cell phone vibrated under her pillow and she slowly remembered why she'd set the early and quiet alarm. Sheer determination overrode her woolly-headedness and the pain in her hips. When she was pregnant with Ivy and Gracie, she'd never been bothered by pregnancy hormones softening the ligaments of her pelvis, but this time it felt like there was a red-hot poker burning into her hips.

She'd resisted the suggestion of wearing a support belt but this morning was fast changing her mind. To the orchestra that was Adam's snoring, she slipped out of the bedroom, closing the door softly behind her before tiptoeing to the laundry.

Once inside, she turned on the light, opened the dirty laundry basket, fumbled under a pile of clothes and picked up the plastic bag she'd planted the morning before. Dressing quickly in the clothes she'd bought in Geelong, she doused the lights, opened the door and jumped over the crushed gravel path to avoid the crunch. She landed on the grass.

Pain lashed her and she bit her tongue. Jumping was obviously not something she should be doing. The moon was waning but the stars still shone. Shivering, she made her way down to the bottom of the drive where she'd deliberately parked the car. She'd told Adam it was to free up space closer to the house for their visitors. The truth was she'd parked it there so the noise of the garage door wouldn't wake him this morning.

She swung up into the driver's seat, gasping as another streak of agony tore through her. Pregnancy shouldn't feel like this. She sucked in a deep breath and started the car. She had two precious hours before the household woke, and the drive into town was predictably and thankfully quiet. She didn't pass another vehicle, which was part of her plan, but Bec knew too well that plans were not worth the paper they were written on. She turned off the road and her headlights lit up the old bluestone pillars that had once supported ornate gates.

Moving slowly and carefully, she got out of the car. Once oak trees had stood tall, shading the graves, but now there were just tiny saplings and a promise. She knelt beside the slab of marble that was covered with fresh bunches of native flowers. She pressed her palms against the cold stone and then lowered her lips. When she raised her head, she let her words flow.

"I wanted to bring you sunflowers because they remind me of you. You lit up my life and I treasure our time together as much as I hate the last two years without you. But I can't bring you flowers so I've brought you an acorn. Remember the one we planted over that dead chicken you brought up from the farm in the cooler?

"I was horrified, but you told me it was the best manure. You were right. It grew. I hope it's still growing. I haven't been able to see it recently, but I'm going to try during January when I take the girls to Melbourne for a vacation."

She ran the acorn along the stone. "I miss you so much. Why do people say it gets easier? It doesn't. Your mom understands, but as much as I want to her tell her that I do too, I can't. Sometimes I wonder why I'm keeping you a secret, but when I think about telling people without you by my side, I'm just not brave enough. And who would believe me? Why, why did we wait so long? Why weren't we spontaneous instead of trying to cover every base and do things the right way? Even a week earlier and you'd still be here. We'd be far away from Myrtle, this baby would yours and Ivy would be happy."

Bec sniffed as tears trickled down her cheeks. "I think Ivy knows but I only realized it yesterday. When we were waiting for you in Lorne, I told her you were coming to visit and you were bringing a puppy. I was sowing a seed to prepare her for the news that I was leaving Adam. I've always assumed the girls thought I was frantic that afternoon because of Adam, not because my heart was breaking for you."

A wet nose suddenly snuck in under Bec's arm and then a tongue was licking her face. She sat up with a start. A merle-coated puppy bounded into her lap. The ache in her heart intensified. *Oh, Hugo.* This puppy looked like Turbo.

Oh, God, it must be the Langs'. What were they doing in the cemetery at dawn the day after the anniversary? Yesterday was their day. Panic rattled her. *Leave now!* But how? Her gaze frantically flitted around the cemetery before focusing on the fence. If she clambered through it, she could get out onto the road. She scrambled to her feet, but pain snagged at her like barbed wire.

She'd only taken two steps when she heard, "Bec? Is that you?" She wanted to run but her body wouldn't cooperate. Her head throbbed as she squinted into the dawn light. Wasn't it supposed to be soft and muted? This was as intense as the noonday sun. She felt herself sway.

"Phil!" Julie called.

The puppy barked.

The roar in Bec's head was as loud as the bass at a rock concert. Julie's outline lost focus, suddenly elongating like the reflections in the crazy mirrors at a carnival. She could hear Julie talking but the words sounded as if they were spoken underwater. Adam flashed into her head. Adam with a rope. Sweat doused her. Her legs buckled.

A strong arm went around her. Then she felt the chill of the marble underneath her and the pressure of a hand pushing her head between her knees. Another image hit her. Adam pulling her head. She screamed and threw back her head. Unlike the hand in her flashback, this one fell instantly away.

"Bec, it's okay. It's Julie and Phil."

"Sorry to scare you, love." Phil sounded contrite. "But you fainted. Didn't want you cracking your head open."

Bec tried to look at them but the light hurt her eyes.

"Will I ring Adam?" Phil asked.

"No!" It shot out of her mouth and she didn't know why, only it felt right. The only clear decision in a tangled mess of confusion.

The puppy barked and Julie's hand touched her shoulder. "I'm worried about you and the baby. I'm calling Claire. She can meet us at the clinic."

Bec remembered fractured scenes from the night before—Josh and Sophie. "She's in Geelong. With Matt. Isn't that great."

"It is great. But they got back late last night."

"Do you think if you lean on me you can walk back to the car?" Phil asked.

"What about Julie?"

"Don't worry about Jules. She's stomping around on that boot pretty well now."

"Claire's fifteen minutes away," Julie told her.

Phil and Julie's concern wrapped around her like a soft blanket and suddenly the strain of keeping Hugo a secret was beyond her. "You're probably wondering why I'm at Hugo's grave at sunrise, aren't you?"

"Little bit."

"The thing is, I loved ... I love him." She rushed on, needing to get her story out before they said a word.

"We'd been seeing each other for over a year. The day he died was the day we were officially starting our lives together. He was supposed to meet me and the girls in Lorne after Claire's wedding. We were having two days' vacation and then we were going to tell you. We'd rented a house in Melbourne and Hugo had a job lined up with the Department of Agriculture. Except the fires happened."

Julie stared at her open mouthed before giving a strangled cry and wrapping her in a hug. "Oh, Bec! I wish we'd known."

"No one could know. Especially not Adam."

"You poor girl." Julie stroked Bec's forehead. "At least we've been able to publicly grieve for Hugo."

Bec bit her lip. "Hugo texted me just before the fire hit. He told me he loved me. I was in agony trying to find out if he'd survived when a police officer at the hospital told me he hadn't. I couldn't believe life could be so cruel. The man I loved was dead and my husband, who I didn't love, was fighting for his life. My fate was sealed. I couldn't leave him."

"For months, Hugo was the happiest we'd ever seen him. We thought he must have met someone but we couldn't work out who." Phil's voice broke. "Thank you for loving him."

Bec buried her head in Julie's shoulder and allowed herself to cry.

CHAPTER TWENTY-NINE

CLAIRE USHERED BEC INTO THE TREATMENT ROOM AND HELPED her up onto the examination table. The woman in front of her had good color and didn't look like she was about to collapse. Perhaps the muesli bar Julie had convinced Bec to eat had done the trick and bumped up her blood sugar.

Claire was utterly bewildered as to why Bec had been in the cemetery at the crack of dawn on the verge of fainting. All Julie had said was, "Hugo," as if that explained everything. It explained nothing.

"How are you feeling?"

"I don't know. I just don't feel like me." Bec grabbed Claire's wrist tightly. Frantically. "I'm scared, Claire. I know this sounds crazy but I've got this premonition that something awful's happening to me. But I don't know what. I've had no energy for weeks. Nothing tastes right. I hurt all over, but today's worse. I mean, every part of me aches like I've slept on rock-hard ground."

As vague as it all sounded, Claire had learned long ago that listening was her best diagnostic tool. "I can examine you, but I understand if you'd prefer to go to Colac."

"I don't have time to go to Colac ... God, what time is it?"

"Six thirty."

Bec paled and struggled up from her pillows. "I have to go. The kids will be waking up and Adam needs breakfast."

"I'll ring him."

"No!"

Claire recoiled. "How about I do a quick examination and get you out the door." She started with pulse and blood pressure. As she slid up Bec's sleeve, she noticed bruises on her inner arm. "What happened here?"

Bec stared at the florid marks. "I don't know. I've been bruising easily lately. I've got a lot on my legs too. I just figured I was clumsier than usual."

"Let's take a look." Claire was trying hard not to jump to sinister conclusions but an exhausted pregnant woman who was bruising easily needed a blood test to rule out a nasty blood disorder.

Bec shimmied out of her capri pants. Remembering Bec's comment about sexy underwear, Claire was surprised her underpants were as plain and boring as her own. She saw the bruises she'd been talking about. "Can you roll onto your side?"

Bec moved gingerly, sucking in little gasps of breath. Claire stifled her own gasp, thankful Bec couldn't see her shocked face. Bec's lower back and buttocks were streaked with purple and red welts. In one place the skin was broken. Claire carefully eased Bec onto her back.

"I'm just going to check the baby and examine you down there, okay?" Claire checked the baby's position and then listened to the heartbeat, thankful it was thundering away at a healthy rate. "I know it's uncomfortable but can you lift up your bum?"

She eased down Bec's underpants and asked her to press her ankles together and drop her knees to the side. Pulling the examination light into position, she carefully inspected the area. This time the gasp slipped out.

"What? Am I bleeding? Oh God, I knew something was wrong."

Claire covered Bec with the modesty sheet and tried not to cry. "The baby's fine, Bec. It's you I'm worried about. Has someone attacked you? It's just it looks ..." She forced herself to say the words. "It looks like you've been raped."

"Raped? Don't be ridiculous. I'd remember if—" Bec's bewildered face suddenly crumpled and her body shook. "Oh God. Oh God. I get these flashes of Adam that come and go. They make no sense but they leave me feeling sweaty and sick."

Claire felt ill. "Did Adam rape you last night?"

"I don't know. I know that sounds stupid, but I can't remember." Her voice broke. "I can't remember anything. I'm losing my mind."

"You're not losing your mind, but I've got to ask you this. If there's any part of you that believes Adam is capable of raping you, please tell me."

Tears slipped down Bec's cheeks. "Once, in our kitchen, he said it was a game but it felt like rape. I convinced myself it wasn't. But I remember it happening. I don't remember anything about last night except for these flashes. I've had them before but today they're a lot worse. They terrify me."

Claire's mind didn't want to go to the dark and awful place it was fast sliding toward. A place where men treated women like meat. "You've been saying for weeks nothing tastes right. That you're forgetting things. Do you think—is there any chance he might be drugging you?"

"Surely if he was, I'd know—" Bec's eyes widened into shining blue pools. "When I told him I was pregnant, he started making me peppermint tea most nights."

"Started? He didn't used to?"

"No. I just thought he was being considerate because I was so tired."

"Does the tea taste odd? Sorry, you've told me everything tastes odd at the moment. Does it make you sleepy?"

"I'm already exhausted when he gives it to me!"

"Right, okay." Claire's mind was running though scenarios. "Since you started drinking the tea, do you feel different in the mornings?"

"Yes." Bec said it softly but it was the first thing she'd said with authority. "I wake up woolly-headed and I don't have any energy until the afternoon. I thought I had a virus that just wouldn't go."

"I don't think you have a virus but I can't say for sure until we do blood tests."

"Oh." Bec's head dropped and her shoulders sagged—it was like watching a facade fall—and the proud and condescending woman disappeared. "Claire?"

"Yes?"

"Things with Adam are awful. Before the fires, he could be difficult but now ... He controls everything I do, from the clothes I wear to where I go. Before I got pregnant he was insisting we do some kinky stuff but I never thought he'd ..." A tear ran down her face.

Guilt slammed Claire for every assumption she'd ever made about Bec. "I'm so sorry. So very sorry. I didn't know."

"No one knows." Her hand gripped the sheet. "Just like no one knew I was leaving Adam for Hugo."

"*You* were Hugo's mystery woman?" Claire knew she was gaping. "We thought she must have been someone in Melbourne."

Bec raised her face with a familiar chin tilt. "No, it was me."

Claire didn't hesitate—she leaned in and hugged her tightly. As she did, shame flowed through her veins reminding her that two years earlier her reaction to this news would have been very different. "Although he never told me your name, he told me how happy you made him. He loved you to pieces."

Bec gulped in a shuddering breath. "He was my soul mate. And the universe took him and left me with a burned and damaged husband. It was awful. I was utterly alone and grieving for Hugo, but I had to consider the girls. I mean, what sort of woman leaves her husband when he's disfigured and a hero? So I stayed. I've tried to make it work."

"Well, you don't have to try to make it work any longer!" Anger bubbled through Claire hot and strong, and all of it directed at Adam Petrovic. "It doesn't matter that Adam's your husband. Or that he saved lives. Rape is rape. He has no right to hurt you. I'm going to take photos and swabs and we're testing for drugs. We need to call Shane."

Bec sat up fast and winced. "The girls!"

"Do you think Adam will hurt them?"

"I don't think so. God, I don't know. But he's going to wake up very soon and notice I'm not there."

"I'm guessing he doesn't know you were at the cemetery, right? I know! Text him and tell him we're having a CWA breakfast meeting. Say you're so vague, you've only just realized you didn't leave him a note. Then ask him to take the girls to school. After that, Shane will be involved."

"He'll see my car at the cemetery."

"Phil can park it behind the clinic."

"Oh God! Oh God!"

Claire caught Bec's flailing hands. "Bec, you're not alone. I'm going to make sure you get all the help you need. Is there anyone you want me to call? Your mother?"

"No! She'll tell me I'm crazy and how lucky I am to have him."

"You're not crazy. Please remember that. It's the drugs making you feel that way."

"Like everything's going on around me but I'm not really part of it?"

"Yes, and it's screwing with your memory. What if I call a friend for you? A mother from school?"

Bec shook her head. "Since the fires, my world's gotten so small. There really isn't anyone except the CWA."

The sting of self-reproach bit Claire hard. All these months she'd actively fostered her childhood dislike of Bec when the woman had been keeping her at bay so Claire didn't twig to what was going on with Adam. What Adam was doing to her. Why, why, *why* had they always been so bloody competitive? She was determined it stopped now.

"You've got the CWA. We're a motley bunch, but we're here for one another. And I'm here for you, just like you've been here for me recently. I really appreciated that you didn't gloat when Matt left. Thank you."

"Claire, I'm petrified of what Adam might do if I go to the police."

"I understand." She knew this was a very real fear for many domestic violence victims but every fiber of her being screamed to protect Bec. "The important decisions are always the hardest, but this isn't the first time you've decided to leave him."

"But I had Hugo to protect me."

"Now you've got us. And Julie and Phil. Bec, you deserve so much better than that bastard's—" Claire heaved in a breath. "Than his treatment of you."

Bec buried her face in her hands. "I thought I was protecting the girls. I think I've made everything worse."

"No. Don't go there. We can only make decisions based on the information in front of us at the time. Back then you did what you thought was best. Now, the situation's changed and it's time to reassess."

"Image is everything to Adam. He'll try to get to me."

"I promise we'll do everything we can to protect you, but to do that we need to involve the police. Do I have your permission to call Shane?"

It was a choice too many women before her had been forced to make—a choice between two types of hell.

"Yes."

It came out so softly, Claire barely heard her.

THE ENTIRE DAY held a surreal quality—an awful nightmare that Bec couldn't wake up from. Staying alert was difficult. Whatever Adam had given her last night seemed much stronger than the other nights and it was affecting her more dramatically; she'd dozed on the drive to Geelong. Everyone at the rape crisis center was kind and gentle and Claire stuck to her like glue, never leaving her side. Bec held her hand and the few times she tried to let it go, panic surged and she gripped it again.

"Sorry."

Claire squeezed back. "No need to be sorry. And just so you know, I'm not going anywhere. Well, I might have to pee soon but you can come in with me if you need to."

"Thanks, but I'm traumatized enough already," Bec tried to joke.

Claire cried.

Drawing on a well of resilience she didn't know existed, Bec got through the forensic examination and the excruciatingly detailed police interview. As humiliating and shameful as it felt to have somehow failed to realize her husband was drugging her—let alone doing things she couldn't think about without shaking—telling the story of her post-fire life with Adam felt like she was taking back some sort of control. It held her up just enough to keep going.

While Claire was on a bathroom break, Bec's cell phone rang yet again. It had been ringing nonstop all day and the call log said Adam had rung forty-seven times. His voice mail messages had slowly transformed from, "Babe, since when did breakfast go past ten?" to "Where the hell are you?", finally culminating in terms that made her shudder and sweat. The police had advised her not to speak to him and to disable any location tracking devices on her cell phone.

This time when Bec checked the caller ID it was Scotty. She hesitated but gut instinct made her take the call.

"Bec, thank God. Where are you?"

"I can't say."

"Why? I'm worried about you. Adam's gone nuts. Are you okay?"

"No." Her heart hammered. "I've never been less okay."

"Bec." His voice agonized over her name. "Please tell me you're safe."

She fought tears. "I'm safe now, but I've had enough, Scotty. I'm not doing it anymore. I've tried to stand by him but now he's violated me in ways I can barely comprehend, let alone cope with. I've got to protect myself and the girls."

There was a gulping silence. "I should never have left you last night. I knew he was riled up—"

"It wasn't just last night." Her voice broke. "Scotty?"

"Yeah." His voice wavered with emotion.

"He might have saved your life, but he's not worth giving up yours for."

"I promise I'll fix this." Scotty sounded desperate.

"You can't." As she ended the call, she heard his strangled sob.

ON JULIE and Phil's insistence, Claire drove Bec from Geelong to the Langs'. When she woke in their spare room it was dark and she immediately tensed. The distant sound of the girls playing with Charger reassured her and she sank back onto the pillows. They were safe. Shane had arrested Adam and his bail conditions meant he couldn't come anywhere near her or the girls.

"Hey, sleepy head." Claire was sitting in a chair at the end of the bed, crocheting.

"You've become an Afghan addict."

"It relaxes me. How's the head?"

"Feeling a little less fuzzy." She heard Ivy laughing and she was suddenly frantic. "Claire, how am I going to tell the girls?"

There was a tap on the door and Julie popped her head around it. "Bec, the police are here. They want to talk to you."

"Again?" Bec sank back onto the pillows, trying not to cry. "But it's late. I've already told them everything I can remember."

"Shane says it's to do with another matter."

Claire rose and Bec said, "Please, stay. I don't have a single secret left that you don't know."

Claire gave her a sad smile and sat as Shane and an officer she didn't know walked in. "Sorry to bother you again, Bec but Scotty Ferguson came down to the station a few hours ago. He's made a rather interesting statement about your husband's business activities."

"Does Bec need an attorney?" Claire asked.

"I'm not involved in the business, if that's what you're asking," Bec said. "The only time I've had any input was when Adam was in the hospital. Even then it was only marketing and design advice."

"Have you ever seen the accounts?"

"No. Adam never wanted me to have anything to do with the business. When he was ill, Scotty managed that side of things. Why?"

"What can you tell us about the tomato crop?" the other officer said.

She had no idea what he was asking. "Do you mean the varieties? I think it's Romas and Black Russians. Maybe some cherry…"

"Have you visited the greenhouse?"

"No."

"Have you ever visited the property before or since the fires?"

"No. There was never a reason for me to visit. Before the fires, Adam used the old sheds for framing and Scotty lived in the house."

The barrage of questions was making her sweat and it promoted an old memory. "Oh, wait. I did go there once. It was a year before the fires. I remember, because we were on our way to Lorne for our summer vacation and Adam made a detour to the vineyard. It was hot and Gracie wanted to get out of the car and talk to Scotty. Adam insisted we stay in the car. Have I done something wrong?"

"Shane, is this absolutely necessary on top of everything else?" Claire asked crisply.

"Just one more question." Shane sounded every inch a police officer. "Do you have any knowledge of your husband's million-dollar cannabis crop?"

Bec stared at him open-mouthed.

"Good. That's exactly what Scotty Ferguson told us. You're in the clear, Bec. Thanks for answering our questions."

"Cannabis?" she squeaked. "He's been growing *cannabis*?"

"For years, apparently. Scotty's given us a very detailed account of the business before and after the fires. It explains Adam's behavior on the day of the fires. He certainly saved two lives but his motivations were not as pure as we've been led to believe."

She'd been living with a stranger. "I can't believe it. Is that what he's been drugging me with?"

"No. Your blood tests show he was using a mixture of prescription sedatives."

"That's why you've had a bitter taste in your mouth and a constantly runny nose," Claire said. "It will all go away in a few days once the drugs are out of your system."

"But I don't understand. If Scotty's known about the cannabis for years, why did he confess today?"

"You'll have to ask him that," Shane said. "He's currently in the lockup but he'll appear in front of the magistrate in the morning. We're not opposing bail. Adam's been re-arrested and we've transferred him into custody in Melbourne for Scotty's safety. Given the rape charges and the cultivation and sale of cannabis charges, he won't be getting out any time soon. I hope that gives you some peace of mind."

It gave her safety, but peace of mind? Would she ever have that again?

CHAPTER THIRTY

"IF YOU DON'T GET A WRIGGLE ON, YOU'RE GOING TO BE LATE."
Matt wrapped Claire's hair around his fingers.

They were in bed and she was snuggled in next to him, loving the
feel of the rise and fall of his chest under her head. "I'm taking the day
off."

"You sick?"

"No. But five hours after we committed to putting our relationship
first, all hell broke loose. I've been at work ever since and I know how
much you hate that so—"

"I'm never going to resent an emergency, Postie. I only got
frustrated because I thought you were creating work to avoid the farm.
Now I understand why you were doing that." He grimaced. "And
talking about my family, what do you want to do about Christmas? We
can run away somewhere for a few nights if you want. Maybe go
camping, just the two of us?"

Her heart rolled in appreciation. "That's a lovely idea but it's not
going to fix anything with your family, is it?"

"No, but it will be a hell of a lot more relaxing. I don't want you
sitting down to Christmas lunch if it's going to upset you."

Claire knew going away was too much like their early days of cocooning themselves in a bubble, but it wasn't enough to stop her saying, "I'm tempted."

He kissed her. "Yesterday, when you were helping Bec, I did something I should have done a long time ago. I called a family meeting. I told Mom and Dad and Tamara that you're the most important person in my life whether we're married or not, and that you come first. Then I gave them an ultimatum. Either they love and accept you and fully welcome you into the family wholeheartedly and unreservedly, or they lose me."

Love and sadness spun through her. "But part of you would die if you left the farm."

"The last few weeks have taught me that more of me will die without you."

"Oh, Matt. What did they say?"

"I don't know. I left them to think on it and went out for a long hard gallop."

She supposed they'd find out the Cartwrights' decision soon enough. "Can I work on the farm with you today?"

"I'd love that, but don't you need to check in on Bec and Sophie?"

"I can do it by telephone. When I told Bec I'd visit this morning, she told me with a hint of her old officiousness that she had an appointment and I needed to spend the day with you."

"God, how can she even think about other people after everything that's happened?"

"Right now it's probably easier than thinking about herself."

His eyes dimmed. "Will she get through this? Will Josh? Is this town ever going to get out from under the shadow of the fires?"

"It's going to be slow, but if the Stitch Bitches have anything to do with it, our gang will not only survive, we'll come out stronger."

"Thought it was the CWA Nightlights now?"

"Officially, but never in my heart."

He laughed. "Your mom warned me you were a rebel. I told her I loved you anyway."

It was the first time Matt had mentioned her mother in months and her heart did another somersault. He'd really heard her at their counseling session. "Well, I'm your rebel now."

She kissed him long and deep, reveling in the joy of being able to touch him again. "And talking about breaking the rules, this farmer's going to be late for work."

AT THREE O'CLOCK, Matt had gone to supervise a delivery of feed, leaving Claire alone in the honey house. She was happily loading the honey frames they'd removed earlier from the hives into the extractor. Today was like one of their pre-fire days together on the farm—loved up and happy—although she couldn't delude herself that their problems were anywhere close to resolved.

As much as she appreciated Matt's supportive stand for her against his parents and the hope it gave her that their relationship had a fighting chance, she couldn't shift the feeling that if they had to leave the farm, their departure would create a whole new set of problems for them. Matt loved his family and he loved the farm. She didn't want to be the reason he was estranged from either.

However, she was determined not to take second best from the Cartwrights any longer. Given that Matt had backed his mother into a corner and Claire didn't trust Louise to be reasonable, things were likely to get harder before they got easier. What did that really mean for them as a couple in the long term? Sick of thinking about it, she switched on the extractor and busied herself sterilizing jars.

"Knock, knock." Louise stood in the doorway. "May I come in?"

It was the first time Louise had ever sought her permission about anything. Claire tried to smile. "Of course."

"You're looking tired, Claire."

"It's been a hellish few weeks and an exhausting couple of days."

"The whole town's abuzz about Adam Petrovic. It's outrageous on so many fronts. How could he do this to Myrtle? And Bec, poor Bec." Louise shuddered. "One feels quite useless in these situations."

"At school, Rebecca Sendo was one of the most determined girls I knew. I'm going to do everything I can to support her so she finds the strength not only to survive this, but to come through it whole. She deserves to know trust and happiness again." To her horror, Claire realized she was crying.

Louise switched on the kettle. "It's a woman's worst nightmare."

Claire swiped her eyes with the backs of her hands. "Pretty much."

"Well, she's fortunate to have you as a friend."

Claire sniffed. "I don't think so. I've let her down. If we hadn't been so tied up hating each other for years, maybe I might have known what she was dealing with. The shameful thing is, I can't even tell you why we were locked in a stupid feud."

"It's my experience that women who are similar clash."

"Bec and I are chalk and cheese."

Louise passed her a mug of tea. "Oh, I don't know. I think you're more alike than either of you are prepared to admit. You're both driven. Despite your protests that you're not a perfectionist, Claire, you are in the things that matter to you. I think if Bec had been allowed to stay on at school and had the same educational opportunities as you and Matt, her life would have turned out very differently."

"I'm pretty sure she wanted to be a hairdresser. I remember her bragging about it at parties."

Louise cocked her head. "If you were forced to do something you didn't like, wouldn't you brag a bit to make yourself feel better?"

It was like the crystals of a kaleidoscope falling to create a new pattern and for the first time in her life, Claire felt she finally understood Bec. It also made her feel small and slightly diminished. More determined than ever to be a real friend.

"Unlike your mother, who loved you dearly, Anja Sendo is an awful woman."

This was the strangest conversation Claire had ever had with Louise. Was this her way of extending an olive branch?

Louise cleared her throat. "I assume you know Matt called a family meeting yesterday."

Claire tensed. "He told me this morning."

"I love my son, Claire."

"I know you do. I love him too, Louise."

"Recently, I've had trouble seeing that."

Don't buy into it. "And Matt loves me."

"He does." Louise sipped her tea and Claire let the silence hang.

Louise eventually broke it. "The last time we spoke I was very angry at you for hurting him. Matt tells me that he takes a large share of responsibility for your current problems and he wants to do everything possible to try to rebuild your relationship. But I have a question. Do you feel the same way?"

It rankled that Louise felt the need to ask. "Absolutely. We've committed to counseling."

"Good."

Good? What was she supposed to do with that? With nothing to lose, Claire gripped the bull by the horns. "I'm sorry you were sad and upset when Matt broke up with Taylor. I'm sorry I'm not the daughter-in-law you wanted. I'm sorry you find it hard to see your son in love with me. But I can't change any of the feelings you have. All I can do is love your son the way he deserves to be loved and try to make him happy. That's all I've ever tried or wanted to do."

Louise studied the pattern on her sandals. "And I haven't made that easy for you. I apologize for that. The thing is, Claire, as much as we may not like it, you and I are similar ... You're a far stronger personality than—"

Claire knew Louise had just stopped herself from mentioning Taylor.

"I can't undo the things I've said and done, but if you're amenable, I'd like to draw a line and work on building bridges. I appreciate things are not going to change overnight and despite our best efforts, we may never be close, but we both love Matt. We are family."

Claire knew Louise well enough to know that this was an apology of epic proportions. This was *the* olive branch and she'd be foolish not to accept it.

"Thank you. And for my part, I know I didn't show you my full appreciation for the help you gave me with Mom and Dad's funeral. Or for how much you and Bill did for us when we lived in the homestead."

Louise made a strangled sound. "That was duty. I blame my WASP upbringing, but practical help has always been easier for me than dealing with emotions."

"Still, it doesn't mean having us living in the homestead for eighteen months wasn't a huge inconvenience to you."

"Nonsense." Louise, sounded more like herself. She waved her hand dismissively. "It's what family does. Bill and I love having the house full. I miss the days when Tamara and Matt were teenagers and the house overflowed with their friends and they'd sit in the kitchen and chat to me.

"I hope one day you'll—" Again she stopped abruptly and gave a wry smile. "Sorry. Matt was very specific that we're not to mention a couple of topics. Tell me, what are your and Matt's plans for Christmas?"

The idea of her and Matt alone and kayaking on the Glenelg River tempted her in the same way the apple had called to Eve, but if she and Louise were to have any hope of forging a relationship, they needed to be around for Christmas. "We're on the farm. Would you and Bill like a year off and everyone can come to the new house?"

Claire watched the struggle on Louise's face and she threw her a bone. "Or, if it's not too much work for you, we can come to the homestead as usual. Perhaps this year, I could bring something?"

Louise relaxed. "Yes, do come to us and bring the brandy cream sauce for the plum pudding. If you want to host something, you and Matt could take over the cousins' barbecue on the 27th."

"That's a great idea and I'm happy to cater it this year but can we take a raincheck on hosting until we have lawn and a garden?"

"I see your point. The children would have a field day in the dust."

"Did you miss me—" Matt walked in talking. On seeing his

mother, he crossed the room to stand next to Claire and slung an arm around her waist. "Hello, Mom. I didn't know you were here."

"Hello, darling. Claire and I were just discussing Christmas."

"Oh?" He glanced between them, trying to gauge the mood.

"We're having lunch at the homestead," Claire said. "You're making brandy cream sauce."

Matt grinned and his body relaxed into hers. "Too easy."

SOPHIE SAT opposite Scotty Ferguson in a Geelong motel room, unable to wrap her head around what he was saying. "Josh did *what?*"

Scotty scratched the back of his hand. "What you need to understand is that Adam's a master manipulator and blackmailer. It's why he didn't charge you labor for the house: it gave him leverage over Josh. He would have spun some line about loyalty, job security and community values to get Josh to install the bypass.

"I promise you, Josh didn't know about the cannabis until the stress of the bypass got to him and he came to the greenhouse to pull it out. Even if Josh had threatened to go to the police, by then Adam had him over a barrel."

Anger fizzed over her disbelief. "If you knew this about Adam, why did you let this happen to Josh?"

Anguish pulled at his mouth. "I didn't let it happen. I tried keeping Josh on the building sites and away from him. But the moment Adam got wind of his electrical experience, it got out of hand."

"Out of hand! It's more than out of hand. The stress of it's combined with his PTSD from the fires and tipped him over the edge." Tears threatened and she batted them away. She was too furious to cry. "He's seriously ill, Scotty. Have you ever looked at someone and realized they're not there? That's Josh. The drugs are keeping him calm but his eyes are dull and his essential self is missing."

"I'm sorry."

"Gee, thanks."

He shuddered. "I'm trying to make amends. Has he said anything about the bypass or the police?"

She thought about Josh's terrifying rantings on the block before the sedative calmed him. "I remember him saying Shane Radley couldn't be trusted. It didn't make any sense."

"Adam would have told him that but believe me, Shane's as straight as they come."

"Does he know about the bypass?"

"He knows it exists but not who installed it. He has no reason to connect it to Josh."

"How do you know that for sure?"

"If Shane suspected, he'd have visited the hospital and requested to see Josh but he hasn't. When Josh installed it, only Adam and Travis knew about it. I only learned about it the day Josh went to pull it out. I won't tell Shane. Travis has scarpered and with his history he's not going to talk to the police either. Josh was a just a bit player and if Adam's going to take anyone down with him, it's me for ratting him out.

Scotty scratched the back of his hand. "Sophie, I want to tell Josh he's safe. I want to reduce his stress. While I'm out on bail, I'll finish the house."

"How can we ever live in that bloody house after what it's done to Josh? I pushed him to work with Adam so we could get it finished." She stared out at Corio Bay. "Oh God. I'm to blame too."

"No! You're not. You didn't know what Adam was up to. He sucks people in with his largesse and suddenly, before you know what the hell has happened, you're in too deep. At least you can sell a completed house."

She fought a rush of gratitude before turning on him again. Over the week, a part of her had hardened to steel. "Did you stand by and let Adam hurt Bec?"

He blanched. "No! I had no idea. I'm gutted."

"Good."

He rose to his feet, his body sagging under the heavy load of his choices and decisions. "When Josh is up for visitors, can I see him?"

"No."

"Please?"

The legacy of the fires hung between them. Scotty might go to prison for being an accessory to a crime and Josh was currently in a prison created by his mind. "Pray he recovers and comes back to me and the kids."

WHEN SCOTTY CALLED BEC, asking her to meet him at the office, she knew she couldn't return to the house. She never wanted to walk into her bedroom again. Erica, Claire and Layla had all offered to pack her clothes and bring them to Julie's place, but she'd refused. Except for half-a-dozen items, she'd never wear any of them again. When she felt up to it, she planned to burn the lot.

Erica hadn't questioned her decision. Instead, she'd clapped her hands and said, "Right. Shopping expedition."

Layla and Julie had taken the girls back to the house and helped them pack their clothes and favorite things. Gracie had complained bitterly. Ivy had silently obliged. The sullen and angry Ivy of the previous weeks had vanished. In her place was a girl who played with Charger and snuck into Bec's bed each night, cuddling in close. Every time Bec looked at her and her loss of innocence, she wanted to cry. Had Ivy sensed what was going on? At least Adam hadn't touched the girls.

Now, in the shade of Julie's garden, Scotty arrived looking as shattered as Bec felt. He walked straight up and silently wrapped his arms around her. It took her a moment to realize he was crying.

"I'm sorry. I'm so sorry," he said. "I hate the bastard. I want to kill him."

She disengaged his arms and sat down on the bench, working on keeping herself together. "You're in enough trouble already. What the hell, Scotty? How long has this been going on?"

He stared off into the middle distance. "Since Adam bought the vineyard. I only found out after he convinced me that paying rent was a waste of money. He offered me the house in exchange for looking after the property. Two months after I moved out there, I discovered what he was doing. Apparently, he'd been growing the stuff for years in a house in Gellibrand. The vineyard meant he could increase operations."

"Why didn't you dob him in then?"

He turned to look at her, his face a complicated mix of regret and resolve. "He threatened my sister and her kid. And I knew he'd carry it out so I figured if I wasn't growing the dope or selling it, there was no harm in keeping the secret.

"But it got to me. I wanted out. I moved my sister to Melbourne and I told you I was leaving, remember? I was going to move on the day of the fires but then you asked me to keep Adam busy for the weekend. You were planning some sort of surprise in Lorne and you didn't want him turning up early. I've never been very good at saying no to you, so I figured I'd help and then leave on the Monday."

An old seam of culpability shifted inside her. "I'm sorry I used you."

"You didn't use me."

"I did. Adam had already told me he wouldn't be in Lorne until the Tuesday but I was worried he might change his mind and arrive early. I couldn't let that happen." She owed Scotty the truth. "That weekend I was leaving Adam for Hugo Lang."

Scotty's eyes widened in shock. "I—you—I didn't know. I thought you and Adam were... God. Sorry about Hugo."

She heard his sincerity but she was confused by the flash of hurt in his eyes. "Thank you."

"Then that bastard fire fused both of us to him and neither of us could leave."

"I've kept telling you to go."

"Yeah." He sighed. "But nothing's that easy, is it? Adam came out to the vineyard that day to stop the CFA from turning up and discovering the crop. He got burned because he stayed too long trying to grab equipment, but his arrival alerted Travis and me to the fire. He saved our lives. Owing him for that got tangled up in his web of secrets and blackmail. Plus, you were distraught. I couldn't leave you to cope with Adam and the business alone."

His fingers started scratching again and shoved his hands under his thigh. "Those months you and I worked together were the best of my life. The thing is, I fell in love with you. Stupid, I know, but after that, I didn't want to leave. When Adam offered me the partnership to shut me up and keep me close, I told myself at least I'd get to spend time with you."

Bec stared at him, stunned. "But we've hardly seen each other since he got out of the hospital."

"Yeah. Those burns turned him from a regular bastard into a jealous bastard. He warned me off. A couple of times he punched me, but not once did I think he'd ever hurt you. Hell, he talks about you and the girls all the time. If I'd known how screwed up he was, how unhappy you were, I'd have got you out of there."

His voice broke. "When I think about what he did to you ... me telling the police about the crop was suddenly easy. I hate that my years of indecision have caused you and Josh Doherty so much pain. I'm going to live with it for the rest of my life."

Enduring other people's reactions to her trauma sapped Bec's strength and she gripped the edge of the garden bench. "Will you go to jail?"

He grimaced. "Probably. Maybe. It's up to the judge. I've told the police everything including the ways Adam laundered the money, so it might mean a lesser sentence. He's a bastard but the one thing he did right was keeping the construction side of things separate from the cannabis so there are still houses to build. You don't have to worry about money, Bec. Just concentrate on getting well, okay? If there's anything I can ever do for you, just ask."

She got a flash of being laid across the kitchen counter. The time she'd convinced herself that Adam hadn't raped her. That it was just a sex game that had gotten out of control. She thought of her counselor saying, "take small steps."

"There is one thing you can do for me."

"Thank God. What?"

"Change the name of the company. The words "Petrovic" and "family" don't belong in the same sentence."

EPILOGUE

THE FIRST WEEKEND IN JANUARY, TWO YEARS LATER

The sun shone and the sun-screened and hat-wearing crowd picnicked under the trees at the third annual Myrtle Tall Trees Fun Run, Stroll and Family Day. Claire surveyed the passing parade from the CWA tent. The market—farm-fresh food and crafts—was in full swing and the food trucks were doing a roaring trade with long lines at the ice-cream van and the Nguyens' coffee cart. The crack of a whip shot through the air, making her smile. This year, Oakvale Park was out in force. Bill was teaching city-slickers to crack whips, Louise was giving wool-spinning demonstrations, Tamara and Lachlan were busy running a berries and pancake stall while she and Matt were selling honey.

"What do you reckon, Harper?" she said to the red-headed toddler in her arms. "It's bigger and better every year."

Harper grabbed for Claire's sunglasses. She laughed and hugged her.

Bec walked into the tent holding an enormous string bag filled with 200 plastic ducks. Harper squealed in delight, pumping her chubby arms out toward her mother.

"How's she been?"

"Great. You're my secret weapon, aren't you, Harps? She says, "waffull," and everyone goos and gahs and buys five dollars' worth of raffle tickets. I might have to keep her."

BEC SMILED at one of her dearest friends, choosing not to remember the years they'd wasted detesting each other. "Thanks for having the girls last week. They love it out at Oakvale Park."

"It's our pleasure. Did Ivy tell you she took her first jump the other day? She's got your seat."

"We've brought coffee and scones." Erica strode into the tent, her fun-run winner's medal for best time in her age group swinging proudly around her neck. Sophie and Layla followed, carrying the food.

"Excuse me," a woman asked. "When I was here two years ago, I bought the best tomato sauce and chutney I've ever tasted. Do you have it again this year?"

"No," the five of them said in unison.

The woman startled.

"Sorry," Claire said hastily. "There was, um ... a crop disaster. But the Oakvale Park tent in the next row's got bottles. They use the same recipe."

As the woman walked away, Bec said drily, "A crop disaster? I suppose it was in a way."

She could hardly remember the first Put Myrtle on the Map day. She'd barely been functioning, but Claire had sat with her in the CWA tent making her feel involved even when Bec could barely string a sentence together.

Bec hadn't seen Adam since the court case. He'd been found guilty of all charges. If she had her way, she'd never see him again. Thankfully, she had another ten years before she had to worry about it —the judge had given Adam the longest possible sentence for each of his crimes.

The counselor had recommended the older girls decide what sort of contact they wanted with their father. As hard as it was to honor this, Bec tried. Ivy refused to read Adam's letters but Gracie occasionally sent a reply, usually when she'd won a sporting event. Harper didn't know Adam at all and Bec was happy with that. She hoped she never would.

Julie and Phil walked past the tent with Penny and her kids and gave her a wave. Bec's heart filled with gratitude and love. During the black days in the months following Adam's arrest, when she and the girls struggled to make sense of what had happened, the Langs had welcomed them into their home and their family. They'd lived with them for a year and a half and Bec didn't know what she would have done without their care and support. Well, she did know—she'd have fallen apart and risked landing up in the hospital and losing the girls.

With Charger as her constant companion, Ivy had healed. Gracie, who was remarkably resilient, had channeled all her confusion into sport. Harper's arrival had given the three of them a new focus and despite everything, she'd been a happy baby with few difficult days. There'd been times when Bec was concerned Penny might be unhappy about them living with her parents but all Penny had said was, "You loved Hugo. If he'd lived, you'd be my sister-in-law, so how is this different?"

Bec had cried.

With the help of a raft of health professionals, the Langs' love and the friendship of the original Stitch Bitches, Bec had slowly put herself back together. There were still tough days, and for a while she'd seriously considered moving to Melbourne. Part of her wanted to leave town and all the memories of Adam, and live the life she and Hugo had planned. But she'd realized in time that without her support system, she'd not only flounder but likely fall over. The girls didn't deserve that and neither did she. Ironically, it was Adam's ex-business —the legal one—that had played a big role in her recovery.

Bec ran the company, now named Myrtle Constructions, with Scotty. In the eleven months before his trial, he'd taught her every facet of the administration side of the business. Her organizational skills were a perfect match to the tasks required. With the assistance of a trusted builder mate of Scotty's, the business had weathered the six months Scotty spent in a minimum-security prison.

"Spill the beans, Bec." Erica passed her a cup of coffee. "Nathan and I saw you and the girls having pizza with Scotty on Tuesday night. Are you two dating?"

Bec didn't know what they were doing or even what she wanted. She'd loved Hugo—she still did—but he'd been dead four years. She trusted Scotty as much as she'd trusted Hugo but she hated that he'd been under Adam's control. Hated that she'd been there too. But was that even an issue anymore?

"We're business partners and friends, and the girls love him. That's enough for now."

"He loves you," Layla said. "Everyone sees it on his face."

"When does Scotty finish his parole?" Sophie asked.

"It was last week."

"He should have a party and celebrate that it's all finally over."

"He just wants it to slide quietly away so he can get on with his law-abiding life."

"I can understand that," Claire said. "He's doing a great job with the youth group. There's nothing like a real-life story of someone making the wrong decision and paying the price to shock wayward teens. But I'm worried he's still doing penance. He needs to be kinder to himself."

"I don't think he's totally forgiven himself for what happened to Josh either," Erica said. "He told Nathan as much."

"Well, we've forgiven him," Sophie wiped cream off her mouth. "For a while there, I didn't think I could, but then I realized he was as much a victim as we were. I hope he knows that."

"I'm sure he does. Don't he and Josh play basketball together?" Claire asked.

"It's more like one on one. Josh reckons Scotty needs to write "must play basketball" into all the building contracts for the newcomers so we get some adult players in town."

Claire laughed. "Good luck with that. Mind you, as the new recreational officer, he can indoctrinate the kids."

"That's his plan. Look out, future Myrtle."

TWO YEARS EARLIER, Sophie hadn't been able to envisage a future for her and Josh in a town that had caused her husband so much pain and suffering. During that terrifying time, guilt had consumed her. She couldn't shake the feeling that her almost petulant desire to be a stay-at-home mom had not only played a role in him viewing himself as the stoic provider, but had exacerbated his sense of failure when the fire had forced them to live in a shed and caused the loss of his job. She was haunted by Josh's misguided belief that he was protecting her by not telling her exactly what had happened to him on the day of the fires. But her thundering hatred was reserved for Adam Petrovic. His blackmail, not to mention the potency of his marijuana, had tipped Josh over the edge. For three awful weeks, while Josh floundered in a psychiatric hospital, Sophie had feared her stubborn, prickly and determined husband would never come back to them.

Her boss had been amazing, giving her flexible working hours and remote access so she could work and visit Josh. As promised, Scotty had finished the house but she immediately put it on the market, knowing they could never live there. In an unprecedented piece of luck, it sold quickly and Sophie had moved her family out of the shed and into a short-term rental in town. Janet and Craig had moved in with them, looking after Josh and the kids while Sophie worked and looking after her at the end of the day. She'd been surprised at how her job became a refuge and her previous resentment at working full time disappeared.

Aileen had visited once or twice, asking perfunctory questions about Josh and the kids before quickly turning to stories of Kylie's baby. Kylie was far too busy to visit and when Sophie received texts that said things like *Between the baby and Lex, I barely have time to get my nails done,* Sophie was thankful for the 120 miles separating them. One of the advantages of having some counseling was recognizing that her mother and sister weren't capable of supporting her in ways she needed, and that was okay, because she had other people in her life who did the job so much better.

As Josh recovered, they'd discussed where they should live. The thought of moving back to Melbourne and starting over after a long absence daunted her. As did the idea of leaving her friends, all of whom had been there for her in different ways during the ordeal that was Josh's PTSD. It became obvious that reducing Josh's stress was vital to keeping him well and this included the likelihood of him only ever working part time. They considered moving to Colac so she didn't have to change jobs but neither of them could muster much enthusiasm.

When the house next to Erica and Nathan's came up for sale, it was Janet and Craig who suggested they look at it.

"Living in Myrtle's too hard for Josh," Sophie had said, immediately scotching the suggestion.

"Living on the block was too hard," Josh said. "Let's take a look and see how it feels."

Josh's illness had forced Sophie to examine her own behavior—her tendency to put her own needs and the kids first and Josh second. They were both working on unlearning unhealthy behaviors. After building two houses and making decisions about everything from doors to floor coverings, Sophie had expected a ready-built house to lack soul, but the property had wrapped around her. But instead of squealing and saying, "Yes! This!" she'd stayed silent and carefully observed Josh.

If their marriage was to survive, his mental health must come first. If he couldn't picture himself living there, there was no point in her expressing an opinion. She'd watched him walk around the large backyard, study the pool and stare out to the horizon. The garden lacked the dazzling view of the hill top block.

He took her hand. "The kids will love the pool."

"Sure, but all they want and all I want is a happy you. Can you see yourself living here?"

"Yeah. I can." He gazed at her, a faint glimmer of old Josh in his eyes. "And if we're living in town and close to the house next door, better the neighbors we know, eh?"

When they told Janet and Craig they were staying in Myrtle, her in-laws had smiled and promptly bought a house two streets away. Sophie had cried with happiness and relief. Josh did so much better with his family close by. They all did.

When she looked back on the early years of their marriage, she recognized they'd often fought each other, determined to win their own way. It was a miracle their relationship had survived at all. Her life now was very different from that naïve vision of being a stay-at-home mom with three kids and a husband who brought home the bacon.

She'd reluctantly given up her dream of a third baby in exchange for a healthy husband. Josh didn't need the stress of another child and, if she was honest—and that had been hard—as she was the main breadwinner, neither did she. Knowing that didn't stop the pangs of regret or the kernel of sadness for the baby that would never be, but when she saw Josh relaxed and happy and being a hands-on dad to Liam and Trixie, she told herself it was enough. Besides, in the last two years, both Bec and Layla had given birth and her empty arms got their fill of cuddles. Plus, there was something liberating about handing babies back when they got fractious.

"Mommy!" Trixie ran into the tent followed by Liam and Josh. "Is it time for the ducks?"

"Soon, Trix," Claire said. "I just need to find Matt so he can turn on the siren and clear the creek of kids."

"We'll do it," Liam and Trixie chorused, tearing back outside.

"They just want to press the siren button." Josh gave Sophie a quick kiss on the cheek. "Coming to the bridge?"

"Wouldn't miss it."

It was now a Doherty family tradition to stand on the bridge and watch the plastic ducks rush past before they held hands and ran to the finish line. If the last few years had taught Sophie anything, it was that sharing simple moments of joy like this mattered. She picked up the ducks. "See you all down there."

"I've got to shoot home to get ready for tonight," Claire said. "If my duck wins, give the money to Matt. Oh, and don't be late."

"This from you," Bec said good-naturedly.

"Hey, emergencies excluded, I'm reformed. I believe you were the one who was late to our last meeting."

"Client crisis." Bec rolled her eyes. "Well, the client thought it was a crisis, because we can't source the tiles she wants. Honestly, sometimes I want to tell people our stories and give them a perspective check."

"Osman and I will be there with a plate with food on it." Layla laughed. "Not like when Erica tells me to bring a plate so I bring an empty one. Do you need help getting ready, Claire?"

"Thanks, but I'm all good. It's just a casual barbecue and Bec and Louise helped me set up yesterday." Claire turned her attention to the crowd outside the tent. "If the Tall Trees Fun Run and Family Day keeps growing like this, in a few years we'll rival Lorne's Pier to Pub."

"Don't wish those numbers on us," Bec said.

"We don't want to lose our tranquil, small-town feel," Erica added.

"We won't. But don't you get a buzz knowing that despite everything that happened two years ago, we not only pulled this together, we've grown it? We've created something special that not only brings money into Myrtle but that people look forward to all year. And I know we have help from the Lion's Club and the Men's Shed and all the new Nightlighters, but we started it. I'm so proud of us, sometimes I want to cry."

Sophie laughed. "Don't go all soppy on us."

"We've definitely put Myrtle on the map," Layla said.

Erica smiled. "And tonight, we're celebrating."

"Oh!" Bec clapped her hands. "Did Nathan get a case of the real stuff again for Christmas?"

"Hell, yes! I've got it on ice so it's ready to go."

MATT GAVE a low whistle as Claire walked out of the bathroom. "Is that a new dress?"

She twirled in front of him, pleased to see he was wearing the clothes she'd laid out for him without protest. "It is. Do you like it?"

"I love it." He pulled her into his arms. "But aren't we a bit dressed up for that lot out there?"

She linked her hands behind his head. "That lot are our family and closest friends."

"That's true." He glanced out the window. "Jeez! Don't get upset, but Mom and Dad are greeting people like this is their place."

It had been a long time since Matt's parents had upset Claire. She and Louise had forged their own path and slowly forced respect had given way to genuine warmth. It wasn't anything like the closeness Claire had shared with her mother or what she shared with Julie, but it was far from frosty. Tamara had been a harder nut to crack.

Things had been cool between brother and sister for a long time. Whether Louise and Bill had finally spoken to Tamara or she'd sensed a losing battle, one day her de facto sister-in-law asked if Claire would mind if she joined the CWA Nightlights. Since then, things had settled into a pattern of acceptance. Claire sometimes wondered if Taylor Norris's marriage to an accountant in Geelong had helped Tamara let go of her animosity.

"Relax, Matt. I asked your parents to help. And I feel a bit mean about Tamara and Lachlan, because they've been busy all day making pancakes, but they're on welcome drinks."

Confusion crossed his face. "I don't get it. I thought this was just a casual barbecue."

"It is and it isn't. I thought tonight might be the perfect occasion for you to announce we're pregnant."

"Really?" He grinned at her, his eyes full of love and hope. "That would be fantastic."

"I know the secret's almost killed you."

He bumped his belly gently against hers. "Longest three months of my life."

In the end, the decision to have a baby had been a lot easier to make than her decision not to have one. Claire still worried she couldn't protect a child from all the awful things life might throw at it, but with Matt's unwavering love and support and his family's caring acceptance of her, the prospect of being a mother was a lot less terrifying. And she had dear friends. They were the embodiment of the saying "it takes a community to raise a child."

Over the previous two years, they'd all helped with the children. Initially, Claire, Layla and Erica had circled Sophie and Bec but as things improved, they'd given back, assisting Layla in the final weeks of her pregnancy when she was confined to bed rest. Claire had spent so much time with Harper in the last eighteen months, she and Matt considered her half theirs. Now they were having their own.

She kissed him, giving thanks for having this man who'd proved stalwart and patient. "I'm lucky to have you."

"Yeah, you are." He laughed and swung her round, staggering slightly. "You're heavier."

"Carrying twins does that to a girl."

He grinned widely, pride riding off him. "I knocked you up real good."

"You did, and that's why I've decided to make an honest man of you."

"What?"

"Honey, we're getting married. That is, if you're still up for it, four and a half years after you proposed."

"But ... what about the paperwork?"

Claire laughed. Usually she was the practical one and he was the romantic. "We'll sort out the legal stuff next week. Come on."

She grabbed his hand and they walked outside. People stood chatting and drinking and kids ran around barefoot on the lawn. Erica waved from the end of the veranda, flanked by Layla, Bec and Sophie, all of whom wore pretty dresses and wide smiles. They looked suspiciously like bridesmaids. So much for Erica and Bec keeping things a secret.

"Hurry up, Matt," Erica called out. "Get down here so we can start. I don't want the champagne getting hot."

Matt's parents, who were in on the plan, walked their son to the wedding party. Then Julie and Phil linked arms with Claire and walked her to Matt. When Erica asked, "Who gives this woman to this man?" Julie and Phil said, "We do, on behalf of Heather and Ron."

Matt squeezed her hand and she squeezed it back, but not out of sadness. Today Claire was happy and everything finally felt right.

When Erica announced them husband and wife, a cheer went up and champagne corks flew.

"I love you, Postie." Matt wrapped his arms around her and gave her a long and lingering kiss to a soundtrack of wolf whistles.

"I love you too."

"THIS IS the first Australian wedding I've been to," Layla said later, watching some impromptu dancing on the lawn.

Sophie sipped champagne. "They're not usually this casual."

"The first time Claire tried to marry Matt, she'd planned a very traditional white wedding," Julie added, "but this suits them perfectly."

"And in most Australian weddings, the bride's not preggers," Erica said.

Bec laughed. "But this is Claire, remember."

"What's me?" Claire slid into a spare seat after relinquishing her husband to a game of bocce.

"Breaking all the rules and having a shotgun wedding." Bec raised her wineglass. "And oh my God! Twins!"

"That's what happens when you start at thirty-three."

"Double pregnancy hormones. No wonder you were all soppy before the duck race, saying how proud of us you are," Sophie teased.

"I was just softening you up cos I'm going to need help. I'm already worried about not having enough arms."

"I will cook for you," Layla said.

"I'll draw up a roster," Erica offered. "Between Matt, the Cartwrights and us, you'll be fine. At least Matt doesn't have to commute."

Julie smiled. "I'm looking forward to knitting caps and booties for winter babies."

"I'm so excited for you," Bec said. "It's going to be the scariest and most amazing ride of your life."

"Gee, thanks. That's hardly reassuring."

Bec laughed and patted Claire's arm. "We're all here to pick you up and cheer you on whenever you need it just like you've always done for us."

And right then, Claire knew no matter what happened, she was in good hands.

FEELING DISTRESSED?

If anything in this book has distressed you and you wish to talk to someone ...

USA
National Suicide Prevention **988**
National Domestic Violence Hotline
1-800- 799-SAFE

UK
24 hour National Domestic Abuse Helpline
0808 2000 247
Help for Suicide Prevention
https://www.nhs.uk/conditions/suicide/

Elsewhere please Google the helplines in your country.

ACKNOWLEDGMENTS

This book couldn't have been written without a support team. Huge thanks to Country Fire Authority (CFA) fire captain David Webb-Ware who answered my many questions, gave me a tour of the Glenburn CFA and let me sit in Bert and turn on the siren. Thanks to the North Geelong Men's Shed for their warm welcome and for chatting to me about their programs. The Geelong Central Nights Country Women's Association (CWA) are a sensational group of women. Thanks for letting me gate-crash your AGM and later your craft night. The Victoria Police Film and Television unit were amazing, responding to my many and varied questions about police procedures, crimes and the law. A special shout-out to Acting Sergeant Adam West who went above and beyond, contacting me a month later when new information came to light. I couldn't have managed the crime thread in the book without their help.

Jamie Moran from Lonsdale Tomatoes briefed me on growing commercial hydroponic tomatoes. John Edmonds from Edmonds Honey explained about bees and Roslyn Groves filled me in on what's currently popular in toddler and preschool land. Mel Scott talked me through fractured ankles and Ris Wilkinson (author Melanie

Milburne) shared her Thermomix story. Tahlia Lowe and Matilda Currie gave me the scoop on Girl Scouts and Rose Goodall-Wilson provided me with a sounding board. Brad Bolden shared his joys and frustrations as a stay-at-home dad, Lesley Menzies answered all my dog questions, Diane Green sent me in the right direction for the flora and fauna of the Otway Ranges and writing mate, Marion Lennox, came up with the perfect title. Thank you!

Researching this book took me to some harrowing places and I heard some devastating stories. My heart goes out to the survivors of natural disasters who deal with situations most of us will never encounter.

Writing a novel is one thing, polishing it so it shines is another thing entirely. Thanks to Rachael Donovan, Annabel Blay and Kylie Mason for editorial advice on the Australian and New Zealand edition and to Norma Blake for her help Americanizing the language in this 'rest of the world' edition.

The Lowe men provided advice, listened to me rant about computers and the rainbow ball of death, and provided more meals than they probably ever expected to prepare. I like to think I've given them the opportunity to improve their cooking skills. Pekoe the cat added to the manuscript often, enjoying lying on the keyboard. Any random characters are courtesy of her.

Last but by no means least, many thanks to my loyal readers who not only use their hard-earned money to buy my books, but make the effort to catch up with me at library talks and take the time to write to me and chat on social media. I appreciate your support very much.

ABOUT THE AUTHOR

FIONA LOWE has been a midwife, a sexual health counselor and a family support worker; an ideal career for an author who writes novels about family and relationships. She spent her early years in Papua New Guinea where, without television, reading was the entertainment and it set up a lifelong love of books. Although she often re-wrote the endings of books in her head, it was the birth of her first child that prompted her to write her first novel. A recipient of the prestigious USA RITA® award and the Australian RuBY award, Fiona writes books that are set in small country towns. They feature real people facing difficult choices and explore how family ties and relationships impact on their decisions.

When she's not writing stories, she's a distracted wife, mother of two "ginger" sons, a volunteer in her community, guardian of eighty rose bushes, slave to a cat, and is often found collapsed on the couch with wine. You can find her at her website, fionalowe.com, and on Facebook, Twitter, Instagram and Goodreads.

BOOK CLUB QUESTIONS

- For some people, support groups play an important role in their recovery from grief, loss and trauma. Do you think single-sex support groups work better than unisex groups? If so, why?

- Post-Traumatic Stress Disorder is usually associated with soldiers who have seen active service. Do you think it is misdiagnosed in the general community and why?

- When a community suffers trauma, studies have shown that the rate of domestic violence rises, including in relationships that had never experienced violence. Why do you think this happens?

- Claire struggled to be accepted by her in-laws. Do you know anyone whose relationship has suffered difficulties due to interference by in-laws? How was it resolved? Did the relationship survive?

- Erica talks about how hard it is to break into the town when she hasn't experienced the fire and she doesn't know people's stories. If someone doesn't share their story, does this lessen their right to be upset when someone blunders in?

- What events in your town have pulled your community together?

- Family traditions are considered to be an important glue in families. What are your traditions?

BUY LINKS

Daughter of Mine *Out Now*

Birthright *Out Now*

Home Fires *Out Now*

Just An Ordinary Family October 12th 2020

Please join my VIP newsletter and be first to hear about new releases, competitions and giveaways.

fiona lowe.com

Romance Novels 2006-2018

Fiona has an extensive backlist of romance novels set in the USA and Australia. For a full list head to fionalowe.com

Lightning Source UK Ltd.
Milton Keynes UK
UKHW011059090920
369617UK00001B/18